W9-AUB-037

## Books by Michael Mewshaw

# Blackballed

# BLACKBALLED

*Michael Mewshaw*

*New York* **Atheneum** *1986*

This novel is a work of fiction. Any references to historical
events; to real people, living or dead; or to real locales are intended
only to give the fiction a setting in historical reality. Other names,
characters, places, and incidents either are the product of the
author's imagination or are used fictitiously, and their
resemblance, if any, to real-life counterparts is entirely
coincidental.

Library of Congress Cataloging-in-Publication Data

Mewshaw, Michael
    Blackballed.
     I. Title.

PS3563.E87B5  1986     813'.54     86-47664
ISBN 0-689-11837-6

Copyright © 1986 by Michael Mewshaw
All rights reserved
Published simultaneously in Canada by
Collier Macmillan Canada, Inc.
Composition by Maryland Linotype Composition Company,
Baltimore, Maryland
Manufactured by Fairfield Graphics, Fairfield, Pennsylvania
Designed by Harry Ford
First Edition

*For* Beth *and* Jonathan Hayes,
*in gratitude for their help and hospitality*

# Contents

*Part* **One**

*The Comedown*

# *Chapter* One

Call me an agent.

Stick on any label you like, my name is Eddie Brown and Latif Fluss was my Lana Turner. I midwifed his birth. I brokered his rocket-burst arrival in the big time. I watched him crater, then witnessed every step of his comeback. Start to finish, I saw it all.

Not from the front row for every scene, not even from the balcony for some. I confess I kept my distance during his trial by tabloid and conviction in the court of public opinion. And, up front, I'll admit I never visited him in prison. I had my own legal problems; cops, corporate bounty hunters, IRS agents and process servers were clinging like bloodsuckers to both cheeks of my ass.

But I was there for the rest of it, stage-managing the fame that grew with his talent and fed on unprintable rumors, pandemonium at press conferences, fistfights at discos, freakouts in luxury suites, prosecutable obscenity on talk shows, stumbling on-stage appearances with rock stars, and snap-shots of girls in G-strings announcing in newspapers they were carrying Latif's baby.

Carrying it where, I always wanted to ask?

We're talking here, you probably guessed already, about pro tennis, the Teflon sport. People had been slinging shit at it for years. There'd been exposés about doped-up players, millions of bucks kicked back under the table, cooked figures in every accounting book, tanked matches, matches orchestrated for TV, phony winner-take-all events in Las Vegas. Whenever investigative reporters got sick of digging up dirt, the agents and Pro Council officers who controlled the game took to pissing on each other. They filed lawsuits charging restraint of trade, monopolistic practices, antitrust violations, and conspiracy to commit fraud. They even trotted out the RICO Act, a federal crime statute, and accused one another of racketeering.

But none of this crud stuck. Not till it hit Latif and me.

I'd like to think we were singled out on account of race, color, and creed. Lots of lunk-headed reporters writing about our case claimed Latif Fluss had been the first black since Arthur Ashe to win Wimbledon and the U.S. Open, the first black since Yannick Noah to take the French Open, the only black ever to sweep the Grand Slam.

But the thing of it is, Latif isn't black. He's blue, a bedouin from the Sahara, a member of the Tuareg tribe. These dudes dye their clothes with indigo that leaks out all over their skin. Lay a hand on Latif when he's sweating and you get an inked-up fist; you're ready to be fingerprinted and flung into the slam just like he was.

Me, I gave one final, fatal interview, then took it on the lam. Staying underground, staying away from the States, I supported myself with low-level scams, barely keeping nostrils above water. No matter what anybody tells you, there's not millions to be made pushing time-share programs with embassy personnel, peddling high-risk insurance and low-grade aluminum utensils to GI's, or leasing pirated cassettes of *Wall Street Week* to corporate ex-pats. But it keeps you in the hustle. That's the point—staying in practice, poised to get back in the game.

It goes without saying I missed pro tennis and the annual swing to Stuttgart for a new Mercedes, to Antwerp for diamonds, to Johannesburg for Kruggerands, to Basel for one-stop, wrap-around banking, to Houston for highly leveraged real estate, to Bogotá for cocaine—all these goodies gratis just for guaranteeing Latif would play tournaments.

I missed the high-fashion clothes, the high-tech toys, the high-cheeked models with their go-to-hell hairdos and fuck-me high heels. And, yes, I missed Latif. Okay, toward the end he was way off in the Bonzo zone. I wasn't in love with how he started calling me the Evil Dwarf and, when he was really mad, Mange Head. But he was, like I said, my masterpiece, my Lana Turner, and I loved him.

After three years of being jammed up, he had dropped so deep into the black hole of anticelebrity his prison release didn't rate a line on the sports page. First I knew about it, I received this package with a note saying, "Want to try again? Meet me at the Hotel du Lac in Tunis. I'm waiting for you."

I had problems with two out of three lines in his letter.

*Try again.* Try what? Tennis was out of the question. Latif had been banned for life.

The only money-making avenue open to us was to tell his side of the story, complete the autobiography he had been spieling into a recorder the last months before his arrest. Matter of fact, that's what was in the package—half a dozen tapes.

The plan back then had been to hire some hack to mold a saleable manuscript out of Latif's maundering. Maybe the project was salvageable. Mass murderers found buyers for their books. Why not us?

*I'm waiting for you.* That sentence sent forked lightning sizzling down my arms and legs. I didn't read patience or friendship in it. I read menace.

Well, I'd been waiting too. Waiting for a chance to explain why I hadn't hurried to the States to stand up for him. It wouldn't of done one damn bit of good. We'd of hit the skids together and wound up in neighboring cells.

In case he needed proof no journalist, judge, or juror was about to buy my word, I had a video cassette of the final, fatal interview I mentioned before, an on-camera spot I did for British TV. I had thought I was dealing with a reporter who was more than sympathetic. I thought the son-of-a-bitch was in my pocket.

Point of fact, Iain Richards had been in everybody's pocket. A typical tennis octopus, he had tentacles that slimed into the dirtiest cracks in the business. Nothing was too low or too petty for the bastard. He'd stoop down to steal the nickles off a dead man's eyeballs. One time or another, and often all at the same time, he had been a tournament promoter, an agent, a racquet dealer, a clothing rep, a TV commentator, and editor of a yearly tennis anthology entitled *Class Guys*.

Far as I could tell, a class guy in Richards's book was anybody who didn't break wind too much in mixed company.

But what can I say? He had been my first choice to ghost Latif's autobiography. So after the bust when he called to say he wanted to air our side, I assumed he meant to protect our mutual interests.

Often as I been around him, I don't have a clue where Richards lives or what passport he packs. Hearing his name, watching the way he folds his pipestem legs, the way he eats, holding the knife the whole time in his right hand and the fork in his left, the way he walks, swanking around like his thighs are chafed—you'd bet he's British. But then he opens his mouth, flashing a full set of caps, and his accent oozes all over the map. It sloshes across the Atlantic, leapfrogs the Channel, and rolls around Europe like a greased ballbearing. He can't finish a sentence without switching languages.

We rendezvoused at Schiphol airport outside Amsterdam, and he looked at home there. The second I spotted him, it hit me; this is where Iain Richards lives. He lives in transit areas, duty-free shops, and VIP lounges. And he always looks like he's just back from a safari. Summer and winter he wears a bush jacket, khaki slacks, khaki hair, a kind of khaki tan—maybe he squeezes it from a tube—and a moustache of sweat on his upper lip.

"It's the pockets," he once explained about the bush jacket. "That's the *primo* consideration—a place to put notes and plane tickets and receipts. *Beaucoup* space for *beaucoup* things."

That day at Schiphol he had an English babe as his producer and a Dutch camera crew, and while they were setting up next to a newsstand, Richards told me in his greasy accent what a great favor he was doing me.

"Tried to call Latif. Terribly decent sort, Latif. High-strung, but decent. He sent word that his lawyers advised *silencio*. I respect that. Still, I think it's important to present your views to the public. *D'accord?*" His bony hands did a ballet to the singsong of his voice.

"Yeah," is all I answered. I was having trouble following him. Ever since Latif's arrest, it'd been this way, with me trancing in and out, like the blood was draining from my head. Of course what was bleeding from me was money. The sun never slept on my case. All around the world a meter was running. You name the time zone and continent, and you can bet I had lawyers there charging two hundred dollars an hour.

I didn't feel so dizzy when I focused on the chick, his producer, who was mumbling orders to the crew and chewing her cuticles. First glance, you wouldn't call her a beauty. She was pale with messy hair. Looked dirty to me, but maybe it was a new fashion. She had dark circles around her eyes and was wearing pink espadrilles, wrinkled white pants that would of fit a house painter twice her weight, and a blue tee shirt. Her nipples, tense as pencil points, seemed to be scribbling a message.

"They're a rum lot, some of these tennis reporters," Richards ran on. "No professional responsibility. Ready to let the yellow press devour Latif."

The chick introduced herself as Honor Heather or Heather

Honor. The name hardly registered. It was the sweet, shabby, dead-end kid look of her that appealed to me. I wasn't falling in love. I was falling into something far sappier. I was letting myself trust her, believing she'd broadcast the truth and rescue Latif and me.

Richards blotted his upper lip and powdered his face a darker tan. I refused makeup. A mistake. On film I wound up looking phlegm-complected.

"Your hair is teddible," Heather murmured, smiling.

I touched it. Bristly as a Brillo pad. "It doesn't want to stay combed."

She brushed at my shoulders. I had on an Italian suit, shiny silk, metallic grey, with these tufts of thread like somebody with long fingernails had been scratching it. Heather, she didn't recognize the fashion. She mistook it for dandruff and kept brushing.

I noticed her fingers were bleeding. She'd bitten them down to nubs. I offered my handkerchief as a tourniquet. "You look tired," I said.

"Eighty hours last week doing a documentary in Belfast. Seventy-two the week before in Zimbabwe. Next week Beirut."

"Poor kid."

"The price you pay."

When Richards jabbed a microphone in my face and the crew closed in with the minicams, Heather Honor drifted away.

"I'm here with Eddie Brown, Latif Fluss's agent, mentor, and, some might say, *éminence grise*. Tell us, Eddie, what's the latest on Latif?"

"He was set up. Framed. This is a vendetta—"

"Did he do what they say he did?" On camera, Richards had the kind of voice you hear only from news commentators and actors playing God.

"Latif hasn't done anything illegal . . . if that's what they're saying."

"They say he's about to be indicted."

"Who says?"

"American television. Every network. Are you denying Latif Fluss is a drug dealer?"

"Absolutely!"

This wasn't the sort of softball interview I expected. Richards, famous for serving up easy, ass-kissing questions, was coming on now like a cross between Mike Wallace and Attila the Hun.

"Look," I said, "my man's innocent of all charges. If there are any charges. And I doubt there'll be any charges because Latif hasn't done anything that isn't standard practice in pro tennis. Pippo Scarcia tried to fix—"

"Are you denying Latif and you demanded guarantees?"

"Our position is, like I said up front, our position is he hasn't done anything wrong. Nothing against the law."

Then I skirted back to Pippo Scarcia and how he was the one railroaded us. But Richards didn't have the microphone cocked in my face anymore. It drooped between us. Sweat had popped through his makeup. He swatted me on the shoulders like he was helping me with my dandruff.

"*Molto buono*, buddy. Sorry if I sounded a bit *feroce*," he said in his off-camera croon. "Professional neutrality, no way around it. Now let's shoot some establishing shots." He handed me a magazine. "Move next to the newsstand. Relax. Look natural. *Perfecto!*"

"Hey," I said, "what's that business about me being eminent grease?"

"Just a figure of speech. Leaf through the magazine."

I glanced at this Belgian weekly called *Humo*. It carried an article about Latif, "*Van Dollars, Dope, und Dattumme.*" "What's it say?" I asked.

"Quiet," Richards said. "Pretend you're reading."


Weeks later, during Wimbledon, I kept clear of the All England Club and everybody that blamed me and Latif for bringing the game into disrepute. I holed up in a London hotel waiting for Richards to set the record straight. Seemed to me once the truth aired on British TV, the American press was bound to pick it up, and the charges against us would crumble and disappear.

Instead, I crumbled.

Maybe you saw the program and remember how I looked lurking there beside that newsstand, flipping through the pages of *Humo* which on account of the camera angle came across as *Homo* Magazine. My expression changed when I spotted the article on Latif. It was a grimace. No one could say I was grinning. Nobody but that fuckface Iain Richards.

In voice-over, he laid the word of God on me. "Why is this man laughing? Why, when his client Latif Fluss, the number-one tennis player in the world, awaits indictment as a heroin dealer, why when millions of fans hold their breath and hope Latif will say it ain't so, why does this man hide in the corner of an international airport thumbing through pornographic magazines?

"On the pro circuit, they call him the Evil Dwarf." The cameraman switched lenses. Suddenly he was examining me like a specimen. I looked about six inches tall. "Others call him Mange Head." They showed a shot of what must of been matted monkey fur. Swear to Christ, it wasn't my hair.

"His real name is Eddie Brown. Or Edwin B-R-A-U-N, as his birth certificate reads and as he is known to law-enforcement agents in the United States. Surely the most hated man in professional tennis, Brown is the Rasputin who directs the shady affairs of the game's most contro-versial star. While Latif Fluss faces life imprisonment, Brown has managed to elude U.S. legal authorities. But our crew spared no expense to track him down and return with this exclusive footage."

I was on camera fifteen minutes, but got to say not a word, not a syllable. There was just me slobbering over *Homo* while Richards flogged his twisted version of events and quoted the shock and outrage expressed by past Wimble-don champions and camp followers.

The way they worked me over with the camera, it might as well of been a proctoscope. They got some great shots inside my ears and nostrils. What they liked best, though, was showing how I refused to face the music when Richards read the list of charges. Actually, I was staring off at Heather Honor, watching her suck her stinging fingers, wishing I could help her.

I suppose that's what hurt most. I should of known Richards would sail whichever way the wind blew. But I felt betrayed by that tiny, tired, waiflike doll.

# *Chapter* Two

There was never a chance I wouldn't fly to Tunis. I packed my bags, tossed in Latif's tapes and a Sony Walkman, then dressed in my best threads. These days, all I had to wear was out-of-date designer duds I had picked up as comps on the tour.

Even back then it was strange stuff and now that it was years out of style I was the target of surprised stares wherever I traveled. A guy my age, pushing fifty, five feet seven and a hundred and forty pounds, his best bet is a three-piece suit, conservative cut, preferably pinstriped. But I had leather ties and silk shirts with French cuffs and no collars; double-breasted jackets with one shoulder padded, the other not; pegged pants with balloon legs and flies cut on the bias so I had to pee around a corner. The budget I was on, I couldn't afford to clean out my closet and start over.

After takeoff I ordered a vodka gimlet, clamped on the Walkman, and listened to the tapes. They started with Latif's childhood and early career, but also contained lots of screwy self-defecation, and I realized straight off it would of been disastrous to let some tennis reporter, specially Iain Richards, listen to them. It wasn't just his crackpot comments undermined the image I had created. These cassettes were full of info that could of laid us both wide open to blackmail and maybe landed him behind bars sooner. But since neither of us has to worry about that anymore, here's what he said.

# *Tape #* 1

Testing, one, two, three. Testing onetwothree. Is this thing working? I mean the tape recorder. Not my thing. My thing is definitely not working. Last night in Copenhagen I couldn't get it up. Tonight in Stockholm I couldn't get it off and get it down.

I was stiff as a graphite racquet. And less sensitive. After a few hours I lost track. I know what you'll say, Eddie. Concentrate!

I *was* concentrating. But on the wrong things. The lady was a little distant. They all are, these Ingas and Ullas, Ebbas and Bibbis, these bland bimbos provided by Scandinavian tournament directors. I found myself recalling the lively whores we have back home with henna designs on their hands and the first line of the Koran tattooed in tiny letters over their shaved cunts.

Then my mind wandered to the smorgasbord laid out on tables in the players' lounge. I was tempted to take a break and call room service. But I played on, giving it what the Code of Conduct calls "best effort." Only when I felt her attention waver—maybe she was hungry too—did I stop and assure her I was satisfied. I explained I practiced tantric yoga and that self-denial was the ultimate orgasm.

"I now don't trust you one word," she said. "You are lying totally." She rolled out of bed and began dressing.

"No, listen. Conservation of seed is an act of sharing."

"This sharing I don't know. Important is only you are pleased and you play well tomorrow. This is what I am told to do."

"I appreciate that."

"Appreciate the tournament director." She went on hooking and zipping. "He sends me."

"Now I send you." I opened the door. "By never seeing each other again, we'll remain on intimate terms."

"It is true what the newspapers tell. You have many kinky things on your head."

"Hairs."


Is this what fans want, Eddie? Life in the fast lane? The glamour, the girls, the star's wayward whang?

I'm in Stockholm, they tell me. Afraid I can't provide any local color. There was no limo at the airport. Two men in a laundry truck met me and explained there had been death threats from a terrorist cell that takes violent exception to my position on nuclear power plants. What is that position, Eddie? Did you release a statement? You know I like to be briefed about what I believe.

The men with the laundry truck hid me in back under bags of dry cleaning, then sped me to the sports arena. I saw nothing of the city and not much more of the arena. Entering through a tunnel, we rolled to the locker room door.

In the unlikely event you're interested, I beat Zippi Rodriguez seven-six in the third set. It wasn't scripted that way. Zippi came to me and complained he had a sore throat and a fever. The court here is laid over a hockey rink. Very cold on the feet. Rodriguez didn't want to stay out there for hours and catch pneumonia. We agreed to go two sets; whoever took the first took the match.

But then Zippi did an obvious el foldo, bagging it six-love in about ten minutes. The crowd was furious. Can't blame them. I was too. It made me look bad, being party to a blatant tank job. I decided he needed disciplining.

Second set, I kept the score close, hitting the wrong shot at the wrong time, serving a few double faults, developing a glitch in my forehand that landed inches behind the line. The crowd didn't catch on to what I was doing, but Zippi did and worked harder to dump the set. I beat him to the punch and forced him to play a third.

By now he was gasping and coughing and cussing during changeovers. But I kept every ball in play, pushing it back at half speed, making him run till his tongue dragged. I carried him into a tie-break, then finished him off with a few rallies that lasted fifty shots.

Zippi's going to need a body transplant before the next tournament.

Later, the laundry truck brought me deep into the bowels of the hotel, and the girl and I boarded a freight elevator to my room. I can't say much about the place except I have a hunch I've been here before. By any chance, do we own it?

The room is hot and there's a beige carpet that crackles with static electricity when I walk on it, which is what I'm doing now, moving over to the window so you can hear what I've been listening to.

At first, I thought it was in my head. The noise. But something's sizzling against the glass. It sounds like the blowing dust of the Sahara, and I feel the way I always did during sandstorms—my mouth dry, my eyes stinging, my skin tingly. Suddenly, here in the parched heat of this hotel, with sleet buzzing at the window, I'm reminded of nights in my father's hut when the *harmattan* howled and the air hummed with the voices of the dead.

The standard story—you probably planted it, Eddie—is that just as Arthur Ashe discovered Yannick Noah in Cameroon so Noah later discovered me in the desert. The truth is, I discovered myself, taught myself, imagined the world outside and launched myself upon it. With an assist from you, of course.

We Tuaregs are a noble tribe of warriors, hardened by the Sahara, trained from infancy to be self-reliant. Once old enough to walk, our children never cry or whine, never show weakness or fear. Nomads free to roam, we once ruled from the spiny mountains of the Hoggar to the sparse grasses of the Sahel. Other tribes feared us, and we exacted tribute from strangers traveling through our territory.

The Romans, then the Arabs, tried to conquer us, but we resisted. Though we eventually embraced Islam, we preserved our rituals and taboos. Among the Tuareg, it is men, not women, who veil their faces, wearing an indigo-dyed cloth, the *tagilmoust*, wrapped around their heads.

Legend has it we are descended from Christian Crusaders who strayed off course en route to Jerusalem. This accounts for our chivalric code of conduct and our use of the cross as a decorative device on the saddles of our camels. It also explains why many of us, including me, have blue eyes and copper-blond hair.

When the French invaded, we fought them too—our swords and raw courage against their rifles and cannons. For decades we held them at bay. But finally, in 1902, at the Battle of Tit—that's right, Eddie. Tit! Don't laugh and defame the dead—we were defeated. Still, we were never colonized. The French drafted our warriors into elite units of their camel corps.

Although most Tuaregs are now so poor they've had to sell their weapons, others, like my father, became night watchmen and bodyguards. Expecting me to follow his profession, he taught me early how to handle a sword. When I took up tennis, the strokes seemed instinctive; an aggressive slashing style was second nature. I swung at every ball as if to draw blood. Latif Fluss's famous strength of arm, the unerring hand-eye coordination were already there and needed only to be harnessed to a new kind of combat.

The most recent foreigners to invade Tuareg territory had no use for camels. Arriving in giant trucks, rumbling over mountains and the vast, pebble-strewn wastes of the *reg*, they brought plastic bags and bottles, sunglasses, women with naked legs, ballpoint pens, gasoline-powered pumps, and Donkey Kong.

My father called them *kaffirs* and *toubabs*, whiskey-guzzling, Christian pigdogs. Actually they were Texans who had come to work the oil fields. As tall as Tuaregs, but twice as wide, loud as braying camels but seldom as mean-spirited, they spoke no Tamahaq, no French, and very little English. Their peculiar dialect depended on the repetition of key phrases which changed meaning according to emphasis and intonation. "Hidy!" "Bye-bye," "Good buddy," "I luv it," "Awright!" "Hey babe," and "Goferit!" could be made to express the full range of their emotions.

Despite their poverty of language, they were rich in technical knowledge. They built an airstrip, a cluster of quonset huts surrounded by a chain link fence, and a pool that attracted mosquitoes and many small creatures that hopped, scuttled, and crawled but could not swim and therefore drowned and drifted around on the chlorinated water. They also constructed an asphalt tennis court, and my father, whose job was to protect these people he hated, convinced them to hire me, twelve years old at the time, as a sweeper, flyswatter, and flunky.

More a mascot than an employee, I spent happy hours at the court fetching balls and drinks and towels for the sweaty *toubabs*. I liked them and their sunburnt wives who played mixed doubles, drank Lone Star beer, and singed chunks of beef over a charcoal fire. They never minded that I ate what they left on their plates or that I saved the skinned-down balls they tossed into the trash bin.

From a slab of plywood I fashioned a racquet, whittling something the size of a Ping-Pong paddle. At night, in the intense light of the moon, I sneaked on court, tightened my *tagilmoust*, dovetailed my *gandourah* between my legs, and ran barefoot onto the asphalt. Alone, I began by bouncing and hitting balls, imitating what I remembered of the forehand and backhand.

Then I invented a more difficult drill. I lofted high lobs, raced and vaulted the net, and tried to reach the ball at the far end of the court before it bounced twice. As my speed and stamina increased, I could keep the ball going for twenty strokes.

Months passed before I dared play during the day and even then I did so between noon and four o'clock when all the *toubabs* retreated indoors. The court radiated heat and blinding light, and it rippled under my blazing feet like a mirage. I kept at it on those hundred-and-twenty-degree afternoons, driven not by ambition but by the boyish pleasure of jumping, swinging, hitting. I had no idea such things could be done for money.

After so much practice, I longed for praise. So one day I remained on court until the *kaffirs* came out and clung to the fence watching me, shouting, "I luv it!" and "Goferit!" as I dashed around chasing my own lobs. I hoped they'd let me play with them, but of course they didn't. When your pet dog surprises you by learning to drink from a glass, you don't invite it to dinner. You pat it on the head and go about your business. That's what the Texans did.

It was over a year before Jim Guy Benton arrived at the oil camp and asked me to hit him some lobs. He needed to work on his overhead, he said. For fifteen minutes, I lobbed, he smashed. Then his partner showed up and I cleared off.

Maybe because it had been a good workout, maybe because he was kind, Mr. Benton invited me to warm up his smash every afternoon. Then he let me return his serve. Soon we were hitting ground strokes, getting him grooved for keener competition. Finally, other men started using me as a practice partner. They never let me play sets with my Ping-Pong paddle. They just liked to loosen up against a steady retriever. But I was ecstatic.

Looking back, I believe every early disadvantage gave me an edge later on. After hitting with dead balls and a racquet carved from a board, I had a feeling tennis was ridiculously easy when played with regulation equipment. From practicing alone at night I learned the importance of listening, anticipating, depending on all my senses, not just sight. From scorching afternoon workouts, I gained endurance and the confidence that I was in condition to go five sets at Roland Garros, to handle the heat in Australia or at Flushing Meadow. Because in the beginning I never had much time on court, I developed a fast-paced, forcing game. I moved at a gallop, gathering up the balls, never pausing long between points, never sitting down during changeovers. All this put pressure on my opponents, rushed them into errors.

When I tell reporters Yannick Noah did *not* discover me, they still pester me to say what the turning point was, as if my career hinged on an isolated incident rather than a series of related events. They're not interested in the years it took to polish a top spin forehand or backhand slice. They demand instant drama.

So I recount the story of how I acquired my first real racquet.

On July Fourth the *kaffirs* celebrated their national liberation day by roasting an ox in a pit and swilling barrels of beer. Then they joined their wives in zany athletic events. They stuck their feet into burlap bags and hopped madly toward a distant line drawn in the dust. They flung raw eggs at each other until there was gooey slime all over their fingers. Their women stretched out face down on the ground, and the men grabbed them by the ankles, scissored their legs wide, and lifted them like so many goats they meant to mount. Then they pushed them like wheelbarrows, the men shouting "Goferit!," the women paddling along on their hands, their pink tongues dangling. All this jubilant activity was punctuated by peals of laughter, loud belches, and exploding firecrackers.

Although at first not invited to participate, the citizens of my village were allowed to watch. Most men stood in pairs, holding hands, staring through the narrow slits in their *tagil-mousts*. Behind them congregated the women, their faces tattooed, their eyes kohl-rimmed, their wrists and ankles manacled with bracelets. Far in the back frolicked a passel of *bouzous*, the blacks who had formerly been our slaves.

Eventually the *kaffirs* organized a contest open to the entire tribe, and Jim Guy Benton announced that the champion would win one hundred dollars. Since the annual per capita income in my region was then, and is now, less than eighty dollars, everybody was eager to compete in what the Texans called the Raghead Racquet Races.

In groups of twenty we were herded onto the fenced-in tennis court and each handed a racquet as Mr. Benton explained the rules of the game, which sounded no odder than others we had seen. Acting out his instructions, he pressed the butt of a racquet handle to his forehead, then bent forward so that the other end touched the ground.

While we imitated him, teetering like three-legged beasts, he said that on his command we should start spinning and keep spinning with our heads down, our racquets to the ground, until he told us to stop. Then we were to race to the gate in the fence. First one through won the preliminary round. Winners of the preliminaries would fight it out for the championship.

The name of the game, the equipment, the place it was played, all persuaded me Mr. Benton had arranged things expressly for me. He wanted me to have a hundred dollars so I could buy a real racquet. My gratitude was so great, no effort seemed unreasonable. I had to win. Or collapse trying.

He set us spinning and let us whirl for a full five minutes. Some contestants dropped in their tracks, dizzy and sun-drugged. Others caved in the instant he shouted to straighten up and run.

The asphalt buckled under my feet. The desert and the sky were reversed. I walked on blue air, staggering, bouncing off the fence, bouncing off people, tangling my feet in the net, skidding on the scalding asphalt, retching through my *tagil-moust*. But I found the gate and lurched through it first.

Crawling in the dirt like a sick dog, groaning and heaving, I tore off my *tagilmoust*, exposing my mouth in public for the first time since puberty. It was either do that or choke.

After a few preliminary rounds, the women, elders, and holy men refused to play on. But I wouldn't quit. It came down to a question of maintaining my dignity or winning the money, and since I believed there was no shortage of nobility in my blood, I decided I could spare a little pride.

As I took my place for the final spin-off, I was more nervous than I would be years later walking onto Centre Court to meet John McEnroe. My opponents were mostly young boys and muscular *bouzous*, all as desperate as I for the hundred dollars.

"Ready," Mr. Benton hollered. I bent over, forehead against racquet handle. "Rotate," he shouted. I whirled like a dervish. My belly quaked, my mouth filled with bilge. "Goferit!" he screamed. I reeled and floundered, falling, scrambling, delirious, half-demented. I bumped other boys aside, stepped over them and on them, ran through them when I couldn't run around them. I flailed the racquet like a sword, thwacking anybody in my path. They were dishing out the same punishment. But I felt nothing as I pitched forward, grappling along the fence until I found the gate and fell through it.

I lay on the ground, an imbecile in the eyes of my father. Worse, an infidel, as shameless and crazy as any *toubab*. But I didn't care. I had won.

## *Chapter* Three

Ask anybody. Eddie Brown doesn't rattle easy. But I'd be bullshitting if I denied the tape upset me. I couldn't believe—I didn't want to believe—it was Latif talking. Oh, I had no trouble recognizing the matter-of-fact manner he discussed his mondo-bizarro experiences on the circuit. I knew that world. But this description of his childhood sounded schizy—half hip, half hick. He changed his tone, his attitude, about as often as Richards switched accents.

Of course, I knew he came from, how do you call it, humble origins. I had supposed that meant he was some kind of farm kid and his autobiography could be shoehorned into the standard formula for sports heroes—strong boy works hard and plays hard, bulks up on good simple food, learns the basic skills from Dad, then goes out and whips the city slickers at their game.

But Latif, his career catapulted him from trash to flash,

with the added twist he wound up back in the crapper. I always blamed his sweet tooth for dope—toward the end, he couldn't turn around without a toot of this or a taste of that— on the pressures of the game. But no wonder he needed nose candy, considering how he started out. It made me feel double bad how he ended up.

At airports in this part of the world it generally takes hours to fetch your luggage. Then, you have to clear customs where a soldier with a machine gun and a droopy moustache that is actually out-of-control nasal hair shakes you down for a bribe. But in Tunis it wasn't ten minutes before I cruised through the passport check and into the waiting lounge where I bumped into this dildo with a sign that said WELCOME BLIND GROUP.

I was mulling over that message when somebody shoved me from behind. A couple guys carrying cameras raced past, but not before I recognized the shover. Swear to Christ, it was the original dead-end girl, Heather Honor with the bitten-down fingernails, tee shirt, and painter's pants.

The air turned thin; blood boiled behind my eyes. I charged after the bitch and, at the same time, spotted what she was here for. Yasir Arafat, surrounded by an armed guard of moptops, swept through the lobby smiling and waving and muttering, "No comment, no comment" to the TV twinks. PLO plug-uglies were pistol-whipping people out of his path, and when I grabbed Heather, she thought I was rescuing her from a gun butt in the face.

"Thanks awfully," she said. "But I'm fine."

I twirled her around. "Remember me, sweetie?"

Her hands right away flew into her mouth. She didn't act afraid or surprised. More like confused. "I never forget a feature," she said.

"Yeah, I got a real memorable face."

"Faces I forget. It's features I remember. Something about tennis? Am I warm? Wimbledon a few years back?"

"You and Iain Richards fucked me over royally."

"Richards maybe. Not me." She took the fingers from between her teeth. "He wrote the script. He cut the film. I never saw it. I flew to El Salvador for the revolution."

For all her frumpy clothes and fly-away hair, she had one of those British accents, classy and crisp. It's hard to stay burned at somebody who keeps so cool. Trying to stoke myself up again, I gave her a shake. Inside the tee shirt, her tense little tits jiggled.

"You enjoy ruining people's lives?"

"Not in the least," she said. "I go where they point me. Shoot what they say. Sorry you were hurt. Tell me what happened."

"Catch you sometime when I feel like talking for hours." I let her go. What else could I do? Coldcock her?

She blew on her cuticles and nails. Her eyes, I noticed, were grey. Very nice. "You oughta stop chewing your fingers," I said.

Heather shrugged. "Bad nerves. But I like bang bang."

"Gang bang?"

"Bang bang. Wars, insurrections, the odd shoot-out. That time with Richards I was between rebellions."

I nodded, not knowing why it mattered, but feeling better that she wasn't part of his permanent staff.

"Crew's waiting," she said. "Again, sorry. But you should take it up with Iain."

"Tell him you saw me. Tell him . . . tell him I'm considering a comeback."

"Glad to. Cheerio."

She left, and I was alone with the cluck waiting for the blind group. He had his beady eyes on me like he thought I should be carrying a white cane. "Forget it," I said. "I see perfect."


I caught a cab, and we circled a lake choked with weeds and trash. Camels and goats were grazing on the garbage,

and veiled women and men in striped burnooses kept the
animals from blundering into the traffic.

As we cruised into the white sugar-cube town of Tunis, I
suddenly wasn't positive I wanted to be there. After listening
to the tape, then bumping into Heather, I had a hard time
believing anything was going to run smooth today. I hadn't
the foggiest what I'd say to Latif. Worse, I couldn't guess
what he'd say or do.

Hotel du Lac was shaped like a pyramid balanced on its
point. Looked like a stiff wind would tip it over. The lobby
was chock-a-block with birdcages, big blue and white jobs
crammed with everything except birds—balloons, lanterns,
leather goods, native handicrafts. I would of ducked into the
bar for a bracer, but a local band, The Mullahs of Invention,
was belting out a Golden Oldie which, the way they sang it,
sounded like Evany and Ibory.

What I'm trying to explain, everything in the last hour
had worked on my head like a whiff of helium. So when this
freeze-dried chick waltzes over and says, "Eddie Brown?" I
really wasn't responsible.

"Who's asking?"

"Latif Fluss," she said.

I looked her up and down and went for a cheap laugh.
"Gee, that's a great set of jugs you grew in jail."

The wrong lead line with a lady like her. Not exactly prissy,
not a dog by any stretch, but buttoned down in a tailored suit
and white blouse with a man's tie. She didn't blush or get insulted. She acted very patient like she'd had plenty of practice
handling half-asses and half-wits.

"Lenore Fenstermacher." She shook my hand. "Latif asked
me to meet you."

She had a book in her free hand, a finger marking her page
in a paperback called *Justine*. Her hair was shiny black,
straight and tucked under at the shoulders. Her eyes were
dark as her hair. Jewish myself, I spotted her for a JAP who
could pass as a WASP except for this almond-eye Oriental
expression that swept over her face when you least expected.

She wasn't Latif's type, not even as a temporary, one of his Kelly Girls of Cunt. He had a hard-on for Amazons in mesh stockings, iron-pumping rock singers, leggy models in satin jumpsuits. This Fenstermacher babe was a 105-pounder, maximum.

"Where is he, Latif?"

"Tozeur," she said.

"Toe-where?"

"A town down in the desert. He's waiting for you."

"I don't get it. He said here, Hotel du Lac." I exhaled, acting annoyed, but secretly relieved to have more time and to have Lenore around. I figured Latif was less likely to get physical in front of a witness. "When's the next plane?"

"We'll drive. I've got a car."

We split from the upside-down pyramid in early afternoon, a bright day for February. All the birds that belonged in those cages had roosted in trees along Avenue Bourguiba and set off a screeching racket. Talk about a shit storm!

Not that much of it hit us. Manhandling her little Fiat with a hell-bent abandon that didn't fit her persnickety personality, Lenore sped out of the city and into the countryside.

"How'd you meet Latif?"

"Prison." Her dainty feet were doing heavy-duty work on the gas and clutch like she was driving a semi.

"Cellmates?"

"I taught him."

I chuckled. "I bet you did."

"I was his literature professor," she said. "An off-campus program at Sing Sing organized through the state university." Despite her demolition-derby driving style, she spoke in a slow, precise voice like English was a foreign language for me. "He was my best student. Barely literate at the beginning, but gifted with verbal genius. In no time he was reading the classics, writing poetry. I can't claim much credit.

He had the advantage of coming from an oral culture. Have
you heard him recite the Koran?"

"I must of been out of the room when he did it. What
brings you here? Continuing education?"

"He's determined to keep up his courses."

"That all he's keeping up these days?"

She shot me the sort of lethal look she must of laid on
the cons when they cut up in class. "Latif warned me about
you."

"About what?"

"Your mouth, your attitude toward women."

"I love women. Why'd Latif go and poison you against
me?" I wasn't just horsing around, needling Lenore. I
wanted to worm out whether she was a major player in
his life. I was also curious how much she knew about the
bad old days and the silence of the last three years.

"Don't act innocent, Eddie. In your marvelously sopho-
moric manner you're fishing for information about my sexual
relationship with Latif."

"Hey, that's none of my business."

"You're right. Where you're wrong is your insinuation that
I'm just a white chick wild about black cock."

"Nice talk for a lady."

"It's called candor. I want us to understand each other
from the start. I'm not a tennis groupie." She was really
pumping the foot pedals now. "I didn't bribe a doorman and
sneak up to Latif's apartment. We met in a maximum security unit. It was six months before we so much as held
hands. I'm one of those women, you love a man, you stick
by him, go with him. But even after his release, I didn't rush
things. He wanted to get married right away. I said let's wait.
Let's see how you feel when you've been free a few months."

"Smart move. Very mature." I pulled the Walkman out of
my bag. "Now you don't mind, I gotta review some tapes."
I clapped on the headset.

Relieved, I'd heard enough to realize Lenore wasn't going
to be part of the program long. Same old Latif. Slap him

behind bars, enroll him in Slammer U., and he still had this
way with women. He'd tell them anything—except the truth.

What I'm saying, Latif was married. Had been since he
was a kid. That's the custom down where he comes from.
When he went on the circuit, he parked his bride back home,
mailed her money every month, but never let on to the press.
Which was fine by me.

For a star player—hell, any performer in the public eye—
the wrong kind of marriage can reduce his endorsement
income twenty, thirty percent. With his name, his navy blue
tan, his being a Moslem from a country nobody cares about
except when there's a drought or new disease, Latif already
had built-in problems. Sponsors are put off by a low-rent,
high-visibility background. So how are they going to relate
to a little lady, barely over the age of consent from what
Latif told me, who's got a face full of tattoos and silver rings
in her nose? Somehow I don't see this cute couple shilling
for Sears & Roebuck or plugging real estate for Century 21.

The secret wife served a second purpose. With Mrs. Fluss
out of the picture, but still in the frame, so to speak, Latif
wasn't free to hitch up with any of the new bush that blew
into his life. On the tennis tour marriage has a downside
a mile deep. It's not just a wife'll occupy too much emotional
space and eat up practice time. Odds are, sooner or later, the
marriage'll fall apart, and the woman'll turn into a potential
whistle blower, a time bomb. Say the player refuses to cough
up the outrageous alimony she demands, she threatens to
throw him to the IRS. She's got leverage like a crowbar to pry
out fifty percent of all his assets, including what the star
palmed in secret guarantees, bribes, and kickbacks, and deposited in Switzerland or the Cayman Islands, then laundered
through dummy corporations in Liechtenstein.

I peeked at Lenore Fenstermacher in profile—the almond
eyes, the shiny black hair, the fixed expression—and thought,
Thank God. The Jewish Egyptian Princess, soon to be a minor
motion picture in Latif's past.

# *Tape # 2*

My arrival in Oklahoma was heralded by sirens and the shriek of motorcycle police escorting me to my motel. I had stayed in Ramada Inns before, but for the first time it occurred to me the chain must be owned by Moslems. Yet my mention of this and of Ramadan, the month of fasting and sacrifice, was met by befuddled expressions. When in an effort to explain things to local dignitaries, I repeated the names of the sacred months—Shawwal, Dhu-l-Kada, Dhu-l-Hijja, and Muharram—their befuddlement swerved toward fear. They thought I was on drugs. In fact I was—which made me anxious to convince them I wasn't.

During an unscheduled ceremony in the lobby, a man I took to be the mayor handed me a brass key which I took to be the key to the city. Attempting to rise to the occasion and correct any confusion about the Islamic calendar and my condition, I improvised an elaborate speech of gratitude, holding forth about the friendliness of Oklahoma and the importance of pro tennis to international understanding. The tournament director, a splendid fellow in boots, Stetson, and a Brooks Brothers suit, squeezed my elbow and cut in, "Latif's real tired, folks. Been up thirty hours flying here from Jakarta. Y'all don't mind, he'll hunker down in his room and sleep off his jet lag."

It seems the man I took to be mayor is the motel manager. The key to the city is the key to my room. Actually there is no city. I've landed in an unincorporated enterprise zone equidistant from three population clusters. The place consists of an airport, the motel, and a building called the Metroplex Multipurpose Dome where I'll play my matches.

Next morning a message was slipped under my door, words clipped from newspapers and pasted to a square of cardboard.

"I admire you very much," it read. "I watch all your matches. You're my favorite player. I want to be you. If I can't, I intend to kill you."

Then came a phone call. "Drop dead Jew nigger gook!"

Somebody's lumping us together. I guess I'm the nigger. You're the Jew, Eddie. Who's the gook? Do we have a gook on the payroll?

Later the same day I won my match, but barely squeaked past the press conference. The reporters sounded so sincere, so earnest, I was tempted to tell the truth.

As always they wanted to know the turning point in whàt they imagined to be a life-and-death struggle. I might have reminded them this is the first round and I'm getting a hundred-thousand-dollar guarantee. The semis and the final are scheduled to be televised this weekend—if I'm still in the tournament. Is there any chance promoters are going to let me lose before then?

My opponent, a Bolivian boy with the face of an Incan emperor, understood his role. He didn't bother checking into the motel. He left his luggage at the airport, performed a respectable charade of resistance, then bagged it. The turning point? I suppose, Eddie, that was last summer when you muscled these people for appearance money.

The other questions were inevitable. What went through your mind at match point? Did the lights bother you on overheads? Will Bjorn Borg ever make a comeback? Do you agree John McEnroe deserves to be put to sleep?

A lady journalist asked, "Who was your childhood hero?"

I answered, "Tracy Austin."

In fact, my father was my hero, even though he disowned me as his son.

After I won the Raghead Racquet Races, my life, at least on the surface, continued as before. Each morning I woke to the cry of the *muezzin*, crouched toward Mecca, and mumbled my prayers. Five times a day I praised Allah. But I lived as if tennis was my god and my fate depended on the Texans.

As soon as Rashida, the bride chosen by my parents, menstruated for the first time, we were wed with much ceremony, much drinking of goat milk and camel blood. Women rattled tambourines and pounded *tinde* drums. Then everybody settled in to await the birth of our son.

At the oil compound, my father insisted my wages be raised to suit my status as a married man of fifteen. The Texans didn't object. They liked me and now often asked me to play with executives who flew in from company head-quarters in Houston. Some of these men were former college stars still serious about the game. I learned a lot from them.

I learned even more when the compound acquired a video machine. Along with cassettes of sit coms, Kung Fu movies, and NFL highlights, the home office sent tapes of tennis tournaments, and I remember watching them in awe much as our tribal tambourine shakers might ogle Tina Turner in concert. Yet, miraculously, what I saw, I could imitate. And what I heard the expert commentators describe I could soon do.

Seeing McEnroe beat Borg in the '81 Wimbledon final, I grasped how to open the court with a wide serve and close the point with an angled volley. Watching Connors crush Lendl two years in a row in the U.S. Open final, I discovered the trick of taking the ball on the rise and rifling it back, using an opponent's pace against him. When Noah defeated Mats Wilander for the '83 French Open title, then cried in his father's arms, I realized that even on clay an aggressive player could defeat a base-liner. And I prayed I would some-day become a champion and my father would embrace me in front of the world and accept what I was doing.

But during those years as I honed my strokes, he did every-thing to discourage me. He berated me in front of the Texans, cuffed me with his hands, whipped me with sticks, swatted me with the flat of his sword. Still I refused to stop playing.

He screamed that I was dishonoring him and disobeying the Koran. Did I imagine Allah had created me, as He had created all men from clots of blood, in order that I should cavort with *toubabs* in underwear chasing after a yellow ball with crooked sticks? "The life of this world is a sport and a pastime," he reminded me. But there was a life to come, and he warned me what to expect unless I repented. Evil would be my drink, dismal my resting place, filth my food, the filth that sinners eat.

Why? Because I had forsaken Islam. Because I had betrayed the tribe by removing my *tagilmoust* and revealing the hideous hole of my mouth. I preferred a tennis racquet, a *kaffir*'s toy, to a Tuareg sword. I scavenged for cast-off clothes, unclean garments the Christians had thrown in the trash. I dressed as a woman, he screamed, pointing at my feet. I wore a pair of ladies' blue Tretorns and low-cut socks with pink pompoms at the heel.

No wonder my seed was weak and I had had no sons, not even a daughter. "The Prophet has written: 'Women are your fields; go, then, into your fields as you please.' Plow the field Allah has provided you," my father pleaded. "Don't go to that other field, the one with the fence around it and the mysterious markings on the ground."


My father was not alone in pressing religious arguments upon me. The *toubabs* also believed in a god, a spirit world, and life after death. But they stressed that tennis, all sports, far from being sacrilegious, were based on faith and morals. They felt no shame at praying for an ace or praising the Lord when they smacked a passing shot. After a workout they were apt to ask, "Say hey, Latif, this desert climate, what do you recommend, gut or nylon?" Then in the same cheerful voice, "Say hey, Latif, have you accepted Jesus Christ as your personal savior?"

Along with God and sport, education made for a trinity of *toubab* beliefs, and their temple was a school in Texas where many oil men had been trained. Called College of the Holy Sepulcher, it was a fully owned subsidiary of the

Church of the Holy Sepulcher, whose Tabernacle and executive offices were housed on campus in a beacon-lit tower.

According to its brochure, the motto of the church, the college, and its athletic teams was "Make a Miracle Happen." The glossy pages showed snapshots of students frowning over test tubes, frozen on diving boards, arms outstretched in imitation of their crucified prophet, riding horses and wrestling cows, massed around a fire clapping and ululating like Tuareg women before their warriors do battle.

Although the brochure repeatedly referred to the powers of the spirit world, the pictures emphasized the wonders of "the physical plant." The immense buildings, Olympic swimming pool, and healthy well-fed bodies were, in my opinion, the miracles their god had made happen, and I was moved deeply by the idea of a religion of amazing energy and achievement.

The Texans swore I was Holy Sepulcher material. They pointed out that I spoke English (with a Texas accent), I worked hard, lived clean, and worshipped a deity, although not, they regretted, the true one. I also played terrific tennis.

Up until then my education consisted of learning a little about numbers and memorizing verses from the Koran. Although I recognized brand names on tennis equipment, I neither read nor wrote English. I had never left the Sahara and had no money.

No problem, the *toubabs* said. God would provide; Holy Sepulcher would provide. At universities throughout America, Africans were already running high hurdles, heaving weights, and slam-dunking basketballs. They named famous Nigerian power forwards, Moroccan milers, pygmy sprinters, Masai javelin throwers. There were even a few tennis players, the best, unfortunately, white South Africans.

I'd have plenty of friends, they promised, to ease the pain of leaving my wife behind. It was impossible, they explained, to bring Rashida. The dorm had no facilities for married couples, and she'd feel uncomfortable because of her nose rings and tattoos. Besides, she'd meet no coeds her age. She had just turned fourteen. It would be better to visit her during summer vacation.

For months I did not mention Holy Sepulcher to Rashida or my father. I knew better than to expect them to appreciate the value of an education or the challenge of world-class competition.

How could I account for it? The ambition that seized me before I learned the word to describe it? What began as child's play had become an obsession. I wanted to find out whether anybody in Texas, anyone anywhere, could beat me.

If this sounds like a simpleminded aspiration, I confess I had more complicated motives for longing to escape my village. Ashamed of producing no sons, I was sick of Rashida and her laments and fumbling henna-flecked fingers. I was tired of her waking hours before dawn, baring her shaved mound, and pressing it against me cold and prickly as a plucked chicken.

I could have repeated *Tallaqtuki* three times, the Koranic formula for divorce. Or I could have discarded her with the ancient Arabic dismissal, "Be to me as my mother's back." But I recalled a proverb the oil men sometimes muttered. "This sucker's a dry hole. Let's mosey along and drill another."

In so many words, that's what I told her finally. She shed no tears, didn't beg me to stay, didn't bother asking when or whether I would return.

My father took the news harder. He drew his sword and fell into a fighting stance. He threatened me with dismemberment, death, damnation. He swore I was not his son, not a man at all. I was the issue of a crow that had coupled with a jackal. I was the scum at the bottom of the latrine.

It is frightening, believe me, to be shouted at by a man whose face is masked, whose curses come through a *tagilmoust* weirdly muffled, whose eyes betray his own pain while his hands, the only other visible parts of his body, clench to cause you pain.

I appealed to his pride in our traditions, assuring him that like those warriors who had enriched the tribe at the expense of strangers, I regarded my trip to America as a raid, a fierce campaign into fertile territory. After ransacking Holy Sepulcher, I would return with great wealth and vivid tales of my exploits. What I was doing was no different than the old days when his own father set off on a caravan to the Sudan and brought back ivory, gold, incense, ostrich feathers, and slaves.

"The difference," he said, "is that you'll never return. You'll become a pig eater. Your name, which is my name, will stink in the nostrils of men. Go," he shoved me, "and meet your ruination."

He chased me from the hut and dropped to his knees, scraped up fistfuls of sand and scoured his arms to rub out the last trace of me.

What my father did after I left for Texas I know only from the secondhand reports of oil company employees, and they depended on eyewitness accounts that may have been mistaken or mistranslated. The Sahara is a natural medium for distortion.

Having no camel of his own, apparently he rented one from a man who made a living snapping pictures of tourists mounted on haggard, flea-bitten beasts. He rode into the *reg*, where oil pumps bobbed up and down, up and down, like giraffes bending to nibble coarse grasses. Then he drew his sword, kicked his heels at the camel, and launched his final assault, a warrior's farewell.

Incredible as it sounds considering my father's age and the animal's broken-down condition, they struck with sufficient force to kill him, cripple the camel, and put an oil pump out of commission. Some say it was suicide. I disagree. When he couldn't bring himself to kill me, he attacked the next best target, a symbol of the foreigners who had stolen his son.

Morning dawns at the Ramada Inn with the sound of flushing toilets and the drone of vacuum cleaners in the hall. On the drive to the Metroplex Multipurpose Dome, I sit up front in the courtesy car with a chauffeur while the tournament director and a major sponsor, the owner of several Taco Bell franchises, perch on the back seat, leaning forward, asking urgent questions. Is John McEnroe still in love with Tatum? Don't you think Guillermo Vilas was a better poet than a player? What about those beaver shots of Patti Connors in *Playboy*?

I can't follow the conversation. For one thing, I hoovered a few lines before leaving the motel, enough to keep my sinuses clear, my head crystalline. For another thing, a cold wind, a blue norther, buffets the car, almost flipping us over.

Also I am thinking again about my father. Were he alive, how would I smell in his nostrils now? A pricey line of toiletries bears my name—his name—and I anoint myself with these scented powders and colognes twice a day. Far from wearing discarded clothes, I have a million-dollar contract with an Italian designer and after each match I strip off shorts, shoes, socks, shirt, and jock and drop them on the locker room floor, never to touch them again. I assume some flunky launders them and saves them for himself. Or else auctions them off unwashed, rich with my musk.

Everything I endorse, everything I touch, everything I excrete has value. Children clamor for my sweatbands. Despite constant death threats, many consider me a lifegiver. Sperm banks and lonely women request jars of my gism. Homosexuals invite me to urinate on them. "Give me a golden shower," they beg. Even my piss is likened to money.

My net worth approaches the gross national product of my native country. I own a quadriplex on Central Park, a *finca* in Spain, an island off Fiji, a chalet in Gstaad, a fleet of cars, and half a dozen holding companies. Like this sparsely populated stretch of Oklahoma, I am a highly profitable, unincorporated enterprise zone. Yet I'm convinced my father curses me from the grave. In his nostrils I still stink.

"What the fuck's that?" the tournament director hollers.

We're doing a legal fifty-five miles per hour when something overtakes us. Low-slung and aerodynamically sleek as my Lamborghini, it crowds into our lane, skids, and crashes on the median strip. At rest, it is revealed as a plastic and aluminum lawn chair.

"Wind musta busted it loose from somebody's backyard," explains the utterly unfazed Taco Bell franchiser. "Tell me, Latif, is it true what they said about Borg? His racquet was strung tighter than a gnat's snatch?"

I am laughing so hard the tournament director asks twice, "You okay?"

"I thought I saw my life pass in front of me. But it was just a lawn chair going sixty miles an hour." This breaks me up again. Nobody else gets the joke.

I lost in the second round, Eddie. My earliest exit in three years. I tried. I honestly did. And the umpire and linesmen tried even harder to protect the tournament's investment. But it wasn't enough. I kept having laughing jags. I couldn't forget that speeding lawn chair and slaphappy Mr. Taco Bell anxious to get back to a truly important topic—how tightly Borg was strung.

## *Chapter* Four

I lifted off the earphones and let them flop around my neck, the rubber pads closing under my chin like a collar. It hit me again how tough Latif had had it, and not only at the end when he turned into such a sick ticket.

"I can't believe Latif's life, what he went through."

"I can believe it. I was there." Lenore had both hands on the wheel, but was swerving all over the road.

"I'm talking about before pro tennis and prison. I'm talking about his home life and how he lost his father."

"The law is an ass. Read Dickens." She followed her line of thought same way she steered her zigzag course. "Read *Bleak House*."

"Don't need to read it. I been living there the last three years."

"No, Latif's the one that lived there."

"Tell me about it." I gave up. "How was he in the slam?"

She tossed her head, shaking her dark hair, then combing it with her fingers. "Ever do time?"

"County jail, never state or federal. Never more than a month."

"Night and day. Worlds apart." Something happened to her voice, her vocabulary. "What you have to understand, Latif went indoors with a high profile and low status."

"Get serious. He was rich. A world-famous athlete."

"Wrong kinda rich, wrong kinda fame." The egghead Lit. Prof. was talking hardboiled now, showing off what she picked up from her students. "His rap—tax fraud, financial flimflam, soft-drug habit, hard-drug smuggling—doesn't carry any weight with cons. They respect a guy that goes into a gas station with a gun and heists a bag of dough. Better yet, blows somebody away. It's a macho jungle in there."

"Latif's a macho guy."

"You kidding?" She cut her eyes toward me, almost plowed into a ditch, then swung back on the pavement. "He could play that Superfly, stone badass act on the circuit. But look who he was up against. A munchkin Connors's or McEnroe's size came on strong in the joint, they'd doll him up in shortie pajamas and pass him around like a toy. You think they play tennis in there? You think they tune in to Wimbledon?"

"All the publicity he got, don't tell me they didn't realize who he was."

"Sure. That was part of the problem. The networks covered his bust, the plea bargain, his transfer from the detox center to the pen. Live TV every step of the way. Understand what I'm saying? The inmates watched him walk off the screen and into his cell. One minute he was a star on the tube, next minute he was another con with a number on his back. Everybody took a look and said, 'Here's a fat turkey. I'm carving off a piece.' They sold photocopies of his fingerprints, negatives of his mug shot. The jerk in the next cell got an assignment from the *National Enquirer* and reported Latif's first days in prison. All the whites hated him because he was black. All the bloods hated him because he was blue. Even the Muslims didn't like him. He was too threatening. He could quote the Koran in English and Arabic."

"Jesus, how'd he survive?"

"First few months, he was in isolation. Guards were scared somebody'd shank him. They held him on a tier with other high-risk cases—squealers, deviates, drag queens, transsexuals who'd been sentenced before the hormone treatments finished kicking in. By the time they threw him into the general population, he'd learned a lot. Stayed to himself, didn't ask favors. He still didn't have the status of a murderer or armed robber. To them he was just a white-collar weenie. But then something put him over. Guess what?"

"He told them about his fling with Martina Navratilova."

"What fling?" She cut her eyes from the road again.

"Watch where you're going and tell me the story."

"He was offered a transfer to Lompoc. Heard of it?"

"Don't think so."

"Sure you have." She was back in class now. No more tough cookie talk. She sounded like she was correcting commas, encouraging slow learners. "It's a minimum-security institution in California. A country club prison. Lots of Watergate people did easy time there."

"Yeah, now I remember."

"Some politician pulled strings. Couple of his campaign contributors wound up at Lompoc and they were tennis nuts. They wanted Latif there as a full-time instructor."

"You're kidding. In prison?"

"Lompoc has tennis courts. It seemed like a nice way for these VIPs to work off a six-month sentence, practicing with the best player in the world. So the fix was put in for him to be transferred."

"I never read this. I watched the papers for news about him."

"That's because Latif refused. He told them he had already spent too many years hitting tennis balls with crooks."

I had to laugh. "Fucking Latif. A mind of his own."

"He told me he'd feel guilty getting a break when other

guys had to serve their sentences straight up. He preferred
to do his time at Sing Sing."

"How'd they take it, the other prisoners?"

Now she was the one laughing. "They thought he was
a lunatic. Said he had to be to stay in maximum security. But
they started to accept him."

"How's he feel about tennis now?" There was an unspoken
kicker to the question: How's he feel about me, the fellow
that put him on the tour that put him behind bars?

"You'll have to ask him." Then after a beat, "I've got a
question for you. I couldn't trust Latif to tell the truth."

"If it's about his fling with Navratilova—"

"No, not that. Did he have a clothing contract with a
company called Honky?"

"Yeah."

"He actually walked on court wearing that label?"

"Sure. It's an Italian line of leisure wear. Good contract,
good product."

"It didn't strike you as wrong for his image?"

"The company didn't have a hint what Honky meant. They
just liked the sound."

"But you knew. He knew!"

"Look, it was a business deal. Only time I ever turned
down an endorsement was for a French soft drink, brand
name of Pschitt! Pronounced exactly like I'm saying it. There
I drew the line. No client of mine is saying, 'I drink Pschitt!
and I love it.' "


We had reached dry, empty land, with cactus plants next
to the road and thorny mountain ridges in the distance. Sort
of reminded me of the scenery around Palm Springs, only
here there weren't any high-rise condos or golf courses, and
the small town streets were named after a dictator or the day
a holy man was martyred, not Bob Hope and Jerry Ford.
I saw women down in an irrigation ditch scrubbing clothes
in water the color of a Hershey bar, and more women draped

in black from skull to ankles gliding along with bundles of sticks balanced on their heads.

Going through Gafsa, we got stuck behind a guy pushing a cart piled with loaves of bread big as sewer lids. But west of the city, the land seemed to tilt downhill, hurrying us across what Lenore claimed was an ancient seabed. We raced the sun toward the ragged horizon. It won and dropped over the edge in a splash of gory red. Then it went dark, and I couldn't see a thing except moths fluttering back and forth in the high beams.

In Tozeur, the hotel lobby was crawling with midgets and dwarfs. Scratch that. Crawling's the wrong word. They were digging out fast as their stunted legs could carry them. Because right on their asses was a hyena pack of local yokels smacking them silly. It looked like a rough game of tag that maybe started off fun—the locals were still laughing—but now the little people were screaming bloody murder, slinging cigars and beer glasses, dodging behind furniture, tipping over potted palms, doing anything to escape the Tunisians.

When one goofball in a burnoose whacked me between the shoulder blades, I knew whose side they put me on. I didn't appreciate that one damn bit and took a swing at the bastard. He ducked. I was about to go after him when Lenore Fenstermacher grabbed my arm.

"My fault," she said. "Should have known better. This happens here all the time."

"What happens? What the hell's going on?"

"I'll explain. Wait in the car. I'll find Latif and catch you outside."

It was cold in the Fiat and my breath fogged the windows. Drop-outs from the Punch and Judy show surrounded the car, rapping knuckles on the door, laying fingers to their lips, doing a pantomime of smoking. Maybe they were begging cigarettes. Or peddling hash. I could of used a joint. Or just a quick change of venue. I didn't relish a reconciliation scene with Latif in a car covered with geeks pressing their runny noses to the windshield while inside the hotel their friends played grab-ass with midgets.

I couldn't help suspecting someone was setting me up. Latif had a warped sense of humor. Flying in a flock of midgets, having them harassed by a band of boobs, might be just his idea of how to welcome back the Evil Dwarf.

Lenore bustled out of the hotel alone, cut through the crowd, and swung her trim bottom in its tailored suit into the driver's seat. "Whew! Things are getting crazy in there."

"Where's Latif?"

"Never seen it this nutty."

"Latif," I said.

"You've probably read about Tozeur. They're shooting a *Star Wars* sequel here. The place has gone to pot completely. They imported these midgets to play, you know, robots and androids and Ewoks."

"Latif," I repeated, putting a lot of lung into it.

"I'm trying to tell you." Unlike my snarl, her voice was soothing, saintly. Sometimes she must of pushed the prisoners too far. "What the movie people didn't understand, there's a local superstition that it's good luck to touch a dwarf."

"Touch! They're slapping them shitless."

"Sometimes things get out of hand."

"Where the hell's Latif?"

"Haven't you been listening?" She ignored the nincompoops that had their kissers against the glass like guppies slurping at the side of an aquarium. "He took one look at the mob scene and moved to another hotel."

"Where?"

"Next town. Nefta."

"This I don't believe!" My voice rang in the metal bread-box of a car. "You two are doing a number on me. Leading me on a snipe hunt."

"Eddie, you're acting a tad paranoid. Nefta's less than an hour's drive."

"You're dragging me all over the goddamn country."

"I'm not dragging you anyplace," she said, the soul of patience. "You'd rather not meet Latif, that's your choice. But I've got to. If neither of us shows up, he'll be sick with worry."

"Okay, Nefta," I said. "No farther."

"Fine. But I don't see well at night. I'll have to ask you to drive."

Relieved she wouldn't end this horror show by wrapping us around a palm tree, I moved to the driver's side, and she lifted her rump over the gear shift and deposited it in the passenger's seat. Before starting off, I dug a sweater and a pair of gloves out of my suitcase.

"Brrr, cold," she said, perky and cheerful like we were on a hayride.

It was no easy trick to see. Those kibitzers had left their nose and lip prints all over the windshield. And it was dark, damn dark. West of Tozeur there wasn't a street light, a lantern, a campfire, another car.

First I knew we were in Nefta, a dozen giant albino bats fluttered out of the night. Naturally, it was more dimwits in *djellabas*. I had to slow down. That or clobber them full speed. They had no fear of darting in front of us, doing their smoking pantomime.

"Where to?" I asked Lenore.

"The Sahara Palace, I suppose."

"What's this 'I suppose' crap? You didn't ask?"

"You were waiting. I knew you'd be anxious, angry, upset."

"Save the psychoanalysis. Just where's the hotel. I don't see a sign. Haven't these ninnies heard about the invention of neon?"

"Better ask directions."

The instant I stopped, the Sahara Soul Train clamped onto us, mashing their mugs to the glass. I cranked down the window an inch, and in slithered an octopus-worth of fingers, tongues, and hands.

"Where's the Sahara Palace?" I shouted up one guy's nose.

"Sahara Palace," Lenore repeated, putting a little French into it.

They agreed it was uphill, to the right. One fellow kept fiddling with the locked door, just dying to pile in with us. I gunned the gas and eased out the clutch. "Step back, boys. Thanks for the directions. Keep in touch. Write. Call when you're in town."

I was rolling—slow at first, then faster and faster, fighting to shake free of their suction-cup palms. Finally with a burst of speed I broke loose and left them flopping in our wake.

"You could have killed them," Lenore wailed.

"What'd you want me to do, wait there while they licked the chrome off the car?" I roared uphill.

"You're getting upset and angry again."

"Damn right. I'm ready for a shower and a drink and dinner and another drink. Then a long talk with Latif to find out why—"

I was so busy beating my gums I drove through a barricade. Plowed straight into a two-by-six laid across a couple barrels. Lucky the board was rotten. It exploded into sawdust. But not before bashing in a headlight.

"This Latif's car?" I hissed through clenched teeth.

"Relax. It's rented."

I rolled to a halt at the top of a hill and saw the Sahara Palace down below, dark except for a sign saying it was closed for renovation.

"Guess he's at the Marhala Touring Club." Lenore talked in a sleepy drawl, like she smashed through barricades every day and was so bored she could barely keep from yawning.

"Where's that?"

"The other side of town."

"Great! Now I gotta drive back through that herd of dipshits that'd like to tear my face off for running over their toes." I wrenched the wheel and spun around, spraying gravel.

"Maybe one of these side roads leads to the Marhala."

I turned where she pointed, the beam of the left headlight wobbling like the bent feeler of a bug that's been tromped on. We entered an antheap of houses, all stacked higgledy-piggledy, built of mud and palm trunks. The street I was driving down was like a tunnel dropping into an underground garage where the curves are tighter than a corkscrew and you're always half an inch from scraping the wall.

I had my hands fixed so tight to the wheel, they were sweating inside the kangaroo-skin gloves. We squeezed through a spot no wider than a doorway and the pavement disappeared, just fell out from under us, and we went thundering down a flight of stairs, Lenore giggling and whooping, me hollering and holding on to save us from ramming into a wall. Axles clanged against stone, the exhaust pipe snapped off, and I banged my head against the roof. Then we hit bottom and sat dazed in the throbbing bell of the Fiat.

"Wow! Rough ride." Lenore smoothed her skirt over her knees. "I believe we take that street to the left."

"What street?" I screamed. "There's no street. That's a hallway!"

"You're hallucinating, Eddie. Put your head between your legs."

"Put your head up your ass. We're in somebody's living room."

A guy in an undershirt and saggy drawers opened a door in front of us, shook his fist, and start caterwauling. I didn't understand his lingo, but I knew what he was bitching about. We had crash-landed outside his bedroom. Behind him a woman and a baby were crying.

"You like to explain to him what happened?" I said. "Or do I turn down that hall and race him to the front door?"

"The engine's on fire." She didn't sound specially upset.

But seeing smoke pour out of the motor, I panicked. All I could think was the Fiat's going to explode and the man'll be studded with shrapnel, his family fried to cinders. I cut the ignition, popped the hood, and sprinted to the front of the car.

The radiator was steaming. I reached in and unscrewed the cap. Right away, I recognized my mistake. Boiling water and rusty metal erupted and blew off my hand. I saw it fly in slo-mo past my face, the fingers black and mangled. Hor-

rendous as the pain was, it was more the sight of my char-
broiled fist zooming toward the ceiling that knocked me to
my knees, then knocked me out.

I revived with my head on Lenore's lap. Where my hand
should of been I felt nothing but flames shooting from my
elbow to my wrist stump.

"Are you all right?" Lenore said.

"You stupid bitch. How can you ask that when I just lost
my hand?"

She slapped something soggy into my face. I peeled it off
my cheek. A wet kangaroo-skin glove. No bones, no blood in
the shriveled sack of leather. I forced myself to look at my
right wrist. The hand was still attached. Blistered and burned,
but there.


We hoofed it to the Marhala Touring Club, following the
fellow in scorched underwear who, after some cash changed
hands, dressed in a *djellaba* and toted our luggage. Far as I
was capable of thought, I was thinking, He's doing this to
me. Latif, he planned everything, paid off everybody, put
them up to it to punish me for abandoning him.

Crowded with backpackers, bikers, punks with chain belts
and studded leather bracelets, the Marhala had all the charm
of a Greyhound terminal. Every direction I turned, some
open-mouth breather was eyeballing Lenore.

But the owners were friendly. They cleaned and bandaged
my hand in a ball of gauze, then relayed a message from
Latif. He had crossed the border into Algeria and was waiting
at El Oued.

Lenore was hot to hurry and catch up with him. Didn't
even ask why he had left without us. But it was too late to
rent a car or flag down a bus, and cooler heads here doubted
the Algerian customs officials would let us pass till daybreak.
They said we should stay the night. Not in a room. The
Marhala was full.

I began making noises, not crying, more like moaning. I
was thinking how terrific it'd be back at that upside-down

pyramid hotel, the one crammed with birdcages. Hell, I'd
of settled for the midget tag-team wrestling arena in Tozeur.

"Let's eat dinner," said Lenore. "Something'll open up."

"Yeah. Probably a hole in my head."

We had to share a table with four tan, muscular Americans
with butch haircuts and clipped moustaches. They went on
talking like they never noticed we were Americans too.

"I wouldn't eat it," one guy said.

I thought he meant the *couscous.*

"I would," said a second guy. "He's cute. Looks clean."

"And the eyes," said a third, "he's got both of them. I was
beginning to think all these guys had only one good eye."

They were talking about the waiter, a kid wearing a wool
cap about the size of a yarmulke.

"It's the flies," one of them said. "Gives them trachoma."

"I hate to think about the diseases they're carrying."

"The flies?"

"These waiters."

Cradling my bandaged hand in my lap, I downed a straight
Scotch I had brought from the bar. Then I filled the glass
with wine.

Lenore nudged my elbow, whispering, "Remind you of
Gide?"

"Sheed?"

"You know *The Immoralist?*"

"Not personally. But I'm familiar with the type."

She drew back and did a double take. "You're tired. We'd
better find you a place to sleep."

"What do you suggest? Outside with the sand fleas and
scorpions? Or in here with the trouser snakes and spiro-
chetes?"

"Trust me."

"Trust you?" I tried to snort. I didn't even have the
strength to do that. A mouthful of wine bubbled up my nose.
"Look, lay it on me straight. Is this an obstacle course?
Some kind of test? Or simple torture, revenge?"

"What do you mean?"

"I mean, if Latif has no intention of meeting me, he just

wants to jack me around, say so and save everybody a lot of trouble."

"Eddie, you're way off base. Of course he wants to see you. He's been talking about you for months."

"Oh? What'd he have to say?"

Crossing her legs, she picked at imaginary specks on her dress and frowned, wrinkling her nose like she couldn't figure whether to confide in me. "I'd rather he tell you himself. But I will say this, he has a lot of affection and loyalty left for you . . . considering."

"Considering what?"

"Oh come on," she said in a light, bouncy voice. "Be honest. With yourself, if not with me. Even a conniver can sometimes face the truth."

"Is that what Latif told you? I'm a conniver?"

She laughed. It was a throaty laugh I would of liked if I hadn't been on the receiving end. "No. The first time he ever mentioned you was one day in class. I quoted Oscar Wilde's definition of a cynic, and Latif piped up, 'I know that man. His name's Eddie Brown.' "

"What's this Wilde quote?"

She flung it in my face like the soggy glove. "Wilde said a cynic is someone who knows the price of everything and the value of nothing."

Drinking the wine left-handed, awkward and unsteady, I tried not to show how much it hurt. "You're right. I *am* tired. I gotta get horizontal for a few hours."

"I'll arrange something and be right back." Before she left, she patted my knee. "Latif really is looking forward to seeing you."

## Chapter Five

I wound up bedding down on a table, wrapped in a red and white checkered oilcloth, my carry-on bag as a pillow. The way my hand was pulsing with pain, I never expected to sleep. But next I knew, it was eight hours later, the sun was shining, and Lenore was singing, "Good morning. I've ordered breakfast."

After I ducked into the bathroom to splash my face with water and beat my wiry hair back into shape—neither easy to do one-handed—I found Lenore on the terrace, sitting in cold sunlight, warming her hands on a coffee mug. The Marhala was on a hill, looking out over a palm grove. Seemed like you could step off the patio and pad across a springy carpet of green fronds.

Lenore poured my coffee and buttered a croissant and told me she'd been up for hours. She didn't say where she spent the night, and I didn't ask. What she was wearing, she might of bedded down with the bikers and got her clothes mixed with theirs. No more prim schoolmarm. She had on a black turtleneck and a pair of grey, wet-look slacks with zippers at the hips, thighs, calves, cuffs, and crotch.

She'd been on the telephone, she said, informing the car rental company the Fiat was wrecked. She'd also arranged for us to ride on a German tour bus. "I spoke to Latif. He'll meet us at the Souf Museum in El Oued."

"He promised to wait?"

"Yes. But he stressed he'd understand if, in your condition, after all these inconveniences and changed plans, you decided it was no go."

"Why can't he come here?"

"Didn't say. But that's the point, Eddie. If you're going to stand on ceremony and insist he come to you, or if you're on a tight schedule and have to get home, then I'll take you back to Tunis."

I sipped my coffee and stared over the steamy edge of the mug. What could I say? I didn't have a "schedule," hadn't had one for three years. No "home" either, not in any sense Lenore could fathom.

Suddenly it swept over me, like it did sometimes, and I was mooning about America, all the things I missed. I wanted my own place, my old life back. I wanted a thick bloody steak and a baked potato. I wanted Wild Turkey bourbon and all-night delis and NFL football and Home Box Office and junkets to Vegas and my own car on a real highway and that great feeling that I was onto a good thing, driving to a place that led to something better.

But I knew there was just one way to get there. Go full circle. Rejoin Latif and try to come back together. "When do we leave?" I asked Lenore.


The standard rap against German tourists, they're loud and boisterous. But not this bunch. Maybe it was an affinity group of strong, silent types. Maybe they were traveling on business, not pleasure. They studied the countryside like scouts from Kentucky Fried Chicken. Occasionally someone called out a word of Kraut, pointing to a pack of camels or a boy herding goats. Otherwise, they kept their opinions or cost estimates to themselves while we crossed a stretch of land that looked like it had been left in the oven too long.

Fiddling with the zippers on her pants, Lenore was reading a book, a new one today, *The Sheltering Sky*. I hooked myself to the headset.

# *Tape # 3*

After twenty-four hours in a plane, I bumped down through the clear air turbulence of west Texas to see wiry plants twisted by wind, sand dunes, and dun-colored buildings rising from dun-colored ground. The arid air, hot as it had been in my village, crackled with dust, and I smelled the same burn-off from oil wells. In patches of shade, the same dark-skinned *bouzous* waited to carry my bags and drive me to the campus.

These similarities between home and here were more disturbing than consoling. I didn't want to believe I had abandoned my birthplace, bringing down the curse of my father, only to trade one desert for another. So for weeks I sought out and exaggerated the differences. In the dorm I set my window air conditioner on Maxi-Kool and slept under blankets. I hauled buckets of ice from the machine at the end of the hall and popped the crunchy nuggets into my mouth like peanuts. I stepped into the shower stall and let the spray— hot or cold according to my whim and a twist of my wrist— stream down my body and gurgle through a grille in the floor.

Water, a substance beyond price in the Sahara, the dribbling capillary of life, was worthless here. While I squandered gallons of it, a peculiar spinning device below my window spat more of it onto plots of ground where shrubs grew. Although these plants sprouted delicious-looking flowers and berries, neither men nor animals ever ate them.

At Holy Sepulcher, eating was as symbolic as the pretty plants on the lawn. Three times a day, students congregated in the dining hall, a building bigger than any mosque in my country, and there, at the training table with the athletes, I heaped my tray high with charred meat, limp vegetables, spongy white bread and sugared pastry. Then after a brief ceremony of chewing and chatting, we marched to a tin barrel and scraped kilos of food into plastic bags. I assumed this was a ritual of sharing, that the *bouzous* who cooked and cleaned for us bore these bags away to their huts and gobbled what we left, just as our slaves would have done.

One day I followed the blacks and discovered that they dumped the leftovers in a dry riverbed. This, too, I assumed was a ritual, a sacrifice the *bouzous* offered their god, praying to be spared from flash floods. But no, it was called "landfill." Food was so cheap, so unimportant, people used it instead of dirt to fill gullies.

Before class, students scrubbed themselves clean. Men shaved and girls painted their faces brighter than the tattooed women of my tribe. Then we gathered on wooden chairs under fizzing fluorescent bulbs while the professor, as heavy with knowledge as any *imam* or *ayatollah*, distributed lists of books and names and dates. In the still and quiet of so many souls crowded close, I recalled the long hours I spent learning the Koran, the difficult verses I mastered by rote memory. "I swear by this city (and you yourself are a resident of this city), by the begetter and all whom he begot: We created man to try him with afflictions."

But strangely, at Holy Sepulcher, nobody was tried with afflictions. We did not chant nor did we listen, heads bowed, bellies tormented, to the fulminations of the professor. We dialogued, we interfaced, we laughed, we disagreed. We ended each class by asking, "Is this going to be on the final exam?" If it wasn't, we forgot it.

In spite of a fear that my failure to read and write English would, once exposed, put me on the next plane home, I did fine. Along with many foreign students and no small number of Americans, I enrolled in English as a Second Language and Remedial Reading. I also registered for History of Film, in which I watched movies; Current Events, for which I studied the nightly news; and Radio and TV, during which I pretended to be a sports commentator.

While class work proved easier than I had expected, college tennis was harder than I could have conceived. There was nobody on the Holy Sepulcher team I could beat. Unlike the *toubabs* at the oil compound, these fellows were my age, stronger, and more experienced. I could not overpower them and I didn't know enough to outsmart them. That came only after hours of arduous drills with the coach, Clem "Snake" Wiegnard.

"Stop right there. Point's finished. You lose," he'd scream whenever I made a mistake.

"Hit for the lines and take the net," he'd hammer at me. "You don't, the other guy will. He'll ram it down your throat."

Semicrippled, he'd hobble on court to demonstrate, his eyes shaded by a green visor, his elbows and knees wrapped in Ace bandages. "Why hit wide when this guy eats up angles? Work him down the middle," or, "Don't just keep the ball in play. Every time you hit it, have something in mind," or, "You catch a man at the net defenseless, never let him forget it. Take his tit off. Nail him in the nipple."

Wiegnard worked wonders with me. He broke down my bad habits and built up my confidence, shortened my backswing and lengthened my follow-through, quickened my ground-stroke preparation and slowed down my service motion, taught me to save a step rushing the net and improved my volley. By the end of the fall season, I could beat everybody at Holy Sepulcher; by spring I could handle any college player and many pros.


Thousands of miles from home, I had resigned myself to loneliness. But this was one more mistaken expectation. My teammates quickly befriended me. Only one thing was lacking. Although I didn't miss Rashida's whining, I had virile needs, and these were not satisfied by a weekly bus ride to a bordello across the Mexican border, a hundred miles south.

During my second year at Holy Sepulcher, I met a plump blonde named Noreen. She had a space between her front teeth, a sign of healthy sexual appetite among my people, and she wore low-slung blue jeans and skimpy tank tops that left bare an inch or two of tanned flesh at her waist. The sight of her navel, a tight slit glinting with a few golden hairs, made me light-headed.

Sitting next to me in the darkness of History of Film, she let her round thigh rub against mine. She touched my arm when she talked. Strolling past the stained-glass windows of the Tabernacle and executive offices of the Church of the Holy Sepulcher, she once raised a hand high and pointed to a biblical scene, and I was tempted to bury my face in the moist hairless hollow under her arm.

Yet although after a movie or a taco off campus she would come to my room in the open dormitory, where all the doors were bolted shut, she would not let me put my hands under her clothes. Cupping her breasts or dipping between her legs, I had to keep a layer of fabric between my palm, calloused from years of tennis, and her soft skin, sweet with suntan oil.

When it came to touching me, however, she didn't hesitate to unzip my trousers, peel down my underpants, and whack away with startlingly swift hands. I erupted like a geyser, shooting off onto the walls, the ceiling, the floor while Noreen danced clear of the torrent of gism, laughing in girlish wonder.

When I begged to make love to her, she said, "No way, Slick."

When I suggested she at least let me caress her, flesh to flesh, as she had me, she said, "Forget it, Bubba."

Whenever I attempted to ease a finger under the leg band of her shorts, she said, "Whoa, pardner."

Finally she explained that although she was without racial prejudice, she had stern religious scruples. Since I was a

Moslem and she was a member of the Church of the Holy Sepulcher, she couldn't in conscience let me do more than fondle her bunched-up clothing.

"Unless, of course," she said, "you'd consider converting."

I told her I'd consider anything.

"There's another problem," she added. We were in my room, the sound of the sprinkler below my window competing with the whir of the air conditioner. "I'm almost too embarrassed to tell you."

She lowered her eyes to her right hand which clutched my erect manhood in much the same manner as it gripped the gear shift of her peppy Fiero when she was driving. Her lips, a glossy pink, were slightly parted and judging by the tilt of her head, the loose tension of her neck, it seemed possible she was considering taking me in her mouth. I raised my hips, hinting.

But she let go of me and scratched her knit shirt, one tinted fingernail fiddling with the tiny mounted horseman who wielded a mallet near the crisp nipple of her left breast. "It wasn't like I meant to hide it," she said. "I just didn't see how it could become an issue, not even after we started, you know, started dating." She faced me now, the gap between her front teeth going dark, then pink, as her tongue darted back and forth. "I sleep with a retainer."

My sturdy Tuareg dirk dissolved into a length of limp meat. Delirium, delight, anger, interest swept through me, wave after wave. One instant I was aroused by this confession; the next instant I was outraged that she had bestowed on a *bouzou* the favors she refused me.

In History of Film we had watched *Birth of a Nation* and *Gone With the Wind*. So I knew all about retainers, whether faithful darkies, proud bucks, fat mammies, or treacherous mixed bloods.

"You're still doing this? Now? Here at Holy Sepulcher?"

"Yes." She nodded. "Whenever my roommate's away, whenever I don't have to worry somebody'll see me." Her voice cracked. "I can't help it."

"Why?" I roared.

Blushing, she turned away. "Isn't it obvious?"

"Not to me." I pulled up my pants and zipped the fly.

"I go a week without it and I, I . . . I just, you know, fall apart. I feel myself starting to spread. There's an ache."

"Always the same retainer?"

"Gimme a break, Slick. Can't you see I'm dying of shame?"

"I have to know."

"Of course it's not the same one. I've been spreading since I was twelve. But things change—my size, shape, what fits, what feels right. Now you happy? Now you know all the gross details."

Again her brutal honesty about her body and its appetites excited me as much as it hurt. I could guess how it had started—some dusky, donkey-dicked family employee slinking into Noreen's bedroom late at night, wading through the Cabbage Patch dolls and trainer bras, the Madonna and Prince tapes, tipped off by the Michael Jackson posters that she yearned for what he loosened from his butler's uniform.

At the age of twelve, had she understood what she was doing? Yes, of course. Rashida wasn't much older when she married me.

At Holy Sepulcher no student had a personal retainer. But there were the *bouzous* from the dining room and dozens more who buffed floors and scrubbed toilets in the dorms. If they weren't enough to ease Noreen's ache, there were the men from the Buildings and Grounds crew. I imagined a herd of black stallions pawing the turf below her window, waiting for her roommate to go away for the weekend. Apparently all that qualified them and disqualified me was their faith.

"How long does it take to convert?" I asked.

Her lovely face brightened. "You mean you'd do it? For me?"

"That depends." I stood up.

"I'd love to save someone's soul."

"Then you'll have to make a choice. Me or the retainer."

"You're kidding. It bothers you that much? Is it a cultural thing?"

"I can't express in English how much it sickens me."

"I know it's not nice but—"

"Nice!"

"Okay, it's ugly and disgusting." Her lower lip quivered. "But some men would make allowances."

"No man in my tribe. No man who loves you and respects himself."

"Do I have to quit right now?"

"What do you want? One last night? A few weeks?"

"I thought while you were taking instructions you wouldn't mind."

"Wouldn't mind?" I exploded.

"I'll start to spread."

"Where's your willpower? What about me and my feelings?"

After a pause, she said, "All right, I'll give it up. I want you to know I care for you. Jesus cares." She stood up and ground her plump mound against me. "But you've got to promise to convert."

My head swam. My manhood stirred. "I promise."

Her hand went under the waistband of my trousers and yanked the dirk from its scabbard. I unzipped her jeans and this time she didn't stop me when I slipped a finger into the fluffy nest. But that was as far as I got. Those fields that had been plowed for years by Christian retainers would remain off bounds to this Moslem until he completed religious instruction.

Conversion, I discovered, consisted of sitting for several hours a day in a darkened room watching movies about Holy Sepulcher's founder, L. Robert Jimson, who rolled into West Texas late in the nineteenth century with a wagonload of Bibles and a shotgun. Believing in a political interpretation of Scripture and a religious reading of the United States Constitution, Jimson prophesied the discovery of oil in the Permian Basin and promised his followers earthly riches and heavenly salvation. An early advocate of the abolition of taxes and the passage of an oil depletion allowance, he had, by the end of his life—he died in a head-on collision in 1951 outside Muleshoe, Texas—established churches, drilling operations, and tool and die companies on three continents.

When pressed, I replied that I had no problem embracing the truths found in these films. Fortunately I was not asked to identify them or to repudiate the Koran, in which I continued to believe. I viewed this not as cynicism, but as a right-thinking attitude. Why not convert if that rescued Noreen from the corruption of the retainers—and saved her for me?

First, however, I had to prepare for the sacraments of Public Testimony and Total Immersion Baptism. Whereas Baptism required only the purchase of a black, wrinkle-proof, preshrunk polyester suit, Public Testimony entailed an extensive examination of conscience, and by the time I entered the Tabernacle to confess my past wrongdoings to an assembly of students and professors, I was convinced I would disgrace Noreen and disgust everyone else.

She stayed by my side, sitting next to me in the front pew, smiling encouragement. She told me not to worry. It was natural to be nervous before Public Testimony. Everybody would understand and forgive me. "Just be honest," she said.

After an organ recital and an introduction by the deacon, I turned to the ranks of white faces. Beaming brighter than the rest, Noreen blew me a kiss. Then I was on my own. I raised my eyes, staring off at the stained-glass windows, swaying as I unburdened my soul. The list of Christian sins I had memorized tumbled out like those verses from the Koran that had been drummed into me during torrid desert afternoons. Caught up in the chanting rhythm, I had to take care not to break into Arabic.

"As a boy," I admitted, "I lied, I stole, I disobeyed my parents, I lost my temper, I bullied small children, teased weak and crippled people, and robbed the blind."

I felt a tug at my trouser leg—Noreen urging me on. She knew these childish wrongs were nothing compared to the sacrileges of my later life.

I launched into my adolescence, still looking off at the jeweled light of the windows. "For years I played what we in my country call *frapper le saucisson*. Literally, beat or agitate the sausage. But I'm sure you know what I mean. I did not realize this was wrong."

A sharper tug at my polyester trousers. Noreen caught me before I rambled, excusing myself through ignorance.

"Then it was on to goats and sheep. Sometimes my father's flock. Sometimes a neighbor's, thus complicating illicit sex with a property rights violation. But in a rural village, not unlike some small towns in Texas—"

She grabbed me with both hands, goading me to get it over with. I didn't dare look down until I had finished and was forgiven.

"From doing jig-jig with livestock, it was a short step to women. I'm ashamed to say . . ." I hesitated. Even Noreen didn't know this. "I slept with slave girls, *bouzous*."

Noreen groaned. A sigh of relief as she realized she was not alone. I was guilty of the same sin.

"It is an act," I said, "not unknown in your country and on this campus. Sleeping with a retainer you call it. In my village, we say—"

"Shut up," she shouted. "Jesus Christ, please somebody shut him up."

Startled, I glanced down. Her face glistened with tears. The gap between her front teeth had widened.

I peered at the rows of pews, at my professors and fellow students. I wouldn't confront such expressions again until that year at Wimbledon when I committed an outrage in front of the royal family.

"Sit down," the deacon demanded.

I should have done that—shut up and sat down. But my mind was reeling. "I know I am weak, and when my teammates say, 'Let's roll down to the border and rip off a piece of spic ass,' I lack the courage to refuse. But once I have converted—"

"Call Security."

"Sit down."

I began babbling in Arabic, chanting verses, seeking security in the familiar rhythms. "Tell them of the man to whom We vouchsafed Our signs and who turned away from them; how Satan overtook him as he was led astray. Had it been Our will, We would have exalted him through our signs. But he clung to this earthly life and succumbed to his desires."

Some believed I was possessed by demons, speaking in tongues. Others who had lived in the Islamic world recognized a few words from the Koran. But everybody regarded my outburst as an insult to the sacrament of Public Testimony and a mockery of their faith. I was shouted, then roughly shoved, down.

As they dragged me from the Tabernacle, Noreen trotted at my side, took an amulet from her purse, aimed the semi-circle of wire at my eyes, and hissed, "I wear it on my teeth, you retard. I wear it on my teeth."


Snake Wiegnard saved me from expulsion and a one-way flight to the Sahara. At my trial by the Student-Faculty Disciplinary Panel, he swore my behavior was injury-related. During a team match against Southern Methodist—a match, he stressed, I had helped Holy Sepulcher win—I had hurt my head diving for a drop shot. Ever since, I was apt to pop off with the most peculiar remarks. He convinced the panel to put me on academic probation and review my case after the match against Ouachita Baptist College.

That's when we met, Eddie. Remember? You showed up and introduced yourself as a talent scout. In your white Stetson, lizard-skin boots, and tan leisure suit, you resembled those runts at Texas county fairs who get chased by Brahma bulls or lassoed by bronc busters. A rodeo clown, that's what you looked like.

But the first syllable you spoke, I knew you weren't from Texas. You had an accent like Ratso Rizzo in *Midnight Cowboy*, a movie we had screened in History of Film, and you spoke from the side of your mouth, as if whispering a secret you didn't want your cigar to hear.

Immediately I was on guard. After skidding off the rails during Public Testimony, I feared you had been sent by the college to tempt me, test me.

"Listen, kid," you said, "I don't know what you're getting here, but—"

"I'm getting a good Christian education and the friendship of my fellow students."

"Okay, I'm not prying for a dollars-and-cents figure. But I bet we're talking about the regulation free ride for athletes —books, room and board, laundry money, and an occasional blow job from a cheerleader."

"Wrong!" I bellowed, eager to have Holy Sepulcher people hear how much I had learned from my mistakes. "I know what a retainer is. I know a retainer has nothing to do with sex. It's not a coed sleeping with a black man."

"Hey, hold it down. These clowns got no right to know our business. You wanna talk retainers, we'll talk retainers. A lump sum down. Seed money to cover your expenses. I get it back later by pocketing a larger percentage, on a temporary basis, of your earnings."

I was lost. I had no idea how to answer—which is why I asked a question. "Have you accepted Jesus Christ as your personal savior?"

You smiled, Eddie, and cigar smoke streamed from your nostrils. "No, kid. I've accepted you as my personal savior. We can go places."

"Where?"

"The pro tour. You're too big for this burg. Where you from anyhow?"

"Africa," I said. "The Sahara."

"What's your name?"

"Latif Fluss."

You squinted against the cigar smoke. "A handle like that could be trouble. Tell you what, you shower and get dressed. We'll drive into town and discuss this over dinner."

I still wasn't sure whether you meant to trick me and turn me over to the Disciplinary Panel. But I knew you had told the truth about one thing—I was ready for the pro tour.

When I returned from the locker room in my black baptism suit, you blinked and shook your head. "Jesus, kid, what are you studying to be, a mortician? Right after your name, we gotta do something about your wardrobe."

Your car, a white Lincoln Continental, had orange pin-striping and a padded dashboard of genuine cowhide. The hair was still on the hide. We drove to Shoney's, my choice, not yours, and a waitress escorted us to a table with a view of a heat mirage on the parking lot. I picked Shoney's because it had colorful menus with pictures of specials and platters. Even after two years of English as a Second Language and Remedial Reading, I was sometimes reduced to pointing at what I wanted.

"How did you happen to be at the match?" I asked after we ordered.

"No 'happen' about it. Heard about you. Word spreads fast in the talent industry. Major act, they say. Hurry over and sign him up."

You removed the Stetson. *Bouzou* hair, was my first thought. Bushy and crinkly. Your scalp was red. Your face seldom shows your true emotions, Eddie, but from the start I could read on your head the changes in your mood.

"About your name," you said, "it could be a loser in lots of markets. Let's change it to Larry Fields or Luke Feeney so you don't have to throw out your monogrammed underwear."

"If my name isn't good enough for you, I'm not good enough."

"Hey, don't get touchy. It matters that much, then keep the name. We'll change everything around it."

"I'm not going to lie about who I am or what I am," I said, disappointed nobody from Holy Sepulcher heard me resist temptation.

"Who's talking lies? We're choosing, selecting. That's how you build a winning image."

"You don't win tennis matches with an image," I said.

"Lemme tell you a secret, kid." You leaned across the table. "I don't care what the game is, image has a helluva lot to do with winning. Looking at you now, I see a dozen details I could change that'd improve your performance."

"For example?"

"For example that fucking undertaker's outfit you're wearing. I'll dress you in something with style, flair. You look like a loser, you can't be a winner."

I fingered the lapel of your leisure suit. "Can you get me a discount on a rodeo clown costume?"

"Don't jump to conclusions about this shitkicker gear. I represent a couple Country and Western acts. Sometimes I have to dress down."

You pulled a cigar from your breast pocket, tore off the cellophane, passed it under your nose. "I'm gifted with a sixth sense—built-in radar for guys ready for the big time. I know you can handle any kinda tennis competition. Problem is, you can't prove that unless you get a shot at a Lendl or a McEnroe. That's where I come in. I'll put you in the action, put you in the game. That's what losers never learn—you can't win if you're not in the game going for the jackpot."

"*Knute Rockne, All-American,*" I broke in with a name of another movie I'd seen in class. "Win one for the Gipper."

"Don't knock the Gipper." You lit the cigar. "Positive thinking, going for the gold, it works miracles. Look where the Gipper wound up."

"Dead."

"No way. In the White House, president of the free-enterprise world."

The waitress brought our orders. I reached for the salt and pepper shakers to season my gravy-smothered chicken-fried steak. You grabbed my wrist.

"You tasted that?"

I shook my head.

"No, 'course not. That's why you need personal management. You're an impulse-type guy. It helps your game—being aggressive. But off court there's people in this world that'd watch you salting meat you never tasted and think here's a kid I can snatch bald-headed without him even being aware." You let go of my wrist. "Me, I'll protect you, teach you, swim between you and the sharks."

After sampling everything on the plate, I reached for the salt and pepper again, then ate warily, watching you work at your food. That's what you did, Eddie, you worked at it— cut it, seasoned it, sliced it, never took a bite.

I can't recall exactly what you said about traveling first class and living like a champion, but I remember your energy, the jittery vigor out of all proportion to your size. You touched everything on the table—ashtray, plastic flowers, wire frame full of sugar packets, each piece of silverware, including mine—and you never stopped talking. Logic, syntax, and grammar sometimes escaped you, but you never lost sight of what you were saying.

You saw through my self-protective lies and tossed aside the truth as being of no interest. Like an athlete with an instinct for his opponent's secret weakness, you laughed at my inexperience and ignorance, then argued that such a client, half-formed, still a boy in many ways, offered a special opportunity for your genius.

Just as you never ate, only rearranged your food, you never really smoked. The cigars were a prop. You lit them one after another, punctuating your sentences with a jab of the smoldering butt, blowing away my remaining doubts like so much smoke.

"So what do you say, kid? Sign with me and it's up, up and away." You made a missile of the cigar.

"What am I signing?"

"A contract that I represent you worldwide. In return I get twenty percent of the gross. I'll stake you for six months."

"It may take longer."

"Okay, a year. I'll travel the circuit with you, hire a coach, set you up with the best contracts."

"I'd have to leave Holy Sepulcher. My education."

"What can they teach you I can't? And can they make you a star?"

"You're serious?"

"Kid, I'm always serious. Even when I'm joking. Specially when I'm joking."

We drafted a deal memo on a Shoney's napkin.

# *Chapter* Six

Seeing a German tour group with beery faces and knockwurst knees, soldiers at the Algerian frontier surrounded the bus. Ready to fight off an invasion, they stood guard with automatic rifles next to a bivouac of shacks, tents, and tethered goats. They lowered a barrier across the road, one of those striped poles like at the entrance to a pay parking lot.

It didn't take me ten seconds to size up the situation. I'd been through it dozens of times. All the countries you never wanted to visit in the first place, they thought they were doing you a huge favor just considering letting you in. They demanded to see your passport, your pocket cash, your return ticket, your itinerary. Everything except your life line and a blood test.

When they began calling us off the bus one and two at a time, I knew we were in for a long wait. Lenore knew it too and never quit reading. Me, I changed the cassette in the

Walkman, but held off pushing the start button, still thinking about the previous tape.

I never let on to Latif that I didn't come to College of the Holy Sepulcher to watch his match. I wasn't in the area scouting Country and Western bands either. What I'd been doing down there, I'd been beating the bushes for oil lease investors when my car, a brand new Subaru, conked out. Naturally, that type town, there was no dealer, and I had to cool my heels while they flew in spare parts.

A local grease monkey loaned me the Lincoln, and I cruised five minutes in one direction and five in the other; every street led back into the desert. Nothing to see out there except a yellow line and dead armadillos. The main drag wasn't much better.

So I took a spin over to Holy Sepulcher. Like most religious nut colleges, it looked like it had been designed by Walt Disney on drugs. Every building was shaped like a carnival ride or flying saucer full of statues and paintings to teach the kids a lesson.

I didn't give those lessons a second glance. I was more interested in the prime tenderloin prancing across campus. That's another thing about church schools—the coeds tend to have shapes as fantastic as the buildings.

I got to following a few of them, drifting at their flanks, admiring what healthy babes they were. The girls were headed to the tennis matches. They cold-shouldered the rest of the players and crowded around one court, pressing their tasty tidbits against the chain link fence, watching Latif. I couldn't take my eyes off him either.

Later, seeing him in his mortician suit, I decided he not only didn't know anything about clothes. He didn't have an inkling how his appearance affected people. At first glance, he was—no better word for it—terrifying, but so exotic nobody ever left off after just one look. You kept on staring and before long started thinking he was more terrific than terrifying.

Tall, about six feet three, and broad-shouldered, he had lean-muscled arms and legs, and his stretch fabric tennis shorts looked like a fishnet bulging with two clams and an electric eel. Dead still, he vibrated strength. When he moved he was pure menace, a panther, blue-black, the blue highlights coming clearer when he sweated. His hair had a ginger tinge, and his face was delicate, except for a strong, curved nose, and he had these blue eyes that'd break your heart. I kept thinking here's a kid I could definitely market.

A confession up front—till that day I never watched a tennis match the whole way through. Like most Americans, I favored contact sports—football and fucking. But Latif converted me on the spot. That's star quality, that knack of grabbing people's attention, changing their minds.

Another confession—although I had never been a fan, I followed the business side of the sport and knew on the basis of prize money alone, not counting endorsement contracts and secret rake-offs, tennis players were the richest athletes in the world.

What intrigued me, all this dough floating around, all these players with the cash flow potential of rock stars or drug dealers, they seemed to have immunity to the troubles that went with the territory. Time after time guys got caught dumping matches, splitting prize money, orchestrating games to fit a TV time slot, taking bribes and payola. And what happened? Nothing!

It didn't add up. You slip some eight-foot-tall kid a shoe box stuffed with cash and tell him to shave points in a college basketball game—not necessarily lose, just keep the score close—you go to jail and so does he. You do the same thing in tennis and a sleek fat cat with a world-class tan and an alligator on his shirt explains to the press and the cops that the game only went pro twenty years ago. Any problems crop up, that's predictable, no big deal, certainly not indictable because the pro circuit is still on its shakedown cruise. The tennis tour is too young, he claims, to be held accountable.

As a legal defense, that wouldn't save a sixteen-year-old

shoplifter. Yet somehow when millionaires copped this plea, it carried.

Tell you the truth, I was more than intrigued. I wondered whether the fix was in at a high level with tennis-loving DAs and prosecutors. Or had they never focused on what was happening? Whatever, I had wanted in on this airtight scam for a long time, and when I spotted Latif at Holy Sepulcher wowing the crowd and walloping the no-hoper he was up against, I knew I had found my ticket to ride.

When it came our turn, the customs guards marched Lenore and me off the bus, told us to pick up our luggage and carry it into a concrete block building. Lenore shut the novel on her finger, marking her page like she expected to get back into the story while the Algerians rummaged through her bags.

But these guys were no respecters of literature. They plucked the book off her finger the way you'd unpin a sock from a clothesline and fanned it, searching for heroin, I guess. Two more guys were making mulch of what was in our suitcases when the head man noticed the ball of gauze around my fist. "What is?" he asked in English.

"A bandage."

"But what is in?"

"My hand."

"I must to see." He grabbed my arm at the elbow and wrist, twisting like he thought it was detachable. "Remove."

I unspooled about twenty feet of gauze. It didn't hurt too bad till I wound down to the last layer that was stuck to the scab where the burn blisters had popped. I tore it off like adhesive tape.

"Now we are making a nice progress." The head honcho pried up a flap of dead skin on my palm, checking for contraband cigarettes and radios. When he didn't find any, he nodded I could rewrap the bloody mess.

With a fat finger he tickled one of the zippers on Lenore's fancy pants. "What is in?"

"Nothing."

"Empty your pockets."

"They're not pockets. They're decorations. Just, you know, fun things."

"Open. Show me fun."

"Forget it."

"Open or my mens open."

"Have it your way."

She passed me the book. Then with the soldiers bunched around, all slack-jawed and hairy-knuckled, she yanked at the zippers, rasping them open, pulling her pants apart like a jigsaw puzzle. A minute later she stood there in a pair of short shorts showing a lot of leg. Nice, but nothing to set anybody's blood bubbling back in the real world. Here on the Algerian frontier, however, it cocked every soldier's pistol.

"I'm not hiding anything. Want to feel for yourself?" She handed the head man a fistful of flimsy scraps. They slithered through his fingers and snaked to the floor. One soldier chuckled. Then another. Suddenly everybody was yucking it up at the officer's expense.

He ordered them to shut up. He ordered Lenore to collect her pants and put them on.

Stooping and straightening, fiddling and hitching, she zipped together the legs, pulling them on one at a time, smoothing them up over her thighs like silk stockings, then fastened them to her short shorts. Reminded me of a scene from Naughty Nylons, a specialty act for leg men. I'll guarangoddamntee you, the Algerians, head guy included, didn't blink, didn't breathe during her performance.


Back on the bus, rumbling toward El Oued, I began to revise my opinion. Maybe Lenore Fenstermacher was Latif's type after all.

She took her book from me. "I shouldn't have done that. But they made me so damn mad with their leering and bullying."

"Really out of line for the lady Lit. Professor."

"You don't know me."

"I'm beginning to. Ever done that sort of thing for money?"

She laughed, blushing. "I used to take modern dance lessons. My ex-husband made me quit."

"*Made* you quit? I don't see any chain marks, any scars."

She was studying her fingernails, snapping them with her thumbnail. The nail on her ring finger had split on a zipper. "He was the one left with scars."

"Are we talking emotional damage? Or did you break a Perrier bottle over the Cuisinart and carve up his gizzard?"

"I ran over him with a car."

"What model?" I challenged her. "What year?"

"Volvo. Brand-new turbo diesel."

"You serious?"

She turned to me, smiling again. "I'm always serious. Even when I'm joking. Specially when I'm joking."

"Hey, look who's stealing my lines. Where'd you hear that, Latif?"

"Second-rate artists borrow. First-raters steal."

"Okay, it's established you're a thief. Are you a killer too?"

"My ex-husband didn't die, if that's what you mean. I didn't hit him full speed. There wasn't enough room."

"Should of given the guy a fair running start."

"Fair? I caught him with a woman. In our house, in our bed. I said, 'That's it! Finished!' He followed me to the garage, saying we should talk it over. I said I was sick of talking it over. He stood in front of the car and told me if I left, it would have to be over his dead body." She shrugged. "I stepped on the gas. But like I said, there wasn't enough room to build up speed."

"Jesus. How bad was he hurt?"

"Internal injuries. Superficial lacerations. A few weeks in the hospital and he was fine."

"You wind up in jail? That how you got into teaching prisoners?"

"No. He didn't press charges. He was chairman of the English Department where I worked. He didn't want our marriage and his mistress and internal injuries spread all over the newspapers. But I had to find a new job."

"No wonder the cons didn't hassle you. They were scared of you."

"You're laughing. But I have a feeling you don't approve." She was needling me now.

"Hey, why would I hold it against you? A minor moving violation like that? I'm a sucker for passionate women."

She went back to flicking her nails. "Afraid I'm already spoken for."

I let out another nervous laugh. "Which raises a question. Has Latif heard how you monogrammed your husband's forehead with a Volvo hood ornament?"

"I mentioned it."

"Maybe you oughta mention it again." When she found out about Rashida, I figured there'd be hair, teeth, and eyeballs all over the highway.

"We don't have any secrets. We've both been candid about our pasts."

"Great! Whatever's right. Me, I'm just catching up on his past."

I clamped on the headset and clicked the start button. Holy shit, I thought, I'm with one maniac on my way to meet another.


# *Tape #4*


. . . New Orleans and I feel I'm underwater. When I mention this to a tournament hostess after a lazy game of leapfrog, she says I *am* underwater. The city is below sea level and only a system of levees and dikes saves us from drowning.

I insist I *am* drowning. Mashing my face to her belly, I

slide down her slick body until my mouth fills with seaweed.
I nibble and chew until the desk clerk calls to say the courtesy
car is ready to drive me to the arena.

This doesn't mean I'll play anytime soon. Every week,
everywhere around the world, it's the same aggravation. I
fly from the Philippines or Nepal or Buenos Aires, crossing
continents, oceans, tropical and temperate climates, and
more time zones than I've got fingers. I rush to make connections. I gobble pills to stay awake. I'm met at the airport
on the runway by a limo with the engine racing. Then we
speed off to the courts—where I'm told I have to wait.

Tonight I arrived more blown away than normal. But no
one in the locker room noticed this or mentioned the tee
shirt I had had stencilled down on Bourbon Street. OLD
TENNIS PLAYERS NEVER DIE. THEIR BALLS JUST LOSE THEIR
FUZZ.

Everybody was shaving something. A few guys were at the
sinks, scraping foam from their faces. More were at the
trainer's table hacking hair off their ankles before being
taped. Side by side in plastic chairs two fellows were talking
cars and Quaaludes and really bearing down with their razors.
One was cutting calluses from the soles of his feet; the other
was slicing a hard crust from the palm of his racquet hand.

Flaminio Flamini, the best and prettiest Italian player
since Adriano Panatta, readied himself for the razor by
lathering his upper torso. Once he had mowed down the
curly hair on his chest and belly, he turned around and let
his agent shave him from his shoulders to the waistband
of his shorts.

"What's this?" I asked.

"Contract," said his agent, Pippo Scarcia. "New cloth-ess
contract."

"What's the deal? Some company weaving winter clothes
out of Flaminio's body hair?"

"No, he is posing for bathing suit ads." Pippo rinsed the
razor. You know him, Eddie, always dressed in white, the
Good Humor Man, the guy who brings the sweetest gifts.

He grinned and his freckles looked like rust pits. "The photographer, he sees this"—Pippo pointed to the layer of hair lining the sink—"and he says *che schivo*. Disgusting. On film Flaminio is looking like a tarantula in underpants. So we are shaving to save the contract."

"Already I feel a body ache," said Flaminio. "I am itching all over."

No matter what the message was on my tee shirt, I had not thought this through. I didn't do it to dump on Flaminio. I was feeling foggy in that dank, sub-sea-level locker room, and with all the razor play going on around me, it was the power of suggestion that prompted me to fetch my twenty-nine-cent Bic, endorsed by John McEnroe. I stepped up to the sink beside Flaminio and did what everybody in my village does during hot weather. I shaved my pubic hair, let my privates breathe.

Flaminio took it all wrong. Backbone tufted with Noxzema foamy lather, he lunged at me, screaming. *"Che cazzo.* Don't be making fun of me, you focking knee-gair."

I did the worst thing imaginable. I laughed. It's a humorless black man—or blue man, for that matter—who can hear himself called a "focking knee-gair" and not crack up. But how could I explain this to Flaminio as he rushed me, swinging wild rights and lefts?

I didn't want to hit him, not after that bout of bad publicity for fighting at Wimbledon. So I sprayed him with shaving cream. That blinded him, and Pippo pulled him away, screaming.

When the Grand Prix supervisor and two security guards showed up, they accused me of inciting a riot by sexual innuendo. Be prepared, Eddie, to pay a fine.

Also be prepared to file suit against that meat-packing company in California that keeps marketing a poster of me holding a huge weenie dripping what I hope is mayonnaise. It's a trick shot, my head on someone else's shoulders. I'm smiling like an axe murderer as I mouth the company slogan, "Bite my Fluss-furter."

We've been over this before, Eddie. They're selling the poster without my approval, without paying me, and I want it stopped. I'm sick of being exploited.

Everybody complains I should clean up my act. But I'm a prisoner of my image. It's ads like this that get me blamed for everything on the circuit from rainy weather to fatal overdoses.

Tell you another thing I'm tired of—having no cash in my pocket. I'm worth millions. At least that's what I read in the papers. But yesterday I had to borrow a dollar from a hostess to tip a bellhop.

I've heard you brag how you handle my finances. I've heard you describe taking forceful positions, pitting strength against strength, going eyeball to eyeball with the opposition, shoving somebody to the wall, shutting him down, kicking his ass up over his shoulder blades, scoring big, winning. I think you think you're the athlete, the world champion, and I'm just some dumbass out here doing the donkey work.

I want this to stop. I want more allowance. I want better representation. I want—

# *Chapter* Seven

I hit the stop button. He wanted, he wanted! Hell, he couldn't of had more effective wraparound representation if he hired ten guys in wing tips and tortoise-shell glasses to do my job. You think it's easy managing millions, moving it around, making it grow, then making it disappear before the tax people can touch it? Have another think.

I spent my days reviewing investment portfolios, silent partnerships, mom and pop operations about to be swallowed by conglomerates. I read up on Ginny Maes and bearer bonds and gold futures and genetic firms ready to engineer a technology for cloning cocks. I studied exchange rates, cost-price ratios, inflationary spirals, stagflation figures. I had to know what countries were going communist, where they had declared martial or Sharia law, where the dictator's been dead for years and they're just dragging around his mummy in parades.

Then on top of hondeling with lawyers and spitballing ideas with economic experts, I had to *try* to explain things to Latif. One time I proposed a leveraged buy-out, and he thought I was saying beverage buy-out, like we were going to corner the market on Mountain Dew.

Another time I said, "I been wondering whether we should get into a yen straddle, you and me."

Latif popped his cork. "You try that, you ever touch me that way, I'm gone. I'll leave and sign with Dell or McCormack."

What Latif never did, he never learned the facts of financial life. I didn't let him carry a lot of cash because he was the easiest mark I ever met. To have him flashing a fat roll would of been disaster.

I tried to convince him to travel with an entourage. It actually would of been cost efficient to transport everybody he needed everyplace he played. I pointed out most stars had bodyguards, coaches, trainers, dieticians, all-purpose ass kissers. WAGs they call them on the circuit—Walk Around Guys.

Sure, these people were mostly parasites. But they would of been *our* parasites, and whatever they stole was tax deductible. Elephants lumbered along with birds that ate bugs off their backs. Sharks swam with tiny fish that nibbled their teeth clean. Lions lived cheek by jowl with vultures and hyenas. It was a law of the jungle, I told Latif. You were successful, you had to surround yourself with lowlifes that took care of the scut work.

But he didn't want to hear it. That was his trouble, Latif. He never listened, never looked through a wide-angle lens.

I explained the concept of shrinkage. Given his gross income, there were bound to be checks that bounced, companies that paid late, sleazebags that used his picture without permission in ads for enema powders, hair straighteners, and breast-enlarging lotions. No sense bitching about every grifter who nicked him for a dollar.

But Latif, he was in bad shape his last months on the circuit. More and more paranoid. Did he suspect I was screwing him too?

I confess I'd sometimes tell tournament directors I'd deliver my man—for a fee! A kickback for me on top of a guarantee for Latif. Why not? It wasn't coming out of his pocket. I never—okay, almost never, maybe ten times—I negotiated a $100,000 guarantee and told Latif I got $80,000.

Another thing, I handled his banking. Every penny poured into my account. After I covered our expenses and deducted my percentage and paid whatever taxes I couldn't dodge, I transferred Latif's share. But I can't claim I was quick about it. Sometimes I let a million bucks take a breather in my account for a few weeks while the interest piled up.

I wasn't proud of the things I did, and I'd like to think if I'd known his problems, I'd of done better. I'd like to think Latif believed this. More than anything, I'd like to think none of this was going to cause problems when we had our face-to-face.

The loose dust that had been blown out of Tunisia had piled up in Algeria. Dunes hundreds of feet high crowded the road, and wind-driven sand came fizzing across the asphalt. Inside the bus, I tasted grit.

As we rumbled into El Oued, Lenore started lecturing about the palm groves we were passing through and how the dates from this region were famous. The city, she said, was "a splendid example" of something or other. The architecture had influenced a fellow she called "Corbu." She allowed I probably knew him as Le Corbusier. Wrong. I never heard of the guy.

And I sure as hell never saw a town like El Oued. All the buildings were round and low and even the smallest hut had a dome. Lenore called them cupolas and barrel vaults. But I was reminded of hundreds of beehives humming with life. Through the bus windows, I caught flickering glimpses, like pictures on a video tape in fast-forward, of camels in courtyards, guys pounding brass trays, boys kicking a ball of old socks.

The driver turned down a boulevard lined by palms and

oleanders and dropped us in front of the Souf Museum. Blowing dust swarmed over me, stinging my skin. The sun stung too. I felt it needling my skull. A suitcase in my good hand, Lenore's overnight bag under the other arm, I followed her toward the museum where a dead man—some kind of sun-cured mummy—was slumped in an upright coffin beside the entrance. This antique stiff was in terrible shape, its beard speckled with sand, its ratty brown *djellaba* in tatters.

Laugh-a-minute Lenore, she reached right into the casket and yanked the mummy's sleeve.

The leathery corpse came alive, babbling, *"Bienvenu, benvenuto, bienvenido,* welcome, *willkommen."*

Son-of-a-bitch was a museum worker wedged in a ticket booth. He saw our suitcases and jerked his thumb up the street. *"L'hôtel."*

He would of nodded off if Lenore hadn't tugged his sleeve a second time. "We're not looking for a hotel."

"No baths," he warned us in English. "No beds."

"We're here to meet a friend."

He gave her the once-over, then glanced at me and put his fingers to his lips. The smoking pantomime.

"No cigarettes," I said. "Used to smoke cigars. Big smelly Cubans. Can't afford them these days."

He wasn't interested in excuses. He burrowed deeper into the booth, dropped his chin onto his chest, and shut his eyes.

With Lenore in the lead we went into the museum, schlepping our luggage. It was dark. I don't mean dim. I mean pitch dark. Lenore found a switch and while the lights were blinking on, she was singing, "Latif. Latif, honey, we're here."

"What is this?" I said. "We're in the wrong place."

"He promised he'd be at the museum."

"This is a museum?"

It was the size of a cluttered storage shed. Beside me stood what looked like the busy end of a feather duster. A stuffed ostrich. A sign said it was the last one seen in the Sahara. Shot by a French Legionnaire in 1937. My suitcase clattered to the floor.

"Obviously we're early. Or late," said Lenore, the loony voice of reason. "Or else he came and when he didn't see us, he went to the Hotel du Souf."

"You just said he promised to be at the museum."

"Why don't you go to the hotel and have a drink? Have lunch. I'll wait for Latif. We'll join you there."

"I'm not moving another fucking foot." My voice rattled glass cabinets all around the room.

"Have it your way." She brushed at her hair, shaking loose a little sand. "You browse here. Get your temper under control. I'll check at the hotel."


Browse, she said. Control your temper. Like I was the one to blame. What kind of bullshit was this? That's what I couldn't figure.

Usually I'm a quick study. I don't need to spend hours pissing blood over a problem to get to the bottom line. But I couldn't think straight, not here surrounded by samples of every creepy, deadly creature in the Sahara.

There were venomous snakes the size of earthworms, intestinal worms the size of boa constrictors, scorpions the size of ten-dollar lobsters, horned beetles as big as Princess telephones, hairy and clean-shaven spiders, lethal lizards and bloodsucking centipedes.

The prizewinner, though, was a wineglass filled with formaldehyde and fat grey blobs floating around like rotten grapes. I suppose the locals had no trouble recognizing the display. But for tourists, a typewritten card identified "Blood-Engorged Ticks."

I whistled through my teeth, watching the ticks float clockwise, then counterclockwise, according to the tune I blew. When Lenore came back, face flushed, dark hair damp with heat, all her zipper gizmos jiggling like she'd had to hurry on my account, I told her, "This is a fascinating place. I'm going to visit every year."

"Afraid I have bad news."

"Lemme guess." I fought to hold my voice level. "Latif's not here."

"No, but—"

"But he's waiting for us an hour up the road."

"As a matter of fact—"

"As a matter of fact," I boomed, "he can go on waiting till engorged ticks suck his dick dry. I've had it. I'm out of here."

"Well, if that's how you feel—"

"That's not half of how I feel. Where's the airport?"

"I presume you can find out at the hotel," she said, fighting heat with frost.

"Point me to it, babe. Or is that too big a favor to ask?"


The Hotel du Souf bore a really uncanny resemblance to a normal tourist trap. It had a lobby and a switchboard, a reception desk and a dining room, a courtyard and a swimming pool. Since all I needed was a plane reservation and lunch, I figured I was home free.

I bellied up to the reception desk and rang the bell. Nobody. Nothing.

The place was definitely open. Four fellows sat in the dining room having a terrific time fiddling with a wooden matchbox. They took turns setting it on the edge of the table, flicking it with a thumbnail and, what I guessed, counting how many times it flipped before it hit the floor.

I didn't want to barge in and interrupt the game, but I coughed so they'd know I was there. I waited another minute before asking, "Anybody speak English?"

They glared. I'd made them lose track of the score.

"Arabic," one guy growled.

"French?" I asked, thinking I'd have to lean on Lenore.

"Perhaps you have not heard," the same guy said in near-perfect English. "We defeated and expelled our colonial oppressors thirty years ago."

"Hooray for the home team. You fellows work here or what?"

"I am the manager." He stood up, a tall dude in a shiny brown suit. He had hair wiry as mine and must of carved a part in it with a woodburning iron. "Do you require a room?"

"No. What I require, I require food and some information on flights."

"When do you and madame wish to depart?"

Lenore had moved up beside me. I put some space between us. "I want out of here soon as possible."

"Tomorrow morning."

"Nothing sooner?"

"Tomorrow morning is the airplane to Algiers." He hadn't left the table. His friends were itching to get on with the matchbox contest.

"Then I will need a room. And a reservation on that flight."

"We do not make reservations."

"Who does?"

"Air Algérie in Algiers."

"Don't they have an office here?"

"To make reservations it is necessary to go to the Air Algérie office in Algiers."

"Can't I call them?"

"You can. But they will not make reservations over the telephone."

"So what you're saying"—grainy dots spun past my eyeballs; the madder I got, the redder they got—"you're saying I can't make a reservation unless I go to Algiers. But I can't go to Algiers because I haven't got a reservation."

"Not at all. I am saying you must go to the airport tomorrow morning. Perhaps there will be a seat on the airplane. Perhaps not. Do you still require a room?"

I was woozy, confused, furious. "Let you know after lunch. You do serve food here?"

"But certainly." He waved at all the tables where no one was eating. "What do you desire?"

"A sandwich and a bottle of beer."

"No sandwiches. No beer."

I staggered to a table, desperate to sit down. "Lemme see the menu."

"No menu."

I groaned and collapsed into a chair. Lenore sat opposite me. "We'll have whatever you suggest," she told the guy. "And a bottle of mineral water." She held my good hand, like she was checking my pulse. "Cool your jets, Eddie. A climate like this, a man your age, you'll have a stroke."

I groaned again. "Why are you and Latif doing this to me?"

"You're doing it to yourself," she whispered. "You're acting like an Ugly American. These people are very proud, very independent."

"Too proud to have a menu? Too independent to make plane reservations?"

"They haven't entirely adapted to tourism. They equate service with subservience. They don't like to humble themselves waiting on foreigners."

"I didn't ask for humility. I asked for a sandwich."

Propping my head in my hands, I stared into the courtyard where some yahoo with a pole was stirring the swimming pool. It had a coat of green scum so thick I could of scribbled my name with my finger. The first course was pea soup, I'd starve before I'd eat it.

"Where's Latif?" I couldn't help whining.

"Touggourt. A town about sixty miles south."

"Why? Why didn't he wait?"

"Trouble with his ex-wife and her family."

That sent a jolt through what little was left of my nervous system. I lifted my head, looking at her, wondering had I heard right.

"Please," she said, "don't pretend you didn't know he was married."

"It's just I'm shocked you know."

She shook her head, pitying me. "You keep assuming I'm another of his one-night stands. You keep assuming Latif hasn't changed. You keep assuming you knew him to start with."

"No, after listening to the tapes, I don't assume that. You said ex-wife. He get rid of Rashida?"

"Of course. He had to divorce her before he married me."

The second jolt hit me harder. "You said yesterday you decided not to get married till he'd been out of stir a while."

"He's been out six months."

The man in the brown suit brought our lunch on a tray made out of a Trivial Pursuit board. He spun the bottle of mineral water, flashing a label with a purple snake on it, like that was the mark of a fine vintage. Then he served up plates of rice and lemon chicken. "*Bon appétit!*" he quoted his old oppressors and disappeared.

Still groping to digest the news, I toasted Lenore with mineral water. "Congratulations."

She kept her glass to herself. "Latif wanted you to be the first to know. Hope he's not too disappointed he didn't get to tell you himself. He also wanted you to be along for his comeback. But you—"

"Comeback? He was banned for life."

"But you're not very loyal." She was fooling with her zipper thingamajigs. "You balk at traveling a few miles out of your way."

"You're telling me things you should of said before. What's he been, reinstated?" I was talking between bites. I was so hungry I could of eaten the arms off a rag doll.

"You're excited now. You see something in it for yourself. But what's in it for Latif?"

"I'm a damn good agent."

"That's not why he asked you to meet him. He likes you." She squinted, trying to see what Latif saw.

"I like him too. I love the guy. About this comeback—"

"I shouldn't have brought it up." She shoveled in a forkful of chicken, chewed about sixty times, and patted her lips with a napkin. "It's strictly between you two."

"How do we get to Yoghurt?"

"What?"

"The town where he's waiting. How do we get there?"

"Touggourt. By *louage,* a long-distance taxi service that runs between towns."

"Can we catch one this afternoon?"

"We'll check in the marketplace."

"Great! Hey, this chicken's not half bad." I hoisted my glass again. "Here's hoping you and Latif are nothing but happy."

"Oh, Eddie, you're such a fraud." But she was laughing as she raised her glass and chinked it against mine.

We waited in a flyblown, shit-flecked marketplace for the *louage* driver to rustle up customers to fill his Peugeot. I was trying to weigh the news of Latif's marriage against his comeback. But every time I mulled over a question— Did Lenore expect to travel the circuit with Latif? Would sponsors honor his old contracts? Had he been practicing since his release?—Lenore kept interrupting.

A brass hand dangled from the Peugeot's rearview mirror. A good luck charm, she told me. The Hand of Fatma.

This wasn't your average Arab bazaar, she said. These Algerians, citizens of a socialist country, wouldn't bargain. Solemn-faced and proud, they sat tight and waited for somebody to buy their oranges and bananas, their buckets of sheep eyes and goat balls.

Once we were on the road, Lenore was buried in her book. But now there were worse things to distract me. The driver barreled out of El Oued at seventy miles an hour, one hand on the horn, one hand twirling the radio dial, his knees working the wheel. Plus which he hogged the middle of the road. Anybody had been headed our way, we'd of been hamburgered.

Other people had already gone through the grinder. The countryside was strewn with gutted cars. I covered my ears with the headset, closed my eyes, and listened to Latif for the rest of the cannonball run to Touggourt.

# Tape # 5

The problem is no one prepares us, no one warns us. As they slog through uncharted country, new players remind me of the first white men to cross the Sahara searching for mythical cities, pursuing mirages of gold. Those who didn't die of hunger or thirst were captured by hostile tribes, my own among them, and hacked to pieces.

That's how it is on the tennis tour. People have passed this way before, but not many have returned intact. Even fewer have had the urge or ability to share their knowledge. Instead they treat newcomers as invaders and savage them to protect their turf.

Only in rare unguarded comments have I caught glimpses of what other players have gone through. McEnroe said of life on the circuit, "No one gives a shit about anyone else deep down. Everybody's just out for himself. It stinks."

Before Guillermo Vilas's career hit the wall when he was turned in for taking an illegal guarantee, his coach Ion Tiriac told a reporter, "Our life is the worst life ever, the worst life anybody could ever dream. Guillermo is working like nobody else ever did. Now he is doing exorcise."

Exorcise? Yes, having had enough exercise, he started exorcising. His mind? His humanity? Struggling to explain, Guillermo coined a new word to describe his condition. "It's really *extenerating*."

Yannick Noah seemed to be suffering a fatal dose of exteneration in 1984 when, after considering suicide, he flipped out and fled Paris, babbling, "The press, the pressure, the fear of being eaten raw by ducks, television, the radio, and all my whole life, my personality dissected into pieces, little phrases, little photos that boomerang on me and break me for good and divide me against myself like a schizo. The press creates monsters and I don't want to be one."

I wonder about Bjorn Borg. A decade after he dropped off the tour, reporters still ask why he quit. Some quote that interview in *Rock & Folk* magazine where Noah seemed to hint Borg was on amphetamines. Was it drugs, these drippy journalists demand, that forced him to retire?

I tell them I never played Borg. I just watched him on video cassettes the Texans showed at the oil compound. But from what I saw, he appeared to have the metabolism of a three-toed sloth. If it took drugs to hike him up to that quasi-comatose level, maybe he didn't retire. Maybe he hibernated.

Then there's the other rumor, the one that insinuated Borg realized if you're a millionaire, you can fuck anyone you want. During his last days on the tour he was seen with a succession of rock stars, actresses, petty royalty, and teeny-bopper models. Was that, reporters ask, what ruined his game?

I always answer, "I hope so." I truly hope it was pussy that persuaded him to quit tennis. I'd like to think he was seized by an obsession, that he somehow reestablished contact with a basic human drive. Because if it happened to Borg, who knows? maybe it'll happen to me. Maybe I'll wake up one day and discover I'm wild about a woman, an idea, a cause.

I'd like to find something equal to the emotion I used to feel hitting a ball with the hackers at the oil compound, hearing the sound of a shot smack against the sweet spot, savoring the solid vibration up my arm, deep into my chest. Later that feeling came only with winning. Then only with being Number One. A narrower and narrower rush, until eventually it disappeared.

I'm still driven, but not by love of the game or of winning. Titles mean as little as money. It's the fear of losing, of sliding backward, falling. Into what? I've traveled so much, gotten so far ahead, there's nothing behind me now except a howling emptiness.

Remember how it was at the beginning, Eddie? I played; you schemed and wrote my script. The greatest difficulty wasn't raising the level of my game. It was getting me to memorize my lines, then deliver them on camera. You saw my reluctance as a primitive dread of having my soul sucked away by photographers. But that was only part of the problem. We Tuareg warriors are taught to be dignified, reserved.

But Eddie, you undermined every value that had been drummed into me as a child. You trained me to project, to exaggerate my anger in defeat and my joy in victory, to taunt other players and bait spectators. A month after we met, you had me shaking my fists, shooting the finger at linesmen, waggling my fanny in front of thousands of fans.

You claimed you had compiled profiles of the top players for the past two decades, and anybody who wanted to avoid being swallowed in the anonymous pack had to decide whether to be a white hat or a black hat, whether to imitate Stan Smith or Ilie Nastase, Arthur Ashe or Jimmy Connors, Bjorn Borg or John McEnroe. A player who lacked a definite identity was bound to lose millions in endorsements.

What's more, he was likely to lose matches since tournament directors took steps to ensure that fellows with the right images made it to the finals. There was a self-fulfilling prophecy—a classic circle jerk, you called it. Players became stars when they won major titles. But once they were bankable, they continued winning titles *because* they were stars, because they were too important to be allowed to lose.

With Ashe still an influential figure, you said it was foolish to market me as a thoughtful, responsible black. And since Yannick Noah filled the role of affable African, it was silly to package me as a pale—in my case, an inky—carbon copy.

"You want to max your potential," you said, "you gotta be the first bad nigger in tennis. Lots of people are going to take one look and figure you're something that swung down from a tree. So play the part. Play it big. Go out there and gorilla the other guys."

On your orders, I studied tapes of Sonny Liston, Thomas (Hollywood) Henderson, Marvin (Bad News) Barnes, Idi Amin, Mr. T, and Muhammad Ali. The trick, you told me, was to push my act to the limit, then shove on through to the other side. Be so abrasive, so offensive, that reporters found me funny as well as frightening. Come on as such a weird menace, spectators wondered whether I was kidding. For every threat I had to throw in a joke. Every obscenity had to be offset by a grace note. You groomed me to be the player half the public loves to hate and the other half hates to love—and these halves flipflopped from week to week.

My first tournament win, a late summer warm-up for the U.S. Open, took place at a club that had been bulldozed out of hundreds of acres of corn next to a Federal Reform School for Boys. The exit sign on the interstate read EZ OFF, EZ ON. But some delinquent had changed this to HARD OFF, HARD ON.

For me nothing was hard that week. I stampeded through my early round matches without losing a set. Then in the final I eked past Stefan Edberg, who was less bothered by me than by the heat. The Swede seized up with cramps and had to be carted off court like a gigged frog.

My joy was shortlived. Surrounded by TV crews and commentators, I labored to remember the lines we had rehearsed. I wasn't convinced I could say them—not to John Newcombe, Tony Trabert, and Iain Richards. But you had programmed me well, Eddie.

NEWCOMBE. (*Because of his jaunty moustache and dazzling teeth, he always seems to be smiling. But up close I thought he might be grimacing.*) Welcome to the big time. Grite win, Lerteef.

ME. (*Glaring.*) The name's Latif. Better get it right. You'll be hearing it a lot from now on.

TRABERT. (*He had the typical look of the aging jock commentator—a little boy's face poised atop a mud slide. His hair was dyed, his wrinkled sunburnt skin caked with makeup.*) You put a lot of pressure on yourself today, going for aces and winners. Was that your game plan?

ME. (*Still glaring.*) My plan was to kick his butt. Get him down and kick him again. You saw what happened. They had to haul that no-talent turkey out of here on a stretcher.

RICHARDS. (*He was wearing eye liner, lip gloss, and tan make-*

*up.)* A lot of fans don't know you, Latif. Tell us a bit about your background.

ME. No background. I'm all foreground. I'm up front, in your face. I'm big, I'm blue, and I'm beautiful. I'm lean and I'm mean.

RICHARDS. You also sound remarkably like the old Muhammad Ali.

ME. Right! I'm the greatest. I'm Number One.

RICHARDS. In point of fact, just so our viewers won't be confused, you're Number 425. You had to qualify for this tournament.

ME. *(Thrusting an index finger at the camera.)* I am the uncrowned champion. The Third World Avenger. You tell Lendl, you tell Connors, Becker, and McEnroe, I'm coming after them. I'm going to whip them like they're babies.

TRABERT. *(Chuckling, looking around for someone with a net.)* Well, you'll get your chance at the U.S. Open. That's played on Deco Turf. A lot faster than the Har Tru here. What's your favorite surface?

ME. A mattress.

Then I sprinted to the locker room, bolted myself in a toilet, and was stricken with diarrhea for the rest of the day.

Next week, during the qualifying rounds for the U.S. Open —I still wasn't ranked high enough to get straight into the main draw—I tried to avoid the press, but you, Eddie, wouldn't permit that. At every opportunity you shoved me in front of a camera or foisted me off on a reporter scratching for a story during the slow days before the start of the tournament.

"I am huge," I repeated to everybody. "I play huge. I live huge. I love huge. Other players hate me because I refuse to humble down. I hope Jimmy Connors has the juice to reach the second round. Because I'll be there waiting for him. Anybody who likes the old man better come and watch because when I'm finished, there won't be anything left of him but a gooey white puddle."

Flushing Meadow! The name carries no magic for me.

Instead it recalls those days of intestinal distress when my nerves were tight, my bowels loose. Flushing! Never was a place more aptly named. I spent a week with the roar of the toilet and the name of Jimmy Connors ringing my brainpan.

Then in his late thirties, Jimbo was still beating younger players—destroying them!—with stark power. His backhand had lost little of its sting; rushing the net against his return of serve was like running down the barrel of a bazooka. He was the seasoned champ who had made his reputation as a scrapper. How could I expect to survive after insulting him?

The common strategy was to work to his forehand with low, off-speed shots. But Eddie, you didn't care to discuss tennis tactics. You promised Jimbo could be beaten before he stepped on court if I did exactly as you instructed.

The day of the match, the locker room was quiet, tense, heavy with humidity from the showers and from hundreds of sweaty socks and jocks. Yet Connors appeared cool and supremely confident as he strutted by with a towel wrapped around his waist.

A curious touch, that towel. Other players walked around naked. Jimbo never did. Not ever. You wondered why. So did I.

I stood up and started toward him, advancing slowly, careful not to alarm him. Then when I was next to him, I shot out a hand, grabbed his towel, and spun Jimmy like a turnstile, flouncing his bangs, stripping him bare. Following your script to the syllable, I laughed.

I expected him to lunge at me, arms and legs whirring. Or pick up a racquet and brain me. But he crouched and covered his crotch. His scrubbed, chipmunk cheeks blushed as he grappled for the towel.

"Put on your diaper, little man," I said, "and get ready for an ass whipping."

He didn't stomp his feet or shake his fist in my face. He didn't shoot me the finger or grab his gear and pretend to jack off on me like I'd seen him do to hundreds of linesmen and umpires. Small and sad and suddenly ancient, he shuffled off, dragging his toes.

Minutes later, he strode onto the stadium court like a bantam cock. But he was never in the match. He had no rhythm, no timing, and no stomach for hanging tough and treating the New York crowd to another afternoon of his famous gut spilling. He cratered in straight sets.

I almost felt sorry for him, almost regretted what I had done. But that didn't keep me from inflicting a final insult. When he trotted to the net to shake hands, I rumpled his greying locks and patted his fanny, like he was the callow rookie and I was the condescending old pro.

Force-fed a cruel dose of his own medicine, Connors never presented the slightest problem for me. By the time he retired, shortly after his fortieth birthday, I had shellacked him twenty matches in a row.


I was slated to meet Ivan Lendl in the quarter-finals and I didn't give myself a chance. Earlier in his career he had had a reputation as a choker, a guy who crumbled in Grand Slam finals. But the flaw had been in his technique, not his head. Lendl couldn't change pace, couldn't play inside the service line. Now he had much greater variety to his game and wasn't afraid to rush the net.

"Forget that technical crap," you told me. "We're going to hit that Commie with the complete Eddie Brown treatment."

"Have you seen his inside-out forehand? I can't handle it."

"You won't have to. He'll give up before the first game."

"Another towel trick?"

"Relax, kid. Study the script. I'll take care of the rest."

That evening, you arranged a press conference where reporters asked my prediction for the Lendl match.

"I'll win easy. Ivan's a robot. He's got a mechanical brain and one gear. Every point, I know what he's going to do."

"Because you scouted him? You spotted a pattern?"

"I always know what every opponent's going to do. Besides being the best player and baddest mother on the tour, I have psychic powers. Lendl, he's such a simple study, I take one glance and get a clear picture of his game plan, his love life, his financial posture."

Whether because they thought I was colorful or crazy, reporters broke out laughing.

"You don't believe me? I'll prove it."

Lowering my eyelids to half-mast, I mimed deep meditation and delivered the lines you had drilled into me, Eddie.

"Looking into Lendl's mind, the first thing I see is dollar signs on a sheet of paper. Seems to be . . . yes, it's his bank statement. Anybody who doubts my powers, here's Ivan Lendl's numbered Swiss account."

I rattled off the digits you had supplied. I can't say where you dug them up or whether they were accurate. But the press turned serious and sent out stories.

Next day Lendl got serious too—seriously sick, according to his agent. He withdrew from the U.S. Open, giving me a walkover, and flew to Zurich for "emergency medical treatment."

I've owned him ever since. Maybe Ivan's afraid I'll tell reporters what Eddie found out about his financial dealings with the Hunt family in Dallas.

That left John McEnroe as the last barrier in my headlong leap to the U.S. Open final, and he popped my bubble in three easy sets. He read my game the way I claimed to read Lendl's mind. Over the next nine months, he had so little trouble trouncing me, I was close to conceding he was Number One and I was forever doomed to be a distant runner-up when Eddie, you concocted a strategy so awful, I am ashamed to—

## *Chapter* Eight

I clicked the stop button, cutting Latif off. I'm not a damn bit ashamed of what we did to McEnroe, which is what somebody should of done a decade before.

Don't get me wrong. I like John. And there's no denying he's box office. He puts asses in those seats from ringside all the way up to the rafters.

I know the reasons people disagree and don't see John first and foremost as a drawing card: they see him as crazy. One year there was a story in the London *Sunday Times*—not the raciest scandal sheet in circulation—that quoted a family friend saying Junior "has a severe personality problem" and needs psychiatric treatment.

Now I grant he's always scratching his head and eating his fingernails and, yes, he likes ice in his beer and in his milk and he chews with his mouth open and lets half of every meal dribble out on the table. But does that prove he's a basket case?

I do think he's obsessed with his old man. Every time he looks up into the stands, he sees Daddy Mac, a bald, fat guy jawing a stick of gum, and realizes how he's going to end up and it freaks him out.

With a few hair and physical shortcomings myself, I can sympathize why he blows a fuse whenever some porker or chrome-dome hassles him. Like that linesman at the '82 Wimbledon final who gave Connors a close call and McEnroe ripped him, "Baldy! Bald eagle!"

At the '84 U.S. Open he hollered at a fellow who was going thin on top, "Grow some hair."

Then at the '85 Masters he let an overweight woman have both barrels. "Drop twenty-five pounds, lady."

But I don't feature Junior as a rubber-room candidate. You notice he's not drooling on his own fur coat. My opinion, he's a hustler—hands down, bar none, the greatest con artist I ever met.

Here he is, a pasty, soft, potato-face kid that pretended to be Conan the Barbarian and got away with it. This Yuppie from the suburbs of Long Island, this nerd from Trinity School and Stanford—kind of guy, you picture him carrying a book-bag and a lunchbox—he sold himself as a street fighter, a hardass in a black leather jacket and skin-tight Levis. He made a career—and tens of millions of bucks—giving people grief, slinging sawdust in their faces, daring them to fight, pushing reporters around hotel lobbies, spitting on them, lashing at TV cameramen with his racquet, drawing blood, brow-beating anybody who hinted he knocked up Tatum O'Neal . . . before he announced in the newspapers he had. Then the topper, at the '85 Australian Open, he hollered at Slobodan (Bobo) Zivojinovic, this hulking Yugoslav that's six-six and weighs two-ten and is beating him bad, "You're going to pay for this. I mean it!"

And no one calls his bluff! Not ever! No one except Martina Navratilova, that is. She said McEnroe was built like a wimp. Smart man, John didn't mouth off back at her. In a *mano a mano*—I'm talking about a duke-out now, not tennis—my money would be on Martina.

Latif's first year at Wimbledon, to prepare my client, I did my homework, read back through the history of McEnroe's horror shows, and found a tidbit buried in an article about the '84 French Open. During a third-round match, Mac griped so long and loud about court conditions, a ground crew was called in to sweep the clay. Turned out the crew was these three fellows named Amar, Hadj, and Mabrouck, brothers from the Sequeni family, members of a minority, if you get my meaning.

They trucked onto the court, hosing down the dirt, patting and stamping, trying to do what Junior wanted. But he's a tough customer to satisfy. Afterward he sounded off to the press, "These workers think they're doing us a favor by being here. They do absolutely nothing. It's an absolute disgrace."

When I showed Latif this piece about the Sequeni brothers, he exploded, "McEnroe's an anti-Islamic racist."

"Hard to deny that."

It was the night before the Wimbledon semifinal, and the adrenaline was already screaming through his veins; his crescent-shaped nostrils were flared. Swear to God, I didn't tell him what to do. I didn't have to. I just said, "You want my advice, based on I went back through the files and all the films on the man? McEnroe's a front-runner. You can't let him have the whip hand. You're bigger, stronger. What do you got to be scared of, a scrawny guy like him?"

"Eddie," he said, "if I go after him—if I threaten him, forget hitting him, just threaten—they'll default me."

"Well," I said, "you don't figure to win anyway, do you? He's beaten you, what, six, seven times straight. But there's the future to think about. And there's your pride. Your race and religion."

"They'll fine me."

"You got money."

"They'll suspend me."

"Maybe. But that's from tournaments. There's exhibitions to keep you in shape and in the headlines."

"Look at the bad press I got just for rumpling Jimbo's hair."

"Different case altogether. A guy Connors's age gets the sympathy vote. You rattle McEnroe's chain, they'll pin a medal on you."

"Jesus, Eddie, Princess Di and her sons will be in the Royal Box."

"Wonder where the Sequeni brothers are? Think they received engraved invites to the Royal Box? Think anybody but you and me cares what became of those fellows?"

I don't guess I gotta describe what happened. You didn't have to be there or among the millions following the match on the tube. You were anyplace in the free world—for all I know, anywhere behind the Iron Curtain—you caught it on the nightly news or the front page or in the weekly sports roundup or in the hundreds of replays and specials that featured isolated stop frames.

There's some debate what triggered it. Latif accused Junior of calling him "boy." John explained from his hospital bed he had been calling the ball boy "boy." But since the ball boy was black, that hardly let him off the hook.

Whatever the beef, Latif jumped the net, and in the cemetery silence of Centre Court, you heard this collective insuck of breath, followed by a yelp. The yelp was from McEnroe. Slashing his racquet like his ancestors did their swords, Latif whacked him across the ass hard enough to burn a waffle iron print on Junior's buns. Then he threw away his Rossignol and attacked barehanded, banging at Junior's belly.

For three minutes, as timed by news analysts, he throttled Mac by the neck and strummed him. He looked like some boss bass fiddle player plunking out rhythm for a hard-charging number. One network showed the film clip with Michael

Jackson wailing "Beat It" in the background, the sound track synched with the punches Latif landed. It became a major hit on MTV.

As the tape bears out, the linesmen and umpires were *not* paralyzed by fear. They really wanted to, they could of stepped in and stopped it. But they were getting a kick out of the show same as everybody else. Some of them were laughing; two guys clapped.

Up in the stands, reaction was mixed. Mac had his supporters, Latif his. Fistfights broke out in the standing-room section. Princess Di tried to hide her sons behind her, but there wasn't enough of her to go around. They kept popping out, one side or the other. The Duke and Duchess of Kent were on their feet, and a post-match replay revealed with the help of a lip reader that while he mumbled, "I say, bad show," she was saying, "Jolly good!"

Finally, a few bobbies lumbered out. Latif was arm-weary and would of had to let Junior drop in a second anyway. When they dragged him off, he played the curtain scene like a pro. He shook a fist and shouted in a voice that carried through Centre Court and was picked up letter perfect on worldwide TV, "Remember the Sequeni brothers! Power to all Third World people!"

Mac had curled up near the net cradling his belly, a white slug on a bed of green grass. Kneeling next to him, a bobby waved for a stretcher and they carried him away. Any honest applause meter indicates John didn't get as big a hand as Latif.

It took me ten minutes to reach the dressing room where players were giving Latif a standing ovation. But the All England Tennis and Croquet Club was giving him something else entirely—the bum's rush. The club chairman refused to let Latif speak to the press anyplace on Wimbledon grounds. In fact, he refused to let him shower and change. There was some talk of having him arrested for assault and battery. We split pronto.

By the time we got to the Westbury Hotel, news vendors

were hawking special editions with six-inch headlines. LATIF
LUMPS MAC. ROYAL FAMILY REVOLTED. SUPERBRAT BROUGHT
LOW. MAD MOOR RUNS AMOK.

The desk clerk handed me telegrams from Howard Cosell,
the *Today Show*, CBS 60 *Minutes*, ABC *Nightline*, and the
*MacNeil-Lehrer Report* requesting interviews. There were
also messages from King Hassan, King Hussein, the Saud
family, Khaddafy, Khomeini, Mubarak, Arafat, and the
Islamic Jihad, expressing support for Latif.

Up in our suite watching BBC, we waited for the rest of
the returns, the ratings so to speak. And they weren't slow in
coming. Public opinion, based on call-in shows around the
world, was running 60–40 in our favor.

More important, offers were pouring in by telephone. An
emissary from the OPEC nations proposed a series of exos
between McEnroe and Latif, one in each oil-producing country
at $500,000 a pop. Don King made a pitch to promote a Heavy-
weight Championship of Tennis in Vegas. Sun City promised
to change its name to Fist City for a weekend and pony up a
million bucks for a winner-take-all rematch.

The way things were moving, I decided I better contact
McEnroe's father, who, of course, is his agent and lawyer. I
had a bellboy hand-deliver a letter to his hotel. "Reserving
all my client's rights and admitting no guilt, I want to assure
you we can work this out in a businesslike fashion to everybody's benefit."

We did just that. Latif paid Junior's medical bills and
granted him a generous percentage of future grosses. He also
paid a $20,000 fine to the International Tennis Federation
and made a donation to the British Lawn Tennis Association
for desecrating Centre Court. He was supposed to serve a
six-month suspension, but we appealed and, with an assist
from the network that owned the TV rights to the U.S. Open,
we got it reduced to six weeks.

Meanwhile, we set up a summer of exos and raked it in at
the rate of a million a week from all sources. I'm talking tee
shirt, doll, and headband sales, department store and shopping

mall appearances, and guaranteed prize money. The Mc-
Enroes must of done as well or better.

I have to hand it to Junior. He was a trooper. He didn't
let hard feelings or a hobbling injury stand between him and
a monster deal. When the bell rang in Las Vegas or Little
Rock, Kuala Lumpur or Caracas, he charged out of his
corner swinging.

Jesus, those were great days. I'll take exhibitions over
tournaments anytime, and not just because of the money.
They give a guy like me a chance to get involved, get creative.
I ran the fog machine that made the court resemble the
Scottish moors. I stage-managed the spotlights for Mac's
entrance, then Latif's. At outdoor arenas, I arranged for
glitter to be dropped from low-passing planes; at indoor
arenas I arranged balloon releases that rivaled the Republican
party convention. I hired hostesses, brought in local cele-
brites, movie stars, and rock singers for mixed doubles, and
in every town found a band that'd play the themes from *Rocky
I, II, III, IV, V, VI, VII,* and *VIII* during the warm-up and
changeovers.

But my greatest triumph was how I choreographed the
media coverage. First, I huddled with Mac and Latif and
got them to accept a few ground rules. Every match had to
go three sets, the last one a sudden-death tie break. They
agreed to keep the games and series close. This way I could
build excitement for the final in Freeport, tell TV networks
what kind of time slots we needed, and promise the writing
press they'd never miss a deadline.

Couple journalists thought they had a scoop when they
charged that these matches were fixed and said the scores
should be printed on the entertainment page. But this never
hurt the gate. Paying customers just wanted a good show
and they got one, specially in the final that was played honest
and that Latif won in a walkaway.

This gave him the confidence to go into the U.S. Open and
take his first Grand Slam title. By the end of the year, he
was Number One on the computer, universally feared, if not

loved, looked at as larger than life, stronger than dirt, more dangerous than death—this sweet blue kid I picked up in an undertaker's suit at a religious nut college in Texas. Life's a funny old dog, as they say down there.

The question in my mind, could we do it again? From what Lenore said, he kicked drugs in prison. Maybe he pumped iron, too, and slapped a nerf ball against his cell wall to keep his hand-eye coordination sharp. Still, to come back, he'd need the full-stroke Eddie Brown treatment. I couldn't wait to start. But first I had to find him.

The *louage* dropped us at the Hardt-Citroën monument, a stone pillar dedicated to these dipstick motorhead Frenchmen that drove in 1902 from Touggourt to Timbuktu. A trip I had zero interest in retracing.

I didn't have much more interest staying in Touggourt. The town was divided into mud-pie houses that had just been built and hovels that were crumbling back into sand.

A boy about nine with a shaky smile and a shaved head cruised by us, then circled back. "Help you?" he asked, proud of his English.

Lenore described best she could where we wanted to go, and he puckered his brow, thinking. "You know I am not guide. I am student. In Algeria we are rich with oil. We do not need tourists. But this one time I take you."

Scooping up Lenore's luggage, leaving me to carry the rest, he led us into a palm grove past farmers working postage stamp plots of land. Once we were off the main drag, he stopped and lifted his *djellaba*. Under it he had on a pair of blue jeans. He pulled something from his back pocket. "Because you are Americans . . ." He hesitated. "You are Americans, no?"

"Yes."

His shaved head with its three-day growth swiveled left, then right. "Good. Because you are friends, I give something to you—American money for Algerian dinars."

He showed what he had in his hand—a gift certificate from McDonald's, good for a free cheeseburger and Coke.

"Where'd you get it?" Lenore asked.

"Other American friends. They give it because I take them to Grand Mosque and Royal Tombs."

"That's mean," she said.

"Mean?"

"It's not real money," I told him.

"Yes. Look." He pointed to the dollar sign and Ronald McDonald's daffy mug.

"It's a gift certificate. Good only at McDonald's."

"Yes, a gift. Good for friends. I give you. For dinars."

"It's not for dinars. It's for a cheeseburger and Coke."

"But here we do not have. In America you buy."

What was I supposed to do, tell him my life story? How I couldn't go back to the States unless I wanted to wind up behind bars where a Ronald McDonald dollar would buy just about as much as it did in Touggourt? Anyway, Lenore was right, it was a rotten trick somebody played on him. I handed the kid a bill and told him to keep the funny money, but he made me take it. Then he grabbed Lenore's bags and galloped up the path.

"Now don't ruin the gesture," she warned me in a whisper, "by cracking a joke."

The joke was on me. When we got where we were going— a squat cinderblock building painted pale blue, with a black palm print over the door—this sawed-off operator had his hand out for a tip.

"Thought you were our friend," I said.

He nodded his fuzzy noggin.

"Thought you were a student, not a guide."

"Yes." He nodded again.

"But you wanna get paid?"

"For friendship." He flashed his shaky smile.

I smacked the McDonald's gift certificate into his hand.

"This is not real," he said. "This is hamburger money."

Lenore laughed, and I had to laugh too. Here was the son

I never had. "Kid, you and I'd make one hell of a team." I doled out another tattered bill.

He was no dummy. He pocketed the bread and ran.

"A man never stands so tall," I told Lenore, "as when he lets himself get knocked flat by a junior con man."

A few fellows in uniform came out of the cinderblock building. For a second I was scared this was a police station and Latif was in jail again. But then I noticed they were soldiers, not cops.

Lenore knocked at the door, and a woman opened up, her tattooed face gleaming with gold teeth. She had a red bandanna wrapped around her head, and instead of the regulation black sack on every female you saw in the street, she wore a polka dot kimono cinched at the waist.

"Latif?" Lenore said it like a greeting.

"Latif," the woman answered, letting us into what reminded me of a 1950s recreation room in suburban U.S.A. Pastel paint on the walls, pink and black tile on the floor, leatherette chairs, and a TV in the corner. The scene was complete right down to these women lounging around in frowsy robes and rayon housecoats. You overlooked their tattoos and gold teeth, it could of been a coffee klatch gabbing about husbands and hysterectomies.

But I had them pegged as cleaning ladies taking a break before scrubbing this army barracks. A fat soldier sat watching the television. He waved for me to join him. I left Lenore with the charwomen.

"Welcome. I am watching American sex cinema."

What he was watching was an ancient videotape of *Charlie's Angels* dubbed into Arabic. Somebody like me must of saturated the territory with pirated cassettes. This soldier, Commander Salamander, couldn't tear his eyes off Farrah Fawcett. Sometimes when she was talking, the dubber had dozed off. She made shapes with her mouth, licking her lips, wagging her tongue, but there was no sound.

"I would like her doing that to me," said the soldier, rubbing his thighs. "Everywhere! What do you like?"

"A little info on Latif."

"Huh?" He didn't turn from the tube.

"You know Latif?"

"I know many Latifs."

"Latif Fluss. Tall guy. Blue complected."

He shook his head, annoyed at the interruption. The Angels were working undercover, investigating prison abuses. A corrupt warden got the drop on Farrah and clapped her into leg chains. Commander Salamander was riveted. Either he had a keen sense of injustice or he was a bondage freak. Before I found out which, Lenore called me over.

"Do you know what this place is?" Her eyes had the same glitter as Commander Salamander's. Her face was flushed with excitement, and I noticed a dusting of freckles across her nose.

"Beats the shit out of me."

"A brothel," she breathed the word. "These women are Ouled Naïls, a famous tribe of erotic dancers and courtesans."

"You're kidding." I took a longer look at them—the ratty robes and slippers. "Dressed like that?"

"Typical Western attitude. In the Moslem world clothes aren't the opposite of nudity. They're its complement, part of the sexual turn-on. That's what Lévi-Strauss says."

"Sure. He's in the business. You think he's not going to push his product? And what the hell's this got to do with Latif?"

"Eddie, you're hopeless. There's no point telling you things."

"Just tell me one thing. Latif!"

"He told me all about the Ouled Naïls. They have this fascinating custom." She was rasping one of her leg zippers back and forth. "When the women reach puberty, they leave their villages and work as prostitutes until they accumulate a dowry. There's no stigma. In fact, a successful courtesan is considered more likely to make a good wife."

"Yeah, well, these babes are tricking just till they get a dowry together, business must be damn slow. Some of them look older than me."

She sighed, disgusted.

"Lay it on me straight, Lenore. He's gone again, isn't he?"

"Calm down. Let me explain. He hired the little boy to lead us here because he didn't trust anyone else with the letter."

"Letter? He used a whorehouse as a mail drop?"

She pulled it out of her purse—an envelope addressed to me. I snatched it and went back to a chair by the TV. Commander Salamander had switched to *Three's Company*. Lenore sat between us.

"His wife?" he asked her.

"Hardly."

"Where's husband?" Suddenly he was more interested in her than Suzanne Sommers.

"South of here."

"English?"

"Tuareg."

"You?" He chuckled. "Not possible."

"My husband."

Rubbing his hefty legs, he said, "I hope you have many sons."

"*Inshallah.*"

I shook the letter out of the envelope. It was on lined looseleaf paper, the handwriting straight up and down like a school kid's. I can't swear it was Latif's. I never saw him do more than sign a check or an autograph. It sure didn't sound like him. There was a Happy Face at the end of the last sentence.

He started off apologizing—something he never would of done in the bad old days. He was sorry about the postponed meetings. He knew how upsetting that had to be. He was anxious to see me. Anxious to see Lenore too. Did I like her? He hoped that traveling together we'd get to know each other. He explained that a combination of ex-inlaw trouble and a shortage of hotel space and preparations for his comeback had convinced him it was wiser to head for his home village. He'd wait there, eager to discuss plans.

"How many sons?" Commander Salamander gave me a playful poke in the shoulder.

"None I know of." I slipped the letter back in the envelope, trying to sift the facts. Latif was talking comeback, but still heading south, away from me. Had Lenore written the letter as part of some elaborate practical joke? What was the punch line?

"Very bad. A man so old, he should have many sons. What if you die? Who will have your name?"

"The IRS."

"Excuse?" The soldier thumbed his ear, telling me to come again.

"Can we fly to Latif's village?" I asked Lenore.

"Nope. *Louage*."

"Jesus," I groaned.

"You can rest till tomorrow. Latif arranged for us to stay here tonight."

"In a cat house? You out of your mind?"

"No, listen. Today was military day. Soon as this one leaves, they'll lock up. We'll have rooms to ourselves."

"Yeah, rooms and a dose of clap."

"Very clean girls," said the fat soldier.

"I wouldn't sleep here in a full body condom. Let's go. I'm not turning back till I find Latif and he tells me what's on his twisted mind."

# *Chapter* Nine

The Sahara rushed at us in sheets of color —dull bronze dunes, white salt flats, stretches of crushed pebbles burnt black as asphalt. Every day the car sank to its hubcaps in sand and we had to dig our way out, me with my bandaged hand fumbling a shovel like a man in mittens eating with chopsticks.

Nights we slept in reed huts that the wind set humming like Spike Jones's band, a godawful racket of jew's harps, clarinets, and kazoos. We sacked out in hovels where the bed legs stood in cans of insecticide while up on the ceiling lizards battled bugs as big as your fist. At one hotel in a town of religious fanatics all the toilets had been torn out. The management was afraid men would take a whiz facing Mecca.

Lenore, it surprised me, never lost her temper, never bitched about flies or mosquitoes or bottled water with worms at the bottom. Where I was apt to pick at a mystery meal, then push the plate of slumgullion aside, she ate everything and said it tasted like chicken, even when she was talking about pastry.

Whenever I thought she had written me off as an ignoramus, she'd hit me with a minilecture on the formation of *barchan* sand dunes or the handling traits of four-wheel-drive vehicles, debating the merits of Land Rovers, Range Rovers, Toyota Landcruisers, and Steyr-Daimler-Püch-Heflingers.

Sometimes she showed me a more serious side—a damn depressing one—of the desert, and read out loud from *Wretched of the Earth.* Or she'd quote statistics on infant mortality, illiteracy, disease, drought, and famine.

Finally it clicked. Maybe this accounted for all the oddball occurrences since we met in Tunis—why Latif kept retreating, why we took the slowest transportation and stayed in lousy places. She and he intended the trip as one long, hard lesson. They wanted me to experience the size, the sights and smells, the marvels and misery of where Latif came from, what he had gone through, what a miracle it was he escaped here in the first place.

Did they understand it would take another miracle, a bigger one, to escape again?

No matter how I turned it in my mind, I couldn't feature the International Tennis Federation lifting its lifetime ban. Latif had gone too far, and the last few months before his arrest my bookkeeping began to read like the *National Enquirer.*

A minor actress in a major soap opera charged him with heaving her off a hotel balcony. You ask me, her story was full of holes. How the hell did she survive a fall from the sixth floor? Still, I settled.

An employee at an internationally renowned hotel offered to sell me a blood-soaked mattress from Latif's suite. If I didn't meet his terms, he threatened to feed the press an affidavit from a coroner who tested the blood and determined it wasn't human. I told him I'd rather my client was sacrificing a goat in his room than murdering a hostess. But I paid off.

I received a hefty bill from an outfit called Reptile-O-Gram when Latif shipped Gila monsters, no messages attached, to McEnroe, Lendl, Becker, and Connors. The lizard addressed to Connors made the evening news when it was misdelivered to former president Reagan at his ranch, next to Jimmy and Patti's spread in the hills behind Santa Barbara. The Secret Service executed the Gila monster, dispatched it to a lab for dissection, and even after learning it was all a mistake, they shadowed Latif whenever he played on the West Coast.

I started getting complaints from sponsors petrified Latif was attracting the wrong crowd, scaring off the right one. They liked to target customers who bought a lifestyle, a whole line of products. Their opinion, a fan who paid to see Latif, hoping he'd crash in flames and maybe take the building down with him, wasn't a hot prospect for Les Must de Cartier.

I warned Latif, but he kept pressing his luck, making demands. The etiquette for tennis spectators was already ridiculous. No talking, no moving around, no clapping, no flashbulbs. Still he wasn't satisfied competing in the equivalent of a concentration camp. He wanted to tell people how to dress right down to accessories. He objected to anything that shined—earrings, watches, necklaces. Claimed they blinded him.

He also laid down the law that base-line seats were off limits to fans in tennis gear. You know the kind that come ready to play. Like they believe somebody's going to send them in as a substitute. Latif complained they confused him. Said he couldn't keep track of his opponent.

When at a tournament in Tucson, he stopped during a point and screamed at the crowd, "Why are you looking at me? Why's everybody always staring at me?" I decided it was time to travel the circuit, provide a stable influence. I caught up with him in Italy, at a Pippo Scarcia production.

Pippo, the guy Latif talked about on tape, the agent shaving his client's back, was also a tournament director and a clothing and racquet rep. Like most of the Good Humor Man's deals, this one made you think twice where the dough came from. That area of Italy, the annual per capita income less than three thousand bucks, how did he scrape together a quarter of a million in untraceable cash to pay as guarantees?

My guess, the Calabria tournament was a mob operation. It smelled of bleach and detergent, as in dollars tumbling through a laundry.

The afternoon of the final between Latif and Pippo's man, Flaminio Flamini, I bumped into Buzz Murphy bustling from the hotel with his bags. Buzz was Latif's favorite umpire. A dapper guy with white hair and a salt-and-pepper moustache, he traveled with a doctor's kit full of pills—uppers, downers, penicillin. It wasn't for Buzz Murphy, many a tennis event would of had to hang out a sign, CLOSED DUE TO CLAP.

"Where you headed?" I asked.

"Airport. Catch a plane to Rome, then points north." Buzz was my age, a little older, mid-fifties maybe. Looked trim and frisky in a Coq Sportif shirt and warmup pants.

"Thought you'd be working the final. Latif asked for you special."

"Yeah, well, Pippo asked for the opposite. Asked me politely, diplomatically, so on and so forth, to blow town. Wants his friend umpiring."

"And you're doing it?"

"Can't risk offending the Good Humor Man. He puts on first-class tournaments. Don't know where he finds his hostesses. Have you sampled the terrific down there down here?"

Serious as the situation was, I had to laugh. It was a running gag with Buzz, always saying "down there," which is what his wife called a cunt.

"Look," I said, "Latif's one step from the loony bin. Been snorting nonstop. He doesn't lay off the coke, he'll be the first pro tennis player had to retire because of cauliflower nose. You're not in the chair today, he'll throw a shit fit."

"Afraid Pippo and his friends might throw something worse. Have you thought about this match? Way I hear it, Pippo's at the courts right now talking to your boy. Why not join the conversation, serve as the voice of reason, et cetera? Otherwise this could turn into a definite situation."

"Pippo setting Flaminio up to win?"

"Eddie, you're so quick! You shouldn't have any trouble beating everybody to the bottom line."


The tournament site, a private club, used to be in the country. There were still umbrella pines, cypresses, and oleander bushes around the courts, but whenever you raised your eyes from the red clay, you saw apartment buildings. Tall, turd-colored, concrete-slab, sleaze-constructed buildings with TV antennas, a whole jungle of them, on every roof.

The town had swallowed the club, and people in the apartments leaned out their windows or over their terrace rails and watched the matches. These freeloaders took a more serious —anyway, a louder—interest in tennis than the paying customers. They cussed, threw coins and bread crusts, and spat at anybody who beat an Italian.

Under A-1 optimum conditions, Latif didn't figure to have an easy time with Flamini. Clay was the worst surface for a hard charger, the best for a base-liner like Flaminio. With that gang of goons catcalling from the apartments and a team of Italians on the lines and a stranger instead of Buzz in the ump's chair, it looked like an uphill battle. I hoped Latif would recognize this and cut his losses.

I found him in a windowless cinderblock bunker under the bleachers. Pippo Scarcia was with him. The room, full of equipment for grounds keepers, had a pile of sand and a few shovels in the corner. Just in case Pippo didn't already think he was cracked, Latif was sprawled in a wheelbarrow plucking at his racquet like it was a guitar.

I wasn't in love with the way he looked. He'd lost weight, and had these throbbing veins on his arms and neck.

On the circuit, you see lots of guys like Latif, players who say they're on a special low-fat, high-protein diet, say they feel faster, stronger, fitter. They tell you they're planning to market their secret, write a book about losing weight.

Save your money. Don't buy the book. Nine times out of ten the secret is frequent tastes of nose candy or meth or both.

Pippo, though, he was the picture of health. Dressed in white except for a blue tie and matching hankie, the Good Humor Man sat in a metal folding chair, hands resting palms up in his lap. A medium-size guy with freckles and butch-cut red hair, he had this body language that lied and said he was bigger and better-looking than he really was.

"What's up?" I asked.

"He made me an offer he thinks I can't refuse," Latif said.

"My motto, we'll listen to any offer."

"I explain him is not good for Italian player to lose in Italy. The peoples, they get mad," Pippo said.

"What pee-pulls?" Latif parroted his accent.

"Here, Flaminio has fans. The peoples pay to watch him, not you."

"Then fuck the pee-pulls. I'll win for myself."

Pippo turned to me. "You see, I say some reality. But he can't understand."

"I think he understands. He expects a tough match today."

"I too expect a close, tough match. Three sets with tie-breaks. We have television. I am myself announcing in the booth."

"You own the TV rights." Latif spat it out like he had caught Pippo with his spotless white pants down.

The Good Humor Man smiled. *"Esattamente."*

"I carry Flaminio three sets, you and he pick up a bundle from TV escalator clauses."

"Yes," Pippo was glad to agree. "And when he wins, we qualify for the Bonus Pool and the Masters in Madison Square Garden."

"He wants me to tank to his faggot," Latif explained like they'd been speaking Swahili.

From the fact Pippo threw his punches straight from the scrawny shoulder, I figured he must of had plenty of hidden muscle behind him. "Looks like there's a lot on the line for you," I told him. "What's in it for us?"

"What is in?" He pursed his lips. "Let us remember together like good friends. In the long years at my tournaments I pay you more than a million dollars in black money. And for Latif, there are always the little pills he likes and the womens and the white powder up his *naso*."

"You gave and you got," I said. My legs felt weak. I wanted to sit down. But damned if I'd squat on the sand pile or squeeze into the wheelbarrow beside Latif.

"I and the peoples backing me," Pippo said, "we believe it is nice you do us a favor now."

"I'm not tanking to Flamini," Latif cut in.

"Because he call you focking knee-gair in New Orleans?"

"I think what Latif's saying—"

"I said what I'm saying. I'm not tanking."

"Why not?" Pippo asked. "Lose and you still Number One. Lose and you get the same guarantee. And can I recall you, last year you lose here on purpose in the second round to catch a plane to Rawalpindi, and I have to make the hard apology to reporters and peoples with money in my tournament."

"So you think we owe you one. I can appreciate the logic in that."

"You can appreciate the logic in anything," Latif lashed at me. "Anything that makes you money."

"Hey, I remember right, you earned a few bucks in the bargain. Never heard you complain before."

"I'm complaining now." He stood up and started prowling the tool shed. "I'm sick of this."

I sagged into his place in the wheelbarrow. "Let's discuss it later. Right now, we got a proposition from Pippo."

"Fuck Pippo and his proposition." He was whipping the air with his racquet, loosening up his service motion.

"Then my good friends"—Pippo patted his knees, but not hard enough to smudge the linen—"I must go to the International Tennis Federation and confess I am breaking the rules. I am always paying you illegal guarantees."

"Wait a minute," I said. "You'll wind up in some very deep shit."

"Not me. Remember Guillermo Vilas? Remember the Rotterdam tournament confesses it gives Guillermo a guarantee? Who ends up in the shit then?"

"He's bluffing." Latif flailed the racquet close to Pippo's freckled face.

"Wait a minute," I repeated, realizing our troubles with the International Tennis Federation would be nothing compared to our tax problems. I hadn't been declaring Latif's guarantees. The IRS found out, we'd be up to our ass in audits, interest charges, fines, legal bills, maybe prison.

The Good Humor Man rambled on about Rotterdam. "You tell me who is in the toilet? The tournament pays ten thousand dollars fine. Vilas pays twenty thousand. The tournament they play as always. Vilas is suspend one year. Okay, he appeals. But are you remembering how long that takes? Many, many months when Vilas is losing his mind and millions of dollars. He loses matches, he loses his ranking from Number Four to Number Nobody. When they let him play again, he cannot win. No one cares anymore that he loses. All because the Rotterdam tournament becomes honest and turns in itself. Don't make me be doing this to you, Latif."

"I'm going to win."

"No." Pippo sighed. "Now or more later, you going to lose."

"What is this," I asked Latif, "a death wish? Take the long view. We got other tournaments, other deals."

"I'm tired of deals. I just want to play tennis. Every time I go on court now, I never know whether the match is on the level. You've ruined it for me." He slammed out of the room.

Lifting his hands and letting them fall light as fluff on his knees, Pippo sighed again. "More idiot than Latif nobody has been in history. I am feeling sorry what I hafta do."

"Hold on. I'll change his mind." I pitched up out of the wheelbarrow.

Pippo said nothing, just sniffed at his blue pocket hankie like it was a flower.


Latif was alone in the locker room, flat on his back on the trainer's table. He wouldn't look at me.

"Listen, kid," I said, "you're in a dangerous position."

"What better position to have my ankles taped?" His feet, the soles shrimp pink, twitched back and forth.

"This is no time for jokes. Pippo's serious. The people behind him, they're worse than serious. I think there's Mafia money in this tournament. You don't go into the tank, they're liable to—"

"What? Break my racquet hand? Kill me?"

"Could be."

"Eddie, you're such a cornball. I can always count on you to remind me of a movie I saw in History of Film. *Body and Soul, Golden Boy, On the Waterfront*—you've stolen material everywhere."

"Yeah, well, Pippo's stealing his stage directions from the same flicks. You don't want to wind up in a concrete overcoat, you better take a dive today."

"In Arabic there is a saying for what you're suggesting. 'Kiss the hand you cannot cut off.'"

"My sentiments precisely."

"I'm sick of kissing hands. Sick of kissing asses."


There was nothing I could do except sit in the stands and pray for a miracle. Pray Latif would cramp up and quit. Pray Flamini would play over his head. Pray an earthquake would bring the entire tennis club tumbling down around our ears.

But from the start the miracles ran against me. First point, Latif hit a serve, an American twist, that bounced over Flamini's head, up into the bleachers. After that, he went for a winner every shot. He ripped into returns and rushed the net. He overpowered Flamini, smothered him.

Slick with sweat, his skin had a neon glow. His kinky reddish hair radiated electricity. Some players grunt or growl when they serve. That day Latif gave a primal scream, and waiting for Flamini's serve he pawed the ground like a bull. Points lasted two, three strokes maximum; according to the scoreboard clock he ran out the set 6–0 in seventeen minutes. A golden set. Latif didn't lose a point.

The second set was delayed when a flock of pigeons swooped down from the apartments and roosted on the net. The ball boys tried to shoo them off, but the birds lifted and relanded a few yards away. The crowd laughed, some cheering for the pigeons, some for the ball boys. Flamini got into the act, whistling and warbling, beckoning to the birds.

Latif had different ideas. Fed up with waiting, he waded in with his racquet, bashing pigeons. Feathers, blood, beaks, and squawking birds flew everywhere. Ball boys bit the dust, scuttling for the sidelines. People in the stands heaved cushions and Coke bottles. Boobs on the balconies rained down fifty-lire pieces.

Then just as quick as it started, it stopped. The pigeons were dead or dying; the umpire and linesman cringed in their chairs. Fans were freaked into silence. Flaminio Flamini had his pretty face screwed into an expression like a baby that can't decide whether to laugh or cry.

Latif looked frozen—sick at seeing what he'd done. This is our salvation, I thought. The miracle I prayed for. He was paralyzed and couldn't finish the match. Or else he'd be disqualified. There were penalties for ball abuse, verbal abuse, racquet abuse. There had to be one for bird abuse. Forget abuse! Bird slaughter.

But he shook himself out of his fog and stalked to the service line, feathers streaming from his hair, his Honky shirt flecked with blood. Who was going to stop him? Who had the guts to try to kick him off court? Silent as stones, everyone just watched Latif go back to unloading bombs, drilling craters in the clay, serving bullets. Flamini looked like he wanted to crawl into a hole and hide.

Latif ended the second golden set and the match, 6–0/6–0,

with a monster overhead that caromed up and smashed the scoreboard and clock. Time stopped. Numbers scattered everywhere. So did spectators. Fans, officials, reporters, and TV crews fled. Latif offered to shake with Flamini and the umpire, but they turned up their noses. He was tainted meat.

For the first time in my years on the tour, there was no award ceremony, no press conference. The shower room was locked and Latif's street clothes were heaped outside the door, the prizewinner's check for $60,000 pinned to his pants.

The last courtesy car sped off as we raced for it. Cabs passed and wouldn't stop no matter how much we waved and whooped. Toting spare racquets and clothes, Latif's guitar and cassettes, we had to hoof it to the hotel.

Here's where it happens, I thought. Pippo's payoff. Assassins on motorcycles. A hit-and-run driver. We were sitting ducks, dead pigeons, on the roadside.

But Latif could of cared less about my life-and-death worries. I couldn't convince him to cut through an olive orchard where there was good cover, big gnarled branches to duck behind.

"I played the greatest match of my career," he said, "probably the greatest match in history, and nobody applauded. Not a single reporter stayed around to ask questions. You think they'll send out stories? I mean, two golden sets."

"Hard to say, kid. Keep moving. Keep your head down."

"At least there was television. There's a record of what I did. They can't take that away from me. Make a note to order a dub of the video tape."

"With or without pigeons?"

He wasn't listening. "Maybe they'll do a delayed broadcast to the States."

At the hotel, our bags had been packed and dumped in the lobby. The desk clerk refused to say who'd done it. Latif had to clean off and change in the bar. Then still on foot—no bellhop or cabby would help us—we schlepped everything to the airport and caught a plane to Rome.

Even airborne, I didn't feel safe. I wouldn't till we were

out of Italy. Till Latif and I split up. I was almost as petrified
of him as I was of Pippo and his hit men. Call me chickenshit,
but I decided to put distance between us.

"What I been thinking," I said, breaking in on his guitar
practice which once again he was performing on his midsize
Rossignol, not his Stratocaster, "I think you're right about the
match. I should market it in the States. Half hour of sports
perfection. A polished jewel. Why don't you fly on to New
York while I stay and get the tape?"

He nodded. "Later let's talk. What I said before the match,
I meant it. I want out."

"Of tennis?"

"The other stuff. I want out of all that. The deals, the
match dumping."

"We'll make some changes. If you're tired, take a rest. See
a doctor maybe."

"I'm not sick. Just bummed out from being pushed into
things, into people, into places I don't want to go."

I folded my hands to my chest. "No more pushing. We'll
kick back for a while."


Once he was on the plane to New York, I hopped the next
flight available. Destination didn't matter. I landed in Amsterdam. Normally I got comped to the eyeballs—door-to-door
pickup, free rooms, free meals, baskets of fruit, and booze.
But the beauty of Amsterdam, I wasn't there on business and
nobody expected me. I checked into a hotel named for a dead
artist and after dropping my bags, I went out to eat.

I had my heart set on Indonesian food, *rijstafel*, a twenty-
six-dish production they serve in tiny bowls. About three
tasty bites of everything. But I got to strolling beside the
canals under the streetlights and staring into the water at
the squirmy reflections of trees and houses, and before long
I forgot about eating, forgot tennis and my troubles. Like
Latif, I needed to throttle back.

I kept on walking past houseboats and hippies and tall

narrow buildings with gold scrollwork and smaller ones with whores in the front windows like Kewpie dolls in plastic boxes. These whores came in a variety of sizes and flavors, and they dressed to show customers what their specialities were. Some wore spike heels and leather garter belts. Some were gussied up as little girls. Some sat petting Great Danes.

The one caught my attention was watching TV. Decked out in black nippleless bra and panties, she never took her eyes off the tube. I assumed she was screening an S&M video. Two burly cops were dragging a black guy through a jeering crowd, really banging him around.

Only when they stuffed him into a squad car, I recognized Latif. The whore was watching the late news.

I grabbed a taxi to the central post office where there were international lines, and called our New York lawyer, then held on while he placed a call on another phone. Twenty minutes later I was still in the booth, slumped against the wall, listening to the dial tone drill a hole in my head.

Customs officers at Kennedy Airport had shaken down Latif's luggage—a strange thing itself; usually they waved him through—and found a kilo of heroin. They booked him for possession and suspicion of dealing. The size of the stash and the fact that urinalysis indicated he wasn't a heroin user —only coke and speed turned up—they took as proof he intended to lay the smack off on local contacts. The street value was estimated at a quarter of a million. Dealing, the lawyer told me, carried a mandatory life sentence in New York.

But Latif hadn't cleared customs. There was a jurisdiction question. The case might land in federal court. The lawyer was working on that angle and on bail which, Latif being a rich alien and a poor risk, had been set at a million bucks. He needed collateral, preferably not in crisp hundred-dollar bills that had tumbled out of an Italian laundromat.

"It's a setup," I screamed transatlantic. "He was framed, and I know who did it."

"Don't say his name. I don't want to hear it. A little personal advice," the lawyer added. "Make sure everything checks out on your end. Make sure your books, just for instance, are straight. You're going to have more readers than Harold Robbins."

"Latif have anything to say yet?"

"Latif, what I understand, has done nothing but talk since they took him into custody. Speed has turned him into a fantastic conversationalist. Could be the first case in history where cops shoot a prisoner to shut him the fuck up."

"Jesus."

"I'm urging caution, Eddie. The cops and the press are going to air this one out like a pair of dirty socks. They find any holes, they're going to poke their fingers all the way to the bottom. I'd think hard before I moved. However I moved. Wherever. And Eddie, make sure you're clean."

Back at the dead artist hotel, I considered cutting and running, ditching my stuff. But I couldn't bug out yet. I had to pick up my valuables, my papers, and check what else might be in my bags.

The suitcases were where I dropped them on the double bed. I bolted the door behind me and closed the curtains before having a look.

Sure enough, Pippo had squirreled a surprise in with my socks. A plastic sack of white powder. Heroin? Cocaine? Ex-Lax? Who knows? I flushed it down the toilet. Show you how paranoid I was, I crouched down and scrubbed the crapper. Then I washed my hands. I took him serious, my lawyer. I intended to be clean when I left this room.

Going back to the bags, I went through my clothes like I go through a contract, line by line. I ran my fingers over every seam, into every cuff and pocket. Even then I wasn't satisfied. I'd read about cops vacuuming for drugs, lab technicians searching for microscopic traces, dogs trained to sniff it out. Why take a chance?

I saved my passport and IDs, important names and numbers. I burned the other papers and flushed the ashes. Chucking my Vuitton luggage and lots of clothes, I walked away with a bag no bigger than a briefcase, flagged a cab, and figuring anybody who knew my habits would watch airports, I went to the train station.

I roamed around Europe traveling under assumed names, holing up in towns far off the tennis tour, phoning my lawyer from pay booths. Not that I needed him to tell me I was in trouble. At every newsstand I saw familiar faces and another fantasyland account of Latif's and my career.

Pippo Scarcia, I read, turned himself in to the International Tennis Federation, confessing he paid us guarantees—like we twisted his arm. He testified Latif was a drug addict and he suspected we were both dealers. Calling for reform of the game, he came out a hero. The ITF fined him a few thousand bucks and renewed his contract as a tournament director.

Meantime, Latif, the best anyone suggested, he should be banned for life. Congressmen called for his deportation. Some pressed for the death penalty. College of the Holy Sepulcher denied he was ever officially enrolled there, but they charged he had once defiled the Tabernacle with a voodoo hex. His old gap-toothed girl friend, Noreen, claimed he tried to force her to carry his baby.

What people said about me I won't bother repeating. My height, my hair, this scalp problem I have, it all got thrown up in my face. Even Latif's lawyers—which is to say, originally my lawyers—laid the blame on me.

I understood the strategy. They were trial-ballooning the ABF defense. Anybody But Fluss. I played along, drawing flak in public and doing in private what I'd always done. I doled out our dwindling dough, collected what was owed him, and liquidated assets to cover his colossal legal expenses.

While he took the heat in the States, I took it worldwide. I settled what I could out of court, leaving behind as little scorched earth as possible. Granted, I was partly protecting my own ass. But I also had it in mind to save some small shot at the future. You see, even then I was dreaming about a comeback.

# *Chapter* Ten

Traveling from town to town by *louage* was like driving inside a neon bulb. Blinding sun burned down and dust boiled up and every breath was a deep inhalation of hot pepper. I had finished Latif's tapes, but went on wearing the headset to keep the grit out of my ears. I closed my eyes and mouth tight and took swallows of air through a handkerchief I tied across my nose.

Every evening we'd rumble into a village no different from the one we left that morning. There'd be a grand arched entrance leading to nothing much—a marketplace where people sold rusty hinges and camel meat, a mosque like a kid's sand castle, a maze of dark, dung-smelling alleys.

One afternoon when I had sunk into a sort of brain fade and was thinking, "This is good. This gives me some practice at being dead," Lenore nudged me from my coma and called out to the driver.

Another passenger, a guy carrying two shopping bags

stuffed with bread, was clamoring to get off too. The *louage* owner eased to a stop and sat, engines revving, while we wrestled our luggage out of the trunk. Then he sped away, abandoning us to the blowing dust and sun dazzle.

The man with the bread marched up a dune like he meant to open a bakery at the top. Lenore headed in the opposite direction. She didn't need to say we were there, we'd finally reached Latif's hometown. I recognized landmarks from his tapes. The oil field had played out and the compound, once bustling with Texans, was deserted. But a few rigs were still standing like gallows, and the swimming pool was a concrete box with chrome ladders curving out of six feet of sand.

We passed the court where he learned the game. The asphalt had buckled; the lines were bleached and crooked. Goats were tethered to the net posts, and fruit and nuts had been spread out to dry. Wherever the fence wasn't flapping with laundry, people had hooked canvas to the chain link and made lean-tos. Under the biggest patch of shade, a guy with grease up to his elbows was tinkering on, swear to God, an Evinrude outboard motor.

"You wonder why he started," Lenore said, and I knew she wasn't talking about the mad mechanic. "This court could be a set for a Beckett play."

"Take your word for that. What worries me, how's Latif working out?"

"Working out?" She frowned. "Are you referring to our marriage?"

"Tennis. Is there another court in town where he's practicing?"

"That's not my field." She nodded. For emphasis, I thought. Then she did it again, and I saw she wanted me to get a load of the men moving toward us.

Tuaregs! Tall and lean, decked out in pale blue robes, faces hidden by blue-black *tagilmousts*, they paraded like soldiers, shoulders braced, heads high. From a leather strap around their necks hung little leather pouches and silver lockets full of hand-scribbled quotes from the Koran. From another strap swung their swords. Most of them had paired off to walk hand in hand.

"Ever catch Latif dragging around like that?" I asked.

"What fear is that wisecrack supposed to kill? Sexual insecurity?"

"Hey, you married him. It doesn't bother you, it doesn't bother me." What *did* bother me was seeing so many masked men armed with toad stickers. I wasn't convinced Latif hadn't arranged a roughhouse welcome, maybe a little game of skewer-the-Jew.

One fellow broke off from his hand-holding buddy and blocked my path. He had on a pair of mirror-lens sunglasses.

" 'Scuse me." I tried to circle around him.

He sidestepped in front of me. *"Baraka Allahfik."*

"Tell him, *'Takbir!'* " Lenore said.

I gave it my best shot, and the guy peeled off the sunglasses, showing dark brown eyes and an inch-wide strip of inky cheekbone. He held out his hand.

"Shake it," Lenore said, looking at me, not the Masked Marvel.

His eyes, staring from a nest of rags, unnerved me. I stuck out my hand, the one balled up in gauze. He grabbed it and pumped hard.

"Christ Awmighty!" I yelped.

"Sorry, Eddie." It was the Tuareg talking. "Didn't mean to hurt you."

"Latif? Is that you in there?"

"Who else?"

"Jesus, you've gone native."

"I *am* a native." He kissed the hand that had squeezed mine, then touched his heart. "I'm glad you're here. I've missed you."

There were already tears of pain in my eyes. Now the shock and the hand kissing and heart touching nearly turned on the water works. "I can't believe this."

"Calm down, Eddie." His voice, coming through cotton, reminded me of a radio with a dusty speaker.

"But your eyes, they're brown. You had the most famous baby blues in the world next to Sinatra and Newman."

"Contact lenses." He put back on his mirror sunglasses. "Let me show you where we're staying."

I turned on Lenore. "Why didn't you tell me?"

She shrugged. "Wasn't sure myself."

Handling the heaviest luggage, he led us past a padlocked spigot, down a street littered with busted springs and spare jeep parts. When we reached a blue door with a brass knocker, he shoved it open, deposited the suitcases inside, and said, "Welcome home, honey."

Lenore stepped in and shut the door.

"I've got something for you to see." He pushed on down the street that was roofed with reeds. Sunlight poured through them, zebra-striping us like cons.

I wanted to sit down, better yet, lay down, till things stopped spinning. But I figured he was taking me to the tennis facility where he'd been training for his comeback.

"Listened to your tapes. Some dynamite material there."

He didn't answer. His head in a helmet of rags, it was hard to know whether he heard me.

"Had no idea"—I semitrotted to keep up with him—"you had such a tough time as a kid. That's the meat of the story. Whether there's a market for it, we'll have to wait till there's a typed manuscript. Book contracts are tricky."

"I'm not interested," he said. "Books are for later, at the end of my career. I'm at the beginning."

"That's the spirit I like. But why'd you send the tapes, you didn't want me to peddle them?"

"I wanted you to think them over."

"I been doing just that. And you don't mind, I got a question. When did you record those tapes? Three years ago? Or in prison taking courses from Lenore?"

He swung his head around to face me. In the mirror lenses and *tagilmoust*, he resembled a giant June bug.

"They didn't sound like the Latif I knew."

"Maybe there were always two Latifs. Does it matter?" he asked in a voice that didn't invite debate.

"Hell, no," I chuckled and raised a hand to slap him on the shoulder—anything to make solid contact.

"Don't do that, Eddie. Don't touch me."

I let the hand drop.

"Men don't do that here," he said. "They don't slap backs or jab fingers at each other's chests."

"What the hell, they hold hands."

"True. You can hold mine. But nothing more."

"I'll take a pass on that."

We were out from under the reeds, walking away from the town. Sunlight fell on my shoulders and skull, scalding hot. Grains of sand big as boll weevils scuttled around our feet.

"Lenore's a real treasure," I said. "Beautiful and smart and tough."

"She saved my life."

"She said there'd been inlaw trouble?"

"Yes." He was heading toward the dunes. The sand here was like talcum powder; we sank in it up to our knees. Still, Latif kept going. When we started climbing the highest dune, I knew there wasn't going to be any tennis court up there. But what was?

"Great for the legs and cardiovascular system," I wheezed. We might as well of been scaling a volcano, staggering through hot lava, smothering in ashes. By the time I reached the top, Latif had squatted down with his *schmatte* wrapped around him and was tranced-in on the other dunes, a whole ocean of them flowing in orange waves toward the horizon.

"When I was a boy," he said, "I came here every evening to think."

I sank to my knees. My tongue tasted like shoe leather.

"I wanted to share it with you. The only other person I've brought here is Lenore."

"Thanks," I croaked.

"Now that she's told you about my inlaw trouble, you understand why I didn't meet you in Tunis or El Oued or Touggourt."

"Matter of fact, she wasn't what you'd call free with info.

What's the problem? They resent you got a divorce and married Lenore?"

"It's a bit more complicated. Rashida's family expected me to kill her."

"Kill Lenore?"

"Rashida. She lived with another man after I left for Holy Sepulcher. They had a couple of kids. The family wanted me to redeem my honor. Their honor. It's a tradition."

"Hey, you don't have to tell me this." I was in no condition to hear a murder confession. Had he dragged me all this distance to get it off his chest?

"Of course, I didn't do it. I divorced her. Wished her the best with her new life."

I sat cross-legged like an Indian. "Now you're ready to get on with your own career. Well, I've given it a helluva lot of thought, kid. Days of brainstorming while we waited for *louages*. There's the physical aspect of coming back. Then there's—"

"Eddie," he interrupted, "let's not ruin our first day together by talking about tennis as though nothing's changed."

I looked at him a long moment. That is, looked at myself in his mirror lenses. Again I had an urge to touch him, to erase this eerie feeling my hand might pass through the material without meeting anything solid.

"Okay. I know I owe you an explanation."

He shook his head. "I'd rather not talk. I'd rather just sit here with you."

It was dark by the time we stumbled down off the dune. I tripped and rolled halfway to the bottom. After that, Latif took my hand and led me into the rabbit warren of alleyways to his place.


The house was built of hand-molded mud. The beams were palm trunks, the rooms barely furnished. We lounged on carpets and pillows, drinking mint tea off a brass table. The walls glowed a rosy milk chocolate. On hot afternoons as the three of us chatted about the future, ignoring, not forgetting, the past, I felt the place might melt like a Hershey bar.

Me, I had already dissolved into mush. At least my brain had. Often as we ran through it, I just didn't get it. I followed the general drift—Latif had decided to come back—but the nuts and bolts baffled me.

The International Tennis Federation, he admitted, had not lifted its lifetime ban. He hadn't filed an appeal for a pardon and didn't care to discuss what condition he was in.

"For Chrissake, Latif, level with me. When's the last time you touched a racquet?"

"Yes," he said, delighted. "My new racquet. Let me show you."

He stepped over to a cedar chest and removed a bolt of indigo cloth, same material as his robes. Back at the table, he knelt and unfolded it, flourishing a wood racquet like it was a trophy.

I looked at Latif, not it. Indoors around Lenore and me, he lowered the *tagilmoust* off his face, leaving a twisted loop of it tucked under his chin, like a man slipping into or out of a noose.

He handed me the racquet, very pleased with himself. I thought maybe it was the prize he'd won in the Raghead Racquet Race. But then I noticed it was a homemade job, a hefty, old-fashioned club, the kind nobody used nowadays. The wood was dark except for an ivory inlay on the handle. Someone had carved Arabic on the shaft.

"In prison," he said, "I learned woodworking."

"Lucky they didn't have you making license plates. You'd of punched up a tin racquet."

Lenore and he didn't laugh.

"It's not from prison," he said, superserious. "I made it here with local products. It's strung with camel gut."

I sniffed the strings. "Yeah, that's camel all right."

Still no rise from the sunshine twins. I didn't dare look Latif in the eye. Afraid I'd bust out laughing. Next thing he'd tell me, Lenore crocheted all her own bras and panties.

"Translate the inscriptions," she asked him.

"This one, this is the opening line of the Koran. 'In the name of Allah, the Compassionate, the Merciful.'"

"Didn't you mention on the tapes that's what Moslem whores have tattooed on their shaved . . ." I caught sight of Lenore's sizzling Jewish Egyptian Princess eyes . . ." their down there?"

Not a chuckle, not a grin.

"I intend to make my comeback with this racquet," he said.

"Hard as you whack the ball, you'll run through a dozen a week."

"This one will last forever."

"You've hit with it?"

"This one will last forever," he insisted.

No sense arguing. The minute some equipment manufacturer coughed up megabucks, he'd pack this dinosaur bone back in the cedar chest.

"There's still this little problem of the lifetime ban," I said. "No tournament's going to let you play."

"There are ways around it." He took the racquet from me.

"Sure. Go to court in the States, charge restraint of trade, say you served your sentence and they got no right to prevent you making a living. But that'll take years and cost a bundle in legal bills. You got a deep pocket?"

"There's another way. Play under a different name, a new identity."

"Get serious. You think wearing brown contact lenses they won't recognize you?"

"I was thinking of a much more drastic switch in image."

"A sex change operation? Get chopped and channeled and come back on the women's tour like Renée Richards? What's Lenore have to say about that?"

"I say give him a chance to explain." She fished a sprig of mint from her tea and munched on it. "To be honest, Latif, I've been wondering myself."

He was rubbing the racquet handle with his broad pink fingertips.

"I'd recognize you anywhere," I said. "Just looking at your hands, your fingers, I'd know you."

"You didn't know me that first day in the street."

"What the hell, I hadn't seen you in three years."

"Neither has anybody on the tour."

"But, honey," Lenore said, "you were wearing long robes and a *tagilmoust* and sunglasses."

"It's time you two saw something I worked on while I was waiting for you." He left the room, lugging his do-it-yourself racquet.

Lenore was fingerbowling for more mint leaves.

"Where do you stand on his comeback?" I asked.

"Latif wants it, I'm for it."

"But personally, what's your position?"

"It could be educational, therapeutic." She started flicking her nails, index finger against thumb. "A way to regain self-respect. Express himself physically. Work off deep-seated rage. Then again, there's a potential downside."

"Which is?"

"The tennis tour drove him around the bend once. Put him in jail. It could happen again."

"Pippo Scarcia put him in jail."

"Okay, he was arrested for a crime he didn't commit. But you two were into so many rip-offs, tax frauds, currency dodges—"

"We didn't do anything wasn't standard practice."

"—Latif was bound to get busted sooner or later."

"I can name plenty of famous players and agents all did the same damn thing. Nobody bothered us till Latif had that attack of conscience or crazy pride in Calabria. He'd thrown the match, he'd never of done time."

"I disagree. He was headed indoors. If not prison, then a hospital or mental institution. You're lucky not to be there yourself."

"Be where?" Latif glided barefoot back into the room.

Both of us turned. Our jaws sagged and we gaped.

"This is what I'll wear on my comeback," he said. "Nobody'll recognize me."

"No shit," was all I managed to mumble.

He had rewrapped the *tagilmoust* over his nose and mouth. Mirror-lens sunglasses masked his eyes. The thong of leather pouches and silver lockets still dangled from his neck, but the sword was gone. Instead of brand-name shorts and a shirt, he had on baggy blue pants that hit him mid-thigh and a loose-fitting tunic with a scrawl of Arabic hand-stitched in black over his heart. Latif didn't wait for us to ask for a translation. " 'God is as close as the vein in a man's neck.' "

"No shoes?" Lenore said.

He stamped his splayed feet. "No need. I never wore tennis shoes until I was in my teens. My soles are tough enough again."

"They'll let you on court like that?" she asked.

"The Code of Conduct's vague about dress. But I think I can claim this is customary where I come from."

Now that the numbness was wearing off, I began to feel giddy, not just at how he looked to me here, but how he'd come across on camara, the scene he'd create at Wimbledon and Flushing Meadow. I thought of Boy George, Michael Jackson, Prince, Liberace, a raft of professional wrestlers. People, specially kids these days, were crazy about costumes, sexual confusion, cross-dressing. I didn't want to get too excited, but this new format was definitely something I could sell.

"Can you play in that getup?" I asked.

"Count on it." He was bouncing on the balls of his feet.

"You've practiced in this rig?"

"I've got it worked out."

"You've worked out?" I tried to pin him down.

"I think you look terrific," Lenore broke in.

"I was honeymooning with you, maybe I'd say the same. Don't mean to be downbeat," I said, "but you can wrap your face like a mummy and run around barefoot in lounging pajamas and, still, the first shot you hit, fans are going to know you. The Latif Fluss style, it's like a fingerprint."

"I've worked that out, too. I've—"

"I understand what Eddie's saying," Lenore interrupted
him. "The first tennis book I ever read—when I fell for Latif,
naturally I did research—was John McPhee's *Levels of the
Game*. Nice writing. Urbane and fluent."

"Is this a comeback or a seminar we're discussing?" I tried,
but couldn't jerk her onto the track that interested me.

"McPhee wrote, 'a person's tennis game begins with his
nature and background and comes out through his motor
mechanisms into his shot patterns and characteristics of
play. If he is deliberate, he is a deliberate tennis player; and
if he is flamboyant, his game probably is too.' But I don't
buy that," she said. "It reminds me too much of Ezra Pound's
remark that every failure of art is a failure of character. I
simply don't accept that style in art or sport necessarily
reveals a person's psyche."

"Look, Lenore, you're the Lit. Biz expert. Me, I'm Show Biz,
and I'm telling you, soon as somebody sees Latif play, they're
going to know."

"You're assuming I'm the same man. You're assuming I
can't change my game."

"You only know one way to play. Hit for the lines. Take
no prisoners. Go for the jugular vein."

"That was never really me. It was you."

"Me?" I asked so loud it rattled the tea set.

"I never felt right gorilla-ing guys, playing the role of
'bad nigger.' "

"What do you plan? Play left-handed?"

"You'll be surprised. Everybody will." He was swinging
some practice strokes.

I wanted to believe there was nothing goofier about him
than players who wore gold neck chains, diamond earrings,
and nose studs. Why not a quote from the Koran when other
fellows flaunted decals for hamburger franchises, brokerage
firms, oil consortiums, and airlines? The world, specially the
circuit, was one huge hustling nuthouse. Why single out Latif
and say he'd lost his marbles?

The answer of course was what Lenore pointed out earlier.

Tennis drove him around the bend once. It was logical to wonder whether he had a head start on a second trip. "Why do you want to come back?" I asked.

"I love the game," he said, like that explained everything.

"But the way things went last time—"

"It'll be different this time." He knelt at the table, lifted off the bug-eye sunglasses, and gazed at me across the brass platter of oranges and dates. "You've got to agree to that from the start. It's going to be as different as the way I dress."

I chuckled. "We going to travel by camel?"

"How we travel, where we stay, there'll be changes in that area too. Everything's going to slow down." His voice sounded like a record played at the wrong speed. "I want to enjoy where I am, see where I'm headed, who I'm with."

"I got no problem with that," I said. "Other changes?"

"No point discussing them all now. We'll improvise, play it by ear. No matter what, I won't be locked in." His hand was on the racquet, fingertips rubbing the white inlay, skimming the Arabic inscriptions like Braille.

"I follow you, kid. You're coming off three tough years of being locked in."

"No. Much longer, Eddie. From the time I left the Sahara, my life got smaller and smaller. I thought I was trading this village for the big time, but I wound up trapped in a series of tight spaces. I was always stuck on an airplane or in a hotel room or the back of a limo. Whenever I went out to a restaurant or disco, I was surrounded by strangers shouting their names and phone numbers and sexual fantasies."

"I should of looked after you better. I thought you were having fun."

"I thought I was having fun, too. Everybody told me I was. But I was in a kind of jail. Then I landed in a real one."

"That's all behind you."

"No. I intend to keep it in front of me. As a boy, I longed to prove my father wrong. But I did the opposite. I proved him right. I want to remember how I turned into a *toubab* toy, a stink in men's nostrils."

"You're too hard on yourself, kid."

He shook his head, plowing on. "To become a tennis star, I broke the taboos of my tribe and religion. Then once I was a star, I broke the rules of tennis. Broke the law. Nobody stopped me until I refused to tank for Pippo."

"It's what I was telling Lenore. You were set up. Framed."

"The most fortunate thing that ever happened to me."

"What the fuck?" I almost fell off my pillow. "How can you say that?"

"Jail brought me back to my senses. Brought me back to the Sahara." Rocking on his knees, he wasn't so much talking as chanting now while Lenore sat beside him and beamed. "Prison is a sort of desert. Most men can't live there. But my father taught me to survive on dates and a mouthful of water." He grabbed some dates, then let them drop, ringing the tray like a gong. "Getting along in jail was just a question of recalling the lessons I learned as a child."

"Why do I get this impression I'm being pressured to buy a time-share condo in a federal pen?"

I didn't mean to hurt Latif, just lighten things up a little. But he sagged back on his heels.

"Sorry," I said.

"No, I'm sorry. There's no reason you should enjoy hearing about my time in jail."

"I want to hear about it. Really. Like I said, kid, you were framed from start to finish."

"Not the way you mean. But I was cut to measure and displayed to the public in a frame. I was a picture you painted. A scenario you concocted. A story you leaked to the press. I don't blame you. I blame myself for letting you do it."

"We'll rewrite that story, the ending especially."

"Nobody can rewrite the past," Lenore butted in.

"Sure they can."

"You sound like Gatsby, forever yearning for the green light."

"That's me, babe. Gimme the go signal and I hit the ground running."

"Read Fitzgerald. There are no second acts in American life."

"Who's talking American life? He's a Tuareg. He'll have a second, third, and fourth act."

"Please, don't argue," Latif said. "You know, Lenore, how much I admired the books we studied. But in the beginning it was the Koran that sustained me. Alone in my cell I chanted verses. I shouted them against the babble of radios and televisions and curses from the other cells. 'Well have you deserved this doom: too well have you deserved it! My wealth has availed me nothing and I am bereft of all my power.'

"Each verse that came to mind spoke to my problem. 'I seek refuge in the Lord of Daybreak from the mischief of His creation; from the mischief of the envier, when he is envious.' "

"Plenty of them envied you," I said, confused where this mumbo-jumbo was going. "Everybody on the circuit wanted to cut you down."

" 'I seek refuge from the mischief of the slinking prompter who whispers in the hearts of men.' "

"Pippo? Iain Richards?" I asked.

Lenore laughed. "Guess again."

"Fine. It makes you feel better, lay it all on me. I admit I made mistakes. I'm here to set them straight."

"Good," said Latif. "That's why I'd like you to be part of the comeback."

"My pleasure, kid. When do we start?"

"I was a good player."

"The best."

"I was a champion."

"You'll be one again." As I picked up the chant, we sounded like Ayatollah Khomeini and Jesse Jackson singing *cheder*.

"But 'Allah does not change a people's lot unless they change what is in their hearts.' Can you change, Eddie?"

"You bet your ass."

"Don't lie to me." He grabbed my bandaged hand. "I need to know the truth."

"I'm a new man." I winced with pain. "I swear."

"Good." He sat back, but kept ahold of the gauze. It ripped

and unspooled in a blood-encrusted spiral, like innards being pulled from a pig. The healed skin on my fist was pink as a baby's behind. "Eeeyike!" I screamed.

"Did I hurt you?" he asked.

"Nothing to it," I muttered through clenched teeth. "Just tell me, where do I fit in? What do you want me to do?"

"Wait and watch."

"For what?"

"You'll know when you see it."

*Part* Two

*The Comeback*

## *Chapter* Eleven

No more chartered jets, no more first class. Like Latif threatened, everything slowed down and humbled down. By truck and *louage*, we traveled north to Algiers, then boarded a rusty, stinking boat bound for Egypt.

Though we never played it, there'd always been a tournament in Cairo. The prize money was pitiful, $100,000 for a thirty-two-man draw. The champion copped a measly $15,000 —which meant a star with an entourage and a sweet tooth could barely cover expenses, much less pay for toots of Peruvian nasal decongestant. But we had to start modest. At bigger tournaments with millions of bucks above the line and almost as much under the table, entry went strictly according to the Association of Tennis Professionals computerized ranking.

This ATP computer was a mystery to most people, players included. It was supposed to be scientific, foolproof. But I'd seen enough glitches in the system to question what got fed in by the programmer. Some fellows struggled six, eight months without a win and still ranked higher than players that beat them. Guys that dropped off the tour temporarily because of injuries or mental troubles climbed the ladder by not playing. Other guys retired altogether, yet kept a ranking for years.

When Latif wound up in the clink, he became the first player in history to have his name scratched. Overnight, with the blip of a few buttons, he disappeared from the print-out.

Now he was coming back with forged papers and the alias of Ali Ben Baraka. Claiming to be champ in his no-account country, he wrote a letter in Arabic asking to compete in the qualifying rounds at the Egypt Open. If he won three preliminary matches, he'd make it into the main draw, where he'd finally play for money and computer points. Because Cairo had trouble attracting anybody except local hackers and low-ranked journeymen, they welcomed Ali Ben Baraka.

Despite Latif's homemade racquet and space odyssey outfit, I took some encouragement he wasn't entirely lost in cloud-cuckoo-land. He showed genuine scheming skills creating a fake identity and picking a tournament he could snake his way into. I hoped after a few weeks on the tour we'd iron out the other wrinkles in his act.

But then on the boat he began weirding out again. Or rather, he kept doing the same thing—namely nothing. He dropped into a deck chair like a load of laundry laid out to dry. It wasn't bad enough I had yet to see him hit a tennis ball. For hours he hardly budged.

"What's this?" I said. "North African gymnastics? You stay still and let the ocean move?"

"Practice," he said.

"Great! How about running in place? Skipping rope?"

"I'm processing some old brain tapes. Sharpening the reflexes." He reached out to Lenore who lounged in a chair beside him and squeezed her hand. "My game's ready."

"It's your body I'm worried about," I said, though I did have my doubts whether his elevator ran to the top floor.

"No problem." He tapped his turban at the temple. "It's all up here."

"Look, I been thinking, what we're going to have to do—"

"I've been thinking too," he said. "That's the best practice— thinking. In prison, I replayed my matches. First the ones I won. Then the ones I lost. In three years I corrected all my mistakes."

"In your mind?" I couldn't take this standing up. I flopped into a deck chair too.

"That's where it matters. In your mind." He pulled off his sunglasses and spun them by the earpiece. The mirrors blinked a message I couldn't follow.

"What I'd like, I'd like to get your mind and your ass out on a court."

"No need. Every hour of the day, I'm bearing down, work-ing hard. I've started replaying other people's matches. This morning I did the 1984 French Open final. You remember that time when McEnroe zoomed to a two-set lead, then Lendl bounced back to beat him in five. I played it from John's side of the net, then switched to Ivan's. Very exhilar-ating exercise. Instructive too."

"They've done these fascinating studies," Lenore piped up, "that prove Latif's right."

"Who's done them, these studies?" I asked. "And what's right?"

"Scientists. They maintain you can improve at a sport as much through mental imaging, fixing a clear picture in your mind, as you can through physical training."

"I'd just like to see that new racquet in action." I tried a new tack.

"It's a miracle." Latif left it at that.

This Masked Marvel routine, with fortune cookie wisdom filtering through thin cotton, was already getting on my nerves. My motto's Do it my way or hit the highway. But how could I cut bait before I saw how he did in competition? And how could I threaten to bug out when I had nothing to fall back on?

"What you both ought to do," said Lenore, looking in white shorts and a knit blouse like the true athlete in the trio, "is prepare for Egypt."

"That's what I been saying."

"I mean prepare for the history, the culture, the art. Do some reading. Why travel to Cairo knowing nothing about the city?"

"This is a comeback, not a Cook's Tour," I said.

"Tennis is just part of the comeback," Latif put in. "And not the most important part."

"Don't pout. Enjoy yourself," Lenore told me. "Regard the wine-dark sea."

"I ever got a bottle this color, I'd send it the hell back. Who ever saw sparkling blue wine?"

"Stay with me"—Latif was waving his hands—"and you will see signs and wonders."

The first wonder I witnessed was the port of Alexandria.

"Jesus, it's dreary," Lenore said as we docked. "What was on Durrell's mind? Where's the mystery? The romance?"

The wine-dark sea was puke-green here, full of plastic bottles and cigarette butts. Behind the harbor hunched a huge mosque with four domes and a minaret stabbing at the sky like an ivory letter opener.

Latif led us down the gangplank, tossing out useless orders in Arabic as a ragtag army rushed at us. One guy in a khaki uniform—I thought he was from passport control—grabbed the suitcases. "Forget these fools. Follow me."

A bigger guy leveled a piece of chalk at him like a .357 Magnum. "Drop those bags."

The fellow did what he was told and hightailed it. The big guy chalked a mark on each piece of luggage. "Which hotel?"

"We're going on to Cairo," Latif said.

"I take you to train station. My taxi is outside."

"Halt!" another man hollered. Like everybody else, he was dressed in army surplus duds. "Open suitcases."

"Who are you?" Latif asked.

"Customs." He flashed a gun, not a badge.

We let him paw through the luggage while a battalion of goofballs in olive drab, dress grey, and camouflage gear pawed at us.

"Welcome already, I am your guide."

"Hello America. Speak Englees."

"Beau Rivage. Best view on Montazah Palace."

"Union Restaurant. Here comes Churchill, de Gaulle, Montgomery. All is eaten here."

The customs officer wasn't the only lout with his mitts in our luggage. Everybody gave our clothes a feel. Lenore's sherbet-colored bras and panties were specially popular. Latif and I tried to keep the looting to a minimum till finally we made a break for daylight.

Outside, more shock troops were waiting. But we had the hang of it now. You couldn't slow down, couldn't let them smell your fear. You had to lower your shoulder and barrel on through.

Then I heard something that brought me to a skidding stop. A gang of kids surrounded Latif, shouting, "Fluss! Fluss! Fluss!"

The mask, the mirror-lens glasses, the blue robes hadn't made a damn bit of difference. They recognized him.

I shoved him into a horse-drawn carriage, desperate to get away before somebody tipped off the press.

"This'll cost a fortune," Lenore complained, climbing aboard. "We should bargain."

"No time." I gestured for the driver to go, and he went, whipping his scabby horse that was the size of a collie and had even less pulling power. The kids kept up with no trouble, trotting beside us screaming, "Fluss! Fluss!"

"We're finished. Fucking finished before we started."

"What are you talking about?" Latif asked.

"Listen to what they're saying."

"I don't hear anything." Lenore was straightening her bra straps. For all her education, I wondered whether she didn't have inner ear problems—like nothing between them.

"Fluss! Fluss! Fluss!" The kids were banging the carriage door.

"Street urchins in Alexandria see through your disguise," I said, "there's no hope of hoodwinking anybody on the tour. You might as well throw away the Halloween mask."

Latif laughed so hard the rag over his mouth rippled. "They don't recognize me. They want money." He hiked up his skirts, dug some change from his pants pockets, and chucked it into the street. The kids scrambled for the coins, then scattered.

"I clearly heard them saying, 'Fluss.' "

"Which means money in Arabic."

"You saying your name all those years was Latif Money? Should of told me. I maybe could of got us a contract with a bank or brokerage firm. Like, 'Hi, I'm Latif Fluss. Tennis is the game. Money is the name.' "

"Try it with Baraka," Lenore suggested.

"What's it mean, cash and carry?"

"Grace or soul."

"Ali Ben Soul. That's a hard sell."

"My name is not for sale," Latif said.


At the station we hopped a train and for the next three hours sat in an air-conditioned compartment where nobody bothered us except to announce lunch. Frankly, the menu didn't do much for my appetite. The English translation of local delicacies offered a choice of "meat-stuffed paste tubes," "lamb thumbs," "mixed boils," "chickie broth with fingers," and "foul madhammas."

"Why not a helping of each?" Latif told the waiter, a fellow with a thimble-size fez on his bald head.

In my frazzled condition, I was impressed by Latif's cool. Used to be the slightest hassle—losing his hair dryer, breaking a string on his guitar—knocked him pinwheeling into a nose-dive, his schnoz hooked over a hand-held mirror and long rails streaming up his nostrils. Now nothing fazed him. Or if it did, the swami suit screened his emotions. He ever got around to playing tennis, this could be an advantage.

"I'm making a list of 'must-see' sites," Lenore said, scribbling notes in the margins of a guide book.

"Be sure to set aside an afternoon for the Pyramids," he said.

"Here's something I wish I'd read a few weeks ago. 'Immunization against the following diseases is recommended by medical authorities for travelers in Egypt: cholera, infectious hepatitis, poliomyelitis, and typhoid.' "

I was about to suggest we forget the food when the waiter brought a meal that bore no relation to the menu or to Lenore's medical alert. It was shish kebab on a bed of rice with a bottle of Omar Khayyam wine.

"Can't believe my good luck." Lenore grinned at Latif. "I have wine, I have thou. Now all I need is bread."

"Welcome to the club," I said. "Everything depends whether your hubby can still serve."

"Sure I can." He spooned some rice onto my plate. "And a second serve." He ladled a helping to Lenore.

After serving himself, he put a hand to his *tagilmoust*, then hesitated. He didn't yank it down like he usually did at dinner. He slipped food up under it. "From now on," he said, "I suppose we should be careful who sees my face. Careful where we speak English. Anytime tennis people are around, I'll talk Tamahaq."

"Tomahawk?"

"Tamahaq. The language of the Tuareg tribe."

"Jesus. They'll have one hell of a time finding a translator for press conferences."

"That's what I thought."

"But how will the three of us communicate?" Lenore asked.

"You'll learn a little Tamahaq. And there's sign language. I'll be very dramatic."

"I'm counting on it," I said, shoveling in the lamb and rice. He was planning ahead to press conferences, I guessed he must have a game strategy more dependable than daydreaming about past matches.


At most tournaments, players check into the official hotel, probably the Hilton or Sheraton in Cairo, a place that offers a discount in return for promotional considerations. But even at a reduced rate, we couldn't afford first-class digs, and Latif wanted to avoid the tennis crowd, and Lenore wanted to stay with "real people." What I'm saying, after fighting a traffic jam of cars, camels, and donkey carts, we wound up in a fleabag that had a lobby lined by men hooked into hookahs and rooms that were painted gruesome purple so I felt I was floundering at the bottom of a swimming pool.

Next morning I woke the minute the caterwauling started. It was a recorded *muezzin* squawking through a microphone. The needle got stuck and the same phrase repeated itself till I staggered to the bathroom and stuck my head under the spigot.

Shaving at the sink, I glanced out a window at a tall slice of Cairo. Down in the courtyard some men were crouched on a carpet. At first I had them pegged as praying toward Mecca. But they were scribbling with Magic Markers, recoloring a faded rug. For some sucker of a tourist, I suppose.

Lifting my eyes, I scanned the city layer by layer. So much life, so much bustle, there wasn't room for it all on the ground. It spread out on balconies and rooftops. Kids played tag around chimney pots; guys going to work crossed rickety wooden catwalks from building to building. And over everything hovered the dusty brown domes and minarets.

After rinsing off the shaving cream, I stayed at the window and put on one of my out-of-date Italian designer suits, a glittering silver-grey job with ready-made wrinkles. In sunlight I'd look like I was wrapped in aluminum foil.

By the time I finished dressing I felt I'd had the grand tour of Cairo. Latif and Lenore, though, they didn't have the same view from their bathroom and they wanted to go sightseeing. Lenore had put in a lot of donkey work for this day.

But as she rattled off dates and dynasties, the names of dog-faced gods and infant pharaohs, I kept getting distracted.

While I marched through the Egyptian Museum oohing and aahing at the gold and the jewels and the mystery of the mummies, what amazed me most was how much Lenore in her white cotton dress and shiny black hair resembled the chicks in the wall paintings, regal dames with their shoulders straight forward, faces in profile, mascaraed eyes daring all comers.

Another amazing thing I noticed, the bastards saved everything, those ancient Egyptians did. Then they took it with them—money, food, wine, clothes, servants. How're you going to escape the past loaded down with so much luggage? And what kind of life is that, shooting your wad getting ready to go underground?

Cut your losses and travel light, that's my motto. One of them anyway.

I tried to steer us to the National Sporting Club to find out the schedule of play and sign up for a practice court. But Latif insisted on seeing the Pyramids, and Lenore said we should go by bus.

The station was behind the Hilton in Tahrir Square, and we body-surfed through the mob, trusting the current would carry us the right direction. But there was a helluva undertow, a regular riptide, against us. I lost three buttons off my suit, and Lenore came out with a greasy palm print on her behind. "The Hand of Fatma," Latif kidded her, rewinding his *tagilmoust*.

On the bus, it was standing room only. People that couldn't sandwich inside perched on the rear bumper or latched onto the windowsills, hanging by their fingernails. Once we were moving, weight shifted; the bus listed to the left; men moaned; Lenore winced. I clamped one hand on my wallet, the other over the family jewels. Nothing much I could do about my feet. My bunions took a beating.

Where I was wedged I couldn't see much except roadside

shops, signs for nightclubs—the Red Carpet, Sahara City—and irrigated fields. Then after enough passengers bailed out, we spotted the Pyramids, like tremendous tents in the sand.

At the end of the line, another horde swarmed. Tourists and day-trippers heading back to town, I thought.

I thought wrong. They were waiting for us and pounced the second our feet touched the pavement. Shouting and shoving, they peddled soda pop, postcards, pastry studded with flies. They demanded money, addresses, and immediate changes in American foreign policy.

We hurried uphill to escape. But they stayed with us, laying down a line of patter, then laying on clammy hands till Latif lost his temper and screamed in Arabic and Tamahaq.

I was ready to make a run for it back to the hotel when this sawed-off, bowlegged bozo with a swagger stick tucked under his arm pushed through the mob. "Welcome," he said. "I am Champion."

How he carried himself, puffed up with importance, he had me half-convinced he was some kind of official greeter. When a dervishing bead seller started his sales pitch, Champion slapped him with the swagger stick, which I now saw was a fly swatter.

"Welcome," he repeated, showing a picket fence of brown teeth and black stumps. He wore a knit skull cap the same grizzled grey as his beard, and a moth-eaten Adidas warmup suit.

"Lady, please." He cupped a hand to Lenore's elbow. "I am bringing you to Pyramids." In his other hand he fanned the fly swatter, chasing off the riffraff.

"We don't need a guide," Latif said. "Just someone to make these people leave us alone."

"I am not guide." He cracked up, giggling at the very idea. "And when you are with Champion, you are alone."

I couldn't help asking, "What are you champion of?"

Again a giggle, followed by a geek's look of fake humility. "Pyramid." He waggled the fly swatter. "Up and down running. Whole world record."

"When was this?" Lenore asked.

He dropped his hand from her arm, insulted. "Now. Today. Every day. Like to see?"

"No thanks. But I appreciate your company so we won't be bothered."

"No bother." He cupped her elbow again. "Nice lady, to know, how big is Great Pyramid of Cheops?"

"Let me see. It's in my book."

"Champion is not asking. Is telling." We had reached a corner of the pyramid, and he went into a tour guide rap, running everything together without breathing. "Great Pyramid is one hundred thirty-seven meter four hundred and fifty feet high thirteen acre built of two and one half million stone some weigh fifty ton and two hundred twenty five meter wide."

"Wow, that's impressive," Latif said.

"Nice man, I see your desert veil and I think you are coming from a place where is no such thing big like pyramid."

"We have sand dunes in my country about this size," Latif took up for his home turf.

"Allah builds sand dunes. But to know, how do men build Great Pyramid? Remember, olden times don't have deenameat."

"Deenameat?" I said.

"Yes, no deenameat. No boom!" He threw his hands over his head.

"You mean dynamite?"

"Yes, deenameat." He stuck the fly swatter in his back pocket and smacked a stone. "Look at how big long heavy rock. So to know." He pointed up the crooked ledges leading to the tip of the triangle. "With no deenameat, how they fly rocks up so high?"

"You think today they blow bricks to the top of buildings?" I asked. "You think they explode skyscrapers from the ground up?"

"Don't tease," Lenore scolded me.

"Use to, olden people make ramp. Dirt ramp." With his hands he shaped a tit or a tent. "Ramp ramp ramp. Slaves dragging stones up. After, they dick dick dick down." His hands were shovels now. "Dirt ramp go, rock pyramid come." With a flourish he pulled the fly swatter from his pocket. "I run. Up and down. You want to see now, nice friends?"

"No, thanks," Lenore said. "We'd like to go inside."

"No good. Nothing. Empties."

"But there's the Grand Gallery and King Cheops's burial chamber."

"All stole. Smell bad. People use as watering closet. Better to see Sphincter."

"This guy's great," Latif whispered to me.

"Wait till you see his bill."

"To know"—Champion was getting wound up on another spiel—"how old I am?"

"You're a fine man," Lenore, suddenly quite the sugar-booger, told him. "And you've been very helpful. Now my friends and I will go inside and—"

"No. Very old. Guess." He whacked the fly swatter against his leg, smiling, flashing the black stumps.

"Fifty," she said.

He guffawed.

"Seventy," I said. Lenore shot me a look. But Champion guffawed louder.

"No more guesses," Latif said. "Tell us."

"One hundred five year."

"Bullshit."

"Eddie, don't," Lenore said.

"And to know"—he doled Latif a light leg slap—"I race you up and down. And I win."

"Win what?"

"Ten Egyptian pound."

"You're on," Latif said. "But just to the top."

Much as I hated to have my man hustled, I figured what the hell, it was exercise. I'd finally get a chance to check whether he'd left his speed behind bars.

"You'll trip and hurt yourself," Lenore said.

"I'll be fine." Leaving the *tagilmoust* in place, he tugged

his robes up between his legs and tucked them into his belt.
He scuffed the sand, testing for traction with his bare feet.

"This is foolish," she said.

Latif was flexing his arms and legs, loosening up. Champion pulled off his warmup pants.

"You'll fall, scrape your knees, cut your feet," Lenore was warning Champion now.

I didn't give a personal shit about Champion. I was concerned about my client. This early in a comeback, confidence was crucial. I warned Latif, "Watch him. There has to be a trick."

All around us rug sellers, camel drovers, bargain drivers, beggars, and tourists stood on tiptoes, elbowing for a better view. I was sure the locals had seen this scam many times before, but they pretended not to understand when I asked what Champion's angle was.

Kicking off his laceless brown shoes, handing Lenore the fly swatter, he drew a line in the dust with his big toe. Then he crouched down on his pleasure-bent legs. Suddenly he didn't seem so silly. He had that fused steel look of sprinters. "Nice lady, when you like, say 'Go!'"

Latif took his stance, his face a scarfed secret, his body language likewise a mystery to me. His legs looked limp as licorice whips. Where were the stringy muscles? "Bear down," I said. "Think Win! Think Wimbledon!"

"All right," said Lenore, raising the fly swatter like a starter's pistol. "Get ready. Get set."

Champion lifted his ass a little, leaning forward. Latif stayed slack, loose-limbed.

"Go!" She whipped the swatter down. The runners shot out of the blocks; the crowd exploded with applause.

With his longer legs, and him being seventy-five years younger if you believe Champion, Latif hit the wall at high speed, breaking to an early lead. But then the going got rough where the rocks were cracked and crumbly. It threw Latif off stride, whereas Champion, the old goat, he scampered up that slag heap, never putting a foot wrong, sensing what rocks to grab hold of and what to go around. And he was fast, damn fast. Bent low, arms swinging for balance, knees firing like pistons, he reached the top before Latif was halfway up. Then in a grandstand gesture, he cheered my man on, encouraging him to stay in the race.

"I can't believe it," Lenore murmured.

What could I say except, "He's not as old as he claims."

"You mean like he's ninety, not a hundred and five."

"He's not a day over sixty."

Either way, we'd had an ass whipping from an antique con artist. How come, all the no-hope clucks in the world, we had to bump into a Champion just when I was trying to rebuild Latif's winning habit? Okay, they don't play tennis on the tilted side of ankle-twisting triangles. Still, it looked to me like he'd lost a step or two. Or was stamina the problem?

He scrabbled to the point of the pyramid and stood there heaving for breath. Champion gave him this counterfeit gracious handshake. The crowd around us clapped.

"They're waving," she said. "They want us to join them."

"You gotta be kidding."

She wasn't. Neither were Latif and Champion. They were signaling we should climb up.

"You don't suppose he's hurt?"

"That's all I need," I said. "Now I've tracked him all over fucking Africa and finally dragged him to a tournament, he's down with torn ligaments."

"You didn't have to drag him. Let's not stand here arguing. Let's see what's wrong."

The way she went at it, scrambling up that rock pile, no regard for her toes and fingernails or her dress that swirled high as her sherbet underpants, you'd of thought she was racing me. But it was no contest. I wasn't letting her hurry me into a heart attack.

Also I had on these tight, pointy-toe Italian shoes. The soles must of been made of eel skin, they were so slippery. I set my own pace and took off my glinting alumium foil jacket. Read some names and dates people had scratched in stone. Sat down once and glanced back through the heat shimmer and haze at Cairo. Down below, the tourists were bright hunks of candy and the Egyptians were brown beetles scuttling over them.

I reached the top panting and lathered like a drugged race horse. Lenore, Latif, and Champion sat facing the desert where far off it was nearly night. Looked to me like they were on something. Was this whole deal Champion's excuse to coax us up here and peddle weed?

Something had Lenore melting in her sherbet drawers. "Have you ever seen such a view?" she said.

"What's up?"

"Champion's teaching Latif stuff."

"Stuff?"

"Breathing techniques. Muscle control. Training methods. Secrets of the Pyramids."

"The secret is stay at the bottom."

"But look at *that* view." Now she was staring the other direction, off at the city where the sun was half over the horizon, staining the sky like a bomb in a fruit basket. Everything was orange and lemon and apple green and mango, with the Cairo tower, a couple skyscrapers, and the tallest minarets raspberry red. It was enough to make you sick to your stomach.

"Slide over."

She scooted to one side and I collapsed between Champion and her. Latif was overdosing on the desert view. Reminded me of that day on the sand dune down near his village.

"Welcome," said Champion and shook my hand. "You lose."

"I'm lucky to be alive. How do you do it, an old geezer like you?"

He pumped up his chest, breathing deep. "Great Pyramid."

"That's what I'm saying. A fellow your age, how'd you get up here so quick?"

"Pyramid make me fast. Pyramid make me strong." He socked his bare mahogany thighs. "Pyramid make me young."

"Yeah. It doesn't kill you first, I guess it's good exercise."

"That's not what he means." Swooping down off the clouds, Latif leaned forward and looked at me. "He doesn't see this as exercise. He claims his strength comes *out* of the pyramid."

"There is that theory," Lenore said, "about pyramid power. You know, a sort of mysterious energy generated by the geometry of the mass."

"Don't give me this mass of the gas, heat of the meat business. He's hustling Latif for a double-or-nothing re-match."

"You're so cynical," she said.

"Nice lady." This time he socked Lenore's thigh, a little close to the crotch, you ask my opinion.

"I feel it flowing through me," Latif said.

"Yeah, well, it's flowing right out of me." I mopped my face with my jacket. "We don't climb down soon, it'll be dark and we'll need a helicopter to rescue us."

"Run down?" Champion asked.

"Count me out."

"I'll have another go," said Latif, and just like that, they raced off lickety-split. Again Champion crouched low, his feet spread wide, his hands paddling along in front like a chimpanzee's. Latif imitated his technique and made it a closer contest. Still he lost.

How can I describe how it feels to watch your client lose a downhill wind sprint to one of the world's oldest humans?

Lenore looked on the bright side. "He's improving."

Next few days, that's all I heard—his confidence is piling up like flapjacks, he's feeling stronger, getting better. But better at what, I wanted to know? At crab-walking up and down a pyramid? What kind of tennis practice was that? I couldn't even convince him to stop at the club and check the court conditions. All he and Lenore cared about was each other and Champion.

Every day, what they'd do, they'd head to Giza. Their one semi-sane decision was not to ride the bus again. They took a taxi out there and ate a ptomaine picnic treat with Champion, trained with him, asked advice like he was a goddamn guru instead of a top ten bullshit artist. Then while Latif worked out, Lenore sat at the tip of the Pyramid, sometimes watching, mostly reading *Ancient Evenings*.

Once, and only once, I went along and sat sweltering in the sun beside her.

"Ever ask Latif how he likes taking it in the blind-side from your friend Champion?"

She floated up out of her book. "I resent your foulmouth remarks. I thought you'd be happy to see Latif enjoying himself, making such progress."

"Look, honey, I thought this was helping, I'd be happy. But we're not in Cairo, I remember correctly, to compete in some cockamamie steeplechase."

She closed and opened her eyes, giving me a weary-with-the-world's-ignorance expression. The sun, I noticed, wasn't just tanning her face. It was darkening the freckles sprinkled across the bridge of her nose. "Latif told you before, tennis is just part of his comeback. And not the most important one."

"What's more important?"

"Recovering from three years of confinement. Learning to take life on its own terms. Learning that what happened to you two wasn't the end of the world."

"Easy for you to say. You weren't the one left holding the shitty end of the stick."

She slammed the book shut. "The thing I despise most is self-pity. That's the big battle I had with Latif. It's a fight you haven't bothered to start yet."

"We were fucking framed," I shouted. But my voice shriveled to a squeak in that hot sandy space.

"So you've said seventy times. I don't mean to sound unsympathetic, Eddie." She put her hand on mine. "But you act as if you suffered some earthshaking injustice. What you went through was more in the nature of an inconvenience, a career setback."

"What do you call injustice? Your ex-hubby humping your friend?"

"Six million Jews incinerated. That's injustice."

"Thank you, Anne Frank. Now for a special prize, please answer the bonus question. What's your advice for us lucky bastards who only lost all our money, everything we owned, our home countries?"

"If you wanted, you could move back to the States."

"Yeah, and get slapped with an arrest warrant."

"The price you pay. At least you have a choice." She gazed off toward the dusty skyline of Cairo, then let her eyes drop to where Champion and Latif had huddled for a chalk-talk. "Look at Champion. You think he'd let a little thing like tax problems or arrest warrants affect him? He's a life affirmer."

"He's a swindler, a bowlegged putz bilking two adults that oughta know better."

"I'd say you sounded jealous."

"Of a small-time grifter? A two-bit Egyptian gyp artist?"

"I was wrong. There is something I despise more than self-pity. I hate your xenophobia."

"My what?" One hand automatically went up to my hair and dry scalp.

"Everywhere we've gone it's been the same. You've got this typical prejudiced attitude—like 'I am a man and nothing alien is human to me.'"

"How much has he already rooked Latif out of?"

"Less than we'd pay a coach. Less than you'll rake off when the prize money rolls in."

"This heat, I haven't got the energy to argue. Just make sure he shows up for the qualies."

"We'll be there." She went back to the book and was turning a page as I started the knuckle-busting, ass-burning downhill slide.


What can I say about the qualifying rounds? Latif won, but his opponents—a local teaching pro, a gimpy Pole, and a promising fifteen-year-old Polynesian down with dysentery—

put up such pathetic resistance, I didn't want to jump to conclusions. All the bizarre winning shots from Latif, I was ready to write off to crummy conditions.

The courts were dry, about the consistency of Kitty Litter, and the wind, a howling beast called the *khamsin*, whipped up dust devils. Along with tons of sand, it blew in smells strong enough to curl your hair. A tournament official told me he always knew the direction of the wind by its stink. It came from the south, it carried pollution from the steel and cement plants in Helwan. From the north, it floated fumes from the lead and zinc smelters in Shubra El Kheima.

The opening day of the main draw the air was dead still— which didn't mean the stink disappeared, but you had to guess where or who it came from. Me, I also had to guess what was on Latif and Lenore's mind, assuming they had enough grey matter between them to add up to one normal brain. First thing after breakfast, they announced they were headed out to the Pyramids for a final fleecing. Maybe they planned to fly in for the match on Champion's magic carpet.

Me, I went to the club early and alone, but had nothing to do. Till Latif rolled up some good results, some titles, it was stupid to try to cut deals. And anyway, no equipment reps or reporters had showed up in Cairo yet.

Still, it was nice to see the red clay courts swept and wet down and waiting. To watch the grounds keepers puttering with shrubs. To hear fellows on the practice courts, their feet churning the damp brick dust, balls catapulting off tight-strung gut. To feel my own tension build. I realized again how much I'd missed tennis.

"Eddie! Eddie Brown!" Buzz Murphy stepped out of the dressing room carrying his black kit like a doctor on a house call. "What the hell you doing here?"

"Representing a new player." We shook hands. He seemed genuinely happy to see me.

"Thought you were on the shit list, blackballed, et cetera?"

"Latif. Not me. How they going to ban an agent? They got no control."

"Who's your new boy?" Buzz was patting his white locks,

brushing his salt-and-pepper moustache, smacking his flat belly. Three years and he hadn't changed a bit. Even his fidgets were the same.

"Ali Ben Baraka."

"Never heard of him."

"A blue man. Same as Latif."

"Same?" He tapped his kit.

"Not that. This fellow's very religious. A fitness freak. No drugs. What's new with you?" I wanted to beat him to the punch line. "Any spicy down there down here in Cairo?"

"What you have to consider, a man like me, the situation's changed. There's herpes, there's chlamydia, there's AIDS. There's diseases at some tournaments doctors haven't seen since the Middle Ages. These days it pays to be picky about pussy. But the players, they keep putting their dicks in places I wouldn't put my umbrella."

"Thanks for the warning. I'll steer clear of the toilet seats. Anything else I should watch out for?"

"I were you, I'd watch my ass. Some people aren't going to be so glad you're back. It's a brand-new ball game. A lot of the fun is gone. You know, they killed a linesman at the U.S. Open a few years ago."

"They? They who?"

"Guy got hit by a hundred-mile-an-hour serve. Tumbled over backward and cracked his skull."

"I remember. An accident."

"You could look at it that way. But it's bound to put ideas in players' heads. Say I make a few mistakes, bad calls. Is some maniac going to start serving bean balls? When there's millions on the line it stands to reason people'll protect their interests. Look how they came down on you and Latif."

"Yeah, look," I said, keeping my voice light, not giving it much.

"Where is Latif? Still in jail?"

"Far as I know."

"Tragic waste of talent. Had a lot of laughs with him." Buzz scratched at the Coq Sportif insignia—a rooster inside a pyramid—on his shirt. "The circuit's a smaller, drabber place without him. What I should do, I'm seriously considering it, quit the umpire business and go into something better paid. But where else can a guy my age score so much."

"Hell, you're not so old. Met a fellow at the Pyramids claimed to be a hundred and five."

"Gotta run." Buzz went through the full drill, touching hair, moustache, and belly. "If I'm in the chair, count on me. I'll overrule, give your man the close calls, et cetera."

Don't know why I did it. I had no reason to be mad at Buzz Murphy, but I snapped, "Don't give us anything. This kid's a champion. All he asks is a chance to play."


The truth is, Latif was asking a lot more from people, including me, in the way of patience. Two minutes before his match, he ambled on court where the other player had been waiting half an hour to warm up.

His costume drew a crowd. He wore what he showed us that day in his house—baggy blue shorts and a sleeveless tunic. Here in Cairo there must of been Moslems who understood the inscription on his chest, but that didn't prevent there being plenty of chuckles and catcalls.

His opponent, a teenage Swede, one of dozens of Bjorn Borg clones, assumed somebody was playing a joke. He tried to ignore this nincompoop with his *tagilmoust*, mirror-lens sunglasses, and necklace of flapping amulets. He thought a real player would be right out. But he couldn't help sneaking looks at Latif. Shaking back his blond Prince Valiant bangs, he watched him unfold the bolt of indigo cotton and take out the clunky, homemade racquet. That ripped it. He realized he was going to have to play this rug merchant.

He walked over to the umpire's chair, shading his eyes with a nine-hundred-dollar Boron racquet. "This is not correct."

"What?" asked the ump, who I noticed was Buzz Murphy. He must of scooted directly from our conversation and requested this match.

"He is wearing no shoes."

"No rule against bare feet."

"What about . . .?" The Swede passed a hand over his face.

"Nothing in the Code of Conduct against a veil."

The kid stared at the ground, struggling to hold it together. "I am thinking I wish to speak to the Supervisor."

"I were you," Buzz said, "I'd play on. How's it help him to have a mask and no shoes?"

The Swede nodded and went to the base line and hit a forehand. Latif reached out his racquet, and the ball nestled in the loose strings. He might as well of been using a lacrosse stick. Latif gave it a shake and flipped a return that had no more force than dandelion fluff. It hit the clay and died. The Swede was lucky to dig it up and shovel it back short. When Latif pitty-patted the ball over the net again, the kid caught it in his hand, squeezed it, studied the seams, suspecting they were split.

They exchanged—tried to exchange—strokes, but the kid couldn't cope. When he cracked a shot, there was a solid *thwock!* The ball became a yellow blur, zoomed over the net, bounced high and true. Then it snuggled into Latif's racquet, lost its zip, and wobbled back like a wounded canary.

Taking these precise steps, like he was prancing through a field full of mines or horse manure, the Swede returned to the ump's chair. "His racquet, it is not correct."

"How so?"

"Please check it or I stop to play. I quit right now."

"Easy, son. Let me have your racquet. Purposes of comparison, et cetera." He motioned Latif closer. "See your racquet, please, Mr. Baraka?"

Latif didn't answer, didn't move.

"You speak English?" asked Buzz.

Nothing from Latif. Perfect scarecrow impersonation.

"*Fron-say?*"

Still no reaction from Latif.

Buzz swiveled around in the chair, spotted me in the bleachers. "Hey, Eddie, your man deaf or what?"

I came down and leaned across the low green fence around the court. "He hears. He doesn't speak English or French, is all."

"What's he talk?"

"Tamahaq."

"Jesus, you pick 'em. Tell him I need his racquet."

"I don't know much Tamahaq. But I think I can make him understand." Flapping my hands, flickering my fingers, I did my Helen Keller imitation, and Latif passed his racquet to Buzz.

"It's not too long. The racquet face is within the rules. In fact, it's smaller than your mid-size," Buzz told the Swede.

"The strings!" He was steaming.

"They're loose. But they're not double strung. There's no illegal pattern et cetera."

"You have seen his shots? The balls are doing things not correct."

"He's hitting junk. The code doesn't forbid it." He handed down their racquets. "Play on."

Plenty of rumors made the rounds after Cairo. My opinion, they started with this first match and they all had a rational explanation. What I mentioned before, the court was a mess —dry, bumpy, never the same bounce twice. The sun was blinding bright and the Swede had a hard time seeing the ball, much less hitting it. What's worse, the pressure was on him. He beat this blue-robed, barefoot, booby-hatch escapee, nobody was going to give him credit. He lost, he'd be a horse's butt the rest of his career. The crowd was already on his case for complaining, specially the local folks who suddenly adopted Latif as a soul brother.

The Swede won the toss and chose to serve, but never got the ball in the court—forget about the service area. He clobbered four straight double faults that smacked against the back fence. Then when Latif served, the Swede slapped four returns that landed ten feet behind the base line.

The score was five-love, Latif's favor, before the points started to stretch out to thirty, forty strokes like they sometimes do on clay. Here's trouble, I thought. The longer the rallies lasted, the longer the kid kept the ball alive and made Latif work, the more I feared my man would run out of gas.

But he barely ran at all. He sort of glided, like he was on ice skates. He'd always had excellent anticipation, Latif did. Now he was like a magnet and attracted the ball to where he stood. Maybe he hit a peculiar spin so the guy's shot had to bounce back where he wanted it to.

Whenever the kid rushed the net, Latif flicked a top-spin lob. From the same position, same preparation, he could punch a passing shot or a drop shot. More than anything, it was his drop shot that destroyed the Swede. It didn't bounce at all. Looked like it landed in a wad of bubble gum.

Losing 6–0/6–1, the kid ran screaming into the shower room.

When no one asked for a press conference, Latif, who hadn't broken a sweat, told me in sign language he and Lenore were catching a cab to the hotel. This was another move to cut down chances he'd be recognized. His whole time on the comeback trail, he turned up dressed, ready to play, and left without setting foot in the locker room.

I wanted to get away, too, let it sink in what I'd watched. Then ask Latif where he learned his new game. No way he'd win once the shock value wore off. Top-flight talent would gobble up those junk shots, pounce on the short balls and ram them down his throat.

Buzz Murphy grabbed me as I was leaving the club. "What the hell was that?"

"An easy win."

He backed us into a shady corner. Embarrassed to be seen with me? Scared the sun was yellowing his hair? "Your man looks like a space cadet."

"He was holding a lot in reserve. No sense showing it all unless you have to."

"Couldn't see his eyes, but it looked like Lude-city to me."

"No, I told you, he's a health nut. Very religious. He's just got an off-beat style."

"Yeah, well, that beat-off style is going to have people talking. Who's his coach?"

"Doesn't need one. Self-taught."

"Why the bare feet and face muffler?" Buzz brushed his moustache like he smelled something gamy.

"The veil's a tribal tradition. Tuaregs do that."

"And the rest of his rig?"

"We're waiting for some endorsement contracts to change his wardrobe."

"A word to the wise et cetera. Could be problems while you wait."

"Oh?" The hair at the back of my neck stiffened. I was afraid he had guessed the truth.

"The Code of Conduct reads, 'Clean and customarily acceptable tennis attire shall be worn.' They might catch you on that."

I smiled, relieved. "Depends how you define 'customarily acceptable.' Down where Baraka's from they have different ideas about haberdashery."

Buzz grinned too. "You've sold me, Eddie. I like variety and spice."

"Stick around. You'll see more." I slapped his belly before he did it himself.


Call it spice and variety, call it a carnival sideshow, Latif didn't care how people labeled his game. When I cornered him one of the few times he wasn't off climbing pyramids with Champion, he refused to discuss his style. "I'm afraid too much talk will kill it."

In the second round, he treated a peppy South American like a yoyo. Never budging from the base line, he suckered the guy from side to side, back and forth, wrong-footing him so many times he twisted an ankle and had to default.

Latif's every stroke, every gesture was like a slow-motion

demo tape. But when he needed to, he could generate surprising power. In the quarterfinals, he started unloading a top-spin forehand that looped high over the net, thumped the soft clay, then bounced over the other player's head. In the semifinals when everybody was expecting top spin he sliced his ground strokes, peeling fuzz off the ball, sending it skipping crazily over the court like a flat stone across a pond.

Sitting up in the stands, it was hard to tell anything about his serve. It didn't appear to have much work on it, but players complained it was impossible to read. Not that they gave Latif any credit. They blamed his *tagilmoust*, tunic, and flapping amulets. Said he concealed his racquet face behind his body rags. They griped about a glare from his sunglasses. They bitched that in his bare feet he crept around the court so quiet, you never knew where he was. Nobody admitted being beaten. Everybody believed he'd been caught off guard by a novelty act, claimed Baraka stood no chance of winning the next round.

In the final, Latif went up against a Frenchman, Henri Leconte, the one player in the tournament I ever heard of. Back in the bad old days, it would of been a two-fisted slug fest. Leconte's style was what Latif's used to be. A net-charging leftie, Henri didn't have the mind-set for long rallies. He wanted to kill points quick, bim! bam! boom! I figured he'd blow Latif and his puffballs from here to the Pyramids.

Up in the bleachers, I sat with Lenore on one side and Champion—who else?—on the other. Latif's idea, of course. He invited the little gonif along as a good luck charm. My opinion, he was dead weight. Worse, a royal pain in the ass. Every third point, he'd punch my leg and announce to nobody particular, "Pyramid make him fast" or, "Pyramid make him smart."

While Champion was tenderizing my right thigh, Lenore was chewing my left ear with her loony theories about Latif's technique. "It's a holdover from prison," she said. "You notice how he pauses now at doors or before he speaks or takes a bite to eat?"

"Please, Lenore, it's break point."

"It's a result of three years of coming to a cellblock door and waiting for a guard to frisk him, waiting for someone to unlock it. Coming into a room and waiting until a guard told him what to do. Wanting to say something, but waiting for permission."

"Let's watch the match."

"Don't you understand, he's integrated these pauses and hesitations into his game? He's imposing the rhythms of a prison on his opponent. These stutter steps, these lulls in the action, they throw the other guy off his timing. The result is obvious." She flung a hand at the court. "Avant-garde tennis."

"That what we're watching? Looks like Kung Fu to me."

"But he's winning."

I couldn't deny that, and much as I worried this kind of crackpot performance would get him killed against a top player, I found it funny.

Even Leconte, basically a good-natured guy, seemed to get a kick out of Latif. He started playing the part of straight man, applauding shots, laughing, shaking his head, taking a bite at the ball. What else could he do? Henri had only two speeds—off and on, fast asleep or fast assault. The first few games, he tried to bomb this blue man into oblivion. When that didn't work, he had no fallback strategy.

The crowd loved it, and so did I. Champion socked his thigh, socked mine, squeezed Lenore's. When Latif killed the last point, the grizzled little shyster pitched to his feet. "Have won," he hollered, clattered down from the bleachers—compared to the Pyramid of Cheops, this was a cinch—and jumped the fence. Grabbing Latif around the waist, he lifted him high and did a few fast victory laps around the court. I hope somebody caught it on camera—the hundred-and-five-year-old snake oil salesman carrying the Masked Marvel.

Lenore surprised me with a wet kiss on the lips. There were tears in her eyes. "I'm so happy," she said, then scurried down onto the court.

The second she left, someone scooted in beside me. He

said he was a rep for an equipment firm and he wanted to discuss a deal for Latif to endorse his racquets, shoes, shorts, and shirts. It hit me then full force. After years of waiting and weeks of wandering around Africa, I was back in business.

## *Chapter* Twelve

Then Latif wrecked everything. He refused to meet the equipment rep. It didn't matter I warned him his price would plummet if he didn't win another title in the next few months. He should at least be polite, I said, and hear the fellow out. But no dice.

After picking up $15,000 in prize money, he also refused to upgrade the operation. He failed to grasp a basic concept. You cut corners, it costs you in the long run. You get sick from the food, bummed out by the service, and your morale and your ranking fall.

Not only wouldn't he fly first class. He made the arrangements himself and bought tickets at a bucket shop. We wound up with a three-hour layover in Athens waiting to connect with a charter to Amsterdam, where we'd catch a train to Rotterdam. The ABN World Tennis tournament, a Super Series event with $500,000 in prize money, had given him a wild card entry. But we'd be lucky to make it there on time.

"Wait and watch," Latif told me while I waited and worried in the Athens airport. "Patience. Haven't things worked out?"

"So far. But Cairo was small beer. Rotterdam has top-ranked players. How are you going—"

"That's my job. Not yours." He was lounging on a leatherette bench beside Lenore. His legs folded under him, his hands in his lap, he looked relaxed as the Dalai Lama. But what was going on behind the shades and the drapes was anybody's guess.

"What *is* my job? You won't let me cut deals. You won't let me handle the hotels and travel. You got Lenore handling the finances. Which was a big blow to my pride. Why am I here?"

"Trust me. 'Did He not find you an orphan and give you shelter? Did He not find you in error and guide you? Did He not find you poor and enrich you?' "

"Who's this 'He' did all these favors for me? You?"

"Allah."

"Look, I respect your beliefs. But think of Lenore. Think of me. It's tough traveling steerage, staying in flophouses, eating roots and berries."

"I'm fine," said Lenore.

"I give up. Just don't blame me, either of you, when you're defaulted for being late. Or you play like garbage after all this lollygagging in transit lounges."

"We'll make it. My one worry is whether we should have brought Champion with us. And whether there'll be a pyramid in Rotterdam."

"Oh god! Gimme a break."

I went to the duty-free shop, checked labels and prices, leafed through magazines in languages I didn't read. Anything to keep from remembering that monkey business at the Pyramids and Latif's oddball behavior on court and off. I wasn't comfortable with this witchcraft crap. I didn't believe in it anymore than I believed in luck. I believed in facing facts, calculating the odds down to the last decimal place, covering your bets and covering your ass.

Still, I grant there are facts that don't add up. As a for instance, leaving Athens and landing in Amsterdam, who'd of predicted the first person we'd bump into at Schiphol Airport would be Iain Richards? It was like he hadn't budged from the spot where he nailed me three years ago. Like he'd been waiting to take another crack at me on the return trip.

It was winter, a gloomy March afternoon, but Richards had on the same safari suit, the summer tan, the khaki hair, the sweat on his upper lip. He was clowning for his TV crew, tossing a mike from hand to hand, shooting his cuffs like a lounge singer belting out an old favorite.

Tell you what I wanted to belt. I wanted to belt that bastard through a plate-glass window, break his skinny legs, wrap them around his neck and strangle him.

Latif grabbed my arm and squeezed hard. He didn't say a word. He didn't have to. In a millisecond I realized we had something to lose now. Why blow it for the pleasure of pasting Richards?

Iain turned and spotted us, smiled and sang out, *"Ciao, ciao, bambini."*

Next to him I noticed the girl with the bitten-down nails, Heather Honor. She had on a shabby pea coat, corduroys, and jogging shoes.

With Latif goosing us along, we pushed on by the TV creeps.

"Eddie, Eddie, slow down." Richards and crew fell in beside us. "Welcome back to big-time tennis. Fans in Rotterdam are raring to see your *magnifico* new man."

I couldn't tell whether his mike was live. "Go fuck yourself." I figured that'd kill it.

But he shoved it nearer my mouth. "Heard *incroyable* reports from Cairo. Everybody agrees they've never seen anyone quite like Ali Ben Baraka."

"Get that thing out of my face. Who tipped you off we'd be here?"

"Hey, Eddie, this is a bleeding bore, all this running after you when we've been waiting half the day."

"Save your breath and stop running."

"Have a little sympathy for Heather and the crew. They can't keep this pace."

I stopped for Heather, but not out of sympathy. "You fooled me in Tunis, babe. Had me half-convinced you weren't part of this deal with Richards."

"Beg your pardon?" The words were slurred by the fingers in her mouth.

"I know. It's never your fault. You go where they point you, shoot what they say. You're a pistol."

"You asked me to tell Iain you were making a comeback. I did. Naturally, he's interested."

"Naturally." I waved Latif and Lenore on. "Meet you at the taxi stand."

"Forget taxis," Richards said. "There's a limo outside. The tournament told me to pick up Ali Ben Baraka and his entourage and transport them to Rotterdam in style."

"You expect me to buy that? A limo for an unseeded player?" I kept signaling for Latif and Lenore to go ahead.

"Rotterdam's had rotten luck. *Beaucoup* injuries and last-minute withdrawals. They're counting on Baraka to build the gate." He let the mike droop in his delicate hands. "Must say, he's *molto* colorful. What's he look like under the desert drag?"

"Short, stubby, pigeon-breasted. He and Elizabeth Taylor were in the same shower, you couldn't tell the difference."

"Eddie, no hard feelings about the past on my part."

"I got enough hard feelings for two of us."

"The point I'm making, there was nothing personal in that interview."

"Bullshit! You aimed to break every bone in my body."

"You think I was acting as a free agent? Be reasonable, *mon ami*." He went to put a hand on my shoulder. I pulled back. "The issue was a lot bigger than two individuals. Forget petty resentments and think like the businessman you are. Pro tennis is a multimillion-dollar international enterprise. People and corporations have substantial interests, substantial investments in it."

"And they're the ones ordered that hatchet job?"

"Let's just say they made their pressure felt."

"Time to pull the plug on Latif and Eddie Brown. That what they told you?" I was dizzy with anger at something even slimier than Iain Richards.

"*Entre nous*, that's about the size of it. They decided the game needed a more positive image."

I turned to leave. It was either do that or unload on him.

He scurried around in front of me, the crew at his heels. "But that's ancient history. Show you where my sentiments are now, I'm ready to go to bat for you. Let me talk with Baraka."

"He doesn't understand English."

"I speak five languages."

"He only talks Tamahaq."

"We'll find an interpreter."

"Fat fucking chance."

"How do you communicate with him?"

"Mental telepathy." I was walking fast. But they stayed with me, lugging camera and sound equipment.

"I want an interview," he panted.

"Learn Tamahaq and show up after his match for the press conference."

"I want an exclusive." His upper lip was streaming sweat. "I can put him across to the public. Build his image, his price."

"That's what's wrong with you cynical tennis creeps." I remembered the line Lenore lashed me with. "You know the price of everything and the value of nothing."

Richards cocked his head. "Somebody's writing your material. Who's behind this?"

"We're making it up as we go along." I broke into a sprint. "Bye bye, Heather. Why don't you ditch this limp dick and get yourself some live bang bang?"


On the train to Rotterdam, Latif and I told Lenore who Richards was, how he had tricked and trashed me before. What neither of us could guess was what he was after this time. He might be working for the tournament, like he claimed. Plenty of reporters played both sides of the street, serving as PR flacks for events they were supposed to cover. Then again, Richards wasn't the type to settle for small change when he could dip into the deep pockets behind the scenes.

"Look," I told Lenore, "you're going to have media types crawling all over you, asking questions about Latif."

"I can cope."

"I don't want you to cope. I want you to keep quiet."

"Now wait a minute, Eddie," Latif cut in. "She's got a mind and a life of her own."

"My point precisely. She should refuse to answer questions about you, your marriage, or your background on account of your private life is private and she intends to keep it that way."

"You think Richards is on to something?" Latif folded his legs up under his robes.

"Don't know. What I do know, he and every other hack'll be bloodhounding for the inside story. Where you come from. Why you dress this way. The best defense, we don't say anything that might be misinterpreted. Or, for that matter, interpreted."

"That about covers the possibilities," Lenore said. "You and Susan Sontag, dead set against interpretation."

"I learned last time," Latif said, "the less you say, the more people talk. The longer you keep quiet, the quicker they are to speak for you."

"Fine. They're welcome to invent everything. Let them write lies. It's the truth I'm afraid of."

"I don't like this," he said.

"Neither do I. But we're stuck with it for the time being."


A train ride to Rotterdam was a rotten way to shake the jitters. Rotterdam was, after all, the tournament that turned in Guillermo Vilas for accepting a guarantee. What nobody ever fathomed is how it happened. Players had been palming dough for decades. Why single out Vilas? Why, unless it was a double cross like the one Pippo pulled on us?

Tournament officials admitted paying $60,000 in hundred-dollar bills, the way Vilas's coach, Ion Tiriac, wanted it. They delivered it to his hotel in a paper bag, like so many tournaments had done for me. Why did they go to that trouble, take those risks, bilking ABN Bank, a major sponsor, out of the $60,000 with a forged check, then rat to the authorities? Had Tiriac and Vilas welched on some side deal?

What's harder to understand is what happened later, after Vilas's conviction, pending his appeal. Tiriac stayed in touch with the Dutch fellow that fingered them. They met in Paris; they talked by telephone; they turned into regular chatterboxes. And Tiriac, that crafty Rumanian, kept his tape recorder running. Depending on who you believe and how you interpret the tapes, Tiriac was offering him a $300,000 bribe to take the rap. Or the Dutch guy was trying to extort $300,000 in return for which he'd claim he pocketed the guarantee, never paid the $60,000 that had been embezzled from ABN Bank.

Tax fraud, forgery, bribery, embezzlement, extortion—that's the wonderful world of pro tennis. So happy as I was to be back on the circuit, I couldn't forget the rocky tumble we took before. Rotterdam was a city for serious remembering.

"I miss Africa," Latif said as we rolled into the station, a cold, gloomy cave of steam and steel girders.

"So do I." And that surprised me.

"I miss Cairo," Lenore said.

"Me too, sort of."

"I miss Champion," Latif added.

I wouldn't go that far. But the bowlegged old guy's spunk, the sappy, cheerful simplemindedness of his scam did seem appealing compared to people here. They were closemouthed, fat, and rich, and they looked miserable as the weather. I grant Cairo was a madhouse, but Rotterdam was a morgue.

Dead leaves, brown and twisted, skittered like rats along the street outside. Standing in line for a taxi, I realized I hadn't seen a line for the last month, hadn't been anywhere without a swarm of kids and hotel touts rocketing around me.

It felt lonely having people right next to me, not talking, not gawking, not touching.

Lenore let loose a yodel. "Yoohoo! Anybody here alive? Don't bother answering. Just stamp your foot."

The space around us widened.

We got stuck with a cabbie who couldn't or wouldn't talk. He also wasn't crazy about climbing out and unlocking the trunk for our luggage. But he recognized the name of the hotel Lenore told him and sped us past blocks of office buildings, shoebox apartments, and toothbrush-shaped street lamps.

"You don't mind," I said to Latif, "I won't ask this joker whether there's a pyramid in town."

We didn't stay at the Hilton, the official hotel. We drove to a place miles from the tournament site. I was anxious to check in, then cut out for the Sportspalace Ahoy. After a week on slow red clay, Latif figured to have a tough time adjusting to a fast indoor carpet.

But once we were in his room, he said the adjustment had to be in his head, not his game.

"I don't care about surfaces," he told me. "It's the atmosphere. This place is dead. I don't feel any energy."

"You're tired," I took a guess. "A little rest."

"I need to mental-image some matches."

"Okay, kid. But it wouldn't hurt to hit a few balls."

"Eddie, he has to think." Lenore led me to the door.

My room, a single, was the size of a second-class sleeping car. Narrow bed, lamp bolted to the wall, tiny built-in closet, toilet down the hall.

I tried not to think about the Hilton, the big bright rooms, the complimentary swimming pool and sauna privileges for tournament personnel. Most European cities, saunas were coed and nude. Better than singles bars. And there would be free buffets, sightseeing tours, video games. I was itching for something to do. Stuck where I couldn't even find out who Latif was playing tonight.

Maybe like he said, mental-imaging was the answer. I don't know what was going through his mind at the moment, but I thought about what I had to accomplish in the weeks ahead. Get Latif on a reasonable training routine. Get him out of the tribal *schmatte* and into some clothing contracts. Get us out of these fleabags and back on the gravy train.


Posters at the Sportspalace Ahoy gave top billing to McEnroe and Lendl. But both had scratched. Mac was said to of reinjured a wobbly ankle. Lendl was supposed to of been summoned to Prague by some commissar. Who knows? There are always withdrawals. My experience, I never yanked Latif from an event unless we didn't get the guarantee we demanded.

Still, there was plenty of top-flight talent. Latif, it turned out, was slated to meet Boris "Boom Boom" Becker. I was stunned. This was the last tournament I expected Ion Tiriac, Becker's manager, to showcase his meal ticket, the player that Tiriac and Vilas invested in when Rotterdam shoved the skids under Guillermo. But when Latif came on court, there was the stocky, strawberry-blond German, now a veteran of twenty-five, and up in the stands smoking a stogie was the moustachioed Rumanian sending him signals.

The arena was banked with plastic flowers and billboards for products that sounded like insults. NELLE SKAG said a sign. KOK JUWEILER KOK said another. A Porsche, one of the prizes, was jacked up at an angle, like it was about to crash into the umpire's chair.

If Latif wasn't distracted by this, he still had to cope with the carpet, and during the warmup, he moved like a man on hot coals, taking dainty steps in his bare feet. Where he seemed to be swinging a powder puff, Becker smashed each stroke with ball-breaking power.

What most fans never recognized, though, Boom Boom didn't just depend on brute force. Sure, he'd smack his ground strokes and blast his serves. He'd slap volleys straight at a guy at the net or shoulder-bump him during the changeover. But, well trained by Tiriac, he was also a terrific con artist. From the time he was seventeen, that year he first won Wimbledon, he'd toy with players, bait them, do a lot of talking, clown around with linesmen, go ape to get the crowd behind him, stall between points, turn away at the last second as a guy started to serve, pull Mickey Mouse crap to juke an opponent out of his game.

Tonight, he complained about the mirror sunglasses, and the ump ordered Latif to remove them. But this dodge backfired. Latif changed to smoky lenses, then used sign language to say he was bothered by the gleaming gold Ebel wristwatch Becker wore as part of a megabuck endorsement contract. The ump didn't have much choice. He told Boom Boom to take it off, and after a long argument, with Becker reading his lines from Tiriac's cues, the German gave up and got on with the match.

He started off fighting mad, pumping his fists. But Latif was relaxed and rubber-limbed and kept feeding him off-speed shots that Boris belted into the bleachers. When he tried to rush the net, diving for volleys, skinning his knees, Latif dished out spitballs, knuckleballs, floaters, and fork balls that left Boom Boom flat on his bum. We won pulling away—6–4/6–1.

Latif had rewrapped his racquet and was heading for an exit when they called him back for a press conference.

Reporters didn't care they couldn't talk Tamahaq. They were drooling to see him up close, snap pictures, and ask me questions. I felt like Frank Buck on *Bring 'em Back Alive* describing how I supposedly discovered him in Africa—village and country unnamed—and staked him to a season on the circuit.

While I was shooting the breeze about his fictional background, he sat at a raised table in front of the Mitsubishi Grand Prix logo looking like the top figure on a totem pole. He lifted his sunglasses and pressed a towel to the sweaty silver of face between his *tagilmoust* and turban. The towel when he took it away had an ink blot on it, a blurry negative of his eyebrows, cheeks, and the bridge of his nose.

Pandemonium! You'd of thought it was the Turin Shroud. Didn't matter I explained to reporters it was dye leaking from his *tagilmoust*. They crowded in with cameras, cried out for him to do it again. One clown grabbed the towel and ran. Some hacks chased him, others hurried off to file stories.

In the taxi to the hotel, Latif muttered he felt weak, woozy. I felt worse. Next day's papers were bound to describe him as a miracle worker, a medicine man, an extraterrestrial being in baggy drawers.

"It's damn hard," I said, "inventing excuses for how you look and what you're doing. Gimme a few hints what to tell people."

"Tell them," Lenore suggested, "he's the pharaoh's resurrection."

"I start talking about the pharaoh's erection, they'll haul me off in a straitjacket."

"Tell them," she went on with her winning suggestions, "his game is a trick he—"

"It's not a trick," Latif broke in. "I'm calling on what I learned as a boy. Tuareg warrior techniques."

"I can't say that with a straight face. You're putting me in an impossible position. I can't sell you as the Comeback Kid because people don't know you been there in the first place. I can't sell you as Rookie of the Year because I can't explain why your past is a blank."

"Remind them what the Prophet wrote: 'Does there not pass over every man a space of time when his life is blank?' And Eddie, I'm not asking you to sell me. I don't want to be bought and sold. I don't want to be like all the other players— regardless of nationality they're just variations on the American Dream."

As we approached the hotel, I saw the proud smile on

Lenore's face and knew where he learned that line. "So what are you?" I asked.

"The African Dream."


Tell you the truth, I was relieved next night when he lost. The way he sleepwalked through the match, I knew we needed to regroup, rethink. But before we could slip out of the arena, Latif was called back for a press conference. I expected another photo opportunity, silly show-and-tell, a total waste of time.

Reporters, it turned out, were also hot to interview the player who won, Tito Zhukov, a Bulgarian kid with an early Beatles hairdo and breath like garlic bread. You could smell him from one end of the room to the other. He didn't speak English and nobody except his coach and bodyguard, a bullet-headed hulk called Todor, could translate.

Not that Todor was fluent. Far from it. But that's how it is in pro tennis—English is the common, cut-rate language that no one, not even lots of American players, really speaks right.

When some jokester of a journalist asked whether Communist bloc players, in the spirit of socialism, pooled their prize money, a quick-thinking press aide thanked Todor, then hurried him and Tito out of the room. Another aide led Latif to the mike. At the same instant, Iain Richards arrived with Heather and a camera crew. I grant it's not every night on the Grand Prix a Bulgarian beats a Tuareg, but I couldn't believe that called for TV coverage.

Richards had different ideas. He also had his own interpreter, a bald fellow name of Lee MacHose with a British accent and skin so pale it looked like he never left the library much less lived in the Sahara. Still, he talked Tamahaq and started off asking Latif to remove his sunglasses.

Latif nixed that. Said the lights hurt his eyes. I couldn't tell whether he had stage fright, but he seemed to stiffen when Heather held a meter near his *tagilmoust* and signaled Go! to Richards and the crew.

RICHARDS. *(Speaking in his mid-Atlantic news reader accent.)* Where did you learn to play tennis?

LATIF. *(As translated by MacHose.)* In the desert.

RICHARDS. Did you have lessons, a coach?

LATIF. No. I watched players. I tried to do what they did. Maybe I am not such a good imitator. Don't blame anybody but me for losing tonight.

RICHARDS. You have an extremely unorthodox game.

LATIF. It is orthodox for me.

GERMAN JOURNALIST. *(Interrupting Richards.)* What about the whale?

MAC HOSE. Pardon?

GERMAN JOURNALIST. What about his whale?

MAC HOSE. Afraid the word doesn't exist in Tamahaq. And I doubt Mr. Baraka shares your interest in whales.

RICHARDS. He means your veil.

LATIF. It's what men of my tribe wear.

AMERICAN JOURNALIST. *(Calling out from the back of the room.)* Why don't you show us your face?

LATIF. Tuaregs believe a man's mouth is an ugly, shameful hole. All that is evil issues from it.

RICHARDS. *(Motioning for Heather to have the cameraman focus on me standing next to Lenore.)* What evil do you mean?

LATIF. From a man's mouth comes bad air. Spit. Vomit. Lies. Disease. We cover this foul hole.

RICHARDS. Why have we never heard of you before?

LATIF. We have never met.

RICHARDS. Why haven't we heard of you in tennis? At other tournaments?

LATIF. I had little money to travel. And before I went on tour I wanted to be sure that I was good enough and that I could play without betraying my beliefs.

RICHARDS. What are your beliefs?

LATIF. What are yours? You tell, then I will tell.

BRITISH JOURNALIST. *(A snifter of brandy in one fist and a microcassette recorder in the other.)* Let's talk tennis for a change. What do you call those shots of yours?

LATIF. My serves, I call them the red one, the blue one, the green one—

BRITISH JOURNALIST. What the bloody hell?

LATIF. My ground strokes, there's, there's . . . *(It was MacHose, not Latif, stuttering.)* . . . there's the semicircle, the square, the triangle.

BRITISH JOURNALIST. What about that dinky drop shot? That diabolical lob?

MAC HOSE. *(Speaking after a talk with Latif.)* He insists on calling his shots colors and shapes. I believe you'll find a correlation between colors and speeds, and shapes and angles.

BRITISH JOURNALIST. *(Growing belligerent.)* What's your re-action to people who charge you hit nothing but junk? That you win by cheating?

LATIF. " 'He is but a cunning enchanter,' say the unbelievers."

RICHARDS. Do you know Latif Fluss?

LATIF. I have heard of him.

RICHARDS. Have you met him?

LATIF. How could I? He's in prison in America.

RICHARDS. No. He's out now. Odd, isn't it? One Tuareg is released from jail just as another appears on the tour. It must mean something.

LATIF. Yes. The Prophet said, "In the alternation of night and day and in all that Allah has created in the heavens and the earth, there are signs for righteous men."

In the taxi, Lenore was exuberant, talkative. But Latif said very little, and I didn't say much more. I had this awful feeling something was about to happen. Or already had. Richards had started stalking us.

"You were marvelous," Lenore told Latif. "You didn't look a bit nervous."

"How could you tell?" I asked. "You can't see anything except his forehead and his fingertips."

"I loved the way you worked in quotes from the Koran."

"We squeezed through this time," I said. "But we don't

prepare better for the next tournament—I mean on court and off—we're in trouble."

Latif had a hand on his leather purses and silver lockets, running them back and forth on their thong. Lenore had a hand at her neck, too, holding shut the velvet collar of a Chesterfield coat she'd bought that day.

"We've got, what? Five, six days," I said, "before the first round in Brussels. Let's get down there, get in some practice. Just as crucial, decide how to handle the press."

"I was never in the match tonight," Latif mumbled.

"You didn't feel any energy here," Lenore indulged him. "The atmosphere is dead."

"I'm disorganized, disoriented. I need Champion."

"You gotta get tournament tough," I told him. "That's what you gotta do."

"I want to fly to Cairo. Or bring him here."

"I don't believe this." The last thing I needed was that bunko artist horning in on my bailiwick. "You spend three years in the slam kicking speed and Bolivian blow, coping with major-league criminals, dementos, murderers. Then you let yourself get sucked in by a nickel-and-dime chiseler."

"Either I fly to Cairo"—Latif's voice was loud enough to bubble his veil—"and work out with Champion, or we find a pyramid in Brussels and train there."

"Kid, use your common sense."

"They say a pyramid, even a miniature one," Lenore chimed in, "can keep razor blades sharp and meat from rotting."

"I got no trouble keeping my meat from rotting. My razor blades go dull, I buy new ones. What you have to consider, what if—"

"I'll call Egyptair," Latif said. "Maybe there's a plane tonight."

"All right," I hollered, "I'll find a fucking pyramid—on condition we leave Champion where he's at, and we stay at the official hotel in Brussels. We're creating problems, suspicions, living apart."

He nodded. "A bargain."

## *Chapter* Thirteen

You think an agent gets a free ride? You think he doesn't earn his twenty percent? Try tracking down a pyramid in Brussels. Believe me, they're in short supply, and the locals—the Flemish and the Walloons, one of which speaks strange Dutch and the other French—don't knock themselves out giving directions.

But I got a hot tip, rented a car, and the three of us drove through an imitation American suburb to the town of Waterloo. In case we forgot our history lessons, a wise guy had scribbled on a city signpost, "Where Wellington tore Napoleon's bone apart."

Off in the distance I could already see it. Impressive size. Hundreds of feet high. The Butte du Lion was a Waterloo battlefield memorial.

I'm the type guy keeps a poker face and never counts his chickens. But this one time, after all I'd been through, I thought I had a right to crow. "Get a load of that mother. Just what you ordered, Latif."

"Maybe."

He wasn't just playing it cool. The weather *was* cool and drizzly, and no matter how high I set the heater, he'd been freezing since we left the hotel. His normally high-gloss blue-black skin had turned ash-grey.

In the back seat, Lenore had her hands deep in her pockets, her head turtled down in the collar of her Chesterfield. The both of them's blood had been thinned by too much time in Africa.

"Champion himself couldn't of done better," I said, still bragging.

Then I caught a closer look and the bottom dropped out of my belly. The sides of the pyramid were green. Fact is, it wasn't a pyramid. It was a cone-shaped mound of dirt covered with grass.

I started talking louder, faster. "That baby's big. It's got good angles. Got an excellent point on it."

Despite the drizzle, the parking lot was bumper to bumper with cars, tour buses, and bright-painted trailers where people bought greasy bags of french fries smothered in mayonnaise. A Ronald McDonald toy train trucked hungrier tourists off to the Golden Arches while this fat fool in a feathered cap fired a cannon to attract customers over to his candy stand, a dentist's nightmare of jawbreakers and bubble gum.

I parked in front of a combination snack bar and museum.

"This is dreadful," Lenore said. "Terminally tacky."

"Hey, I remember right, Giza wasn't an upscale operation either. We came for the pyramid, not the shopping."

We got out and passed the snack bar/museum with its cups and saucers and platters stenciled with pictures of Napoleon, Wellington, Michael Jackson, and the Smurfs. The only souvenir that tempted me was a corkscrew in the shape of Mannekin Pis, Brussels' most famous landmark—a statue of a little boy peeing in a pond—the screw where his pecker should of been. This joint ranked right up there with the Souf Museum and its collection of blood-engorged ticks.

"Time's wasting," I said. "Light's fading. Let's have a go at the pyramid and get ready for tonight's match."

As we huddled in the misty wind waiting our turn to climb the Butte du Lion, I was relieved neither Latif nor Lenore mentioned its actually being a mound of dirt. Lenore did say, "I suppose the principle's the same."

"Absolutely," I said. "Pyramid in Cairo, pyramid in Brussels, it's all a matter of geometry generating power."

But from the looks of the tourists staggering down the staircase, the Butte was an energy drain, not a generator. They were gasping like greyhounds after a fast trip around the track. Some of them were green at the gills, like they'd caught and swallowed the mechanical rabbit.

"Gonna be a great workout," I yammered, trying to psych up myself as much as Latif.

On account of the crowd, it was a slow climb, but it got my blood pumping, my heart pounding. While Lenore and I hauled at the rusty handrail like it was a lifeline, Latif marched straight up the two hundred and twenty-six steps, his robes ballooning in the wind.

At the top, a brass lion was digging a claw into a cannon-ball. Latif circled it, breathing deep and regular where I was wheezing shallow and ragged. He stared down at the cookie-cutter farmhouses, the *friture* stands, the toy train trundling off to McDonald's.

"Feel it?" he asked. "It's different from Cairo. But it's definitely there."

"What'd I tell you?"

Lenore was shivering. "I feel something too. I can't say what."

Any other time I'd of wisecracked it was the cold and the rain and the gale-force wind she was feeling. But I wanted to get away from this place and these people who eyed Latif like he was an unemployed palm reader. "It's pure jet propulsion. Suck up a month's supply and let's beat it before you catch pneumonia."

"I *really* feel it." He shut his eyes and spread his arms, like a giant kite of parachute silk. Then he sky-dived from the observation deck onto the grass and scuttled downhill. All the tourists rushed to our side, roaring curses or encouragement. I got caught up in the frenzy and found myself beside Lenore shrieking, "Go! Go! Go!" specially when a guard darted out of the ticket booth.

The guy took a stab at Latif, who ducked and hotfooted it back up the slope. Twice more he scampered up the monument, bare feet digging in the turf for traction, arms pumping for power. On the final trip, he waved for us to follow him, and we dashed down the steps.

The guard had gone into the ticket booth to call for reinforcements. Latif wrapped Lenore in his arms and robes, and she planted a kiss on his *tagilmoust* in the approximate location of his mouth.

I heard sirens and pried them apart, leading them to the car, slinking behind *friture* trailers for cover. Catching up to the McDonald's train, I glued our bumper to the back of it, hoping we'd pass for a caboose. It worked. Two squad cars sped by, headed toward Butte du Lion, and didn't give us a second glance.

On the drive to the Sheraton, Latif bounced and bopped with the sort of pep I hadn't seen since his days on speed. He punched the air, punched the upholstery, shouting, "Awright! I luv it. Goferit!"

At the hotel, up in the room, he flicked on television, tuned in MTV, and danced, his moves a mixture of a Tuareg war strut and a hurricane tearing through a sheet factory. He seemed hell-bent on staying at this fever pitch for his match.


I was wrong. As wrong as I had been lately about everything. That night and the rest of the week, Latif shuffled around the court like an ad for Librium, moving so slow he might of been playing underwater. Even the sounds of his shots—*squish! splat! splash!*—reminded me of synchronized swimming, and the ball looked liquid on his racquet as he sprayed high rainbow lobs.

Speaking of which, the newspapers didn't lie. He did hit a lob in the second round that didn't come down. At least not right away.

There's always, you ask me, a rational explanation. How I saw it, the lob had tremendous altitude and got lost in a haze of arc lights and cigarette smoke. Maybe it landed on a girder. Maybe it drifted into a heating duct.

But Latif's opponent, a Malaysian, it rattled him bad. For five minutes he stood there mouth open, staring up at the ceiling, coiled to hit an overhead smash. He didn't care the ump awarded him the point. He was worried where that ball disappeared. Three games later when it plummeted with great speed, struck the supreme Court carpet, and zoomed straight back up into the stratosphere, the Malaysian didn't wait for it to come down again—which, by the way, it never did. He collected his gear and got out of there.

With easy wins in the first two rounds, Latif didn't face a stiff test till he ran into Mats Wilander in the quarterfinals. Junk shots, off-speed garbage, down and dirty balls, nothing bothered the Swede. He scooped them up and pooped them back like a cheerful Sanitation Commission worker. If Latif hit fifty cross-court forehands, Mats hit fifty-one. If Latif looped moon balls from the base line, Mats looped them back. If Latif dumped a dozen drop shots just over the net, Mats chased them down and punched winning returns.

Behind four-love in the first set, Latif switched tactics. Unless you were near the court and listening close, you might of missed it. Wilander lost six games straight, and the set, before he had an inkling what was happening. Then he rushed to the umpire's chair. "He"—he flung an arm at Latif—"has to stop making noises."

"I didn't hear anything," said the ump, a burly American named Frank Hammond.

"Every shot he hits he makes a noise to trick me."

"Play on, Mr. Wilander. I'll listen."

Latif was serving to open the second set. When he slapped the ball up the middle, Mats caught it in his hand. "You hear what I mean?"

"Mr. Wilander, that serve was well in. You lose the point for touching the ball."

"Yes, It is in. But do you listen? The way it sounds, is it flat? Or does he serve with spin?"

"Spin. Sounded like an American twist."

"Yes," the Swede hollered, "it sounds like twist, but it is flat. I hear one thing, then he hits another. You must make him stop his mouth."

"I can't see his mouth."

"Say to him, take off the mask," Wilander said. "I am always most fair play. It is known of me. I am asking only he should be fair too."

"The rule, Mr. Wilander," said the ump, "is he can't make noise when the ball is on your side of the net. When it's on his side, he can make noise—if that's what he's doing."

"You see that it's bothering me."

"Well, sometimes you grunt when you serve. Maybe that bothers him. But there's no rule against it. Play on."

Up in the stands, people were whistling at Wilander, clapping and chanting, "Baraka! Ba-ra-ka! Ba-ra-ka!" Mats went back to receive serve, but shouldn't of wasted his time. He was so busy listening for sneaky sound effects, he was lucky to lay a racquet on another ball. I sympathized. A nice boy, Mats. Latif and I always liked him. But I can't say I was sorry when he swirled down the drain 6–0 in the second set.

Back at the hotel, while Lenore was getting ready for bed, Latif stopped by my room. Something was eating him. He prowled around instead of squatting down in a snake charmer pose. His third lap past the television, I said, "Very entertaining match tonight."

"I wasn't cheating," he snapped, yanking down his veil.

"Hey, who cares? You won and you had the crowd behind you."

He flopped on the bed. "I care. As a boy, I learned from my father how to throw my voice. How to imitate birds and animals and other noises. I don't consider it cheating."

"All the shitty tricks they played on us last time, they deserve what they get."

"Wilander never did anything wrong to me."

"You know what I'm saying—tennis people in general. How I see this comeback, it's no holds barred."

"I'm not out for revenge. I just want to play and prove I can obey the rules—all the rules—and still win."

"Come on, kid. I heard what you were doing half an hour before Wilander caught on. You faked him out of his jock."

"Yes, I faked Mats," he admitted. "At this level of the game, a lot depends on faking. Good players listen to the sound of your strings and hear whether you're hitting flat or with spin."

"I know all this."

"Let me finish. Everybody accepts that it's fair to hide your racquet face and disguise the direction and speed of a shot. Plenty of guys growl like grizzly bears, then pattycake the ball to cross you up. Lendl, for instance, serves underhand if he sees someone standing too deep. So as long as it isn't against the rules, why shouldn't I fox people with sound effects?"

"No reason at all."

"It took a lot of explaining, but I think I convinced Lenore I wasn't cheating."

So that was the problem—a marital spat. "Great. Finally there's something the three of us agree on."

Just then Lenore let herself in. She was wearing a long white *galabeah* she'd bought in Cairo. "It's Lady Dulcinea stopping by to visit her good buddies Don Quixote and Sancho Panza."

"Which one's me?" I asked.

"Sancho. The earthy realist."

"Somebody in the group's gotta keep his feet on the ground."

Grinning, she sat beside me and slipped an arm around my neck. "Your problem, Eddie, you don't know when your feet are on the ground or when you're knee-deep in muck."

In the semifinals, we played Pat Cash, an Australian with a big public relations problem. He should of been an easy sell. He was handsome in a blond, beefy, surfer-boy fashion. But he kept putting his foot in his mouth or through his racquet or threatening to boot it up somebody's ass.

He said whatever popped into his head. Like, he casually owned up to tanking the '84 Olympics. Must of been the first time in history an athlete took a dive at the Olympics. But then, of course, it was the first time there'd been pro tennis at the games. As Cash alibied, he'd played only to get free tickets to the other events. He didn't give a damn about a measly Gold Medal.

A month later, he just about redeemed himself during a five-set match against Lendl in the semifinals of the U.S. Open. But after losing in a tie-break, he heaved his racquet into the bleachers, almost decapitating a couple fans.

Against Latif in Brussels, he didn't wait that long to throw his racquet. He started first game, first set, when four of his hardest serves floated back and fell dead at his feet. Then when Latif served, he caught on to the acoustics ruse— maybe Wilander had warned him—and roared, "That's riley greasy. How bleeding greasy can you get?"

The umpire, a bald-headed Brit, issued a warning for Verbal Abuse.

Two points later, Cash was at the net screaming that Latif had added a new wrinkle to his repertoire. He was mixing it up now, mouthing a noise for heavy spin, leaving Cash braced for the opposite, then hitting a shot that matched the sound. Triple-crossed, Cash nearly had a hernia whiffing empty air.

Later, during a long base-line rally, Latif flicked a drop shot. Cash reached it, tossing up a lob for what looked like a winner. But there had been the distinct *plop! plop!* of a double bounce.

"Not up," said the ump.

"He did it," Cash screamed. "Made that noise with his mouth."

"It was a double bounce, Mr. Cash."

"That's too bloody much. I'm not competing against a ventriloquist. I quit."


In the final we faced Lendl, and the Czech wanted to blow us off the court. But Latif didn't give him any pace, and when Ivan tried to generate his own, he wound up shanking shots left and right. Every ball Latif hit seemed to land on a soft spot, ragged seam, or loose thread in the carpet.

Tell you the truth—and why would I lie?—I didn't catch Latif making any noises. But Lendl blamed him for every let call, every catcall from the crowd, every one of his own hundreds of mis-hits. That was the beauty of what Latif was doing—planting doubts, playing with people's minds, then letting them beat themselves.

After a straight-set loss, Ivan said at his press conference the rules had to be changed. This wearing of masks, these nonregulation racquets and poltergeist voices were turning tennis into a sham like pro wrestling and turning off fans. When a reporter reminded him Baraka's matches had been watched by record crowds, the Czech said he'd rather perform in an empty arena for the rest of his career than go up against Ali Ben Baraka again.

"Are you hinting you might boycott him?" a journalist asked.

"Out of the question is not for all players sometime in the future refusing to play this Baraka. I will be raising the matter at the next union meeting."


.   .   .

Before I had a chance to chew over the boycott threat, the press demanded to speak to Ali Ben Baraka. I didn't understand where the request was coming from till I spotted Iain Richard's personal Tamahaq interpreter, Lee MacHose, who still had the kind of pallor you get spending your days down a root cellar.

Heather Honor, the camera crew, and Richards weren't in the room. But I ran into them in the hall hunting for Latif.

"Small world." Richards greeted me with a smarmy grin.

"You think so? Try walking around it."

"*Amico mio,*" someone shouted.

Where the sight of Richards brought a furious red explosion to my eyeballs, I saw nothing now but white. Pippo Scarcia rushed forward, wrapping me in his scrawny arms, and took two phantom passes, pretending to kiss my cheeks. He reeked of Paco Rabanne and *pasta al pesto.* Swear to Christ, we weren't in public and on TV—Heather's crew had closed in—I would of killed him.

"Eddie, this new boy, he is"—he was talking at the camera, not me, playing the warm, lovable Paisan—"how you say in the States, *sugo buffo.*"

"Socko boffo?" Richards suggested.

"Yes. *Fantastico!*"

I tried to twist loose from his mitts.

"I want him under contract," Pippo said. "I want him in my tournaments. I want him in my cloth-ess."

"You mean in this Good Humor Man suit?" I tugged his lapels hard.

"Eddie, Eddie, always the joker with the laughs. I want Baraka to wear my brand, play in my shoes."

"Long as they're not made of concrete, we'll listen to any offer."

Pippo hugged me tight. "We have a saying in my country, 'There is no lamb so loved as the little lamb lost, then found.' Welcome back, Eddie."

"What can I say?" I mugged at the camera. "Except baaa-aa-aa!"

. . .

The press room was crowded and noisy. Flashbulbs popped, reporters shoved and shouted, cameras clicked like paper cutters, *snick-snack, snick-snack.*

At the eye of the storm, Latif sat perfectly still, ignoring Heather who had one wounded paw in her mouth, the other reaching a light meter near his *tagilmoust.* MacHose tried to take questions in order, but there were so many of them sailing in from all corners it was hard to tell how the Q's connected with the A's.

Q: What was the difference today between you and Lendl?
A: Height. Weight. Color. Nationality. Religion. Internal organs.
Q: No, the difference during the match.
A: I won more games.
Q: At this level, what's the difference between champions and runners-up?
A: Spiritual.
Q: You mean it's more mental than physical?
A: Spiritual.
Q: What's your advice to young players starting out?
A: Stop.
Q: How do you prepare for an important match?
A: Creep down in my bed. Picture the past, feel the present, imagine the future.
Q: What's your reaction to playing Lendl for the first time?
A: He really needs help with his hair.
Q: You just won eighty thousand dollars. How do you feel?
A: A little guilty.
Q: Lendl did a lot of complaining about bad calls. What's your philosophy?
A: "The life of this world is but a sport and a pastime."
Q: I take it you believe the close calls even out in the long run?
A: Yes, and then you die.
Q: Why do you play in bare feet?

A: To stay in touch.

Q: Do you think it's proper for tennis players to wear veils?

A: Only the men.

Q: What if all the players wore masks?

A: Good idea. I don't like seeing their mouths.

Q: Everybody says you're making noises on court.

A: Yes, with my racquet, my feet.

Q: What about your mouth?

A: It's an evil organ.

Q: Lendl thinks the rules should be changed.

A: I think they should be enforced. All of them.

Q: There's been talk of a boycott. Do you have any response to players who might refuse to play you?

A: "More swift is Allah's scheming. Our angels are recording your intrigues."

Q: Are you saying in so many words you'd rather let your racquet do your talking?

A: I'd rather let Mr. MacHose do my talking.

Q: What did you enjoy most in Brussels?

A: The pyramid.

Q: What's your opinion of Latif Fluss?

A: Low.

Q: You think you could have beaten him at his best?

A: When was he ever at his best?

Q: What's your racquet made of?

A: My father.

Q: Not "who" made it. What's in it?

A: My father.

Q: Could we talk a bit about your marriage?

A: I would as soon show you my mouth.

Q: When will you wear real cloth-ess?

A: My clothes are real.

Q: But when will you sign an endorsement contract?

A: Never. I accept only prize money. No endorsements, no guarantees, no special appearances.

Q: Why?

A: Gifts make slaves as whips make dogs.

Q: Has anybody offered you a guarantee?

A: No one speaks my language except Mr. MacHose and he has offered nothing.

Q: Do you condemn other players for taking guarantees?

A: I condemn no one.

Q: Do you condemn endorsements?

A: I endorse nothing.

Q: Do you have a police record?

A: I've only listened to their old songs on the radio. "Tea in the Sahara" is my favorite.

Q: How will you celebrate tonight?

A: Eat a big gopher.

"That's enough," I screamed. "This interview's over. He's exhausted."

One more mondo-berserko answer and I was afraid somebody would bring Latif down with a tranquilizer dart. One more question from Richards about police records, and I'd personally drop him with a tire iron. Lenore and I shouldered through the mob and escorted Latif out of the room.

Reporters and photographers chased after us, shooting pictures, shouting questions. I had a few things to ask him myself. Why the hell make loony remarks like he was going to eat a gopher? And worse, announce publicly he didn't want endorsements and guarantees? With one screwball outburst he was flushing millions down the drain.

As we forced our way from Forest National Stadium, Richards, Heather, and the crew tracked us with a minicam. Then, best I can reconstruct events, five baboons, maybe six, sped up in a van and jumped us. One crud-bud pinned me to the wall. Another got Lenore in a half-nelson. The rest of the gorillas circled Latif, grabbing at his *tagilmoust*.

At least that's how it looked to me. But I wasn't watching a still life with fruit. The gorillas were on the go, and so was Latif—lashing them with his racquet, reminding me of his old self, the savage style that had copped sixteen Grand Slam titles, not the rubber-limbed rope dancer whose strokes couldn't crack an egg. He was really rapping heads, breaking fingers and wrists.

When the guy on me glanced around at his buddies, I brought my knee up into his nuts and doubled him over. Then I slammed into the goon manhandling Lenore. It was only then that Richards and his crew galloped over like Royal Mounted Police to the rescue. By the time they reached us, the punks had bugged out, squealing away in their van.

"Hope you got great footage, you fuck-pig."

"Yes, old man," said Richards. "I believe we have some sensational shots."

"Why didn't you help?" Lenore snapped.

"A journalist's job is to record news, not participate."

Latif stabbed his racquet into Richards's stomach and brushed him aside like a bug. Heather looked about to break into tears. But with her deep-set, dark-circled eyes, it was hard to say.


In the taxi, Latif laid the racquet across his knees and touched every inch of it Braille-style, testing with his finger-tips for cracks and splinters. He had been famous before and survived open season for assholes—all those rabid tennis fans, star fuckers, and psychopaths determined to kiss him or kill him. I suppose it was predictable the same sort of knuckleheads were now salivating to be the first on their block to get a glimpse of Ali Ben Baraka's face. But there was something about those thugs, hardly your typical sports groupies, and about Richards's reaction, that smelled wrong.

Up in my room with Latif—Lenore had gone off to change her torn blouse—I didn't mention my suspicions. Right or wrong, they'd just rattle him, give him a reason to act flakier. Plus which, I had more important things to say.

"The hell did you mean at the press conference? That smartass comment about no contracts, no exos, no guarantees?"

He sat on the sofa—mood indigo on a Scotch plaid cushion. "Right."

"Don't do that to me. I'm not a reporter. Don't gimme an answer that doesn't connect with a question."

He lowered his veil, looping it under his chin. "Guarantees are against the rules."

"A rule nobody cares about. You're getting boring with this law-abiding citizen routine. I understand you did time and don't want to wind up behind bars again." Tonight I was the one pacing the floor, dodging furniture. "But there's nothing wrong with free enterprise. Contracts, exos, special appearances—that's where the money in tennis is. You play tournaments for publicity, to hike up your price for side deals."

"No, this time I play tournaments for the sheer pleasure of competing. For the chance to visit places I played before, but was too spaced out to enjoy."

"So enjoy! What's more fun than making bucks?"

"Once you accept guarantees," he said, "they own you. They can call in the debt whenever they want, just like Pippo did."

"Forget guarantees." I flung that subject and a small fortune behind us. "What's wrong with endorsements and exos?"

"Same problem. You lose your independence. Sponsors start telling you where to play and when. You wind up flying around the world every other week. Anytime you're not on court, you're at shopping malls or supermarkets for promos. You have to eat pills to sleep and pills to wake up. Your schedule's so tight, you tank matches to make plane connections. Pretty soon you're in crummy shape, but promoters fiddle the draw or fix the umpire so you can't even be sure when you've won honestly."

"It doesn't have to be that way."

"And it's not going to be."

"A clothing and racquet deal that doesn't lock you into a crazy travel schedule shouldn't—"

"I've got a racquet. I've got clothes."

I fell into a chair. "The thing that bothers me—one of them—where's this leave me?"

He paused, tucked his legs up under him, let his hands hang limp in his lap. "It leaves you with me, I hope."

"Doing what?"

"Coming back. Earning some honest money. Taking advantage of the travel. You know, last time, you didn't get to see places or meet people outside tennis anymore than I did."

"You make this sound like summer camp. Eddie Brown's junior year abroad. I'm not into that, kid. I need action."

"You'll be busy."

"Like I asked already—doing what? Gimme a for instance."

"Finding pyramids everyplace I play."

"Jesus."

"I realize it won't be easy."

"You don't understand what I went through here."

"I appreciate it. I appreciate everything about you, Eddie. I really do. And I'm grateful."

I was running out of juice. Arguing with Latif wasn't what it used to be back when he was wired. Now it was like punching a rag doll; your best shots got swallowed in cotton. "Whatever you decide about contracts, we still gotta do a definite walk-through before the next press conference. You sounded certifiable. I mean, saying you're going to celebrate and eat a gopher."

"I said *gaufre.*"

"Any way you say it, it's not funny, it's sick."

Latif broke up laughing. "I've eaten a plateful every night. Some with fresh fruit. Some with powdered sugar."

"Quit it! Next thing you'll be claiming it's a Tuareg delicacy like Chinks eating dead rats."

"Rats? What rats?" Lenore came in. She had changed into a black jump suit, one of those glittery second skins chicks wear so you can't guess whether they're test pilots, deep-sea divers, or porno stars.

"I was telling Eddie I ate a plate of Belgian waffles every night. You know, *gaufres*? He thought I said gophers."

Now she split a gut laughing and dropped what she had in her hand—a big burlap sack, looked to me like. Latif picked it up and put on a woolly brown *djellaba* that hid his indigo robes.

Still chuckling, giddy with what a great time they were

having, Lenore saluted him. "Chieftain Iffucan of Azcan in caftan of tan with henna hackles, halt! Damned universal cock, let's get out of here and go eat some gophers."

They nearly wet their pants they were laughing so hard.

"'Bantam in Pinewoods,'" Latif said. "Wallace Stevens. Knew it right away."

This was bad as a press conference. Nothing connected, nothing made sense.

"Come with us," Lenore told me, taking my arm. "We're going to the Grand Place for *gaufres*."

"Yeah, you'll love them, Eddie."

"I'll do my celebrating in the bar."

"Not sulking, are we?" Her voice, her eyes, teased me.

"No, you guys go ahead. Just remember, Latif, keep a tight *tagilmoust*."


With the tournament over, most tennis people had moved on to Milan. The bar at the Sheraton was quiet, uncrowded. Far as I could tell, there were just four fellows from the doubles final in a booth behind me.

I lied to Lenore. I *was* sulking, feeling sorry for myself. It wasn't just being shut out of their jokes and book chat that depressed me. With Latif shying away from everybody on the circuit, I was cut off from the locker room, the lively horseplay, the hostesses. Latif and Lenore had each other, but I had nobody. And the worst part, like a painter without a canvas, a sculptor without a stone, I was frustrated. Unless Latif let me negotiate deals, I couldn't get creative.

The players, two Australians, an American, and a Swiss, were swigging beer.

"See this new fella, Ali Ben Barracuda?" one of the Aussies asked.

"I hate tennis," said the Swiss. "I never watch matches."

"Sort of interesting, this Barracuda," the first Aussie went on. "How do you think he does it?"

"Cash called it right," said the other Aussie. "The guy's

very greasy. But it's not the noises. It's something about his racquet."

"Talked to Iain Richards," the Swiss said. "He told me Baraka says his racquet is made out of his father."

Listening to them, I didn't notice Heather Honor till she slid into the booth across from me. "I have to talk to you."

Automatically, my eyes swept the room for Richards and the TV crew. She seemed to be alone, but I wasn't taking chances. "You want to talk, come to a press conference."

"It's personal. Important."

"Personally, what important thing do we have to talk about?" I took a big icy bite of my Tequila Sunrise.

She raised a hand to her hair, pushing it behind her ears. I expected her to stick her fingers in her mouth and start gnawing, but she crossed me up and kept both hands under the table. She hadn't exactly gone upscale for the evening. No makeup, no dress, just baggy pants and a sweat shirt with blue and red stripes across the chest. "I know you think I'm unspeakable."

"No, you're speakable. You're a typical media shark. Whether you're chewing up dead babies or tin cans, it all tastes the same to you."

That pinched some color into her cheeks. "I want you to know I have nothing to do with Iain Richards."

"You shoot film for him." I sucked at my Sunrise.

"I mean there's nothing between us and I'm not responsible for what he puts on the air. After talking to you in Tunis, I made it a point to look at that feature we did on you and Latif Fluss."

"Proud of your work?"

"Appalled."

"Now, no doubt in mind, you'll demand the network run a retraction. Else you'll resign in protest."

With no fingers to eat, she nibbled her lips. I tried to picture her relaxed, well rested. It wasn't for the messy hair and tired eyes, she might not of been half bad.

"Want a drink?" I finally asked.

"What I want is to talk. But not here." She nodded to the doubles teams.

"Talk about them?"

"About Baraka," she whispered, "and Richards and the rumors going around."

"My room?"

"Yes."


Don't sell me short. I got a built-in, distant-early-warning system against getting screwed over, specially by somebody that's pulled a fast one before. But I won't lie. It was great to cross that lobby with a girl twenty years younger than me and go upstairs. It had been a long time since someone told me she needed to talk personal, in private; she had something important to say. Didn't matter it was business, and maybe tricky business at that.

"Hot in here." I dropped my coat over the back of a chair.

Heather headed for the Scotch plaid sofa. Before she sat down, she wrestled off the sweat shirt. Under it, she had on a tee shirt about six sizes too big. "There are no strangers in Paradise," it said in blue letters across the boobs.

"Don't you have any clothes that fit?" I asked.

"I'm thinking of getting fat."

"Try eating food instead of your fingers."

"Filthy habit." She shoved her hands between her knees.

I sat across from her, my tassel loafers on one side of the coffee table, her clunky jogging shoes on the other. Her ripple soles looked capable of climbing sheer walls.

"Where's Baraka?" she asked.

"Out with his wife. Eating gophers."

"Oouf!" She smacked her belly. "I ate six at lunch."

My business, you gotta be able to outwait the other guy, outwit him. So while Heather shot the breeze about the food in Brussels, I hung tough and locked all instruments on automatic pilot. She cracked first and skittered back to the subject.

"There've been rumors going around. Richards doesn't like

you. Doesn't care for Baraka either. Thinks you're both bad for the game."

"Say we gave him an exclusive interview. How quick would he change his mind?"

"Afraid it's gone beyond that."

"No way, sweetie. That's why you're here, what you're angling for."

"I'm not *angling* for anything." She pulled a hand from between her knees and blew on her fingers like Jimmy Connors waiting to receive serve. "Because of what happened before, I wanted to warn you."

"About what?"

"You understand this is strictly off the record. What British barristers call a 'without prejudice' conversation."

"Are you selling me a used car? Or telling me rumors?"

"He's after you, Richards is. He intends to expose Baraka. He hired those men to tear off his veil."

"It's what I figured." Much as my pulse raced, I acted unruffled.

"Gossip has it Baraka is Latif Fluss. Richards means to find out."

"Ridiculous! Baraka's nothing like Latif."

"They're about the same color, same size."

"So's a tennis ball and a lemon."

"He plans to stay on the story, keep poking around."

"And keep trying to tear off Baraka's *tagilmoust*?"

"Wouldn't surprise me. He's digging into Baraka's past and Latif Fluss's whereabouts. He's paying for photographs, quotes from old girl friends, fingerprints."

"Can't believe anybody'd go to that trouble and expense."

"There's a lot of curiosity. Baraka's become ultrapopular in a very short time. A cult figure in certain circles. The more he and his wife stay to themselves, the more the public demands we get the story, show who he is and how he does what he does."

"But who's footing the bill? No network's going to write Richards an open check."

"People in tennis have taken an interest."

"A financial interest?"

"Is there another kind?"

"Pippo Scarcia?"

"Among others. A few top players are chipping in. They don't like unknown quantities."

"They're wasting their time. It's crazy confusing Baraka with Latif."

"They don't think so. And even if he's not Fluss, they're anxious to strip him of the advantages of anonymity. Some players object that they can't read his strokes because they can't see his face. Others say a masked man's the wrong image for tennis."

"Haven't they heard of the Lone Ranger? He was a box-office king for decades."

At last she started gnawing her nails.

I stood up, stretched, strolled to the window, pretended to look out, pretended to be unperturbed. Inside, I was stewing. All along, I recognized there'd be problems coming back incognito. But I hoped by the time people discovered the truth we'd be so tied up in contracts with sponsors, promoters, and tournament directors, they wouldn't dare kick us off the circuit. Now, the very night Latif publicly nixed any deal that might of allowed us leverage, I learned they were hell-bent on busting us again.

I went back to Heather, reached down, and pulled her raw fingers from her mouth. Near as I remember, I meant to ask a question, but the mood I was in, I could of gone any direction—homicide, suicide, a signed confession. Obviously Heather regarded the hand holding as a chummy gesture. Maybe it was.

After the fact, it's easy to claim one thing led to another. But what happened next came out of nowhere, like one of Latif's wide-swinging hallucinatory shots that followed no predictable pattern. One minute we were tangled on the couch, her fingers in my mouth. Next minute, we had transitioned onto the floor. Then we were shucking our clothes, crawling across the carpet and into bed.

Dressed, Heather resembled a bag lady just back from a

rummage sale. But under the dowdy threads, she had a delicious, pink body that didn't belong in tee shirts and Plain Jane underpants. She also had a hurried headlong style that explained why she always looked tired.

The less said about the way I looked the better. But my style was as big a surprise as her body. I used to be a classic heavy hitter—fierce inside moves, flat strokes, an instinct for killing the point quick. But tonight, with no premeditation, certainly no practice, I played Ali Ben Baraka's game and gave Heather a dazzling display of touch and timing and deceptive placement. With a looped backswing and lazy follow-through, I hit all the corners; I never served the same speed or spin twice; I changed the pace, alternated top and slice, tossed in an occasional American twist, suckered her close with drop shots, then drove her back with lobs. She had great legs and stamina and stayed with me stroke for stroke till the end.

After we'd showered and toweled off and were back in bed cooling down with a few light stretching exercises, I asked, "Where you headed from here?"

"Depends."

"On what?"

"Whether I go on working with Richards, following Baraka and you."

"Say you didn't, what would you do?"

"Fly to Karachi, jeep to the Khyber Pass. Join a group of Afghan rebels and send back footage of bang bang."

"Wish you'd stay on the circuit."

"And report on Richards?"

"That's not the main reason. It's not in the top ten reasons. But if you could let me know what that bastard's up to—"

"The situation wants watching. We'd have to be careful. It could be dangerous."

"Let's not overdo this. Richards is on the wrong track. The only real risk, say he plans more sneak attacks, somebody might get hurt. It'd help to have advance warning."

"That's why I came." She snuggled closer, clung tighter. "Well, one reason."

"And the other?"

"*Nostalgie de la boue.*"

"Now you sound like Richards."

"I was itching for a walk on the wrong side of the tracks. I have a serious question, though."

Most of me went rigid; some parts turned soft.

"What's your secret?" she whispered.

I didn't want to believe it boiled down to this. She couldn't take me for the type sap that spills classified info in gratitude for getting laid. "Baraka's a sweet kid," I told her, trying to worm out from her arms and legs. "He's nothing like Latif Fluss."

"No, silly." She wouldn't let me go. "I'm talking about you. Your secret. How do you do it?"

Everything firmed up now. "I learned it from a man named Champion."

"But what is it?"

I rolled her on top of me. "Pyramid power."

"You're joking. That's ancient stuff, years out of date."

"It still works."

Indeed it did, more to my amazement than Heather's.

## *Chapter* Fourteen

Now that I'd gotten a glimmer of what Champion was up to and Latif was into, I suggested next morning we take a farewell spin out to the Butte du Lion. Not that I had become a complete convert. But I figured, what the hell, how could it hurt? I ran the pyramid with Latif, staggering up the grassy slope and sliding down on the seat of my pants.

After that, we were on a roll. We raced to where Lenore was waiting in the car, sped back into Brussels, caught a train to Paris, and transferred to an express southbound for Nice. In the past, I never would of frittered away hours covering ground a plane crossed in minutes, going deaf listening to rusty wheels screeching against rusty tracks, being trapped in a second-class compartment full of scruffy kids with backpacks, and old wrinklies with their belongings stuffed in string bags. But now I sort of enjoyed it.

Lenore, like usual, was reading a book, *When the Going*

*Was Good.* I was tempted to tell her, the going's always good. After months on the road, I felt friskier than ever. Back on the tour, back on top, I believed there was something healing simply in circulating. Better at any rate than sitting on your ass waiting for a miracle.

We were *making* one happen. Wasn't that the motto of Holy Sepulcher College? "Make a Miracle Happen." Those Bible thumpers might not of had in mind what we were doing. Still, how else can you account for our comeback, Latif's and mine?

At lunch in the dining car, when I reported what Heather warned me, they swallowed the news with no sweat. It went down smooth as the *veau à la crème de morilles.*

"I've been expecting this," Latif said. "From the start . . . in fact, before we started, I saw what would happen."

How could I argue? He'd cleared every hurdle so far. He swore he was ready for any rough stuff Richards might throw his way.

South of Lyons, it was early spring—fields plowed, fruit trees in flower, black branches in vineyards sprouting green buds. As we dawdled over dessert, Lenore sighed and said, "Provence," like that one word summed up how satisfied she felt, how little she was worried.

We went on sitting there looking at castles and churches and villages clustered on hilltops, watching the land buckle, the vegetation get scrubbier. The light changed the closer we got to the coast. By late afternoon, with the sun fading, the trees were dark blue, all the buildings pale pastel.

Okay, I can hear the lip farts. The guy scores after a long dry spell and suddenly he sees the world through gauze. He's living in a beer commercial. An ad for feminine hygiene spray. But gimme some credit. I realized Heather might be planning to feed me worthless scraps, all the while hauling meatier tidbits back to Richards. I had my eyes open. I wasn't about to be the one that got diddled.

Still, even a hard-core cynic like me, ever alert for a double-cross, has gotta admit life doles out bonuses in the same brainless fashion it lays on the bad luck. As we rumbled toward Nice I noticed no more than a couple miles from the next tournament site exactly what I had expected to spend days searching for. Latif and Lenore saw it too.

A pyramid beside the sea!

To be honest, it was a high-rise condo development called Baie des Anges, futuristic in design, triangular in shape. But Latif agreed it filled the bill.

From the train station, we caught a taxi back to Bay of the Angels, talked to the manager about short-term leases, and rented a one-bedroom flat for them and a studio for me. Their place had a terrace, and we stood on it, goose-pimply and shivering because of the cool evening breeze and the breath-catching turnaround that had landed us *inside* a substitute pyramid.

Lenore gazed at the blinking lights of Cap d'Antibes. "Tender Is the Night," she murmured.

"Tough days ahead." I was squinting in the opposite direction, off toward the Nice Country Club and, miles farther east, the Monte Carlo Country Club.

"I feel it," Latif said, staring out to sea, his blue robes bellying like sails that could carry him across to Africa. "Ready for a run, Eddie?"

"Ready."

"Where?" Lenore wanted to know.

"The hall. Through the fire doors. Up and down the stairs. If that doesn't work, I'll climb from balcony to balcony up the outside of the building."

"I'll stick to the stairs," I said.

"I'll stay here and draw up a list of places to visit," Lenore said. "The Riviera's rich in literary history. D. H. Lawrence died in Vence. Fitzgerald, Hemingway, and Dos Passos worked for a while at Gerald Murphy's house on Cap d'Antibes. Somerset Maugham had a magnificent villa on St.-Jean-Cap-Ferrat."

"Bjorn Borg's got one there now."

"Too bad we can't drop in on him," Latif said. "I'd like to

persuade him to come back and play my game. It'd save him a lot of wear and tear. I think he'd enjoy tennis again."

"Graham Greene lives in Antibes," Lenore ran on. "Anthony Burgess is in Monaco."

"Harold Robbins has a mansion in Le Cannet," I razzed her.

"Ugh." She bumped me with her hip. "Hit the stairs."


Down in the lobby, Latif tightened his *tagilmoust* and dovetailed his *gandourah* between his legs. Then off he raced, bare feet slapping marble steps. I kept the pace on the first-round trip, but fell behind on the next four jaunts to the top floor and return. Still, I finished and I felt fine.

I felt that way for weeks as Latif played and won minor tournaments in Nice and Aix-en-Provence, warming up for a Super Series event in Monte Carlo. Since he never practiced and we spent only about an hour a day sprinting through the bowels of the building, Lenore had plenty of time to drag us around sightseeing.

We toured perfume factories and ceramic shops, botanical gardens and picturesque little ports where years ago actual fishermen parked their boats. We ate in a restaurant where, Lenore claimed, F. Scott threw Zelda down a flight of stairs, and we walked through walled medieval villages where all the houses had been tidied up and turned into boutiques. We visited the Léger museum, the Picasso museum, and the Matisse chapel, a room with white tile walls that looked like a public lavatory a talented kid had decorated with a felt-tip pen.

Most of these places, I arranged to meet Heather. She told me Iain Richards was traveling from tournament to tournament a step ahead of us, and she warned me to warn Latif to be prepared—which he definitely was. In Nice, after a second-round match, the loser, a tubby Samoan, waddled to the net, ignored Latif's outstretched hand, and grabbed at his veil. With hair-trigger reflexes Latif flashed a forehand

and a backhand, walloping the fellow up one side of the head, then the other, and escaped with his disguise intact. Days later in Aix, a Yugoslav went to yank the do-it-yourself racquet from his fist and got a busted knuckle for his trouble.

Way it turned out, I had to be every bit as prepared as Latif. Even when Heather didn't have hard news to report, she never passed up a rendezvous. The odder the hour, the more improbable the place, the quicker she was to shed her civvies.

"We've only a moment," she whispered in an empty IMG hospitality tent during the awards ceremony in Aix.

"Here? You're kidding! You said we had to be careful."

"No need to be ultracautious." Color came to her cheeks. Her hair had more life; the tired raccoon rings around her eyes were fading.

"Why not wait till we can take our time?"

"Just a boff *de politesse* for now. We'll take our time later."

She'd goad me on, confident even during a stand-up quickie I'd touch all the bases, run through my full arsenal of strokes. I hit cross court, down the line, inside out, moving like a domino-phenomeno, mowing down any opposition in my path.

After racing hard to get where she was going, she was a slowpoke about pulling on her unpretentious undies, baggy trousers, and tee shirt. In a not unkind voice, she'd turn objective, analytical, like a post-match commentator.

"Not very big, are you? And not what you'd call young."

"Nope," I cheerily admitted, climbing into my clothes.

"Not terrifically dishy either."

"Matter of opinion."

"Yet I fancy you. I truly do." She said this studying her fingernails. She had stopped biting them, and they were growing back. "You've got something, Eddie."

"At this level of the game, there's just one difference between winners and losers." I buckled up, then beat my hair into shape.

"What's that?"

"Spiritual."

Heather gave me a friendly grope. "Whatever your secret is, don't go sharing it with anyone else."


She wasn't the only one trying to find out my secret, which is to say Latif's. In an issue published the first day of the Monte Carlo Open, *L'Equipe*, a French sports journal, devoted two pages to a study of our style, quoting scientists, psychiatrists, astrologists, and literary critics. I couldn't wade through it with my menu and wine-list French, but Lenore provided a loose translation. Latif wouldn't listen. He wandered off on his own while she and I sat on the balcony, a basket of croissants and pot of coffee on the table between us. You wore a windbreaker or a woolly pink sweater like Lenore, it was almost comfortable eating breakfast outdoors.

"Here's an item from *Scientific American*," she said. "An aerodynamic engineer theorizes Ali Ben Baraka has stumbled onto the secret behind the experimental Stealth aircraft which is invisible to enemy radar." Her eyebrows knitted. "He doesn't reveal what the secret is.

"Then there's a psychiatrist, a woman. She contends many professional athletes are sexually insecure. She speculates that Latif's *tagilmoust* frightens players, and his unorthodox style causes them to question their techniques. The more they question, the more inclined they are to performance anxiety and dysfunction."

"Jesus, gimme a break."

"She points out how many stars are superstitious and observes that superstitions are a classic substitute for terror. Vitas Gerulaitis darts a look over his left shoulder before serving. What's he afraid is behind him? Jimmy Connors cupped his testicles at crucial moments during matches. Emasculation panic? This Bulgarian boy, Tito Zhukov, remember him from Rotterdam? He chews a clove of garlic. Dread of Dracula? McEnroe walks off court at right angles, careful never to step on a line. An anal retentive reaction to stress? According to the psychiatrist, most champions have ambivalent emotions and much as they are driven to win, they also harbor a secret desire to be beaten, publicly humiliated. It's this desire that Latif is exploiting."

"Glad to accommodate them." I poured her a second cup of coffee.

"Here's a name I recognize. Luxford Lyons, the deconstructionist critic. He prefaces his piece with a quote from Saul Bellow. 'You know that famous painting of the gypsy Arab traveler sleeping with his mandolin and the lion gazing on him? That doesn't mean the lion respects his repose. No, it means the Arab's immobility controls the lion. This is magic. Passivity plus power.'

"Lyons goes on to break down Latif's game and 'read' each match as if it were a story full of symbols, allusions, signifiers, and textual problems."

"I don't follow."

"I don't want to vulgarize Lyons's thesis."

"Vulgarity's a language I speak."

"Well, he claims Baraka is a conscious parody of sport, an antiathlete who appeals to spectators weary of traditional hero worship. They identify with him because his clowning brings the stars crashing down to earth. He's like Charlie Chaplin, a leveler, a democratic artist."

She frowned, shoving her hair back, silently rereading a paragraph. This must of been what the cons liked, what let them forgive everything else—this deep passion of hers for explaining.

"What McEnroe or Becker or Lendl do, according to Lyons, is overwhelm everybody, beat them the way old-fashioned writers such as Balzac or Tolstoy browbeat readers. In contrast, the postmodernist athlete, like Latif, doesn't *beat* anybody. He engages players in an act of creation which is the drama of their defeat and the dismantling of outdated norms and structures."

"I don't believe a bit of this bullshit." I tore a croissant in two and tossed it over the rail. A seagull snagged one half. The other fell six stories to the swimming pool. "Nobody mentioned pyramids?"

"No."

"Good."

She dropped *L'Equipe*, shut her eyes, and tilted her face to the sun.

"Can't wait for Monte Carlo," I said.

She opened an eye and aimed a schoolmarmish scowl at me. "Somerset Maugham called it 'a sunny place for shady people.' I suppose you feel at home there."

"I take that as a compliment."

"Guy de Maupassant described it as the world center of abjection, arrogance, pretense, covetousness, and greed."

"Yes, yes, yes," I agreed.

Lenore would never understand that what she loathed about Monte Carlo was what I liked. I'm not talking about gambling. Leave the slots, the craps, and roulette to losers who fly in with affinity groups and think it's a privilege to be bilked out of their bankrolls.

Actually the daily drop at the casinos is a spit in the ocean, a small percentage of the revenues raked in by the principality. The real action is in financing, corporate flim-flam, and three-card monte for multinationals. It's, for example, a terrific spot to put together syndicates fronting deals fueled by laundered currency. Small wonder pro tennis holds a tournament as well as organizational and strategy meetings here.

A Super Series event, Monte Carlo offered a million dollars in prize money. But instead of under-the-table sweeteners, it laid its greatest inducement right out in the open. In return for their promise to play here, the Grimaldi family had welcomed as residents a flock of top-flight stars—Borg, Vilas, Clerc, Wilander, Becker, and, yes, in the bad old days, Latif Fluss. Players didn't really have to reside in Monaco. Who'd want to set up house in a seaside safe-deposit box the size of Central Park? What Latif and I did, we rented a studio about as big as a mail slot and flew in every April to renew his tax-free status. Who needs a guarantee when you're getting a break on several million bucks a year?

This spring they all showed up again, not just the tax dodgers, but Lendl and Mecir, Arias and Krickstein, Noah and Leconte, and a slew of Swedes. The tournament even brought back Borg and Connors as honorary referees.

But the big news was John McEnroe was making a rare appearance in Monte Carlo, and the minute he hit town he told reporters, "I'm here to beat this new guy, this Baraka. What I hear, he's got no class, no game, just hits junk. My only worry, Baraka'll lose before I get a shot at him."

Instead, it was Junior almost got knocked out. In the first round against Tito Zhukov he complained the Bulgarian's garlic breath was suffocating him and demanded the match be delayed till Tito brushed his teeth. When he didn't get what he wanted, he called the umpire a moron and Zhukov a "fucking Commie bastard" and squeezed through in a third-set tie-break.

In the second round against Miloslav Mecir, another Commie, Mac started seeing enemies everywhere. For some reason, he imagined Nora McCabe of the Toronto *Star and Mail* was up in the press box, and he bellowed a line he'd let her have it with at the '84 Canadian Open. "You know, you're a cunt," he screamed. "You should get laid more often, lady."

Because the press box was above the royal box, Princess Stephanie decided he was yelling at her. Plenty of tennis reporters circled the wagons and swore Junior's remarks had been taken out of context, had never been intended to insult anyone, especially not the royal family. Still, the Pro Council fined him $5,000 and announced his next major misconduct infraction, he'd be slapped with a six-week suspension.

The betting was Mac wouldn't survive the tournament. Not only was he in a foul mood and acting flakier every minute, he couldn't adapt to conditions on the show court that had been carved out of a cliff. Every few seconds a hang glider swooped off the cliff, and the crowd oohed and aahed, waiting to see whether the glidee would crash into the ocean or bash his brains out on the rocks. If McEnroe ignored this and lowered his sights, he was staring straight at the clubhouse that was a shade of pink looks terrific on a pair of tits, but is lousy as a tennis backdrop.

At the other end of the court Junior served below a patio where high rollers and Eurotrash ate lunch watching the matches. It was like playing in a supper club. The air smelled of olive oil and grilled meat; ice cubes chinked in cocktail glasses; corks popped from champagne bottles; plates and forks clattered against tables.

Mac, who could hear a fart at fifty paces, went ape. Looking more and more like his old man, pudgy and pale, his hairline halfway back his head, he balled up his fists and screamed, "Will you please shut up, pulleeze!" He kicked the clay. "I hate you people. I hate this place."

But, strange thing, at his press conference, he didn't bitch about the noise or the court or the crowd. He bitched about Ali Ben Baraka. Which showed me two things—he was worried about the new boy, and he was hyping a future exhibition tour. I wished to hell Latif would of let me arrange it.

"What I don't understand is why this guy gets away with wearing that totally outrageous gear," McEnroe sounded off to reporters. "I act up in the slightest, they hit me with a fine. But Baraka, whoever the hell he really is under those rags, the supervisor is too gutless to crack down on him."

Next day, and every match after that, Latif had to pay a $250 penalty for "improper attire." They didn't demand he change clothes. They recognized his costume had gate appeal. But they smacked us with a fine, regular as rent.

Then Junior started in on Latif's game. "All this hocus-pocus, phony-baloney, gyp-joint stuff. Are we playing tennis, or is this a circus act? Baraka may not be cheating in the strict sense of the word, but what he's doing, it's not fair, not sporting. I don't mind being beaten by a better player. If he really is better! But I don't like being jerked around by a magician."

At his press conference, Latif was badgered by Iain Richards, eager to whip up controversy. Latif stayed cool and answered through Lee MacHose that McEnroe should read what is written.

RICHARDS. You mean the rules? The Code of Conduct?

LATIF. In the Book it is written, "When Our truth was shown to them they said: 'This is plain magic.' Moses replied: 'Do you call the truth magic? Magicians never prosper.' "

RICHARDS. Are you prospering?

LATIF. I am winning. I shall continue, *inshallah*. So obviously I am not a magician.

RICHARDS. Do you have any message for the number-one player in the world?

LATIF. Tell McEnroe, "Do not treat men with scorn, nor walk proudly on the earth: Allah does not love the arrogant and the vainglorious. Rather let your gait be modest and your voice low: the harshest of voices is the braying of the ass."

Then McEnroe began mouthing off about Latif's homemade racquet. "You've seen the shots this guy hits, the grotesque spins and angles and bounces. There's no way he could do that with a regular racquet. No way." He shook his head and scratched his scalp.

"What I'd like to know, what's in that racquet? It's the same one he's played with all winter, all spring. He doesn't even carry a spare." He went on shaking his head and scratching. "No way a legal racquet ever lasts that long. Somebody should check it out."

That evening, Borg and Connors, the honorary referees, released a statement suggesting Latif "voluntarily" submit his racquet for testing. They maintained this would clear the air and protect the integrity of the game.

I objected on every grounds except the Fifth Amendment. His racquet was none of their business. It had already been examined by Buzz Murphy in Cairo. This was a primitive harassment campaign to psych us out.

And there was always a chance they'd find something wrong. At least claim they had. I remembered the wrangle over the spaghetti-strung racquet. It used to be perfectly legal. "Then look what happened," I reminded Latif.

By double stringing and weaving patterns as complicated as a cat's cradle, a player got a racquet capable of producing extraordinary shots. The ball dipped and hopped and fluttered like a hummingbird on Benzedrine. It baffled net rushers and base-liners alike. For a few months, the hackers had their revenge and a lot of big names bit the dust diving for balls that squiggled across the net like corkscrews. But when Ilie Nastase used a spaghetti-strung racquet to snap Guillermo Vilas's record-breaking fifty-match win streak— Vilas gave up halfway through and stomped off court—the authorities stepped in and outlawed the most momentous innovation in tennis since rubber-sole shoes.

"It was all right," I told Latif, "to play with racquets the size of road signs. It wasn't against the rules to string them tight as a gnat's snatch and build them of stuff that belongs on space ships—graphite, boron, titanium! But they couldn't accept an element of chance, an exciting equalizer. They wanted to protect the stars and their investment."

Latif heard me out, but said he had no objection as long as they tested his racquet in his presence.

Next morning we marched to a tent near the practice courts. At most I expected a couple tournament officials, Borg and Connors as window dressing, maybe a journalist or two digging for a human interest story. But the tent was packed and more people were pushing to squeeze in. Iain Richards, Heather, and the camera crew were there, and Princess Stephanie, McEnroe, and Tatum O'Neal had ringside seats around a Ra-test machine and an X-ray contraption, the kind that screens luggage at airports.

Unfolding the indigo wrapper, Latif handed the racquet to a shnook dressed like a lab technician. With cameras rolling and flashbulbs popping, this *schnorrer* put it through the Ra-test, weighing and measuring it, checking string tension and balance. You'd of thought he was a NASA engineer gauging the throw weight of a rocket.

The racquet, he announced, was hand-tooled, heavy in the head, and strung with animal gut, type unknown. The tension was so low, the strings so loose, Latif might as well of played with a butterfly net. But none of this violated any rule.

Then he ran it through the X-ray, flipped it this way and that, passing it through three times. "The racquet is constructed entirely of wood," he said like he'd discovered a cure for cancer, "except for the ivory inlay and a foreign substance in the handle."

"What substance?" McEnroe barked.

"It appears to be a bone."

"A what?" Richards asked.

"A bone. Human, I'd say. Probably part of an ulna."

"Are you shitting me?" McEnroe roared.

Everyone was shouting now. People pressed closer, clamoring to see. The poles shuddered, the canvas flapped. Thunder rumbled in the distance. A storm was brewing inside the tent and out.

"*C'est sauvage*," Princess Stephanie hissed.

"A cannibal," Richards erupted.

"I can understand a guy spilling his guts on court," said Connors. "But I draw the line at bones."

Lenore and I took our cue from Latif and said nothing. Not that I had any problem keeping quiet. I was dumbstruck.

Richards rushed to center stage, dragging Lee MacHose over to Latif. "The fans have a right to know. What is it?"

"Part of my father's arm," he answered so cool he barely ruffled his *tagilmoust*.

"Your father's arm? In your racquet? Why?"

"To keep him and his memory near me."

"This is maybe why he is playing always the big points so well," Borg mumbled.

"It's not against the rules," I hollered with a helluva lot more confidence than I felt.

"I have visited Christian churches," Latif explained via MacHose. "They are full of bones. Whole skeletons. I have seen people praying, touching them, kissing them. How is it wrong to have part of my father with me? Now give him back."

He rewrapped it, then, holding the racquet like a divining

rod, headed for the exit. Lenore and I followed him.

"And they fine me for throwing racquets," McEnroe ranted. "Here's a guy playing with dead bones and he gets off scot free. You call that fair?"

The sky had turned pearl grey, closing over Monte Carlo like a clamshell. It started to pour, but a procession of reporters and spectators stayed with Latif.

"Eddie, we need to talk, et cetera." Buzz Murphy bustled up beside me.

"Not now. I got problems."

"I'll say. You got problems in spades."

"He's a blue man, I keep telling you. Haven't seen you in the chair all week. Aren't you working?"

"I'm here in a different capacity."

"Somebody break out in chancre sores?"

"Much different capacity."

When we reached the gate to the parking lot, Lenore caught sight of Buzz and blurted, "Jesus, you're a dead ringer for William Faulkner."

"Thank you, ma'am." He dipped his head and flicked a finger at his moustache. "I'm flattered, et cetera."

While Buzz was dipping and flicking, Lenore shot me one of her looks. Who's this case? her eyes asked. Is he spastic or what?

"Buzz is an umpire," I explained. "Old friend. He called one of Ali Ben's matches in Cairo."

"I've gone into a new line." It registered on me then he wasn't wearing Coq Sportif clothes. He had on a blue pin-stripe suit and Sulka tie. "Like to take you to lunch, Eddie. Baraka and the Missus too. Tell you an idea I have."

"Eddie is the idea man. You two go ahead." She broke into a trot, darting through the rain after Latif.

Buzz had a car, a Mercedes stretch limo, and a driver that understood English but had a one-word vocabulary. He opened the back door for us, and it was, "Please." He shut it, and it was, "Please." Buzz gave him directions and got a "Please."

"What happened?" I asked. "You break the bank here? Or bang a rich widow?"

"I now represent certain interests." He unbottoned his pin-stripes. "Sports and leisure apparel, shoes, men's toiletries, et cetera. Like I mentioned in Cairo, it's years I've been considering a career switch. On the circuit, you fall into a rut. I did some doctoring, some officiating, as much muff-diving as I could manage. But where was it leading?"

As the limo zigzagged up the cliffs behind Monte Carlo, I was wondering the same thing; where's this leading? "Thought you enjoyed the tour?"

"Used to. Older I got, the more I worried about the future. There's a lot of miles on these tires." He patted his belly where there was no sign at all of a spare tire. "How do I know, I don't protect myself, don't make some powerful connections, one of these clowns won't cut me down?"

"What are you talking about?"

"Told you before, a linesman was killed at the U.S. Open by a hundred-mile-an-hour serve."

"So you quit umpiring?"

"No, but I'm more selective about the jobs I accept and I've broadened my base. Diversified. I'm out of the pecker-checking business altogether." Buzz stared through the tinted glass at a sea of milky fog. Still driving inland, we had reached some foothills where the rain turned to sleet. "Trouble was, people took advantage. You know this Bulgarian kid, Tito Zhukov, and his coach Todor?"

"Look, Buzz, what's the deal here?"

"Every town on the tour, they took it for granted I'd get their pipes cleaned. Ever stand downwind of them? Those guys stink like they'd rather be alone, but here they are bugging me to find girls. Can't do a damn thing for themselves. Communists. They lack initiative, that Free World go-getter spirit. Didn't even like to get laid. Took too much energy. For them it was blow jobs. Blow jobs or nothing. Have any idea how hard it is to hit a town cold and locate a chick ready to go down on two Bulgarians that smell like a caesar salad? Two weeks ago we're in Kuwait. Not exactly the global blow job capital, and day and night Tito and Todor are begging for deep-throat therapy."

"Why not say no?"

He shrugged. "You get caught up in the challenge. Still, there's a limit. I reached mine the night before the semifinals. Tito's nervous. Todor's jumpy too. Both of them climbing the walls waiting for the chick to show up. She's an hour late, then two. And Todor blames me. Gets hostile, threatens to break me in half. But Tito steps in and says something in Bulgarian. Todor nods. 'Sorry, Booze.' That's what he calls me. Can't pronounce Buzz. 'Sorry, Booze, but my boy needs a nice relax before his match. Tito says you can do it. Blow him and he goes to bed happy.' You believe it?"

"These days I believe anything."

"I decided it was time to bow out. Stay in tennis, but mix less with players, more with management."

The rain that had turned to sleet now turned to snow, big feathery flakes that melted the minute they touched ground.

"Supposed to be a restaurant around here," Buzz said. "Three stars."

"I lost my appetite, hearing about Tito and Todor. What's this got to do with me?"

He leaned into the front seat and tugged the driver's epaulet.

"Please?"

"Anywhere along here. Just pull over and park."

"Please." The driver climbed out and disappeared into the snow.

"April! Ever see weather like this?" Buzz asked. "Say 'Riviera' to people and they think sunshine, they think warm rump- and nipplescape."

"These interests you represent"—I was getting damn impatient—"they the same ones Richards fronts for?"

"Let's say they're parallel. Maybe congruent's a better word."

"Forget geometry. Just tell me why you dragged me here in a blizzard."

He swiveled around to face me. The seat of his pinstripes squeaked on the leather upholstery. "In Cairo you said you were waiting for companies to pay top dollar to put Baraka in their products."

"We've had some discussions. Our attitude is evolving."

"The people I'm with, we want him to wear our foot gear. State-of-the-art stuff. So light, so pliable, Baraka'll feel like he's barefoot." As he ran through his fidgety manual of arms, his eyes, avoiding mine, followed his hands. "Five hundred thousand for a three-year contract. We'll double it if he'll wear our shorts and shirts. As for racquets, he can collaborate with our engineers and design his own model."

"He's already done that."

"Fine. We'll manufacture and distribute it worldwide."

"With whose bone in the handle?"

"Maybe a synthetic. Maybe an animal bone. Depends how the public responds to the news about his father's arm."

"Look, lemme be honest."

"No, don't be honest, Eddie. Hear me out. There's a kicker. We'll pay more—a negotiable figure—if during Wimbledon, Baraka does a TV commercial where he drops his veil, gives a great smile, and endorses our cosmetics. You know, says like, 'I won't show my face unless it's covered with the best cologne, moisturizer, scruffing lotion, et cetera.' "

"He doesn't speak English."

"He can memorize a line or two. Or we'll dub an actor's voice."

"I know he won't let down his veil. And I doubt he's going to market his racquet. On the shoes, shorts, and shirts, I can't promise much either."

Buzz was watching me now, not his hands. "What I heard, he's nixed exos and guarantees too."

"That's what he says. He's got very strong beliefs, this boy."

"Strange beliefs. Where'd he get these ideas? A kid from the boondocks, never been on the circuit before?"

When I didn't answer, he pinched at the seams of his

trousers, pulling to ease the pressure on his crotch. "You're not a naive guy, Eddie. You know when there's dough on the table, under the table, and everybody except you is grabbing for it hand over fist, people wonder whether you're keeping clean for a purpose."

"What purpose?"

"You tell me."

"Baraka just wants to stay out of all the shit on the circuit."

"A great part of this business, Eddie, a great part of life is establishing the proper relationship to shit. Not in it too deep, not too far away—that's the ideal. That's what our friend Latif never learned."

"No, what he didn't learn was to take a dive for Pippo Scarcia."

"He took everything else. It upsets people when a player gets religion at the last minute."

"That's why Baraka stated his position up front. No side deals."

"A word to the wise, Eddie. I urge you to reexamine your relationship to shit. It's like a credit rating. You don't build one by holding back, hoarding pennies. You borrow, you let the system own a piece of you. That's how they get to trust you, and you get a hold on them. It works both ways. One big happy family."

"I got my own family." I stretched into the front seat and hit the horn. The driver rushed out of the fog, snowflakes flying off his epaulets.

"Please," he said, sliding behind the steering wheel, shivering.

"Back to the Country Club."

"No hard feelings," Buzz said.

"No feelings," I said, "hard or otherwise."

As we swerved down out of the fog, the high-rises of Monte Carlo were crowded around the harbor like too many teeth in a shiny denture. The limo left me on the parking lot, and I walked through the rain to the Beach Club. I couldn't figure whether Buzz had been offering actual contracts—the money sounded inflated—or testing me to find out what it took to get a glimpse of Ali Ben Baraka's face. We turned our backs on millions of bucks, would he see it as a tough bargaining position? Or decide we had something to hide?

I didn't like to believe he was hustling me for the same reason as Richards. I'd known him too long, and we'd had many a good laugh. Why not take him at his word? Like everybody else in tennis, he just wanted a tastier slice of the pie and had branched out into a new line.


Latif played the semifinals against Yannick Noah. Back in the days when I was writing the script, I did everything possible to separate Latif from Yannick. Basically it was a marketing move. Here you had two megawatt stars from jerkwater African villages, both tall, muscular, and talented. It didn't matter one was coffee-colored, the other blue-black, that Noah was from the Ewondo tribe in Cameroon and Latif was a Tuareg. The public, hell, even the press, got them confused. So where Yannick was sweet and sensitive, I coached Latif to be mean and tough, to trash Noah on court, then again in press conferences.

But today, in the person of Ali Ben Baraka, he paid his respects as he would to a village elder. He made Yannick look good, let him repeat past glories. He even tossed up a few soft lobs so Noah could gallop back to the base line and return them with his crowd-pleasing, between-the-legs shot. Watching the ball sail by for a winner, Latif clapped along with everybody else, slapping a hand against his camel-gut strings.

I'm not saying he let Noah win. Latif beat him. Politely. Nicely. Then at the net he gave him the sort of handshake I hadn't seen since the Sahara. He kissed his fingers and touched them to his heart. Yannick did the same, and as they walked off court together, the stadium broke into applause and wouldn't stop until they came back for a curtain call.

At his press conference, Noah said, "Ali Ben Baraka has grace and magic. He transforms tennis into a kind of dance."

Asked whether he minded playing against a masked man, he said, "I respect his tribal customs."

"What about the bone in his racquet?"

"My father is alive. My mother too. If they were dead, I would want some reminder of them near me."

When Ali Ben Baraka arrived and spoke through Richards's mouthpiece, Lee MacHose, he said Noah and he hadn't so much competed as participated in a ritual to achieve a higher plane of understanding.

"Was this match arranged in advance?" Richards demanded. "Was it fixed?" It was a question he had never asked a hundred times in the past when he knew players were tanking.

"No."

"You maintain it was a real match?"

"Yes. But not necessarily a battle. In my country a match can be a meeting, a festival, a celebration. That's what you saw today."


Next day, Easter Sunday, the day of the final, the celebration ended. Before the match, McEnroe announced he was playing under protest on account of Latif's nonregulation Tuareg togs and the bone in his racquet. Then after criticizing the clay—too soft; the linesmen—sitting in the wrong spots; and the weather—too chilly; he went out to warm up and complained about the balls—too heavy, too mushy.

By the time Junior was ready to serve, spectators had been hooting and whistling at him for five minutes. But borderline bonkers as he behaved, he played sane tennis—which made me wonder like always how much his bitching was a tactic to punch a hole in the other guy's head. Even on this slow surface, he followed his serve to the net, swinging Latif wide, opening the court, then closing points with precision drop volleys. He crowded in so quick, skimming over the red clay, Latif's off-speed angled returns couldn't do the damage they did to slower players.

For all his griping about Latif's dinky shots, Junior depended more on disguise, placement, and misdirection than power. He had such fine touch he could hold the ball on his racquet till the last second, then flick it left or right for a winner. His hands were fast as his feet, and he hit so many reflex volleys from his hip the ball appeared to be hopping out of his pocket.

With the score knotted 3–3 and Mac serving, a seagull flapped over the court. It circled and swooped close, checking him out like a scrap of fish bait, did a loop-the-loop and swung back for a second glance, dumping a load of green-white lime on Junior's shoes. He tried to down it with an overhead smash, but missed. The bleachers burst out laughing.

The gull dive-bombed again, near enough now to ruffle what little was left of John's hair. He heaved his racquet, hollering, "Get outa here."

Loping to the net, Latif gave a high-pitched whistle and the seagull honed in on him, hurtling full speed, claws first. There goes his eyes, I thought. But the bird spread its wings and made a smooth landing on the tape.

"Oh, Jesus," Lenore gasped, flashing back same as me, digging her nails into my arm.

"No! Don't do it," I screamed. It would of been a dead giveaway. Two tennis-playing Tuaregs slaughtering birds in the same century—no one would buy that coincidence.

Latif set down his racquet, thank God, and held out his hand. After ogling his fingers like tasty eels, the gull hopped onto his wrist.

He carried it over to his chair, chucked it under the beak, and ambled back to receive serve. But Mac wanted that bird out of there. Claimed it got on his nerves to have those beady eyes on him.

Trouble was, nobody could catch it, nobody could chase it off. Every time a ball boy or grounds keeper shooed it away, it sailed out of reach, buzz-bombed McEnroe, and relanded in the same spot on the chair. While some fans pitched *centimes* at the seagull, plenty of bird lovers screamed to let it alone. Latif was with them. Amulets dangling, tunic billowing, he dashed over and shielded it. Lucky he did. Junior slung his racquet again, and it would of clipped off the gull's head if Latif hadn't caught it.

"Warning for Racquet Abuse," the French umpire announced in English.

"Are you nuts?" Mac screamed.

"Warning for Verbal Abuse."

"Listen, you incompetent fool, I'm not about to play with one eye on the ball and the other eye peeled for seagull shit."

"Fifteen seconds to resume play, Mr. McEnroe."

When Junior wouldn't quit carping, the ump issued a second warning, then hit him with a point penalty, and finally a game penalty. Now the score was 4–3, Latif's favor, and Mac had the choice of shutting up or being defaulted. He shut up.

During the changeover, he took a swipe at the seagull, the sort of vicious backhand that had destroyed many an opponent. But it was a clean miss. The bird shot into the air, then resettled when it was safe.

After that butchered backhand, Junior was out of the match. Out of his skull. He claimed the gull was talking. The net-cord judge called a let, and John blamed the bird, said it, not Latif's serve, made the ticking sound. When the judge refused to change his call and the umpire wouldn't overrule, someone shouted, "You fat turd."

Mac swore it wasn't him. Again he accused the seagull, said it was sabotaging him, mimicking his voice. He rushed to the umpire's chair. "I'm being railroaded."

The ump announced a Verbal Obscenity penalty, an automatic $1,000 fine.

"I'm not giving you the satisfaction of suspending me for six weeks. I'm not letting him"—Junior pointed at Latif— "have a cheap win. I'm not saying another word."

But as he spun around, I heard—everybody at the Monte Carlo Country Club heard him—holler at the ump, "Fucking French frog fag."

I say it was McEnroe. I didn't see his lips move. But I assumed it had to be him. "Fucking French frog fag" was, word for word, what he called an ump at the '83 French Open—the most remarkable use of *f*'s since the old Marlboro commercial, "Filter Flavor, Flip-top Box."

He recognized the quote himself and clapped a hand to the side of his head like his brains were bleeding out. "I didn't say that." He turned to the umpire. "I did *not* say that. Swear to God I didn't. It was the bird."

The ump had had it. "Game, set, and match to Mr. Baraka. Mr. McEnroe is defaulted for repeated violations of the Code of Conduct."

The ump began climbing down, but Mac slashed his racquet at the chair and chased him back up into the seat. "I'm not leaving this court. I'm playing on." Junior kept beating the chair.

The ump drew his chubby legs up under him, babbling in the microphone. "Call the security guards. Someone help me."

Latif walked to his chair, wrapped his racquet in the indigo cloth, and whistled for the seagull to roost on his wrist. From where I sat, he seemed to feed it something. A sardine?

"Look! Goddammit, look at that!" Junior ranted. "He did it! He put the seagull up to this!"

"*Au secours*," the ump shouted.

I looked at Lenore. She looked at me. What we couldn't figure—had Latif imitated McEnroe's voice? Or had he somehow trained the gull to say, "Fucking French frog fag?"

"Where you going?" Mac aimed his racquet handle at Latif. It had been a rifle, he'd of been dead. "Don't pretend you don't understand. You did this, you fucking fakir."

The seagull exploded off his arm, screeched, hit Mac full in the face, then winged away. Junior buried his head in his hands, sank to his knees in slow-mo, slumped onto his side, and rolled over on his back. Blood dribbled between his fingers.

Latif was the first to reach him. Then the security guards arrived, six high, wide, and hideous meatballs with .38 Smith and Wessons on their hips and yacht captain caps on their heads. They pried Junior's hands from his face. What Latif told me later, there was a beak mark on Mac's forehead, deep and bloody. They clamped a towel over it, called for a stretcher, and carted him off.

Showing real class, Latif walked along beside McEnroe, clapping, signaling the crowd to join in a sporting round of applause. They booed Mac instead.

Injured too bad for a press conference, Junior sent a written message, "I'll follow that son-of-a-bitch to the ends of the earth."

Latif wouldn't speak to reporters. Even after the Grand Prix docked him a $1,000 fine, he refused. All he'd say was he was too upset to talk and he hoped McEnroe didn't mean he'd follow the seagull.

Foaming at the mouth, Richards cornered me coming out of the locker room. He had actual bubbles, not just sweat, on his upper lip.

"Was that Baraka's bird?"

"You ever see his bird, you'll know it."

He waved for the camera crew to close in tight.

"If the seagull doesn't belong to Baraka, why did it land on his wrist? Why did it attack McEnroe?"

"Baraka's got a very attractive manner with kids and animals. They flock to him. What they do to McEnroe is his problem. I don't represent him."

"The Grand Prix released word John's been suspended for six weeks. Are you and Baraka afraid he'll be out for revenge at Wimbledon?"

"We look forward to Wimbledon."

"You've had two clients who've beaten McEnroe. Latif Fluss did it with his fists, Ali Ben Baraka did it with a bird. What next?"

"Wait and watch."

I pushed past Richards and stepped out to the terrace overlooking the court. Down next to the umpire's chair, a man knelt working on the clay. A grounds keeper, I thought.

Then I noticed the dental-floss white hair. Buzz Murphy was on his knees pouring plaster into one of Latif's footprints.

Buzz didn't give up easy. Once he got the shape of the feet, he could have shoes made to order. State-of-the-art stuff, he'd said. Light and pliable. They were half as good as he claimed, maybe Latif would let me cut a deal. Like Buzz, I didn't give up easy either.

## *Chapter* Fifteen

It didn't grab me as such a great idea to go to Rome for the Italian Open. Pippo Scarcia owned a piece of the tournament, and after the calamity last time in Calabria, I said, "Why take the risk?"

"There's no way around it," Latif said. He couldn't consider it a successful comeback unless he felt confident traveling any place. The threat of Pippo or memories of Calabria scared him away, he'd start seeing shadows everywhere.

Trouble was, he already seemed to be seeing them. They clouded his eyes. Dye from the *tagilmoust* had darkened his skin, and when he let down the veil, I saw smudges like thunderheads across his face. He hadn't lied when he refused to talk to reporters after the McEnroe match—he was upset. And depressed. And irritable.

On the train trip south, we crowded into a second-class compartment with two priests, a nun, and a young couple with a baby. They took one look at us and scrammed. We had turned into a trio of room clearers—the Masked Marvel, the Jewish Egyptian Princess, and me, their sidekick, the trusty wirehaired terrier.

I made a joke of it to cheer Latif up. When that didn't work, Lenore urged him to talk about what was bugging him.

"Is it the bone in your racquet?" she asked. "The way people reacted? The way McEnroe ridiculed you?"

He shook his head. He sat in the lotus position, the racquet across his knees, his fingertips running riffs up and down the handle. With his sunglasses and smooth wrist action he reminded me of Ray Charles at the keyboard.

"What I been wondering, where'd you get the bone?" I asked.

"I'd rather not discuss that."

"Public opinionwise this could fly back in our face. I mean, you didn't dig up his grave, did you?"

"Eddie, he told you, he doesn't want to talk about it. I think it's understandable he's feeling down. It wasn't pretty, what that seagull did to McEnroe."

"An ugly scene," he agreed with Lenore. "Shameful."

"Depends on your point of view," I said. "Your fans are fascinated. Turn me loose on the story and I could sell it around the world."

"There's a video tape. Anyone interested can watch it."

"But that won't tell them why the bird attacked."

"Neither will I."

"Was it you or McEnroe made those remarks to the umpire?"

"Whatever else John is, he's honest. I believe him."

"Believe what?"

"It was the seagull."

"But who taught the bird to talk? You? Is that what you were doing all that time alone this past week?"

"Excuse me, Eddie. I have to do some mental-imaging. I didn't feel sharp in Monte Carlo."

.   .   .

Lenore took the hint and opened a book. I took it and thought back over past Italian Opens. Honky, Latif's clothing sponsor, used to reserve us a suite at the Hassler Hotel and hire a limo with a day driver to chauffeur us to and from the Foro Italico, and a night driver for late rambles to the Open Gate, Jackie O's, and Hysteria.

I never saw much of Rome except what we drove past or what you can take in from the Hassler rooftop. I remembered a lot of domes and bell towers and that staircase full of flowers and hashheads spilling into Piazza di Spagna. I remembered men's hands on women's rumps and the terrified faces of pedestrians. I remembered cops in white gloves waving at speeding cars like they were no more than gnats.

What I didn't remember was a pyramid. And the downbeat mood Latif was in, that could of been the game breaker. No pyramid, no play. But then Lenore sprang to the rescue, reminding me what an important part of the program she was. Something in a guidebook caught her eye. She didn't oversell it. When we arrived in Rome that afternoon, she simply suggested we dump our baggage at an *albergo* near the Pantheon and hop a streetcar up Via Marmorata.

We hadn't traveled more than three blocks before we spotted it at the end of the avenue, bracketed by overhead trolley wires. Flipping pages in her book, Lenore gave us a quick fill on its history. "It's called the Pyramid of Gaius Cestius. Built by a wealthy praetor who died in 12 B.C. It rises one hundred and twenty feet above the Aurelian Wall, which it abuts at Porta di San Paolo. Shelley described it as 'flame transformed to marble.'"

"Looks fine," Latif said. "The best since Cairo."

I'm not, I promise, a sorehead. I didn't resent too much his insinuation there'd been shortcomings in the pyramid I tracked down in Brussels or that substitute we stumbled across on the Riviera. But I had a hunch there was going to be trouble with this one. Where the trolley let us off, I could tell already it was too steep for any easy up-and-down wind sprints. And since it was surfaced with slick white stone, you'd have to be a human fly to scale it and grab what looked like a giant knitting needle at the top.

We walked through the gate—really a two-lane road—in the Aurelian Wall. Traffic thundered beside us. More trouble, you asked my advice—which of course nobody did. There wasn't a prayer we'd have privacy, and cops might not look kindly on our monkeying up and down an ancient monument.

But, as usual, Latif's head was in a cloud of cotton rags and Lenore's nose was in a book. "Afterward," she said, "let's go around to the Protestant cemetery."

"Thinking of putting a down payment on your plot?" I asked. "Better do it before we tackle this mother."

"I'd like to see Keats's tomb and the place where Shelley's ashes are buried. On Keats's gravestone, there's a very touching epitaph. 'Here lies one whose name was writ in water.' What do you want inscribed on yours?" she asked Latif, just in case he wasn't gloomy enough.

"His name was writ in sand."

"And you, Eddie?"

"Writ in shit."

We were standing at a rusty, waist-high railing, staring down into a moat crawling with cats. Before we climbed the pyramid, we had to cross this canyon.

Lenore said, "Can't you just, you know, let the energy radiate and zap you here?"

"Too far away. I don't feel it." In the lenses of his sunglasses, white triangles gleamed, perfect reflections of the pyramid.

"I don't either," I said, and leery as I was of leaping into the moat and shinnying up the marble, I had to try. Latif's ranking wasn't the only one on the line in Rome. Heather was flying in later that week, and I needed to be ready.

"Whaddaya say, good buddy?" I tried a Texas accent, a joking reminder of his earliest days in tennis.

"Goferit," he said, perking up a bit, passing Lenore his sunglasses.

I followed Latif to a point along the railing right above a

thick clump of grass. Lingering till there was a lull in the traffic and no pedestrians, he stepped over the rail, dangled his bare feet, and dropped. After a four-point landing, he bounced up with no damage.

I swung my tassel loafers over the side and, despite plenty of second thoughts, jumped. A swift free fall and a soft squish in the grass. No pain, no broken bones. But I came away with an inch of cat shit caked to my shoes, and squinting up at Lenore, I wondered how the hell I'd scramble out of this deep, smelly ditch—supposing for a second I survived the pyramid.

A crew of mangy cats crept over and watched with me as Latif plastered himself to the marble, making steady upward progress like a snail with gum on his belly. I tried to imitate his technique, but didn't have his sticking power and got no traction from my shit-caked shoes. Kicking them off, I did better in stocking feet, finding tiny toe- and fingerholds between the stones. Higher up, weeds had sprouted in the cracks, and I hauled myself along hand over hand.

Risking a backward glance, I saw Lenore and the cats had company. A dozen cars were parked in the piazza and a crowd had gathered, gaping and yelling. I turned my face to the warm stone, torn between the temptation to slither down and hide—or snake ahead.

I wriggled forward.

When Latif reached the top, he shouted, "Almost there, Eddie. You can do it." Then he unfurled his *tagilmoust* and tossed me one end, a rope to a drowning man. I held tight and he pulled me up the last few yards.

I got a death grip on the lightning rod and hung on, head reeling, throat rasping. It did give me a rush, though, to see how high I'd climbed, to look down at the pygmy figures on the sidewalk screaming and shaking their puny fists.

"Great workout." Latif looked happy for the first time in days.

"None better," I agreed. "But one trip'll do me."

"Same here." He rewound his *tagilmoust*.

A squad car, an Alfa Romeo with a buggy-whip aerial and a blue revolving light, roared across the piazza and bumped to a stop behind the crowd. Two *carabinieri* scrambled out, one toting a battery-powered microphone, the other smacking his holstered pistol. Shoving forward to the moat, they glared at us like that alone was enough to scare us into scuttling down.

Well, it would of worked with me. I didn't want trouble, specially not gunplay. But Latif sat tight, soaking up the power, and I wasn't about to surrender on my own.

The cop with the mike raised it to his mouth. Swear to Christ, it sounded like he shouted, "Jew!"

I looked at Latif. He shrugged. Being blue-black, he'd had worse things yelled at him.

The cop sounded off again. "Shanty Jew," he squawked.

"This far away, how do they know?" I asked. "You don't suppose Lenore told them?"

"Told them what?"

"Listen what they're saying. I shouldn't have to put up with this anti-Semitic shit."

The whole crowd started chanting, "Jew! Jew! Jew!"

Latif laughed so hard he nearly split his *tagilmoust*. "This is gophers all over again."

I thought he was insane, suffering altitude sickness.

"Eddie, Eddie." He gripped my shoulder. "I know about ten words of Italian. But one of them is *Jew*—spelled G-I-U, meaning 'get down.' Nothing personal, no prejudice. They just want us off the pyramid."

"Yeah, well, I'm not turning myself in." No matter what he thought they meant, it rankled me hearing the whole piazza hollering Jew.

"I'm with you," he said. "If they arrest us, it could be curtains. What if they took off my *tagilmoust*? Fingerprinted me?" He darted a look down the other sides of the pyramid.

The cop with the mike read us the riot act in some kind of English. "You are surround. Give loose you 'ostage. What you demands?"

"What *are* our demands?"

"Another Grand Slam for you."

He pointed to where the pyramid angled into the Aurelian Wall. Broad and flat as a sidewalk, the wall led uphill through pines and cypress trees, twenty feet above the pavement, far from the cops' meathooks. "Let's go," he said, and we crouched low and slid down at ass-burning, sole-destroying speed. He hit the wall first and hardly broke stride.

"My shoes," I shouted. "My shoes are in the moat."

"Forget them."

Off to our left, the *carabinieri* and the crowd chased beside the wall yelling, "Jew! Jew!" Or maybe *"Giù! Giù!"* Lenore was screaming, "Go! Go!"

Off to our right were rows of tombstones—the Protestant cemetery. When Latif saw a soft-looking, grassy spot, we jumped, tumbling ass-over-teakettle into the boneyard. Then we floundered to our feet—his bare, mine in socks fast unraveling—and sprinted past columns and marble monuments and a stone man stretched out with a stone dog and a stone book. On the street, just outside the gate, we caught a cab and were long gone before the *carabinieri* had a clue what we'd done.

Laughing with Latif, I said, "What do we do for an encore?"

"Go back to the hotel and wait for Lenore. Drive out to the courts and win a tournament."


After our hairsbreadth, stunt-man escape, I figured we were primed for the Italian Open. We had the old pep back, that positive, winning attitude. At least I did.

Latif was a different matter. One minute he was up, exuberant, awesome. Next minute he was off in the ozone, his game eerier every day. He was still unbeatable, but on the slow, powdery clay at the Foro Italico, hitting heavy Pirelli balls, he seemed to be approaching a sort of zero-degree tennis. His matches reminded me of those karate kings bundled up in floppy pajamas who look like they're only brushing away a fly and wind up busting down a brick wall. Latif barely swung his racquet, just blocked the ball, but it accelerated into a yellow blur, then stopped dead, nestling into the sand. Other times it skidded like a hockey puck. The crowd would sit for an instant of stunned silence. Then they were as likely to break into jittery laughter as applause.

Off court, Latif acted just as weird. He went with us wherever Lenore suggested, did whatever her guidebooks recommended. But where normal people flung coins into Trevi fountain, he threw paper money.

He ordered pasta with every meal, even breakfast. He wasn't so much interested in eating it. He was obsessed with shapes and arranged intricate designs on his plate with shell pasta, corkscrew pasta, cartwheels, sailor caps, pipestems, and change purses. Best I could figure—and this was guess-work—he found in the pasta new angles to try with his strokes.

To take his mind off fifth-dimension geometry, Lenore invented this game, a search for the perfect symbol of Rome. She nominated a flower pot of begonias hooked by a rusty chain to a window ledge. Said it was a microcosm of the city's fragile beauty and brutal reality.

I suggested Center Court at the Foro Italico where the bleachers were surrounded by huge statues of naked athletes. Forget jockstraps, forget fig leafs. At the Foro, they flaunted it. One statue had a stone prick painted fire-engine red. My favorite was a skier standing beside the scoreboard, buck naked. "He's waiting for a clothing contract," I said.

Lenore nodded. "Nice symbol of Rome's surrealism."

Latif reached up under his robes, whipped out a switch-blade knife, and shoved it in my face. Lenore whimpered, "No."

He pressed the button, and a comb, not a blade, popped out.

"I bought it at a gift shop near St. Peter's," he said. "Isn't that Rome for you? A knife turns into a comb."

Lenore's whimper was now a nervous giggle. "Yes! Silly menace and serious narcissism. That's right on the mark."


On Saturday, before Latif went up against Flaminio Flamini, we waited in the players' restaurant while Wilander and Nystrom finished the other semifinal. Everybody, I noticed, gave us wide berth, leaving plenty of space between their tables and ours. I wanted to believe it was an ass-backward compliment, a sign of respect. But I knew there might be another reason. If someone lobbed a grenade at us, they didn't want to be close enough to catch the shrapnel. Like me, they probably remembered the Italian Open didn't take politely to people that rubbed it the wrong way. Few years back, tournament officials dragged a *Washington Post* reporter out of the press box, bounced him down a hallway, and held him prisoner till he promised to retract an unflattering article.

"*Permesso?*" somebody said.

I looked up and saw Pippo Scarcia pointing to a chair at our table. He didn't wait for an invite. "I eat here with my good friends?" He sat down and lifted Lenore's knuckles near his mouth, a kiss that never connected. Then he waved to the waiter. "I order for everybodies?"

"A big salad for us," Lenore surprised me by saying. We had eaten lunch in town. "I'll toss it. Tell him I need a bowl and lots of vegetables and cheese and oil and vinegar."

"For the health, yes? Very good."

"Roughage is important," she lectured Pippo. "Do you eat enough bran and fiber? You don't look regular."

"I am always the regular guy."

He unbuttoned his white linen jacket, touched the knot of his blue tie, sniffed at the matching hankie. Was there a popper in it? Pippo nodded to Latif who sat draped in cloth like a statue under a mosquito net. "He is learning some little English?"

"No," I said.

"In this world we are living in, it is necessary, English."

"He'd rather people learn his language," Lenore said.

Pippo laughed just the way he kissed her hand—making a quick, dry run at it and bringing his palms down like he'd heard a knee-slapper. But he stopped an inch from his spotless trousers. "How you speak to him?"

"Tamahaq. I've picked up a few phrases. We understand each other."

When the waiter brought Lenore a wooden bowl and a platter piled with cheeses and veggies, Pippo ordered himself a four-course meal. "Like I'm telling you in Brussels, I want Baraka wearing my products."

"He thinks your shorts are like a cheap hotel," I said. "No ball room."

He didn't bother going through the knee-slapping charade again.

Lenore got busy slicing and dicing. Chunks of tomato, celery, *mozzarella*, and carrots *thunked* into the bowl. Below us on the practice court, there was a similar sound, a steady *plock! plock!* as two players batted a ball back and forth.

The waiter set a plate of *fettucine* in front of Pippo. He swallowed two bites. "If my mother is serving this to my father, my father throws her and it from the window." He leaned his elbows lightly on the edge of the table. "Can we speak some reality?"

"Remember what T. S. Eliot said about too much reality." Lenore was shredding lettuce, hacking apart radishes, rugola, radicchio.

"Last time we talk, there is hurt blood and many bad feelings. But in my country we have a saying, 'Let the dogs lie.' " He patted his pursed lips and signaled the waiter he'd had enough. "So this time I tell more slowlier the reality. Here is Italy." He rapped the table. "Here is Rome and it is not good for Italian boy to lose."

"Oh?" was all I trusted myself to say.

"The peoples, they get angry to regard Italian boy beaten."

"What pee-pulls?" Lenore did a deadpan imitation of his accent, just like Latif had done that day in Calabria. I had a sinking feeling she and Latif had hoped for this, had insisted on coming to Rome convinced it had to happen.

"The peoples," Pippo said, "like to see a long match, many tie-breaks, three sets, close scores, with Flaminio winning."

"I take it you control the TV rights," I said.

"Yes, Flaminio is playing on television for his country, and I am announcing. For Baraka, to win or lose is just a matter of money. It has no importance."

"Sure it does," Lenore said, swirling the undressed salad, tossing it with her hands. "He wants his tribe to be proud of him."

"His tribe has no TV. I pay him the difference between winning and losing. Better, I pay what the champion gets. This way you lose nothing."

"And say Baraka refuses, what then?" I asked. "You pack our suitcases full of smack? Or you got a worse idea this time?"

He leaned back and let the waiter serve him a plate of cheese that smelled like dirty diapers. He smeared a gob on bread and ate it.

Lenore splashed vinegar into the salad. Latif, for all he said or did, could of been dead and wrapped in a winding sheet.

Pippo wiped his fingers, folded the napkin, and planted an elbow on it. "You know what we need?"

"A little more parsley." Lenore crumpled some leafy stems.

"We need heroes. Baraka," he went on, "is not a hero. Without a face, how can he be? He has no image. Without an image and contracts and advertising, tennis fans are not so interested in him."

"I think you're mistaken." Lenore was pouring on olive oil, oceans of it.

While they debated demographics and audience appeal, my mind raced. I felt Pippo was suckering us into a trap. Latif tanked, the tennis creeps owned us again. He didn't, they'd strike back somehow. Last time I told Latif to go ahead and lose. Was that what Pippo counted on this time? And what did Latif and Lenore expect?

"Look," I broke in. "Baraka plays to win every match."

The waiter had served a gooey dessert, custard covered with meringue. Pippo stabbed a fork at it like he was afraid it'd slither away. He didn't bother tasting it. "You throw this to the wall and roaches eat it and die." Snapping his fingers, he ordered it carried off. I figure he'd eaten a three-hundred-calorie lunch.

Lenore set down the jugs of oil and vinegar. The bowl overflowed with salad. "Like some?"

"No, *grazie.*"

"Sure you do." She stood up and hefted the bowl—it was about as big as a beer keg—then dumped it over Pippo's head, shaking every greasy sliver of carrot, celery, and caper on the Good Humor Man's suit. Chunks of tomato and *mozzarella* cascaded off his shoulders, leaving snail tracks on his lapels, puddling in his lap. Shredded lettuce stuck to his hankie, and vinegar dribbled down his tie. Scraps of purple radicchio caught in his coppery hair. Olive oil dripped off his chin and nose.

Around the room, people jumped to their feet, expecting fireworks. But Pippo sat stupefied. He didn't speak, didn't wipe away the tomato seeds pasted to his freckled cheeks.

Lenore plunked down the salad bowl, paused a beat, then pointed at his crotch, delivering a line she must of rehearsed for months. "Waiter! Waiter, there's a salad in Mr. Scarcia's fly."

Everybody laughed, and that snapped him out of his trance. "*Stronzina!*" he screamed, lunging at her.

But Latif's arm snaked out of his clothes like a cobra, and he jabbed the switchblade at Pippo's Adam's apple. Pippo wilted, sinking back in the chair, his eyes wide and white as radish slices. He thought he'd bought his lunch.

Latif hit the button and out flicked the comb instead of a knife. Snagging the plastic teeth in Pippo's marinated hair, he took Lenore by the elbow and calmly escorted her from the restaurant.

My exit wasn't quite that classy. I walked backward, watching for the goon squad, waiting for some ginzo to pull a gun and waste the three of us. I enjoy a joke as much as the next guy, but Lenore had pressed our luck a mile over the line.

Even, say, Pippo's backers and mobster friends didn't object to him getting a salad-oil shower, they were bound to be bent out of shape by what Latif did to Flaminio Flamini. He didn't just beat the hometown boy. He destroyed him.

It was a rerun of Calabria, only he didn't crush Flamini in half an hour. He toyed with him, wrong-footed him, taunted him with drop shots, tortured him with lobs, made him look like a fool. He won 6–1/6–0, but dragged the agony out for four hours. By the end, even people who'd come to root for Latif were booing him and cheering Flamini.

Back at the hotel, Lenore was furious. "I've never seen anything so petty, so mean-spirited. Why take out your hostility on Flamini? He didn't frame you last time. He didn't pressure you to tank this time. It was Scarcia, and we got even with him."

"Got even?" No more easygoing guru. Latif's voice roared out of the rag cocoon. "You call being humiliated at tennis or having a salad heaved in your face the same as serving three years in the pen?"

"What are you implying? You won't be satisfied unless Pippo and everybody else in pro tennis does time?"

"I didn't say that." He turned on me. "I suppose you're sorry I didn't tank."

"Hold it. Haven't I supported you every step of your comeback? Haven't I been right behind you, even when I didn't have a clue where you were headed? I told Pippo we play to win and I meant it."

He gripped the amulets around his neck, the lockets and leather purses full of quotes from the Koran. "Sorry," he muttered. "Sometimes it's hard."

"Of course it is." Lenore took his hand, soothing and gentling him.

"Listening to Pippo, I remembered last time. Then I remembered all the times in between. The years in jail. The noise and stink." He shook his head. "It's a hard thing to have to remember."

"Harder to forget. Isn't it enough," she said, "to be back in tennis? To be clean? Playing your own game and winning?"

"Not sure."

"Don't be stupid," I said. "That's the thing about today. You played like a dimwit. Why stay out there risking injury when you got a tough final tomorrow against Wilander?"

"I'm just not sure it's enough."

"Think about the titles, the money," I said. "Think about the grins we've had. The fun here in Rome playing Find That Symbol. Think about Paris next week."

"I've thought."

"Goddammit, think some more."

"Easy, Eddie," Lenore said. "We all need a cool shower and some pasta."

"Yeah, kid, we'll sample a new shape—flying saucers or Frisbees. Forget Pippo. We'll have dinner and get ready for Wilander."


Minutes later, wrapped in a towel and dripping wet, I ran to the door of my room where somebody was beating his fist black and blue. I hoped it was Heather. But it was a bellboy with a telegram saying she couldn't make it to Rome. She'd try to meet me in Paris.

The wire had been sent from Tamanrasset. Was she down there with Iain Richards, tracking Latif Fluss, sniffing the trail for Ali Ben Baraka?

I don't know what hit me hardest—the run-in with Pippo or the blowup with Latif, the letdown of not seeing Heather or the upswing in my suspicion she was double-timing me.

That evening when we crossed the Tiber to Trastevere, the sky was rust-colored, the air heavy. Heat lightning forked from cloud to cloud, and stood my hair on end. We sat outside in a piazza that was supposed to be off limits to traffic so folks could relax in restaurants and admire the fountain and the church facade with its famous mural. But the square buzzed with all sorts of motorized vehicles hell-bent on nailing the gang of kids playing soccer and the Gypsies selling dead roses wrapped in cellophane.

We ordered a new pasta, then Latif stared at the fish tank where our second course swam its last laps. What we needed now was a downpour to settle the dust and clear the air. But what we got was a two-minute sprinkle that left red specks of grit on the tablecloth.

A hot wind blew out of the south, carrying grains of sand that stung my face and pinged at the plates and glasses. "The *harmattan*," Latif murmured.

"A *scirocco*," the waiter said, serving pasta that was shaped like—sort of hard to describe, but it was something like belly buttons. Latif stared at them, rearranged them, searched for a pattern, and finally pushed the plate aside untasted. I didn't see it influencing his game.

"I'm sick to my stomach," Lenore said.

"I lost my appetite, too," I said. "Let's get out of here."


The storm blew all night and brought back the Sahara, reminding me of the eye-inflaming, nose-scalding, nut-shriveling wind that howled during Lenore's and my long drive to find Latif. It rattled shutters and drainpipes, tore off roof tiles and TV antennas, ruined any hope of sleep. I laid awake thinking about Heather, mad at myself for imagining what she and Richards might be doing thousands of miles south of here.

Next day, it was blowing harder, and a dull film of dust covered the city. Just breathing, just being alive, was misery.

On the trip to the Foro Italico, gusts of eighty miles an hour slammed the taxi from side to side and bent trees so low their branches raked the car roof. Some streets were blocked by fallen palms. The closer we came to the courts, the more grit was in the air. The storm had scraped up red clay and sent it sizzling through Rome, sandblasting buildings, stripping trees bare.

I expected the final to be canceled. Postponed, for sure. It wasn't just a question of lousy conditions. It was dangerous to be outdoors. Wind collapsed a couple hospitality tents and clipped off an umbrella pine the way you'd knock down a toadstool with a nine iron.

But there was live television coverage throughout Europe and, via satellite, back to the States, and that settled the matter. It meant saving the TV contract, they'd of played in a typhoon.

Before the match, Latif told me his eyes ached with grit. He had to pop out his contact lenses and pray nobody noticed the famous baby blues behind his sunglasses. Lucky for us, his *tagilmoust* screened the sand from his nose and mouth, giving him a huge advantage over Wilander who hacked and wheezed and seemed to be suffocating.

The Swede never did get grooved. Hitting against the wind, he watched every shot fly back in his face. Hitting with it, he couldn't keep the ball on the court. Half the time he couldn't keep it in the stadium. A few of his mis-hits cleared the nickel seats and were still climbing when last seen sailing toward Florence.

Latif, on the other hand, had no trouble. He lofted lobs that chased Wilander to the base line, then fell in a hairpin curve that hurried him back into the forecourt, flinging him headlong toward the net. A dozen of these rainbow balls nicked the tape and dribbled down on Mats's side for winners.

When he served, Latif released the ball into the full-force gale, letting the current swirl it around. Sometimes it orbited the entire court before dropping into the service area. Couple of his twist second serves bounced in front of Wilander, then boomeranged back across the net to Latif.

What flipped Mats, though, was the scoreboard went haywire. The *scirocco* caused a short circuit and strange numbers started flashing. Latif was leading 31–13 when Mats took a last look at the bughouse scoreboard and the buck-naked skier beside it and decided he'd had enough.

But at his press conference, he didn't carp about the blinding sand and airborne debris. He didn't blow off steam about the electrical fritz. He blamed everything on Latif.

"Since he's on the tour, everything is changing. The weather is not the same. The balls once he touches them you cannot trust. Players struggle and don't understand this sport anymore. One tournament, Baraka uses a bird to beat you. Another tournament he is talking through his veil. Now it is this wind.

"You notice the dirty air is never disturbing him. He has eyes, I believe, like a lizard or a snake. I think he doesn't blink. Nobody has seen his eyes. I wonder does he shut them when he sleeps."


Reporters clamored for Ali Ben Baraka. When I reminded them there was no Tamahaq interpreter, they said it didn't matter. They wanted him to peel off his sunglasses and show them could he close his eyes.

He wouldn't do it. Naturally not. Without his contacts, he was scared they'd recognize his blue eyes and jump to conclusions.

They jumped to them anyway.

Next morning when the overnight train chugged into Gare de Lyon in Paris, I bought the *International Herald Tribune* and read where Wilander was calling Baraka a reptile. Unidentified sources speculated Ali Ben had had a special membrane surgically attached to his eyeballs. "More and more players and tennis authorities are demanding," the article claimed, "that Baraka be banned unless he abandons his human bone racquet and submits to an examination by a neutral committee of doctors and scientists."

"First they accuse me of being a magician," Latif said. "Now I'm an animal."

"Oh, honey," Lenore said, "I know how it hurts you."

"Consider it a compliment. You got them terrified," I said. "You'll take the French Open with no sweat."

He shook his head. "This isn't working out the way I wanted."

"Look, maybe"—I spotted an opportunity—"now don't get mad and jump on me the both of you, but maybe, say, you wore regular clothes, newspapers might decide you're normal, and other players wouldn't be so suspicious. In Monte Carlo, Buzz Murphy made a pitch—"

He walked away. Didn't even wait to hear the numbers.

# *Chapter* Sixteen

The official hotel for the French Open is the Sofitel, near the Périphérique, a bypass around Paris. From there players are chauffeured to Stade Roland Garros by a fleet of Citroëns, these low, long-nosed limos that look like rocket sleds but ride like overstuffed sofas. Given all the groupies, gofers, and sticky-fingered camp followers swarming around, there've been problems with the place. One year so many rooms were broken into, so much stuff ripped off, the players started calling it the Sofisteal. Next year, when forty players were knocked flat by an intestinal bug, they called it the Sofibarf.

Still, it makes sense to stay there. It's cheap, convenient, and a gold mine of gossip. But Latif and Lenore insisted on a glass-and-chrome high-rise hotel in Montparnasse.

We arrived in a cold rain. You'd of guessed it was January, not the last week of May. Latif, though, he wanted to hit the streets and search for a pyramid. I passed. I hadn't slept on the train and I needed to hang around in case Heather called. When Lenore begged off too, blaming her upset stomach, Latif stormed out on his own.

Before I napped, I did a quick inventory of the complimentary souvenirs in my room—perfumed soap, lemon shower gel, shampoo and bubble bath, box of chocolates. Then I checked the computerized minibar, a sawed-off refrigerator stocked with champagne, mineral water, whiskey, cheese, and crackers.

There was a magazine on the night table, but I skipped that and fell into the sack. I'd been asleep ten minutes, no more, when the phone rang. Heather, I thought. I'd tell her to hurry on up to the room.

"Have you read the magazine?" It was Lenore.

"No. Something in it about Latif?"

"He's my husband and I love him, but he's not the only subject that interests me. There's a hilarious article on a new nightclub Régine is opening in LA. Like to have lunch?"

I wasn't used to chatty calls or friendly invites from Lenore. I figured something must be up. "Meet you downstairs."

I skimmed the magazine for a clue to her call. It was a slick job distributed free to hotels and hairdressers. Talking in French, with English and German translations on the facing page, Régine described her nightclub: "This is something completely different and much less disco. It is really a big living room called I.Q. I want to start a place where artists, writers, and painters can be themselves and express themselves freely. I.Q. stands for intelligence quotient, above all that of day and night life."

I didn't get it.

Lenore was in the lobby being leered at by a group of men in white shoes and lime-green trousers. A convention of golf pros?

"Very catchy piece about Régine," I said like that was our secret password.

"Yes, doesn't it make you want to drop your membership in MENSA and join I.Q.?" She pulled a scarf from the pocket of her Burberry and tied it over her hair.

"Thought we'd eat here?" I said.

"The restaurant looks dreadful. I swear they're setting up for a Rotary Club meeting."

"I'm expecting a call."

"They'll take a message."

She slipped her arm through mine and led me outside into the drizzle. I wasn't happy about that, not with me wearing a new silk suit I'd treated myself to in Rome. But I went where she steered me, walking up Boulevard Montparnasse under the dripping chestnut trees, past Closerie des Lilas, Le Sélect, and Le Dôme, with Lenore lecturing about which writers used to eat where. She brought up heavy hitters even I'd heard of—Hemingway, Fitzgerald, and Joyce. Then she mentioned, really, no kidding, a novelist named Fordmatic Ford.

"You're joking," I said.

"Not at all. That wasn't his original name, of course. He changed it."

"From what? Lipschitz?"

She was nodding to another restaurant, La Coupole. "On my first trip to Paris, I ate there, and guess who was at the next table?"

"Fordmatic Ford."

"William Styron and James Jones, eating oysters and looking very happy. I was too shy to speak to them."

"Let's go in, see if they're still there." I was ready to sit down and hear what Lenore had on her mind.

"What I crave," she said, "is junk food. The greasier the better."

"Thought you had an upset stomach?"

"I do. But a burger and fries'll cure that."

"You sound pregnant."

She gave me a smiling sidelong glance. I couldn't tell much with her in a raincoat, but I had wondered why, after Latif was winning big bucks, she didn't splurge on a new wardrobe. Maybe she knew she'd soon need a different size.

"Jesus, it's true! Isn't it?" My belly felt like a plunging elevator. "You had the rabbit test?"

"Yeah, I held it in my hand and caught warts." She went on smiling and watching me out the corner of her almond-shaped eyes. "Don't overwhelm me with congratulations."

"It's just . . . it's a little sudden."

"I suppose you hate kids?"

"I never lump them in a separate category. Ever notice, nobody asks, 'You like adults? You detest senior citizens?' I take everybody on a case-by-case basis."

"Bullshit," she said in a cheery voice.

"Was Latif surprised?"

She let my arm slip from hers. "Surprised? No. We discussed it and agreed we wanted a baby. But fatherhood is still emotionally charged for him. He went through a lot of humiliation when he couldn't get Rashida pregnant. And now that we're going to have to make so many adjustments, naturally that increases his stress."

"What type adjustments are we talking about?"

"I can travel with him a few more months. After that, I'll have to stay put. The question is where? Another question is how much he'll care to travel the circuit alone."

"Alone? I'll be with him. What you need is a base of operations. A nice big house for you and the baby. In a country with a favorable exchange rate and a friendly tax policy."

"There are other problems, other conflicts, that have nothing to do with the baby."

"Problems? Conflicts?" My belly was crashing through the basement.

"Here we are."

She nudged me toward O'Kitch, a McDonald's knock-off that had video machines blasting rock at brain-rattling volume. Lenore roosted on a stool at a Formica counter and asked me to bring her a double cheese, maxi-*frites*, and a choco-shake. Her dark hair, when she took off the scarf, had a purplish sheen from the neon.

The kitchen staff at O'Kitch resembled a UN delegation. A Vietnamese worked the grill, a North African hauled wire baskets out of the deep-fat fryer, a Tahitian manned the bun warmer, and a black guy with tribal scars wrote up my order. Still, everything tasted strictly Middle American. We might as well of eaten the Styrofoam boxes the food came in.

"About these conflicts," I asked Lenore after we'd had a few bites of our burgers.

She licked mustard from her lips. "It's hard to discuss without sounding like a dopey self-help book or a pop psychologist. Ever notice how quickly psychiatric categories become conversational clichés, then wind up as song titles? Middle Age Crazy, that sort of thing."

"You're telling me Latif's suffered a midlife crisis at his age?"

She squeezed tartar sauce and ketchup on her fries. "What I'm doing, I'm trying to spare you that kind of mental shorthand."

"Don't spare me. Explain!"

"Let's just say after a poverty-stricken childhood, an unstable adolescence, and an intense spurt of fame, followed by a three-year stretch in a federal prison, Latif has unresolved difficulties." She pinched a sliver of burger from between the buns and dunked it in the tartar sauce. "Now that he's pretty much achieved what he dreamed about behind bars, he wonders whether it's worth the effort."

"We went through this in Rome. He's back in the top ten, headed for Number One. And like you told him, the beauty is he's doing it clean and completely independent."

"That doesn't mean he's not bothered by the dirty dealing going on around him. The backbiting, the smear campaign, the suspicions about his identity. He's starting to feel the pressure."

"Till this past week he's been loose as a noodle. He still looks that way on court." I sucked up a noisy swallow of my strawberry shake. At the bottom it tasted like Pepto-Bismol.

"An illusion, cunningly crafted and maintained with enormous effort. It takes willpower and discipline to create an impression of utter carelessness. He told me if it weren't for the boost he gets climbing pyramids he'd have to go back to his old game."

"Nothing wrong with that. He's a great serve and volleyer. And this new style has a built-in lid, strategywise and otherwise."

"He'd agree with you, but probably for different reasons."

"Tell me his reasons. I know mine." I slurped up a shot of Pepto-Bismol to settle my belly that was boogying to the beat of Twisted Sister.

"It hurts Latif to have players accuse him of cheating. He thought they'd understand, maybe come to appreciate, what he's doing—exploring new dimensions of the game, opening opportunities for all of them. He's especially upset to have Wilander, a fellow he always liked, angry at him. With McEnroe, Becker, Lendl, and Flamini, it shocks him— scares him really—how much he wants to beat them. He thought he was past that."

"He didn't care, he wouldn't be human."

"True. But he doesn't like the way it eats at him. Or at us as a couple. Since he's got a choice and he's proved his point, the question is how much longer he wants to be around Richards and Pippo, tennis people in general." With her fingertip she stabbed at the sesame seeds that had dropped off her bun. "He's reviewing his options."

"Meaning what?" I couldn't eat, my belly jitterbugging like it was. I pushed my plastic tray in front of her.

"Meaning with a baby on the way, knowing we already have some tough decisions to make, he's adjusting to the idea that—"

"He's playing too much," I panicked and broke in. He was considering quitting, I couldn't bear to hear it. Once she said it, I was scared it would come true. "That's a big problem with coming back—burnout. After Wimbledon, we'll cut his schedule."

"That's one possibility." She nibbled the sesame seeds from

her fingertip. "We've set aside a nice nest egg. No matter what we decide, we won't starve."

"What about me?"

"You won't starve either." She went to work on my burger. "You got what, twenty percent of everything he's won? That gives you some breathing space. Occurs to me you may be having the same second thoughts as Latif."

"Me? I been thinking about nothing but another Grand Slam. The French, the Australian, Wimbledon, and the U.S. Open, they're the tournaments that matter. The others are just warmups. Latif must of told you that."

"The only thing he told me, he won't be playing the U.S. Open because you're still wanted in the States."

"He could go to New York on his own. With you, I mean."

She munched a french fry. "That's another thing that's troubling him these days, your legal situation. You seem to have sorted things out over here. At least nobody's slapping you with subpoenas. But back in the—"

"Let me worry about it."

"That's what Latif wishes you'd do—deal with your problems."

"That's what I'm doing by staying out of the States."

"How long can you run? The rest of your life?"

"I remember right, this is lunch at O'Kitch, not a counseling session for cons. And we were talking about Latif and your life, not mine. What do you say we start back to the hotel?"

It was dumb, I decided, to discuss my legal problems, Latif's career, or anything else with Lenore in her condition. What she said might be no more than raging hormones whistling their own loony tune.

That Latif was suffering a letdown, the mental equivalent of blisters and bruises, I didn't deny. After seven straight tournaments, six where he took the title, it was natural he felt stale. Now with a knocked-up wife on his hands, he had another reason to feel played out. She claimed he wouldn't want to travel the circuit alone—like being with me was no better than carrying extra baggage. But a few months with a colicky kid and Lenore down with a terminal case of post-baby blues, he'd be grateful to go on the road again. The solution I saw, we'd park her in Andorra or some offshore island.

While we hoofed it back to the hotel, the drizzle dried up and the sun peeked through. I was beginning to feel a bit better.

"That's terrific news about the baby," I told Lenore who was noshing the rest of my cheeseburger.

"Took you long enough to make up your mind."

"I'm not the fast food type. I try to digest news too quick, I get heartburn."

She bumped me with her hip, laughing. "Oh, Eddie, you're such a fraud. Funny but awful."

She wiped her greasy fingers on my jacket sleeve. "Damn fine burger," she said. "Hem was right. Paris is a moveable feast."


Strolling up the sidewalk to the hotel, I spotted Latif in the lobby with the desk clerk. I couldn't hear him on account of the plate-glass door, but by the looks of it, he was raising hell, shaking his fists, hollering so loud the *tagilmoust* bubbled over his mouth.

Suddenly it sank in. He's talking! Latif's talking! Which meant unless the desk clerk understood Tamahaq, he was speaking English or French. Which meant it must be an emergency. I broke into a sprint.

The same instant, Latif swung around, saw me, and started running too. He reached the door first and didn't stop. Maybe he never noticed the glass. Maybe he'd begun to believe the press clippings about his magical powers and thought he'd pass clean through.

He went through it all right. His forehead hit the glass and jagged fangs of it flew everywhere, spraying blood like seltzer. Still he didn't slow down. He raced to me, babbling, grabbing my lapels with bleeding hands. He'd lost his sun-shades, his *gandourah* hung in rags, and his *tagilmoust* was torn loose.

"They stole my racquet."

"What? Who?"

"They stole it." He collapsed and dragged me down with him.

Showing incredible cool, Lenore crouched and cradled his head in her lap. When the desk clerk dashed out of the lobby and a crowd of gawkers clustered around she tugged the tattered veil over his face.

"*C'est pas possible,*" said the clerk. "*C'est pas ma faute.*"

"Nobody said it was your fault." She was swabbing Latif's cuts with her Burberry. "Call an ambulance."

"But it's expensive, the door."

"Forget the fucking door!" I screamed. "Get a doctor."

A long gash on his left wrist was gushing blood. I tore a strip off his *gandourah* and wrapped it tight. Reminded of my own hamburgered hand months ago in Tunis, I refused to believe this was any worse than that. Mine had healed; so would his.

His eyelids fluttered open—one iris brown, the other blue. He'd lost a contact lens. He struggled to sit up. "It's gone," he groaned. "They broke into the room and swiped my father's bone."

Lenore eased his head back on her thigh. "Shhh."

But he didn't care who heard him holler. "My racquet, how can I play without my racquet?"

The clerk called a taxi instead of an ambulance, and the cabbie wasn't crazy about carrying a hurt Tuareg till we shook a fistful of francs in his face and promised we'd let Latif bleed on us, not his chintzy upholstery. Lenore and I crawled into the back seat and draped him like a dishrag across our knees.

I told the cabbie to rush us to the nearest doctor. Lenore said make it the best. While Latif went on wailing about his dead father's bone, I tweezed glass from his feet.

The doctor's office was on the bottom floor of an apartment building, and the waiting room resembled a beauty salon with flowerpots, frilly curtains, and back issues of gossip magazines. Seeing the three of us stagger in, Latif swinging between Lenore and me like a bloodstained sheet, the receptionist shot to her feet. "*C'est pas possible,*" she said.

In a pinch, that's always their opening line, the French. Whatever you need, they say it's impossible. After that, the bargaining starts.

Right away the receptionist switched gears and asked did we have an account with the doctor.

I came back with what I thought was French. "*Je n'ai pas un con. Mais j'ai beaucoup d'argent.*"

Lenore barked, "Eddie, this is no time for jokes."

"Who's joking?"

The receptionist sank down in her chair, a frozen smile on her kisser. She pressed a button and repeated over the intercom what I said.

A man in a tweed jacket with a stethoscope jiggling around his neck charged into the waiting room, roaring with laughter. "My nurse tells me there is someone"—he spoke pretty decent English—"who does not have a cunt, but has very much money. *En principe*, I prefer patients with both. I am a gynecologist. How can I help you?"

It was like he didn't see this masked blue man being bled white beside me.

"He's cut bad," I said.

"But this is not a clinic, not a hospital."

"Please, he needs a doctor," Lenore begged. "Stitches, bandages."

He bowed, motioning us into a room with lots of bookshelves, a mahogany desk, and these spindly antique chairs nobody'd dare sit in. There was an examining table, too, and the doctor told Latif to stretch out and stick his hands in the stirrups.

For all his oily bedside manner, the guy seemed to know his stuff. He unwrapped Latif's left wrist and had him clench and unclench his fist, then flex each finger. "Not too deep, not grave," he crooned. "No tendons or muscles *coupés*. But, *bien sûr*, he needs sewing."

He cleaned the biggest cut with cotton and alcohol, dug out a few slivers of glass, then started stitching. He didn't offer anesthetic, and Latif didn't ask for it. He just laid there staring up at Lenore, one eye brown, one eye blue, like an alley cat that had bitten off more than it could chew.

She was crying and wouldn't watch the doctor work the needle in and out of his skin. I could of cried myself. I'd of hated to see it end this way. Even if Lenore was right and Latif was dickering whether to retire, I'd rather he leave tennis on his own terms. Not like last time—set up and screwed over. Okay, nobody pushed him through that plate-glass door, but I didn't have any doubt who'd ripped off his racquet.

After knotting the last stitch, the twentieth, the doctor swabbed his other cuts and scratches. None of them needed thread, only disinfectant. Then he plucked at nuggets of glass embedded in the calluses on his feet. "I don't succeed to get everything," he said. "But soak in warm water and soon the glass will work loose."

"How long before he's fit to play sports?" I asked.

"Sport?" He looked Lenore up and down. "What sport?"

I took a risk and told him, "Tennis."

Now the doctor looked Latif up and down, and grinned. I understood how it had to strike him. Here's this camel jockey just went through a meat grinder, and his friend's worried when he can play tennis. It was like someone asking a vet when his monkey would be well enough to study ballet. But I didn't take offense. It was a relief he didn't recognize Ali Ben Baraka, the hottest ticket on the tour.

"Three weeks," he said. "Maybe a month." He loaded a syringe for a tetanus shot. "This may make him a little fever"—he jabbed the needle into Latif's arm—"but it guards against the locking of jaws."

. . .

In the taxi on the return trip to the hotel, Latif began babbling again about his racquet and his father and how he wanted to play Wimbledon. I told him we'd get him another racquet and Wimbledon would always be there. He insisted he had to play this year.

"Great. You'll play and you'll win," I said.

"But there's no time to make a racquet. And what about my father's bone?" Sounded to me like he was having a bad reaction to the tetanus shot.

"There are others." I swear I was talking about racquets, not digging up his father's corpse. But Lenore shot me a killer look.

"We'll drop you at the hotel," she said. "Pack our bags and pay the bill. I'll phone once we're in a new place."

It made good sense to move and leave no forwarding address. Now that they had his racquet, who knew what they'd rip off next? I told the desk clerk I'd call for messages.

He was so grateful I didn't file a complaint with the police about the break-in and theft, he offered a discount on the shattered door.

That made sense too—me not involving the cops, not letting reporters and tennis creeps realize what kind of casualties we'd suffered. I'd scratch him from Roland Garros claiming he caught an eye infection from the sandstorm in Rome.

Cooling my heels waiting for Lenore's call, I went into the bar and ordered a vodka gimlet. In the booth behind me sat a couple in airline uniforms. "Ever notice how ice in Europe doesn't crack?" asked the stewardess.

"Come again?" said the pilot.

"The ice here, it's quiet. In the States, you splash Pepsi over ice and there's like an explosion. Here, it's totally silent. Hold it up to your ear. Am I right or what?"

I was turning to check whether they both had highball glasses glued to their heads listening to silent ice when Heather dropped her canvas tote sack and slid into the booth beside me. "Mind if I kip here, mate?"

You didn't have to be a raving paranoid to be suspicious.

Richards, I felt sure, was part of the plot to steal Latif's racquet. So why hadn't Heather warned me?

I held one of her chewed paws. "Where you been?"

"Where've I not been? I've been in Africa, America, England, heaps of airports in between."

She did look jet-lagged, travel-whipped, her eyes darkcircled again, her hair lank. She had on a grocery clerk's grey smock, a pair of patch-pocket fatigue pants, and a pea green tee shirt, the sort worn by sewer workers and Central American soldiers.

"Tell me about it," I said.

"Not here. Someplace private. A room with a shower, please," she said. "I'm awfully grubby. Hot water and soap would be heaven. Suppose you realize you've blood all over you? What happened?"

"Bang bang."

When I reregistered, the desk clerk glanced at Heather and overacted by not reacting at all. A bellboy brought the baggage up to the room I'd just left. Already it had been remade. I lifted the lid on the souvenir candy box. Either it was a new box or somebody had replaced the single chocolate I ate this morning. While I tipped the boy, Heather hit the minibar for a bottle of Vichy water and a wedge of foil-wrapped cheese with a Laughing Cow label.

"Famished," she said, shimmying out of the grocer's smock. When the boy left, she shucked her counterinsurgency, junglewarfare camouflage pants and tee shirt and stood there in spanking white cotton panties and tight pink skin.

I fought to control the thermostat, keep it at room temperature. After wondering where Heather fit in, I wondered how I'd fit in. I hadn't set foot on a pyramid in a week, and today had done nothing to put lead in my pencil.

She peeled off her lollypop briefs. "Coming?"

I squeezed into the shower stall beside her, shampooed her hair, then scrubbed her back and front. But my mind and other parts were miles away, puzzling over the link between the disappearing racquet and Heather's arrival.

Soaping me, she said, "Tired?"

"Not a bit."

"Not interested?"

"I've known many a man left his game in the shower room. A veteran saves his best shots for the match, when it counts." I gave her what could of passed for a passionate bear hug or a combat grapple, and stopped just short of thumping her head against the tiles, demanding what the hell she'd been doing two hours ago.

I left her to rinse off alone. Toweling myself semidry, I darted into the other room and fumbled through her tote sack. I dreaded getting caught this way—my own sack flapping in the breeze, my hands scrabbling through spare undies and tee shirts, hairbrushes, jars, pill bottles, shriveled tubes. What did I expect? That she'd hid the racquet here?

I steered clear of the bed. I intended to change the atmosphere, the tone, till I got a few straight answers. All business, I sat in a chair at the desk. When Heather stepped out of the steamy bathroom, I crossed my legs and folded my hands on my stomach. "This place private enough for you to tell me what you've been up to?"

"Can't that wait?" She swung her damp bottom onto the desk, bracing a foot against each arm of my chair. For a girl whose taste in underpants was strictly bargain basement, she had a Frederick's of Hollywood fantasy life. Dipping into the candy box, she twisted a chocolate into the slit of her navel. "Eat a sweet?"


You've seen it a thousand times, sports fans. Probably you've experienced it yourself. There are days when muscle memory and instinct desert a player, and heart and desire will carry him only so far. He can't find the groove, and the more he bears down, the more he loses touch.

I started with the new style, aiming for the open spot, moving it around, using Heather's speed and strength against her. I mixed short strokes and deep strokes, top spin and slice, drop shots and lobs. I changed the pace, I hit for angles and out-of-the-way corners, I alternated cross-court and down the line. But I couldn't keep it in play.

Never stick with a losing strategy, the best coaches will tell you. So I switched to the classic power game, hit for the lines and rushed headlong to finish. But I had lost the knack of bullying in close and walloping winners. The quick twitch muscles failed me, my legs felt shot. I was never really in the match.

Heather was polite about it. More than that, she blamed herself. "Seeing blood on you, I knew there'd been trouble. Knew you needed to talk. But it's been such a long time, and I did fancy you."

I rolled over, covering up with the sheet. "I think you'd better tell me what you been doing."

She stood up, stretching for her underpants and tee shirt.

"Please, not that," I said. "Don't put on the guerrilla gear. Crawl under here with me." She snuggled up close, and I kept a finger on her pulse—an improvised lie detector test. "Africa, America, England? Why?"

"Working with Richards. He's closing in. I should say *they're* closing in. That umpire, the one with white hair, the one who refers to fanny as 'down there,' he's in on it."

"Buzz Murphy?"

"Yes. He's pressing his ear to keyholes. Claims he heard Baraka speak English."

"Sure, he's learned a few words and phrases, whole sentences. But he doesn't feel ready to talk to reporters in English."

"Murphy also got a print of Baraka's feet in Monte Carlo. They're planning to match them with Fluss's footprints."

"How they going to find them?"

"That's why we flew to Africa. But Fluss had vanished."

"Poor guy. Probably ashamed to go home to his village."

"No, they say he came back, then left just about the time Ali Ben Baraka appeared on the circuit."

"Coincidence. Doesn't prove a thing."

"They're convinced," she said, "that Baraka is Latif Fluss. They think they're one step, maybe two, from having hard proof. And they're digging up a lot of unsavory stuff about you."

"I bet," I said real breezy.

"They're prying into his wife's past too. Both wives."

"Baraka's got one wife. Lenore!"

"What about the woman he left behind?"

"Rashida? What's she got to do with Baraka?"

"She's quite bitter. Richards interviewed her, and she was rather convincing in the role of badly aggrieved wife."

"She's beating a dead horse. Latif paid his dues, did his time. What's the good of her going on TV telling the world he was a lousy husband?"

"As for his new wife—"

"You mean Baraka, there's no old and new." I wouldn't yield an inch. "There's Lenore. Period!"

"Whatever. Private investigators in the States uncovered some disturbing news. She ran down her first husband in an automobile."

I chuckled. "Yeah, she told me. Sensational story. Spirited gal."

We were cuddling spoon fashion. Heather squirmed in my arms. "Is that what I should do if you're ever unfaithful?"

"I'm dumb enough to stand there and dare you, I deserve it."

"I'd never run you down. I don't want to see you hurt, Eddie. That's why I'm warning you. They're aiming for Wimbledon."

"Aiming what?"

"A TV program. An exposé."

"They don't have proof. What are they going to broadcast— besides Baraka's footprints and pictures of Rashida bitching?"

"Can't say precisely. We've shot a lot of film, and they're still doing research."

"That why they ripped off Baraka's racquet?"

She rolled over, facing me. Because of the dark circles her eyes looked doubly surprised.

"That's right," I said. "They broke into his room and stole it."

"Who?"

"Thought you could tell me."

"This is the first I've heard of it."

"Richards, Buzz, they never mentioned Baraka's racquet?"

"Everybody in tennis talks about it. But I haven't heard anyone discuss pinching it." She sat up. "I suppose it's fingerprints they're after."

"That and maybe they figure he can't win without it."

"Can he?"

"Sure. He could swing a banjo and beat these other stiffs." Looking up into that cute, raccoon-eyed face, I wondered how far to trust her. I decided to tell the truth—part of it at any rate. "Trouble is, Baraka's injured."

"How?"

"Wigged out when his racquet was swiped and walked through a plate-glass door. We're pulling out of the French with a fake eye infection."

"How badly is he hurt?"

"He'll be ready for Wimbledon."

"And they'll be ready for him."

"Where's Richards now?"

"Here in Paris."

"Think you could poke around," I said, "ask about the racquet and any new rumors?"

She frowned and scratched her left breast, its perky nipple. "I feel grotty going back and forth, playing a double game. I'd rather stay with you."

"And report to Richards?"

She blinked, then not telegraphing her moves, threw an overhead right that caught me smack on the chin. Didn't hurt much, but it got my attention. "What a rotten thing to say. What do you think I am? A piece of crumpet who'll do anything to stay in the game? I could be in Afghanistan, you know."

"Sorry. I'm a bastard for saying that. It's just with the way things have been going, I'm suspicious of everybody."

"Of me?"

"Not anymore." I sat up and put my arms around her.

"If you are, I'm leaving," she said.

"No, stay. I believe you."

I half-meant what I said. Forty percent, anyway. I hated to think of Heather hanging around Richards and Murphy, Pippo and the rest of those crum bums. But the other sixty percent of me thought the best way of keeping an eye out for trouble was keeping her near me. I pulled her back under the sheet. I'd of pulled her even closer if I wasn't afraid I'd butcher my strokes a second time that day.

# *Chapter* Seventeen

Pyramidwise, the Eiffel Tower generated absolutely no pep. I went with Latif, who was still hobbling on feet studded with glass, and we climbed the iron stairs. But the result was an energy wipe-out—as Heather could of testified if she wasn't such a patient lady.

Then we tried the gleaming glass pyramid in the courtyard of the Louvre. I don't mean we climbed it. We'd had enough trouble with Latif tripping and plunging through a shredder. But we stood under it for an hour, like bugs under a magnifying lens, and left limp with sweat.

I was beginning to get desperate for Latif and myself when Lenore discovered an estate called Désert de Retz in Marly, a few hundred yards off the *autoroute* running west out of Paris. This rich guy, the Chevalier de Monville, who owned the place in the eighteenth century, had built replicas of ancient monuments all over his property. I'm talking about towers, triumphal arches, Greek temples, and a scale model of the Gaius Cestius tomb in Rome.

Not only did the estate have a pyramid, the Chevalier de Monville had been a terrific player back when tennis matches took place in courtyards and the scoring system registered zero as *l'oeuf*, which is French for egg, as in goose egg. And which is why when today we say "love" for zero we're really mispronouncing *l'oeuf*. This was, I'll be honest, Lenore's greatest find and best lecture.

Another result of her research was a windfall of junk food. Paris, she learned, has over a hundred fast food outlets, and Lenore was determined to sample every one. Each day we'd stop at a different grease pit and buy her a sack of burgers and fries, or chicken wings, egg rolls, and tacos. Then we'd drive out to Désert de Retz and while she ingested her junk food fix, the rest of us dug into a hamper of Brie and Camembert, *foie gras*, and cold ham with hot mustard smeared on fresh *baguettes* of bread, all washed down by white wine and mineral water that we chilled *inside* the pyramid. Seems the Chevalier had designed it to serve as an ice house.

When I say "the rest of us," I mean Heather too. Privately I explained to Latif and Lenore she'd been my spy in the enemy camp. She'd heard rumors Baraka spoke English, but had no way of knowing, regardless what she suspected, that he was Latif. I didn't think she could hurt us, and she might help—as long as Latif kept a tight *tagilmoust* and didn't do much talking. Like me, maybe they had doubts about Heather, but they didn't mention them.

Even when I told them about the TV exposé that included clips of their spiteful exes, they could of cared less. Was it confidence, I wondered? A superstar's unbendable belief he could handle any heat the competition dished out? Or was it simply they'd decided to quit the game? That thought made me half crazy. But I didn't know what to do except hope he won Wimbledon and that that would whet his appetite for more Grand Slam titles.

Those days at Désert de Retz, Latif and I raced up and down the pyramid. It wasn't as steep as the one in Rome and couldn't compare to the originals in Cairo. He could scamper to the top without breaking stride. I set a slower pace for myself, soaking up the sun and breathing the country air. It was so good to be outdoors, I fell into a hustler's heresy and thought, This is enough for now.

Lenore and Heather spent a lot of time together, and I was leery Heather might be chumming up to her to wheedle information. But whenever I eavesdropped, they were talking about babies, the Lit. Biz, or bang bang.

One afternoon, exhausted by Arab aerobics, I left Latif and jogged back to the picnic blanket where Heather lay spreadeagle in her jungle fatigues. Lenore had curled up on her side, watching me. "You're not humoring him anymore, are you?"

"Never did." I was panting. "Never condescend to a client, that's my motto."

"Don't hand me that horseshit, Eddie. I remember Cairo. If Champion could see you now. Sancho Panza has turned into Don Quixote."

"Champion?" Heather hoisted herself on an elbow. "Is he the chap you told me about? The hundred-and-five-year-old bloke who taught you the secret of—"

"Right," I interrupted before this got more embarrassing.

"Sweet, dreamy, romantic Eddie Brown." Lenore rubbed it in.

"He's a love, isn't he?" Heather said.

Blushing to the eyeballs, I galloped back to the pyramid.

When she wasn't razzing me or schmoozing with Heather or sleeping—these days she could doze off anywhere—Lenore read *The Notebooks of Malta Laurids Brigge*.

How I understood it, the book was about a foreign boy who moves to Paris and is so knocked out by the city, he naturally considers committing suicide. I didn't look for it to make the best-seller list, but I liked a few lines Lenore read us.

"I am learning to see," the book said. "I don't know why

it is, but everything enters me more deeply and doesn't stop where it once used to."

Though I hadn't become the kind of daffy dreamer Lenore imagined, I was definitely seeing things different. How could I help it? They *were* different.

For openers, Latif had changed, and it wasn't just a question of a new name, a mask, a new game, a pregnant wife, and after his run-in with the glass door, a new attitude. Sometimes he did things that flabbergasted me more than his solid-geometry tennis game. He was capable of kneeling next to Lenore and kissing her belly which—maybe because of fast food as much as the baby—was pouched out already. "Children are the ornament of this life," he announced.

Ask whether I bought this, whether I truly believed in pyramid power, I'll plead the Fifth Amendment. But I'll admit to something screwier. I was beginning to believe Heather—that she wasn't here to snoop for Iain Richards, that she was convinced my wand was magic. It amazed me how totally my touch returned. Once again I smacked aces left and right, and every shot entered Heather more deeply and didn't stop where it used to.

Before long, Latif quit hobbling, and the calluses on his feet grew hard as bootheels. He never complained about his cut, not even when we returned to the grinning gynecologist who stretched him out with his hands in the stirrups and tweezed the stitches from a bright scar that curved against his blue-black skin like a crescent moon. The way he winced when he rotated his wrist, I knew it hurt bad. This type injury could wreck his toss, his entire service motion. Still he said nothing.

He didn't talk tennis at all, never referred to his racquet or how he planned to replace it. First I realized he was giving any thought to the game, one morning he told us we wouldn't be driving to Désert de Retz. We were moving to London for Wimbledon.

He wouldn't hear of flying. Even the Hovercraft was too

hurried for him. We caught the train to Calais, a slow boat to Dover, then another train to Victoria Station where I bought the papers and learned Lendl had won the French Open and McEnroe was the top seed at Wimbledon. The front page of *Screws of the World* showed a bare-breasted belly dancer named Fonda Peters who claimed she was carrying Ali Ben Baraka's baby.

"Welcome to Jolly Old England," Heather said.

"Rashida?" I asked.

"Ridiculous," Lenore snapped. "Rashida has tattoos."

"I never saw her up close and stripped for gym. Richards's idea?" I asked Heather.

"I wouldn't put it past him. An effort to destabilize the enemy."

"You stay away from Fonda Peters, Mr. Baraka," Lenore ordered Latif.

That got a laugh from everybody.


The Gloucester is the official hotel for Wimbledon, and plenty of reporters and players take advantage of the discount rate and the courtesy cars that run them out to the All England Lawn Tennis and Croquet Club. If bargain-basement prices and free transport aren't enough to attract them, there's the Texas Lonestar Saloon across the street.

Latif and I always stayed at the Westbury, but after his matches he sometimes suffered an acute case of the munchies, and we'd drop by the Lonestar for an injection of Tex-Mex. He maintained it lifted him quicker than straight meth. While he binged on nachos and burritos and barbequed ribs, I'd knock back Tequila Sunrises, and we'd sit there till closing time surrounded by Dallas Cowboy pennants, HOOK 'EM HORNS signs, and posters for the annual chili cook-off at Terlingua, Texas, just down a dusty road from Holy Sepulcher College.

This year as we drove past the Lonestar, I saw the wooden Indian out front, left hand uplifted like Latif might raise his own and ask, How? How the hell am I going to win Wimbledon with a bum wrist and no racquet?

Never letting me know what they were up to, Latif and Lenore had leased a house on Petyt Street, a short hike from King's Road. Four stories tall, it had an extra-ordinary view of the Thames and, more important, was surrounded by a brick wall, protected by a wrought-iron gate and an electronic security system. Much as it hurt that they hadn't asked my advice, I couldn't argue with their choice.

After unpacking, we gravitated to the library, a high-ceilinged room crowded with potted palms and pieces of fat furniture, each poised on brass lion claws. You stubbed your toes on one of those suckers, it'd tear them right off. But Latif shuffled around barefooted, disregarding dangers, hunting for matches to light the sticks and balled-up newspapers he'd piled in the fireplace. It was damn cold, even for England in June.

Once he got the blaze going, he sat cross-legged on the parquet floor, his sunglasses dancing with reflected flames. "I'm ready for you to buy racquets," he told me, talking through his *tagilmoust*, faking an accent for Heather's benefit.

"Why buy? Lemme make a few calls. Some company'll supply a dump truck full."

"I endorse nothing."

"Endorsements aside, somebody'll be glad to have you play with his product. You're silly enough to do it for nothing, that's your problem. My problem!"

"Let's not argue about this again." Lenore had sunk like a bowling ball into an overstuffed couch. Heather and I had hunkered on a divan that was so hard the brocade left a brand on our behinds.

"Okay, I give up," I said. "Tell me the make, the model, and how many."

"Six mid-size wooden racquets," Latif said. "Any make, any model. I'll string them. I have camel gut."

"Think I'm getting camel gut myself," I said, "and it feels just like ulcers."

.   .   .

I bought the racquets off the rack at Lillywhite's, each a different brand, different grip, different weight, different balance. I thought Latif would test them, at least heft them once or twice, and tell me to exchange the other five for the model he liked best. But he said they were all fine and spent the next week in front of the fire, sanding off labels, carving Arabic on the handles.

That was the total extent of his Wimbledon preparation—unless you counted the walks we took. Maybe he was training for the rock-hard grass on Centre Court by squishing through the soft wet fields in Hyde Park. He wouldn't even watch TV coverage of the Queen's Club final where McEnroe whipped Edberg, showing no rustiness after his six-week suspension.

During our daily strolls, every word out of his mouth was a conversation stopper. When he wasn't quoting the Koran, he was answering me with questions. I'd congratulate him about the baby and he'd ask if I wanted one. I'd fish around for his future plans, and he'd ask what I'd be doing next year. I'd say I had a hunch he had something on his mind, and he'd urge me to face my problems.

"Face!" I said. "That's the problem. I can't see your face, can't guess what's going on behind the curtains. Here I am a hands-on personal manager whose client refuses to be touched. It's like you're in a different time zone."

"Sorry, Eddie. I feel closer to you now than ever. But I want to leave you plenty of room to think."

I didn't want to think. I didn't want room. I wanted in on some action. But I completed my own Wimbledon preparation with one trip to the All England Club. After checking who was on Baraka's side of the draw—Flamini, Becker, Lendl—then copping a coach's badge to get into the dressing room and arranging guest passes for Lenore and Heather, I didn't have a damn thing to do. I suppose another agent might of regarded Latif as a bonanza—a low-maintenance, high-return client. But that didn't do much to fill my days.

Back when nobody reined me in from wheeling and dealing, I spent weeks gearing up for Wimbledon. Every agent did. You had to be in shape, you had to hit the ground running, you had to have a taste for the rough and bloody tumble. More than anything, you needed a pair of ears tougher than pig iron because for a solid month—two weeks in advance, two weeks during the tournament—you were on the telephone twelve hours a day haggling over contracts and guarantees. You hear players moan about pressure, but what they endure is Amateur Night in Dixie compared to the vicious competition of agents in hotel suites, hospitality tents, and the back seats of Bentleys.

To understand Wimbledon, you first have to forget everything you learned about it from TV or Sunday supplements or books by authors who nibbled around the fruity edges but never sank a tooth into the red meat of the joint. Sure, there's tradition and wrinkly geezers in uniforms. There's the royal family with funny noses and floppy hats. There's strawberries in cream, champagne and Pimm's Cup, schoolgirls in straw boaters, schoolboys with skinned knees, and gents in green and purple club ties. There's all the walls crawling with ivy and trellised roses, every ledge dripping hydrangeas. But that's window dressing.

The real Wimbledon—my Wimbledon—is a hustler's heaven. While four hundred thousand fans stand around in the rain watching tennis players imitate ice skaters, a few sharp operators rake in money hand over fist. What I like best, you can bet on matches.

In Monte Carlo, I explained why I don't gamble; you have to be a horse's ass to buck the house odds. But for somebody who can size up players in the dressing room and draw his own form chart, betting at Wimbledon isn't a gamble. It's a smart investment. There were times in the bad old days when I bet on Latif and times I bet against him, and I wasn't wrong once.

Used to be you could plunk down your dough at a bookmaker's stall on the grounds of the All England Club. But the bookie got gobbled alive by players and agents in position to do some sharp insider trading. Now you have to travel to a gaming shop in London. Take my word, it's worth a detour.

. . .

I thought I knew every scam you could pull at Wimbledon. But I confess I was thrown by the number they ran on us in the first round.

Latif was slated to meet a qualifier, a sixteen-year-old Turk with a moustache the size of an oxtail. I don't buy that the kid had a brainstorm on his own. I mean I don't see Ottoman Oddnor sitting awake all night with a Turkish-English dictionary and a copy of the Wimbledon Championship Conditions and coming up with this corker.

Latif and I were in the Players' Waiting Room, under the Royal Box, where everybody scheduled for a showcase court fidgets and kills time. Over the entrance to Centre Court there's that famous quote from Kipling: "If you can meet with Triumph and Disaster/And treat those two impostors just the same . . ."

One year there was a scandal when somebody finished off the sentence, ". . . then you don't know your ass from your elbow and don't deserve to win."

Latif, I was glad to see, had obeyed the Wimbledon rule that "competitors must be dressed predominantly in white throughout." He wore what looked like a doctor's scrub gown and a brand-new cream-colored *tagilmoust*. The bandage on his left wrist was white too.

Legs folded up under him, he was lounging beside me, gazing into space through his sunglasses, when the secretary of the club bustled over.

"Awfully glad you're here early." He had a blazer with a coat of arms and blond hair like the gold braid on an admiral's cap. "Frightful bore and a bit out of the ordinary, but Mr. Oddnor has requested that Mr. Baraka submit to a buccal smear."

"A what?"

"Buccal smear." How he said it with his marbles-in-the-mouth accent, it sounded like a specialty act in an Istanbul cathouse.

"Talk to me later. My man's got a match to play."

ng what Latif's going through with the chromosome
he said, "I'm curious about sexual identity on the
's circuit."
f?" I sat up. "You mean Baraka."
you like." She sat up too, and her breasts did a tricky

at I like's got nothing to do with it."
the contrary. It's got everything to do with whom you
Clearly not me."
y, what's this? You asked about the women's circuit."
e swung her feet off the bed and began putting on her

e're still talking about tennis," I said, "I just don't—"
ennis is beside the point." She stepped into her jungle
ues. "I thought—my mistake, my presumption—you had
capacity to grow and trust me." She headed for the door.
Wait. Where you going?"
Downstairs. I promised Lenore I'd fix Latif's dinner."
Baraka!"
Latif!" She slammed the door; that set the camel bells
nging and Hands of Fatma clapping.


Okay, it wasn't the Thrilla in Manila. But it knocked me
t. She knew the truth. No mistake about that.
At dinner Latif and Lenore were showing such strain
emselves, I couldn't bring myself to toss the subject on
e table along with Heather's shepherd's pie. No matter how
ad she was at me, I had to hope—pray!—she'd keep our
ecret.
Afterward, we cleared off the plates and limped to neutral
orners. Heather climbed back up to the Sahara; I slept in
he library, sinking into an overstuffed sofa like one of Latif's
drop shots into the grass on Centre Court.
Next morning, she was gone. No note, no goodbye.
I staggered into the kitchen where Latif was downing a
breakfast of dried dates and Lenore was packing away a

"Afraid this'll have to be now. We'll just scrape some cells from Mr. Baraka's mouth and send them to the la-boor-a-tree. A mere technicality. But Mr. Oddnor is within his rights to ask."

"Are you saying, is this Turkish tit-head suggesting, my man is diseased?"

"Not at all." He clamped a hand over his heart, like he was swearing on his coat of arms. "The test determines chromosomal structure. It's to keep transsexuals out of the women's competition. But theoretically it applies to ladies and gentlemen alike."

"You're saying my man's a woman?" I screamed. "What kind of shit is this? What about McEnroe? Lendl? Becker? You putting them through short-arm inspection too?"

"Please, Mr. Brown, be reasonable. Nobody has seen Mr. Baraka's face, much less his sexual parts. When Mr. Oddnor asked for a test, we felt obliged to comply."

He waved to a nurse who waddled over with a plastic dish and a tongue depressor. She signaled Latif to lift the corner of his veil. Then she spooned into his mouth for some spit, spread it on glass, put it in the plastic dish, and waddled away.

"This mean the match is postponed?" I demanded.

"No. Play on. The result will stand—pending, of course, the lab report."

"You bring back the wrong news," I said, "his wife's going to be plenty pissed off. She's pregnant."

"Mr. Brown, I'm as upset as you are."

"I'm not upset. I'm mad. And Oddnor Asshole or whoever's behind this is going to be sorry. It won't work," I hollered at the Turk who hunched on a bench nearby, not understanding a single word I said. He kept chewing his moustache that was black and greasy as licorice.

If this buccal smear business was supposed to shake Latif, it backfired. Ottoman Oddnor was the one that got psyched out and moved like a mechanical man that's been wound too tight. His arms and legs and brain were totally out of synch. You've heard about hand-eye coordination. Well, Oddnor demonstrated great foot-mouth coordination. He took about fifteen spills, and by the second set had grass stains from his socks to his shoulders.

Latif, meanwhile, got tremendous traction with his bare feet, and his dipsy-doodle style was ready-made for grass. Camping at the base line, he stroked deep, wristy shots, then whenever Oddnor hit a short return, he swooped to the net and dumped a drop volley into the sopping turf. The ball died like cow flop falling in a pasture.

The only changes I noticed, he'd shortened his backswing and sped up his footwork. He also served harder with his new store-bought racquet. His American twist dug up divots so that sometimes Oddnor swung at a dirt clod instead of the ball.

After a straight-set, no-sweat win, Latif skipped the press conference. He told me he'd rather pay the thousand-buck fine than let Richards and other reporters fish for info.

Oddnor passed up the press conference too, and since that cost him almost as much as a first-round loser's prize money, I was doubly convinced somebody had paid him and put him up to this.

That night on TV, BBC broadcast a bulletin about the buccal smear, ending with a wry, dry voice-over. "Is Ali Ben Baraka actually Ali *Bella* Baraka? Stay tuned. The lab report is due any day."

Next day, tabloid writers had a swell time at our expense. On billboards, newsstands, and sandwich boards all around the city the same wisecracks cropped up. WHAT'S BEHIND THE BAREFOOT BOY'S CHEEK? MASKED MARVEL SUSPECTED OF MASCARA. WHAT'S IN THE JEANS AND GENES? TENNIS TYRO'S FUTURE DANGLES BY A CELL.

*Screws of the World* reran that photo of Fonda Peters, the bare-breasted belly dancer, next to a snapshot of Baraka with "Before?" and "After?" captions.

Hard to say how this affected Latif. Around me, he brushed off the abuse, but it had to hurt and it had to ruffle his relations with Lenore. She took to staying home with Heather watching the matches on TV. She blamed her

morning sickness. But I know
those signs that raised doubts

Then the insults slopped ov
round of sixteen, after Latif th
trotted to the net to shake the
didn't shake his hand. He kisse

Latif reared back with his rac
a new part in Flamini's hair. Bu
to the Royal Box, and slunk off w
catcalling.

In the quarterfinals, Boris Becke
smart-ass labels aimed at Baraka.
Tiriac was there to back him up—
Japanese products soon to be test-
America. "Kitchy," they claimed, w
Sweat," they promised, was a spo
"Creap" was supposed to be a nondai
Maid Queer Aids," they swore, were c
thing like a Band-Aid box. I didn't bu
instant. I filed a protest, but the super
won in five tough sets, looking weaker

The tension, the humiliation, began
fell out of the groove again, found it ha
was confident my touch would return; she
But the night of the Becker match, we ha

We were upstairs under the rafters in a
look and feel of the Sahara. The people
house must of spent time in North Africa a
souvenirs here. With bright carpets coveri
handwoven tapestries on the walls, we mi
tent. Belled camel halters and brass Hands o
from the posters of the bed.

We had just finished a one-on-one drill th
hardly set the camel bells ringing and H
swinging. I felt low, real low. Then Heather s
and I sank below sea level.

plate of fried eggs, tomatoes, and bacon. "Have any idea where Heather went?" I asked.

"She left with all her luggage," said Lenore. "What happened? You two fight?"

I sagged against the butcher block. "Yeah, a hot debate whether Baraka's really Latif."

"Who won?" Latif was leafing through a *Mothercare* catalogue as he ate.

"You lost. We lost. She knows who you are. What are we going to do?"

"Not much to do." He didn't lift his eyes from the prams and playpens. "Commend our fates to Allah."

"Nice girl, Heather." Lenore mopped her plate with toast.

"Yeah, well that nice girl's probably running directly to Iain Richards with this news."

"I doubt it," Latif said. Then to Lenore, "*Mothercare* delivers anywhere in the world."

I got out of there before their casualness caused me a coronary. They might not care if his career was finished, but, dammit, I did.


That afternoon while they were off buying a bassinet, Richards called. "We know," he said. "You know we know. Now let's negotiate."

"How'd you get this number? Heather? Who else is in on this?"

"*Beaucoup* people. It's time we got together."

"They all going to be there?"

"Not likely. We'd have to rent Wembley Stadium."

"What do you want?"

"That's precisely what we're going to tell you in terms even you can understand."

We arranged to rendezvous at the Competitors' Lounge at Wimbledon, also called the Players' Tea Room. Stuck like a barnacle on the back of Court One, it's supposed to be off limits to everybody except players and their personal guests.

But the place was so full of agents and entrepreneurs, so loud with backslapping, bargaining, and backstabbing, nobody'd notice unless I carved up Richards with a meat cleaver.

I hiked to the top floor and sat on a foam rubber bench with a view of the room. Three teenage players passed through wearing shower clogs, carrying their wallets and loose change in racquet covers. They took one look at the crowd on the terrace and turned back, found seats, and talked about estate planning and the advantages of limited partnerships.

One thing kept me from giving up hope altogether. Richards wouldn't of suggested negotiations unless there was something he needed and thought we had. We held a bargaining chip. I just wished I knew what it was.

I was in a three-piece suit I'd had made to measure on New Bond Street. For business, I always say, Dress British, think Yiddish. So it surprised me Buzz Murphy showed up wearing an umpire's green blazer, not the pinstripes he'd had on in Monte Carlo.

He shoved a plastic dish under my nose. "Tell me what this looks like."

"Strawberries and cream."

"Try again. Say the first thing pops into your mind."

"What the fuck's this game we're playing? What are you people pulling? That's what pops into my head."

"Poodle scrotums," Buzz said.

"Same to you."

"Eddie, Eddie, I'm talking about the berries. All these years at Wimbledon and it just dawned on me—with cream on them strawberries look like poodle scrotums. You know, those white poodles with purple-pink nuts."

"*Bon appetit*, Buzz." Iain Richards wormed up beside us and offered me his hand.

"Stick it," I said.

"*Ma scusi.* I thought we could discuss this like *amigos.*"

"What's to discuss?"

"We'll get to that soon as Pippo's here." Buzz finished the strawberries, then flicked a finger at his moustache. The salt-and-pepper whiskers seem to be dripping Devonshire cream.

"Pippo regards this as an opportunity to have his laundry bill reimbursed," Richards said. "They tell me Latif's new wife is lethal with a salad."

"The name's Baraka. And you should see the damage she can do with a Volvo."

"I've seen." He sank his skinny ass into a chair. Bending at the knees and waist, crossing his arms and legs, he reminded me of a Swiss army knife with its blades being folded back in. Buzz sat next to him.

"Look, why make a mystery of this?" I said. "I know Heather's been feeding you info. False info!"

"Haven't seen her in weeks. We've got all the information we need."

"What about Baraka's racquet?" I snapped. "You got that too?"

Murphy wouldn't meet my eyes. Richards flashed a thin-lipped smile that barely uncovered his caps. "Fine piece of craftsmanship."

"Richards I'm not surprised at," I told Buzz. "You I expected better of. Case it slipped your mind, over the years I sailed a boatload of cooze in your direction."

"I remember it, Eddie, every morsel, and I'm grateful. But a man's needs change. We discussed this in Monte Carlo."

"We talked contracts, endorsements. Why couldn't you take no for an answer?"

"Told you. I have to plan for the future."

Richards extended all blades and stood up. "*Ecco* Pippo."

He and the Good Humor Man, decked out in a new linen suit, traded smackers on both cheeks. Buzz satisfied himself with a handshake. I satisfied myself with a sneer.

They sat down, and Pippo said, "I think only to end this business before more troubles are beginning. Tell him."

"We've put together a TV program," Richards said. "*Très dramatique*. It proves conclusively that Ali Ben Baraka is Latif Fluss."

Starting with my toes, I tightened and released every muscle, thinking I might be able to smile by the time I worked the exercise up to my face. "You positive he's not Fonda Peters?"

"The buccal smear indicates it's definitely a man," Buzz said.

"Thanks for the news. Were they waiting to break it till his baby was born?"

"We've got fingerprints. They match his prison records." Richards rolled the sleeves of his safari suit. His tan stopped at his wrists. "We've got footprints, voice prints, blood specimens."

"Blood? From the door he crashed through in Paris?" I was acting unconcerned, unsurprised, leaning way back on the bench. "Or the doctor that sewed him up?"

"Both."

"You boys been busy."

Pippo sniffed his pocket hankie. "The busiest beaver is always getting the honeys."

"Very sporting of you to tell me about your program. Anything else on your minds?"

"Just that it doesn't have to be this way," Buzz said. "We could work out a mutually beneficial deal, et cetera."

"The rewards of airing the film wouldn't be inconsiderable," Richards explained. "But we've been discussing an idea that has a longer, more lucrative payoff."

"You're talking blackmail, you're a mile off base."

"Maybe," Pippo said, "we are not showing the film now. Maybe we are showing it later so the Pro Council should let Latif play under his real name."

"You lost me," I drawled, laying out almost horizontal, like I was falling asleep.

"Let me explain, *mon ami*," Richards said. "Wimbledon figures to have a McEnroe-Fluss, alias Baraka, final. The marketplace is responding. The network predicts record-breaking ratings. After the rumble in Monte Carlo, they're calling this the Grudge Buster, the Heavyweight Championship of Tennis."

"Sounds like an exhibition."

"Very quick, Eddie. But that comes later," Buzz said. "You remember 'John McEnroe Over America?' A multimillion-dollar exo tour? Well, after Wimbledon, we're thinking global. We're thinking satellite hookup and simulcast. We're thinking 'John McEnroe and Ali Ben Baraka Over the World.' "

"Cloth-ess," Pippo piped up. "Explain him."

"Each week, your man discards another piece of tribal mufti," Richards said, "and endorses a new product."

"International strip tease," Buzz said, "but with him dressing in name brands as he drops the desert drag."

"He plugs shoes in Europe," Richards ran on. "Shirts in the Persian Gulf. Shorts in India. Sunshades with Porsche Carrera frames in Hong Kong. An autograph line of racquets in Australia."

"Speaking of which," Buzz broke in, "we've manufactured a replica of Latif's racquet, right down to the bone in the handle. Animal, not human. We're waiting for the go-ahead to start mass production."

"Then in America," Pippo said, "he is on television ripping away his *sciarpa* and showing his face."

"Remember when Joe Namath shaved off his moustache?" Buzz asked. "A razor blade company broadcast it during prime time. We have major sponsors lined up for the same type of campaign. Latif'll pitch skin creams, colognes, toothpaste, shampoo, hair oil. We're aiming for an unveiling at the U.S. Open."

"Lemme get this straight. If Baraka's Latif—and I'm not saying he is—why would they let him play the U.S. Open?"

"That's the bottom line," Buzz said. "You cooperate and, like Pippo already said, we'll lead a crusade to have Latif reinstated. Pippo's on the Pro Council. That's one vote in your favor."

"With minor tinkering," Richards said, "our TV program can be transformed from an exposé into a poignant profile that'll mold public opinion in your favor. We're prepared to incorporate more material, maybe a personal appeal from Latif, a description of his misery in prison, then his miraculous rehabilitation. Pictures of him with his wife. The new one, Lenore. Not that harridan with the bad teeth and tattoos. Or if you refuse"—he twisted his wrist, switching channels—"we'll show a different *point de vue.*"

"Gimme a for instance."

"Stock footage of Latif beating birds to death. Crosscut to his former cellmate alleging he and Latif were lovers. A clip of Lenore's ex-husband who can hobble with quite a convincing limp. Coverage of your own colorful, madcap past, with emphasis on your legal difficulties in the States. He'll be blackballed again. This time they'll boot you out of the game too, even if it means passing new rules."

I dragged myself upright on the bench. "Just out of curiosity, what cut of the exo tour and these endorsements you intend keeping for yourselves?"

"Twenty-five percent of the prize money," Buzz said.

"Fifty percent of souvenirs, concessions, and programs," Richards added.

"And McEnroe, it's arranged with him?"

"We've hammered out the contours of a deal. Now we need to nail down the details."

"If I might amplify," Richards said, tempting me to amplify my foot down his throat and out his ass. "McEnroe insists on a few ground rules. No ventriloquism. No talking or attacking birds."

"Are you saying Junior's in on this? He thinks Baraka is Latif?"

"He doesn't care."

"He and his father, they're not part of the plot to unmask Baraka and tie him up in contracts?"

"No. It's a matter," Pippo explained, "of McEnroe the Papa arranging for the son to do something interesting over the summer after he wins Wimbledon."

"He wins Wimbledon." I let it sink in.

"Is better, I think. Three little sets. Less than ninety minutes. McEnroe is old now and it is nice for him to win another title."

"Sure, a quick dive," I said. "You don't own the TV rights. You don't represent either finalist. No escalators on the line. Just what? A bet?"

"Three sets. Over in less than an hour and a half," Richards stressed. "That way neither player will be *trop fatigué* for the exo tour."

"McEnroe Senior aware of this? He's a lawyer. Maybe he'd like to know what you're up to."

"He knows nothing. Neither his son," Pippo said. "If you tell them, your boy goes back to his *negroni* tribe."

"And you go back to selling shag carpets repossessed from bankrupt motels," Buzz said.

"My man craters in three sets, fans'll scream fix. He's lost one match all spring."

"He's injured," Richards said. "Afterward, we'll reveal how badly his wrist was hurt. He'll look like a hero."

"What you're saying, Latif better tank the final or else you'll broadcast your film and have him banned. Then he has to sign for the tour and these endorsement contracts, forking over a share of the dough to you guys, or again you'll clobber him with the exposé."

"*Exactement.*"

I stood up, a little unsteady now. "I'll talk to him. I'll talk to him and think it over and get back to you."

"*Bueno,*" Richards said. "But make it quick."

"You gave me a good piece of advice in Monte Carlo, Buzz. You encouraged me to reexamine my relationship to shit. You three oughta do the same. Look in the mirror. What the hell, look at each other."

## *Chapter* Eighteen

Though they pressed for a quick answer, it stood to reason I had leeway. What did it matter if Latif agreed to tank the final to McEnroe unless they both made it that far? Either of them lost a round early, all bets were off. I couldn't guess what they'd do then with their program. Maybe save it and squeeze us later.

I said nothing to Latif before his semifinal against Lendl. He already had his hands full with the Czech. Looked to me like he was running out of fuel and, worse, out of ideas. It wasn't so much his game had fallen off as Ivan had caught on to it. Everything eerie and unbalanced about his style had become predictable, and Ivan read his shots—what Lenore once called the *avant-garde* poetry of his game—like a jingle. It took Latif seven hours to win 7–6/6–7/7–6/6–7/45–43— the longest match in Wimbledon history.

In the bad old days after a record-breaking performance, we'd of worked the press, allowing Bud Collins all the time he asked for on NBC-TV. Then we'd of hit the city, limo-cruising, cocaine hoovering, with him Fluss-ing chicks and me catching the overflow. But tonight we dodged the media and grabbed a taxi back to Petyt Place.

Lenore scrambled a Spanish omelet, and we ate in the kitchen standing around the butcher block. I debated whether to clue them in now, but decided to wait till Latif and I were alone. There was no need for her to know unless he wanted it that way.

We cleared off our plates and cleaned the kitchen. Then Lenore kissed Latif, whispered, "Good win," and went up-stairs to read about the Lamaze method. He and I moved into the library where he built a fire and brewed a pot of tea.

He had traded his Wimbledon whites for a blue *gandourah* and black *tagilmoust*. Sitting cross-legged on the floor be-tween the potted palms, he looped his veil under his chin and stuffed mint leaves into two tall glasses. I was reminded of our days in the desert, months ago when we were charting our comeback. He had warned me then I had to change, had to accept he wasn't the same man and didn't care to do busi-ness with the usual suspects. But here we were back where we ended up last time—told to tank or we'd be strong-armed off the tour.

As I laid it out for him, keeping my voice level, letting him make up his own mind, Latif didn't seem shocked or furious, just tired. Today's match had drained him. He fixed us a second glass of tea, lifting the pot high and pouring a long stream, then spooning in sugar.

" 'Satan seeks to stir up enmity and hatred among you' "— from his voice, its cadence, I knew he was quoting the Koran —" 'by means of wine and gambling.' "

"No wine. But there's sure as hell heavy betting against you."

"What do you advise, Eddie?"

"Depends how bad you want to win another Wimbledon."

He stared into his tea, churning the mint leaves with an inky finger.

"You gotta ask yourself," I went on, "how long you want to keep playing. Is it better to take the title here and call it quits? Or stay on the tour and win more later?"

"What would you do?" His voice was calm; his face, what I saw of it in its rag noose, was in neutral gear. Most I can maintain, he looked like he valued my answer but his life didn't depend on it.

I wondered whether mine did. There were millions on the line, hundreds of thousands of it mine, depending how he made up his mind. I was tempted to tell him, Tank! Do the exo tour and grab what you can. But I didn't trust my instincts anymore than I trusted Buzz, Pippo, and Richards. Latif might take a dive and they'd stiff us. No matter what, they'd always have something over us.

"I wouldn't do it," I said.

"You'd do what?"

"Play to win."

"I have a wife and a baby on the way."

"Two more reasons not to deal with shit merchants."

"But look what happened last time I refused to tank."

"We'd have to protect ourselves."

"How?"

"I can't quote specifics right off the bat."

Latif sipped his tea. "What if I called the police, told them I was being blackmailed?"

"The cops?" I felt my throat tighten. "No, not them. Maybe an appeal to the International Tennis Federation, ask for a pardon. Point out you've been on good behavior these past few months. You're a changed man."

"You think they'll buy that? Here I am just out of jail and I have an agent who's a fugitive."

"Jesus, kid, why didn't you consider that before?"

"I did. I wanted you to be part of the comeback."

"Look, Lenore and I were talking in Paris. She said we should recognize there's a ceiling on what we can accomplish. You've come all the way back. Now maybe it's time to bow out."

"You really mean that?" He fished a sprig of mint from the tea and munched it. "And blow the money, all those contracts?"

"Yes," I blurted before I changed my mind.

"What'll you do if I quit tennis?"

"We're talking about you, not me. It's your decision. I'll go along a hundred percent."

"Last time I decided not to tank, I went to jail. You didn't go along then."

That hurt. The tea glass squirted from my hand, hitting the floor, splattering Latif with mint. Miraculously it didn't break. Waiting for me to answer, he didn't bother to brush off his *gandourah*. The glass rolled over to a sofa and clanked against a brass lion paw.

"What the hell you want me to do? Promise to go to prison with you?"

"Why not?"

"This is crazy. I tell you to do the right thing and you're arguing."

"Not arguing. Trying to pin you down."

"You have my word, I'll back you every step of the way."

"I don't want you to *back* me. I want to know you'll be with me."

"Okay, I'll go to jail with you if it comes to that. Satisfied? Now for Chrissake, tell me what to tell Richards."

Latif stood up, rising like smoke from a candle. "Do me a favor."

"Name it."

"Clean up this mess. I'm whipped. I need about ten hours of sleep."

"Done. Then what do I say to Richards?"

"Tell him I'll tank."

"What! Why'd you put me through this rigamarole? I swore I'd stand by you. Go to the slam with you. What more do you want?"

"Nothing. You told me what I had to hear. Now tell Richards I'll tank."

Guess I should of felt relieved, elated. I came out looking like a prince, the guy that preached the right stuff and would still get his share of the loot. But stretched out upstairs on that four-poster bed with all the camel bells and Hands of Fatma hanging quiet, I felt lousy.

Part of it was, despite her double cross, I missed Heather. And I was disappointed in Latif. You spend a lifetime hustling, you think you know human nature and can forecast what people will do. But I'd been wrong twice in a row. Three times, counting how far off base I'd been about Buzz Murphy. Was I slipping? Or was the world? A hell of a question to ask that late at night.

Saturday, the day of the Ladies' Singles Final and the Men's Doubles Final, Latif and Lenore rented a car for a drive into the country. Before they left, he told me to line up a limo for tomorrow. He wanted it waiting after his match.

It didn't occur to me till later to ask what the next move was. A short break before the exo tour? A spell away from the limelight to lick his wounds? Would he start hunting for a house for Lenore and the bun they had in the oven? We'd have to iron out our itinerary this evening.

I phoned Richards and told him the fix was on.

"What guarantee do we have," he wanted to know, "that you and Latif won't welsh?"

"You like a contract written in blood?"

"Nothing in writing."

"Then you got the same guarantee we got. None!" I hung up.

It hit home again how naked we were. They held all the cards. What the hell, they owned the deck, the table, the game. Once Latif tanked, what they did depended strictly on the profits they projected from a world tour. He got wiped out in straight sets, I didn't see how that was supposed to build interest in a series of exos. Maybe they'd go ahead and broadcast the exposé and blow us off the circuit.

I found just one angle in our favor. If Latif planned to roll over and play dead, why not lay everything we owned on McEnroe? Then if Richards and the rest of them swindled us, we'd have something to fall back on besides our asses.

I touched base with a few bookmakers, asking the odds against McEnroe winning in straight sets, under an hour and a half. To a man they said they weren't accepting any more action on that bet. Obviously they had all they could cover with what our friends had ponied up.

Stewing and fidgeting, taking a stab at contingency plans, I stayed indoors all day looking for a loophole, a defense against a double cross. I was also hanging around in case Heather called. Better yet, came back.

But nobody called, nobody came. Every hour or so I raised up the telephone receiver to check it was working right.

When it got dark, I called for Chinese carry-out and ate from cardboard boxes. Before I half-finished the moo-goo-bedpan or whatever the hell it was, I suffered an attack of MSG syndrome on top of the world's worst case of paranoia. It almost bent me double. Suddenly I was sure I'd been abandoned, betrayed. Latif and Lenore could of been in Brazil by now, leaving me here holding the bag.

Bag, hell! Holding nothing. If they'd skipped, I wasn't about to stick around when nobody showed up to face McEnroe in the final. I was sweating where I'd find alias documentation, pocket litter, and untraceable financing— what you need to survive on the lam—when the phone rang. It was Lenore.

"Where you been?" I asked.

"A day in the country. Very soothing."

"Where's Latif?"

"In bed. Asleep. We're at an inn."

"You should of called earlier."

"Sorry. Lost track of time. We'll drive back tomorrow. I'll meet you in the Guest Box. We'll be cutting it close, arriving right before the match. Did your reserve a limo?"

"Yeah. Look, I—"

"Good. Afterward we'll go directly to the airport."

"What about your stuff here at the house?"

"Leave it. Cut your losses and travel light. Isn't that your motto?" Clearly they'd been doing some contingency planning too.

"Did Latif tell you what the deal is?"

"More or less. Good night, Eddie."


The Men's Singles Final used to be played on Saturday. For over a century at the All England Club, Sunday was dead. But a six-million-dollar American TV contract changed that. NBC wanted to show the final on Sunday, and they demanded a 2:00 P.M. London start time so they could broadcast at 9:00 A.M. on the East Coast in the States. Breakfast at Wimbledon, they call it.

Not a bad idea, specially this year when Sunday morning a monsoon dumped two inches of rain. The late start gave the ground crew a chance to roll back the tarp and let the grass dry. When the sun broke through, the temperature soared, oh hell, it had to of been all the way into the high fifties. The drowned rats that had camped overnight at the ticket booths straggled into the Standing Room Enclosure and rubbed up against each other for warmth.

In the Guest Box, I sat near Daddy Mac who snubbed me. Not even a nod. This from a man I'd done millions in deals with and was supposed to do more. I didn't take offense, though. I wasn't sure he recognized me.

Where John Junior looked like his father had back in the '80s—a scowling, bald-headed, plump leprechaun—Daddy Mac resembled Eisenhower late in life. Shrunken, hairless, and pink, he'd reached that point where old guys look like newborn babies. Still, he wore his trademark white cloth hat and jawed at a stick of gum.

Lenore checked in just as the linesmen and umpire paraded on court. She surprised me with a kiss on the cheek, then surprised me more by saying, "Is that your friend, the William Faulkner look-alike, up in the chair?"

Damned if Buzz Murphy wasn't officiating the match. They weren't taking any chances.

"You're pale," she said. "Frazzled-looking."

"A lot on my mind. You, though, you look terrific." She had color on her cheeks for the first time since the days at Désert de Retz, and she filled a white knit dress with soft curves.

"Thanks. I feel great. I've only thrown up once today."

"How's Latif?"

"He hasn't thrown up at all." Giggling at her own joke, she grabbed my hand. "He's fine. We found a pyramid in Brightling, a village in Sussex. Another replica of the Gaius Cestius tomb in Rome."

The news registered with a delayed-reaction jolt. Latif was set to tank, why work out on a pyramid?

I didn't have a chance to ask because as Latif and McEnroe came on to knock up, two more people popped into the guest box, and earlier shocks couldn't compare. This one shattered all records on the Richter scale.

Heather! She was back! Ducking her head, she seemed shy about her new hairdo, a halo of springy curls. She hesitated till I called her name and opened my arms. Wearing a tee shirt with "Children Are the Ornament of This Life" stenciled across the chest, she pressed against me whispering, "I've missed you."

"What happened to your hair?"

"I had it permed."

"Looks . . . different."

"Looks just like yours." Then she felt my body tense and twitch. "Don't be angry. I can explain."

She wasn't talking about hair now. She knew what I'd seen over her shoulder.

Chewing the fat with Daddy Mac was a grizzled, bow-legged guy with a four-day growth of beard, a knit beanie, and tobacco-colored skin. He had on the same moth-eaten Adidas warmup suit and was spieling the same loony rap.

"Welcome, welcome." He pumped Mr. McEnroe's mitt. "I am Champion."

Daddy Mac eyed him suspiciously from under his cloth hat.

"To know, nice man, how they build this big place." Champion did a three-sixty spin, admiring the steep banks of bleachers. "Deenameat?"

"Deenameat?" McEnroe mumbled.

"I am Champion. I am loving this place that is so green like the Nile delta."

"I can explain everything," Heather repeated. "Absolutely everything, darling."

"Champion of what?" Daddy Mac demanded.

"Pyramid. Up and down running. Whole world record. You like to race me on these chairs?"

"Get ouda here."

The ballsy little bullshit artist wasn't bothered by this brush-off. He marched over to Lenore and me like a greeter in a Las Vegas lounge glad-handing the crowd. "Good friend, welcome." He wrung my fist. "Lovely lady, we are meeting once more again." He pressed his prickly mug to both Lenore's cheeks. "They say you are starting to make sons. I see it's true in your eyes."

"What is this?" I asked. "Someone wanna tell me what's going on?"

Heather hauled me down beside her. Champion hunkered like a toad between Lenore and me, gabbing about the beautiful building that was so big and green and had a cool, grassy courtyard.

"They wanted him here for the final," Heather whispered.

"Nobody mentioned it to me."

"They knew you'd never agree. They couldn't cope with any more aggro so they sent me."

"You should of told me."

"A secret mission. That's why I left so suddenly that morning. I flew to Cairo to collect Champion. It wasn't easy to convince him."

"But lemme guess. He changed his mind when you waved free tickets and a few bucks in his face."

"It's only fair we paid him. He had to leave his family and profession. And Latif was very keen to have him here."

"Latif?"

"Oh, Eddie, we're not going to have that fight again, are we? They confided in me. They trusted me. Can't you?"

I nodded yes. I was so grateful to have her back, even with her hair french fried into a frizz.

"Quiet, please," Buzz Murphy called from the umpire's chair. Then he read paying customers the kind of riot act you'd hear in a Mississippi holding pen. No moving around, no talking, no flashbulbs, no applauding during points, no time off for good behavior.

McEnroe won the toss and chose to serve. Planting his feet parallel to the base line, he rocked back and forth. On his forehead the scar the seagull had gouged glowed blood red.

At the far end of the court, Latif waved at the Guest Box.

Champion yodeled and waved back. "Welcome to be here. Proud to see you playing."

"Hey, buddy!" McEnroe screamed. "Sit still and shut up!"

"Welcome to you too," Champion shouted. "To know, good friend, please start."


Generally Junior's game goes according to his serve. If he finds his rhythm there, he seems to feel better about every shot. Today he opened with three aces. But with the score forty-love, Latif chipped a return to McEnroe's backhand and rushed the net.

Mac tossed up a short lob that floated down in front of the umpire's chair. Latif drew a bead on it, dancing into position for an easy put-away. Then with all the time in the world, he rushed and butchered the smash.

The crowd saw it as the sort of silly error that happens early in every title match. Typical case of bad timing and tight nerves. Fans tittered and laughed. Latif hammed it up, shaking his head, thumping his racquet like he couldn't believe it.

But I believed it. I'd seen him aim his feet straight at

the ump's chair. Then I'd seen Buzz shrivel in pain as the ball streaked between his thighs, drilling him in the nuts. His worst nightmare had come true.

When everyone understood the man was maimed, Centre Court fell quiet. Linesmen came running. Latif loaned them a hand lifting Buzz down from the chair. He was coiled in agony, hands cupped to his crotch, legs drawn up against his chest. Amazingly his hair hadn't been ruffled.

A nurse, same one that did the buccal smear, galloped out with two assistants and a stretcher. Shooing Latif to his chair—McEnroe had already gone to his—the nurse loosened Buzz's belt. Then they hoisted him onto the stretcher and hauled him away, still knotted in pain, gnawing at his moustache.

I didn't feel a bit of sympathy for the son-of-a-bitch. I'd of cheered Latif for knocking him out of the match—if I wasn't so worried why he'd done it.

With TV time wasting, the club was quick to send in a substitute ump. He announced the score, called for silence, and said, "Mr. Baraka to serve."

Latif realigned the strings on his racquet, rubbed the balls against his belly, and appeared to talk to them. What I mean, he pressed them to his *tagilmoust*, near his mouth, then made these hand signals, like he was telling the balls where to go and how to get there.

Funny thing, McEnroe didn't mind. He ripped into his returns, running off four points in a row, breaking Latif at love. Then before he served, Junior lifted the balls up to his ear, like he was listening to secrets Latif had whispered to the Slazengers. It seemed to be his way of saying, I've heard you, Baraka. I've watched, I've learned.

I'm not claiming Mac had turned into a Tuareg clone. But there was definitely something of the Masked Marvel in his game today. He stayed loose, he stroked the ball with a lot of wrist action, and he produced almost as many off-speed angles and reverse-English toad hops as Latif. He won the first set 6–3 in twenty-seven minutes.

You couldn't tell Latif was tanking. His style was still a

grab bag of garbage balls and geek-show lobs and drop shots. But too many of them floated long or fell short or else Junior chased them down and knocked off winners. With each point he lost, Latif seemed to lose starch too. His white tunic hung limp, his *tagilmoust* sagged.

When Mac wrapped up the second set 6–1, Champion thumped my thigh and growled something in Egyptian. Heather murmured, "He just doesn't have any zip today. The Lendl match must have taken a lot out of him."

I nodded, growled like Champion, looked as long-faced as Lenore. I wasn't entirely pretending. I *did* feel sad. Latif wanted to stay in tennis, I realized he had to go down the tubes. But I hated to see it.

Ali Ben Baraka was supposed to serve to open the third set. But Latif Fluss served instead. What I'm saying, for the first time that season he really cracked the ball. No hocus-pocus now, no dizzy spins or kicks. He whistled four straight aces, and McEnroe was rooted to the grass, shaking his head, struggling to remember where he'd seen that stark power, that savage wrist snap, that low-skidding bounce before.

Same as McEnroe, spectators shook their heads. But where the speed of Latif's serves set them babbling, his return of serve left the crowd thunderstruck and Mac shell-shocked. Hitting the ball on the rise, he rifled a clean winner, belted two unplayable passing shots, and on break point blasted a cannonball that caught Junior in the chest and flattened him.

He hurried over and offered help. But Mac slapped his hand aside and stared, still struggling to remember.

Champion socked me in the leg so hard my foot hopped. "Pyramid make him strong."

"Isn't this wonderful?" Heather warbled.

I wasn't so sure.

Lenore flashed me a wicked grin, the same one she must of given her ex-husband just before she stomped the gas.

When Latif broke Junior a second time and jumped to a 4–0 lead, I glanced at the scoreboard clock—the match was over an hour old—and assumed this was a short burst of brilliance to show what he could do during the exo tour, a demo to justify a high endorsement price. Now he'd fold and let Mac run out the set and the match.

I hung onto that idea for exactly twenty seconds—the time it took Latif to towel off his hands. Then he unloaded another serve that exploded like a mortar, and I realized why he had worked out on a pyramid, imported Champion, and knocked Buzz out of commission. He intended to win, crash in flames like his crazy father charging an oil pump on camelback. Nobody could watch now and not recognize his game.

In case some moron missed the message, after sweeping the third set 6–0, he flipped off his sunglasses, tugged his *tagilmoust*, and let the long twisted rag slither to the ground.

McEnroe saw his face and fainted.

TV cameramen closed in for a tight shot of Junior delirious, then of Latif looking on concerned. From reviewing the video tape later, I learned what television viewers saw. Mac was mumbling, "It's Fluss. It's Fluss." But there was room for doubt. His copper-tinted hair that used to resemble static electricity was cut short, and his features had filled out and seemed peaceful, not speed-wasted. His eyes, the famous blue blinkers, could of cinched who he was, but he had replaced the brown contact lens he lost in Paris.

The ump and the supervisor glanced at Latif and told McEnroe he was imagining things, told him to play on.

Credit where it's due, Mac bounced up to beat the count. A few points into the fourth set and he didn't give a damn who he was going against. He just wanted to win. He didn't whine about close calls, didn't argue with the ump or smart-asses in the bleachers. Caught up in the match, he hurled himself into every point.

Me, I was completely caught up too. There was no chance to calm down and consider the consequences. Like Latif, I concentrated point by point, game by game.

Heather hugged my arm. Champion socked my thigh till it was black and blue. "Pyramid make him fast!" he screamed. "Pyramid make him *smart*." Then he started tenderizing my leg when McEnroe revived and scored with spectacular shots.

"To know," he marveled, "how he do such strange things with a string board?"

"Deenameat," I told him.

Dynamite! That's what it was, each man bringing out the best in the other, stretching for the top end of his talent, digging down deep into his guts.

Latif eked out a win in a fourth set tie-break and held serve to open the fifth set. By now, Junior had regeared his game and was trying to turn Latif's pace against him, raise the level a few notches and zoom into hyperspace. But Latif stayed with him, and the momentum swung back and forth, the crowd rooting for whichever player seemed to be weakening, everybody wanting the match to go on and on.

With Latif leading 4–3 and McEnroe serving, Junior went for too much on a second ball and double-faulted. Love-Fifteen. Then he sliced one wide and got passed down the line. Love-Thirty. Champion quit pounding and got a death grip on my leg. McEnroe served his first ball long, spun in a second serve, but couldn't dig Latif's chipped return out of the grass. Love-Forty. Triple break point.

Now Heather had a vise on my other leg. Like McEnroe, the four of us rocked and rasped a deep breath. Latif crouched to receive. Mac took something off his first serve, rushed in behind it, and volleyed deep to the forehand corner. Somehow Latif reached it and tossed up a lob, a topspinner that looped over Junior's racquet. Game to Latif, 5–3.

McEnroe crumbled in disgust. Latif skidded on his callused feet and crumbled too. But where Junior jumped right up, Latif stayed down.

Silence. Dead silence on Centre Court. He laid there a long time like he was making up his mind whether it was safe to move. Me, I didn't move either.

Finally he rolled onto his hands and knees and staggered upright. Favoring his left leg, he gimped to the net and gestured to McEnroe. What the hell was this? He offered his hand, and after a pause Mac shook it, stepped over the net, and let Latif lean on him as he hobbled to the sideline.

The ump said, "Mr. Baraka . . . Excuse me?" Latif was saying something to him. "Because of injury, Mr. *Fluss* is unable to continue. Match to Mr. McEnroe."

I could of cried. Why? Why quit, leading 5–3? He could of won his serve on crutches.

"Sorry," Champion said. "We lose." But he looked cheerful as ever and clambered over the seats to shake Daddy Mac's hand. "Nice man, you win. But think how better your boy is playing with a pyramid. It's good for the hairs."

Suddenly all ears, Mr. McEnroe asked, "How?" But Champion had moved on.

"A wonderful match," Heather said. "A shame someone had to lose."

"Oh well." Lenore's smile was more wistful now than wicked. "Once they learned who he was, they would have disqualified him anyway."

Below us, Champion vaulted out of the Guest Box and dashed across the grass, dodging linesmen and security guards. The Duke and Duchess of Kent, him with his hands clasped behind his back, her with her hair piled up like a crown, marched down a carpet between rows of knobby-kneed ball boys to present the winner's and runner-up's trophies. But Champion reached Latif first, scooped him up in his arms, and never broke stride, carrying him past the royal couple and clean off Centre Court.

# *Chapter* Nineteen

They tell me Latif got a terrific round of applause when Pippo Scarcia stepped forward to accept the runner-up trophy in his absence.

They tell me John McEnroe pulled a class act at his press conference and said he didn't care who it was, Baraka or Fluss. He hadn't faced a better player since Borg.

They tell me Iain Richards had a coronary in the TV booth. I don't believe that. The bastard never had a heart to be attacked.

They tell me there are hundreds of theories and rumors on the circuit about what really happened. But the simple truth is Latif tanked. Two sets and three hours too late, when it didn't profit him a dime, he took a dive.

The fake foot injury, the exit in Champion's arms, the security and isolation at the airport—everything was set up. Even I had been suckered—me, Eddie Brown, whose business was always shoving skids under other people's feet and jerking them around. Now I was the jerkee.

Within an hour after the final point, the five of us sat in a windowless room at Heathrow. The VIP lounge wasn't private enough for Latif. We huddled in what looked like the hole at Leavenworth. Flat grey wells, furniture bolted to the floor, lights flush with the ceiling, far from my suicidal hands. Having jettisoned our other stuff, we just had carry-ons—Lenore's purse, Heather's and my tote sacks, a Fortnum & Mason paper bag Champion balanced on his knees.

Dressed again in the blue *gandourah* and black *tagilmoust* —his tennis whites he had flung from the speeding limo along with his racquets—Latif sat across from me in the lotus position.

"Why'd you blow it? Give the title away?" I asked.

"I wanted to beat him, Eddie. I wanted to win another Wimbledon so bad I decided I'd better not."

"Is he on something?" I asked Lenore.

"Not that I've noticed."

"Not now," he said, "but a few more tournaments and I would have been. That's what I'm trying to tell you. When you want something that bad, it's better to back off."

Champion rooted in his Fortnum & Mason bag, brought out a Scotch plaid box of Walker's Pure Butter Shortbread Biscuits, and passed them around.

"Besides"—Latif lowered his *tagilmoust* and munched a cookie—"I owed him one."

"Owed who one what?"

"McEnroe. A Wimbledon title. Remember the year I beat him up and he had to be hospitalized?"

"And there's Monte Carlo," Lenore reminded him.

"Yeah. I cheated him there too."

"The bird?" Heather asked.

"Yeah, I trained it."

"To talk? A seagull?"

"I did the talking. The gull did the rest."

"You trained it to attack McEnroe?" I asked.

"Afraid so. You see what I'm saying? A few months on

the circuit and I was already to where I'd do anything, break rules, scar a man, anything to win. Before long, I'd have been freebasing, speeding, fighting, the works. Better to quit and spend some of the money we won."

I had an urge to scratch my head, really rake it. "Jesus, kid, you need to kick back, fine. Take a few weeks vacation. A month. What the hell, the whole summer. Then come back fresh at the U.S. Open."

"They know who he is now," Heather said. "He's banned for life."

"Don't bet on it. Look at McEnroe after he dropped that great five-setter to Borg in '80, the match with the long tie-break. People started to understand how marketable Junior is. It could be the same for you."

"Latif's got a record," Lenore said. "Not a reputation for sassing umpires. They're not going to forgive and forget. Pippo and Richards and Buzz are bound to broadcast their program."

"Beat them to the punch." I shook my head at Champion who was shoving the cookie box at me. "Hold a press conference. Then fly to the States, the both of you, and do the talk-show circuit. Let people see you're a law-abiding fella, a father-to-be, a credit to your race. Beg to be reinstated."

Lenore said, "I'm tired of traveling. And I don't care to be public property the whole time I'm pregnant. This is something Latif and I'd rather experience alone."

"You at least oughta explain your side of the story."

"You explain it," he said.

"It's you people are interested in. They'll have you delivering speeches, lecturing at drug centers, prisons, universities. Won't they, Lenore?"

She sat flicking her fingernails against her thumbnail. "You know the whole story. Why don't you tell it?"

"Nobody'll listen. Back me up, Heather. The camera loves Latif."

"There are people who love you too," she said.

"What is this? What are you guys doing to me?"

"Write a book," Lenore suggested. "Okay, you're not exactly a stylist or a reliable narrator. But your account is bound to have a certain crude vigor."

"Crude? Is this what I get for—"

A gofer in a peaked cap leaned his head in the door. "Mr. and Mrs. Fluss, Mr. Champion, they're calling your flight."

The three of them got up. "Well, Eddie, I'll be in touch," Latif said. "Let me know what you decide."

"Wait a goddamn minute." I jumped to my feet, glanced from Latif to Lenore to Heather, and back. Blood rushed to my head. My scalp was on fire. "I'm going with you. Heather, aren't you coming?"

"I think you two better discuss your plans in private," Lenore said.

"You're ditching us? Ditching *me*?"

"Not at all," said Latif. "Just allowing you a chance to work out your personal life."

"Personal life? What personal life? I got no personal life. I'm an agent."

"And a very good one." Lenore patted me on the shoulder like some sad-assed jailbird that's been passed over for parole.

I looked at Champion's grinning puss. Nothing there I could read. Then I turned to Heather. Her eyes, deep-set, but not dark-circled anymore, didn't give away anything. But there was the sign on her chest, punctuated by nipples. "Children Are the Ornament of This Life."

It couldn't of hit me harder if Latif had sent a seagull to bury its beak in my head. I sagged back into the bolted-down chair. "You're knocked up, too?"

She smiled. "How elegantly expressed."

"Eddie, you're awful," Lenore wailed.

"I don't get it. I thought—"

Champion was on me so fast I couldn't finish. He was pressing the flesh like some insane Egyptian ward heeler. "Welcome, welcome. This is very happy."

"But how?" I finally got it out.

"Pyramid make you strong." He was nuzzling my cheeks with his slobbery hundred-and-five-year-old whiskers. "You must have many sons." Now he hugged Heather. "Nice lady, to know, this is good to give Eddie babies for his aging days. Sons to support him. Daughters to cook. Children to bury him."

"I'm not dead yet." But I felt close to croaking.

The flunky popped his head in the door again. "Five minutes."

Latif grabbed my hand in the Sahara Soul Brother shake. "It's been great. Thanks for everything, Eddie. Couldn't have done it without you."

"I wouldn't have wanted to do it without you." Lenore kissed me, stepped back, then kissed me again. There were tears in her eyes.

"Where are you going?"

"Soon as I hear where you are," Latif said, "I'll let you know. If I were you, I'd head someplace where Pippo's people won't find you."

"Are you ever coming back again?" I asked, fading fast.

"Don't rule it out. But it'll have to be after the baby's born. And after you—"

"I know. I know. My personal problems."

Champion rolled his Fortnum & Mason bag shut; there was a last rush of kisses and goodbyes; then they left, and Heather and I were alone. The way she looked standing there, waiflike in her tee shirt and baggy pants, I was afraid she'd stick her fingers in her mouth and start gnawing. I gathered her onto my lap.

She tried to wriggle away. "This isn't the Dark Ages, Eddie. A woman has a choice. I'm perfectly prepared to—"

"Shhh," was all I managed to say, the strongest commitment I could make at the moment. Desperate for any excuse not to talk, I stuffed her fingers into my mouth and rocked her, rocked myself, back and forth.

How I wound up married doesn't take much to imagine. How I wound up in the States, in federal prison—okay a minimum-security unit, but still a jail—requires some explaining. There's no one simple reason.

Partly I was homesick and fed up with being on the lam.

That's no life for me, much less for a pregnant lady or a kid. So I flew to New York with Heather, powwowed with my lawyer, then copped a plea with the IRS. The result—a whopping fine that wiped out my bank account, and a six-month sentence in this country-club slammer where I got senators, congressmen, corporate execs, and Social Register junkies as dorm mates.

Partly it was also to put distance and a tall fence between me and Pippo Scarcia. The last place his friends figured to search for me was prison.

Then, of course, I had a book to write. And what better place to do that than in here where every second inmate is at a desk half the day drafting an appeal or penning his memoirs? Some of my colleagues in stir and in literature have contracts with publishers, and they've been very generous with advice about editors, advances, and agents—as if I needed one!

Latif has a different notion why I decided to surrender and do my time. He sent a postcard of the Pyramids in Cairo with a quote from the Koran scribbled on the back: "We will inflict upon them the lighter punishment of this world before the supreme punishment of the world to come so that they may return to the right path."

Who knows? Maybe all these reasons add up to the same thing. I'm raring to get back on the right path; I'm far from being out of the running. I'm anxious to finish this book, and begin hustling the film rights. Heather plans to direct and coproduce.

I miss her; it's hard being locked up. But like I learned from Latif, there's always mental-imaging. I've gone back over all our matches, Heather's and mine, replaying the big points, and I've seen refinements I can make, moves and strokes nobody's tried before. Having witnessed what a hundred-and-five-year-old con man can do, I got every intention of living at least that long and coming back over and over again. Look for Latif to be with me. And there'll be Heather and our kid, and Lenore and their baby which I bet is born a beautiful shade of robin's egg blue.